As one of the editors for Reisig's latest novel, I found the action/adventure moved at such a pace that I had to remind myself I was editing. Before you start the book, get a good night's sleep, eat a good meal, and hit the bathroom. Put away the bookmark because you won't need it. You're riding Reisig's Adventure Express and there will be no stops until the end of the line.
— Robert Simpson, Award-winning columnist and editor

Kansas and Will are back again, thumbing their noses at disaster and stumbling into adventure at every turn – lots of exciting twists in this Caribbean paradise that Michael Reisig paints so flawlessly with his words.

This book is not only an excellent addition to Reisig's Key West series, but it's a riveting read for those who are unfamiliar with his previous novels. "The gods, they love a clever reckoning," as Reisig pens, and I'm confident you will love this latest offering from Key West!
— Jay T. Strasner, Publisher, El Campo Leader-News

Once again, Michael Reisig offers vivid descriptions of bizarre characters and intriguing, south of the border settings. He makes you feel like you're dead center in the heart-hammering action. *Somewhere on The Road To Key West* is a tough book to put down.
— Elaine Hodges – SouthernAuthors.us

SOMEWHERE ON THE ROAD TO KEY WEST

Michael Reisig

CLEAR CREEK PRESS

Published by Clear Creek Press
P.O. Box 1081 Mena, AR 71953
1-479-394-4992

ISBN: 978-0-9713694-7-4

A special thanks to the folks of Savanna-la-Mar, Jamaica, and Isla Mujeres, Mexico, for allowing me to take some license regarding their towns and their celebrations.

*To my Lady, Bonnie Lee, who patiently
listened to all the stories long before they
became pages in books.*

_____

The real Kansas and Will, circa 1978

One of the inescapable encumbrances of leading an interesting life is that there have to be moments when you almost lose it.

— Jimmy Buffett —

CHAPTER 1

Fleeting silver clouds whisked across the night sky, blanketing a glowering, orange moon as it rose over the Mocho Mountains of Jamaica. Early evening mists swirled around leaf and bough as the shrill cries of jungle creatures pierced the silence — a wild cacophony of warning, indignant and frightened. They could hear them coming. And so could we.

Angry shouts sliced through the primeval forest. I could just begin to see the bobbles of light — torches cleaving in and out of the dark foliage, dancing like lightning bugs in the distance, forming a semicircle around us.

"Things were going so well — so well! And then you! You!" I grunted as we fought our way along the barely discernable path, clawing at the vines and broad leaves that threatened our passage and clutched at us like spurned lovers. "His daughter of all people — the second largest drug lord in Jamaica and you have to boff his daughter!"

As he stumbled along beside me on the darkening trail, my partner dipped a shoulder in an aggravated shrug. "How did I know she was his daughter? I thought she was his girlfriend."

"Oh, that makes it much better. You're a freaking idiot! You really are."

Will shook his head, inadvertently running his hand through his long, blond hair. "Jeez, Kansas! You saw the 'come-hither' looks she was giving us — like a mink in heat! Hell, it wasn't even my idea. *She dragged me* off to her little hut of ill repute while you were telling him about what hotshot drug dealers we were." Will grinned, that same old half smile somewhere between confident and goofy, blue eyes gleaming. "But man, I gotta tell you. That girl —"

"Save it for the next bar," I growled, glancing at the closing circles of light. The voices were growing louder. "Right now, it doesn't matter. We're screwed three ways to Sunday. You have any idea where we are?"

Will drew a sharp breath. "Yeah, I think we're still headed in the direction of the river."

"You've got the flare gun — for Eddie, right? You still have it?"

"Damned right I do," my buddy replied. "If he's anywhere close enough to see it."

"You still have the medallion, right? Please, for God's sake, tell me you still have the medallion."

Will offered that same goofy smile. "Does a frog have a watertight ass? Of course I've got it."

"A couple more hours, we'd have slid out of there smooth and easy, and disappeared," I wheezed, struggling to stay with the obscure trail. "Jacko's gonna be bat-crap crazy. I mean, the dude is going to be spitting BBs when he discovers that we not only bonked his daughter, but stole his priceless medallion —"

The crack of a rifle shot shattered the darkness and a branch next to me splintered. The voices behind us were rising like hounds that had found the scent. The harsh Jamaican patois could be heard clearly now. But just as our options seemed to have run out, the jungle began to thin and I could smell water. We had reached the river — the Black River that wound its way into Black River Bay below Montego. By all rights, I might have considered that good news — except for the cliff.

We stumbled out into a clearing at the edge of the jungle and ran the last 75 yards to the edge of the cliff. The river was at least 100 feet beneath us — a dangerous jump for anyone who doesn't know the depth of the water. We just as easily could have become mud torpedoes.

"Shoot the flare!" I yelled.

Will never said a word. He just pulled the flare gun from the small of his back, aimed it up at the moon, and pulled the trigger. The crack of the weapon startled us, but the next second a white-red flower burst above our heads, holding its fiery beauty against the night sky for a few moments, then sailing downward as it diminished in intensity.

"We're going to have to jump," I yelled. "There's no choice."

Will, who had a distinct fear of heights, shook his head adamantly and yelled back, "No way, José. I'm not jumping. I don't do jumping!"

Two more shots rang out, and the turf in front of us shuddered with the impact. I could see men clearing the jungle — big, dark men, with machetes, a few with guns. We were standing at the edge of the cliff — the shadowy river water swirling in slow eddies below.

"Not good," Will said nervously.

I took one last look at the roiling river. "You're not dead until you see the devil," I muttered, then suddenly, throwing up my arm, finger pointing to the sky, I yelled, "Look! A pterodactyl!"

Will instinctively glanced upwards. "A freaking what?"

I quickly took one step back and straight-armed my partner between the shoulder blades as he stared up at the sky. He stumbled off the cliff, that Wile E. Coyote look in his eyes, arms wind-milling for a second, then he was gone, his long shriek gradually diminishing in the darkness. Two of the drug lord's minions were closing in on me, machetes raised, the moonlight accenting the whites of their fierce eyes and glinting off their blades.

"Later gators," I said as I turned and leaped off into the night. Their shouts were lost to the wind whistling in my ears as the dark waters rushed up at me.

Thank God I'd had the sense to put my legs together and go in feet first — a fall of that height into water is a lot like striking concrete if you're spread out. Still, I remember issuing a burbling shriek as I cascaded down, the dark, moonlit water rising up at me with a terrifying swiftness. Suddenly, I was buried in the warm murkiness, somersaulting in slow motion with the current while struggling to find my way to the surface. My pulse hammered in my head, and I was desperate for a breath of air. In the excitement, I had neglected to inhale before hitting the water. As I grew panicky, still being rolled with the current, my feet hit the bottom and I instinctively looked up. There above me was the slight, shimmering aura of the moon. Kicking upwards, lungs aching with the first stages of asphyxiation, I slashed toward the light, finally breaking the surface, gasping for air and pirouetting in a quick circle.

A cloud passed over the moon and I spat out a harsh expletive as the slow-moving, dark surface of the river yielded nothing. I spun again, drawing sweet breaths and floating slowly downriver. The angry shouts of our pursuers followed me along the edge of the cliff. An occasional battery of shots ripped the silence, the bullets smacking the water near me.

"Where are you, Will?" I muttered to myself, still sucking in breaths and craning my neck like a neurotic goose. Fear set in, grasping my entrails with tiny fingers. *Where are you?*

Another cloud buried the moon as I frantically scanned the shoreline. Tall mangroves and buttonwoods crowded the water on one side, limestone walls on the other. Our pursuers were still following me on the cliffs above. *Good God! Did I kill him? Did I just kill that rascally, crazy character with whom I had shared a revelry of adventure for the better part of my adult life? Had we finally pushed our luck to the limit?* Panic was just beginning to overwhelm concern when a hand grasped my shirt from behind and practically pulled me under. As uptight as I was, I'll admit I shrieked like a teenager, quickly fighting to get my head above the surface. As I thrashed around that same hand pulled me up. There was Will.

"Where the hell have you been?" I muttered with relief. "You scared the crap out of me!"

"Good," my partner replied. "Now we're even." He paused. "I think I pooped my pants."

The shouts above interrupted our conversation and we both looked up. The moon slid out from behind a fluffy grey cumulus, illuminating the river and the cliff, as well as a handful of our angry pursuers.

Treading water, Will shot them a one-fingered salute. "Screw you!" he yelled, feeling quite confident. "Screw you and the horse you rode in on! Come and get us!" He glanced at me with that funky Lee Marvin grin.

Suddenly, two of them, machetes in hand, looked at each other, then stepped forward and leaped off the precipice, howling as they fell. They crashed into the water perhaps 30 yards behind us, coming up and shaking their dreadlocked heads like dogs. A moment later they were splashing in our direction, grim with determination.

I looked at Will. "Come and get us," I muttered. "Come and get us…"

Will shrugged, still treading water, and held up his hands. "Who would have imagined?"

I took a look at our antagonists, then quickly glanced around at the sky, listening. "Now we're really up the creek. Where the hell is Crazy Eddie?"

"Yeah," Will muttered. "Now would be a good time." He reached into his khaki cargo shorts and pulled out the flare gun. A moment's more digging and he came up with one last cartridge, waterproofed with wax.

The two Jamaicans were closing in, now 20 yards behind us. The current was slowing their progress, but there was no question about their resolve. My partner pointed the gun skyward and pulled the trigger. I flinched, expecting a report, but nothing happened. He looked at me and shrugged, still treading water.

"Not good," I grimaced, looking around for an escape I knew didn't exist, or something with which to fight back.

Our antagonists had closed the distance by five more yards, apparently having tucked the machetes in their belts.

"Toss that flare gun and let's swim for it. Maybe we can outdistance them."

But that didn't seem likely, as I watched the moon bathe their dogged, powerful strokes. Will started to toss the gun, but suddenly I saw him crack it open, pull out the shell, and rub the back of the casing vigorously against his front teeth. He shoved the shell back in, snapped the device closed, aimed it at the moon and pulled the trigger. We were rewarded with the report of the gun and another brilliant red-white explosion in the sky.

"Weak firing pin and too much wax on the back of the shell," Will said with a triumphant smile.

The flare burned brightly — a beacon in the still Jamaican darkness, and we floated for a few seconds to watch it. But in a moment or two it was gone, there was still no sign of our buddy, and our antagonists were closing in. They had drawn their machetes, and while that impeded their progress somewhat, it was a sure game changer for any kind of confrontation.

I pulled Will over to me. "We can't fight them, we need to try something else," I whispered to him. "Let's do this..." When I finished my partner nodded grimly. "Worth a try, *amigo.*"

When the Jamaicans were close enough to raise their weapons, both Will and I disappeared under the water, diving down deep and around them — easy stuff for two guys who made their living in the water. We came up 20 yards downriver and separated by a few yards. Our adversaries would have to split up to get us. They howled and turned to chase us again, but as they did, I heard it — distant, just barely in the wind. I waited, listening carefully, heart starting to trip slightly with hope. There it was again, like a cat's purr, but steady and rhythmic, and it was growing louder. Crazy Eddie!

In less than a minute the purr had grown to a steady drone, then to the throaty roar of those big Pratt and Whitney engines, and suddenly, straight out of the moon on the horizon, like something out of a Harrison Ford movie, came Eddie and his big Grumman Goose. He waved from the cockpit as he soared over us and wagged a wing. The startled Jamaicans were terrified as he passed over their heads close enough to spit on them. Eddie threw the Goose into a rising bank that would have made a crop-dusting pilot proud, dragged his girl around in a wing-over turn, then dropped the aircraft on us with grace and purpose. We were in a section of the river that appeared to be just wide enough for him, but it still looked like a roll of the dice.

As he came in for a landing, the mangroves on each side reached out greedily at his wingtips, begging to grasp him, spin him harshly, and bring his ship crashing into the dark water, but old Eddie, his one eye gleaming brightly (the other lost to a mishap with a feathered lure and a drunken, careless cast, and covered with a black patch), was howling like a wolf, lost to the thrill and the excitement of another wild roll with the dice of life.

Before I could draw two ragged breaths, Eddie had the plane on the water and Will and I were swimming furiously for the hatch. There was only one Jamaican in sight, and after that stunning entrance by Eddie, he had pretty much lost interest in us. I was fairly sure I saw Eddie deliberately hit the other one with his starboard wing pontoon when he landed.

In moments we were at the plane and our friend was hauling us up through the entrance. "Close the freaking hatch door, you runamuckers!" Eddie yelled as he scrambled back to the cockpit, trying to keep the bird centered in the river and out of the mangroves.

We obeyed as we felt the aircraft begin to pick up momentum, and before we could buckle ourselves into seats up front, our buddy was sliding the controls forward and dropping flaps, and the hull of the Goose was slapping rhythmically against the water — Bruce Springsteen's "Born to Run" hammering the cockpit speakers. In seconds she broke her bonds with the earth and climbed majestically out of the dark jungle and into the rising orange moon. As we soared over the shadowy labyrinth, a small, red-and-yellow fireball rose out of the foliage in the distance where Jacko's compound was located. Actually, it was right where our recent host's drug storage facility sat. My partner looked over at me and cocked his head.

I shrugged . "Never store your gasoline near your drugs."

Will and Eddie grinned broadly at each other. Both were cut from the same bolt of cloth. The look in their eyes was an amalgam of electric excitement and teeth-gnashing high energy. It was the elixir of adventure that fed them. God knows I had seen that look many a time — seen it in the mirror...

"What took you so long?" Will said to Eddie. "I was just thinking about climbing back up that cliff and visiting Jacko's daughter again, just to kill some time."

I couldn't help but chuckle. Once again we'd done the damned near impossible — challenged the gods of fate and consequence, and danced away with the prize. But there would likely be hell to pay for it.

CHAPTER 2

Florida Keys Hospital, Key West, 1984

Shane O'Neal lay in the bed, a warm, late spring sun cascading through the window and blanketing him. His left leg was still in a full cast. The bandages had been removed from his head and his right hand, and he was just beginning to regain some movement in his fingers. He'd been there for the last two months. Although that might have seemed like extraordinarily cruel punishment, all things considered, it was a pretty good deal. He'd gambled with the devil and he was still alive. Will and I stood next to him, telling the story of our experience in Jamaica. Shane, of all people, deserved to know. He was why we'd taken on the challenge.

Truth be known, my partner and I had spent a lot of time skirting rules and regulations in the last decade or so of life in the southern hemisphere, occasionally living on the edge of legality. But that didn't make us outlaws. We just had a habit of sailing our own courses. Indeed, one of our best friends, the fellow in the hospital bed in front of us, worked for the DEA. We had met at Sloppy Joe's five years ago, ended up getting drunk together that night, and for some reason a friendship blossomed. O'Neal — a tall fellow with a trim but muscled frame, Indian dark hair, and green eyes — loved the ocean with the same passion as Will and me, and we spent many a day on it diving and fishing. Oddly enough, our friend was a pilot, as we were. Six months ago we had introduced him to a good friend of ours — a lady we held in high esteem (but whom neither of us could seem to win over) — and something magical happened. It was one of those rare, star-wrought miracles, where two souls find each other and recognize a connection that extends far beyond the here and now. You see a face, and the whole world seems to go eerily silent, and funnels down to nothing more than the person in front of you. The eyes, the smile, and the voice are so familiar you just want to say, "Lord! It's so good to see you again!"

If you haven't experienced this, then it all sounds like so much esoteric moonshine, but for those of you whom the gods have graciously allowed this remarkable, perhaps ageless connection, you understand. You're smiling now and nodding your head, because you know exactly what it feels like.

Shane O'Neal married our lady friend, Julie, three months after meeting her, in a quiet but beautiful ceremony on the porch of my home on Big Pine Key. But Shane still had a job, and after a short honeymoon he'd gone undercover in Jamaica in an attempt to nail one of the drug lords there. Jacko Slade was not one of the little people who brought in a few pounds of pot here and there; he was a hardcore cocaine lord with the conscience of a praying mantis, and if he ran pot at all it was in large amounts. He'd become a serious issue for the DEA when several low to mid-level dealers in Key West and Miami had become "floaters" — washing up on beaches, nastily bloated, and badly bumming out tourists. It seemed Slade had decided to notch up his territory, and was peeing on a lot of bushes.

The DEA got involved and our buddy Shane O'Neal went undercover as a stateside pot dealer who wanted to add cocaine to his trade. He spent several months working his way into a position for a sizeable buy of pot, topped off with a little cocaine. The next step would have been to set up a big cocaine buy with Jacko Slade himself. But somehow Jacko got a whiff of Shane's daytime job and decided to end the relationship. Slade had his own landing strip in the mountains of Jamaica. When Shane got there and cut his deal (the operation set for the following week), Slade filled the reserve tanks on Shane's Beech 18 with watered-down fuel. Our friend and his partner made it just past the Caicos Islands when they switched to the reserve fuel. Five minutes later, the engines stopped and the plane became a rock. The crash landing killed O'Neal's copilot, but somehow Shane managed to get the life raft out and inflated — even with a right leg that had been crushed to near uselessness, and a mangled hand that would probably never be right. He would have bled out in the raft, but his ELT (Emergency Landing Transmitter) was working and a shrimper found him only an hour after the crash.

It wasn't our business. We knew it wasn't our business, and Shane knew the risks, but it just burned a hole in my gut — a young couple with the world in front of them, and now this. It was like Will said (quoting from some obscure movie he'd recently watched), "Sometimes a man's gotta do what a man's gotta do."

So, we set out to learn about Jacko Slade, and we had some friends who dabbled in late-night destinations help build us a "profile" of sorts — enough to get us through the doors of Jacko's Jamaican stronghold. We also set about discovering what he prized the most, and one of those things (along with his daughter, who was

in her last year of college in Florida), turned out to be a medallion —
an ancient, damned near priceless medallion originally owned by the
man considered to be the greatest Maroon leader in Jamaica —
Captain Cudjoe.

Cudjoe was believed to have been the son of a Ghana chieftain
who was captured and sold into slavery in Spanish Jamaica in the
1640s. But his father initiated a revolt and led his tribesmen into the
mountains of the island, establishing the first Maroon community.
Cudjoe followed in his father's footsteps and fought the Spanish and
the British so tenaciously and cleverly that the Governor of Jamaica
agreed to a peace treaty with him, offering the Maroons a tract of
land and recognizing them as an independent nation. Typical to most
of the treaties by white men, it didn't last, but Cudjoe had found his
place in history. He wore a medallion on a heavy gold chain, said to
be cast in Maroon forges with Spanish gold and the blood of
Jamaican slave owners. It became the talisman for slaves everywhere
in Jamaica and a symbol of freedom. When he died, the medallion
was passed to his powerful sister, Nanny, who continued to lead the
fight against slavery in Jamaica. The medallion disappeared in 1733,
when she was killed in a skirmish against British troops. It somehow
resurfaced in the late 1800s and became the most prized item of a
Maroon collection in the Kingston Museum, but it was stolen in a
mid-1900s heist and somehow ended up in Jacko Slade's hands.
There's no telling what it would have sold for, but it had become his
talisman, his power emblem among Jamaican gangs, and his good
luck charm. Until recently…

Shane O'Neal looked up at us from his bed and shook his head
incredulously, his green eyes sparkling but not diffusing the wariness
they carried. He handed Jacko Slade's golden medallion back to me.
"You know the son of a bitch is going to bend heaven and earth to
find out who you are."

"We covered ourselves pretty well," I explained as I tucked the
medallion into my pocket. "We met him in Rick's Café in Montego
Bay, in what seemed like purely a chance affair, us insinuating we
were probably all in the same business. Crazy Eddie staged a false
assassination attempt in the parking lot, from which we 'saved'
Jacko." I smiled. "And Crazy Eddie got clean away, of course. From
there it was an easy gig to get him to invite us to his place.
Eventually, we got him alone and squirted his drink with some of

Eddie's *el tigre* — that combination of hashish and peyote buds marinated in 151 Rum for six months. A teaspoon of that can take down a water buffalo. Most of the time Eddie and his friends use it by just putting a drop or two on their tongues. Jacko probably still doesn't know his name, totally lost to the rapture of the stucco swirls in the ceiling."

Shane grinned, but the look in his eyes faded to concern. "Yeah, that's probably true, knowing Crazy Eddie, but you guys pay attention, okay? I got enough to worry about." He stretched his leg and grimaced. "So, what did you think of Jacko Slade?"

"I think he's an act, but most of the time it's pretty much together," Will replied. "I was surprised to find he wasn't black. He's a strange-looking guy — pasty white with shoulder-length grey dreadlocks and dead black eyes."

"Rumor has it his great-great-grandmother was a slave in the islands, but he could have made all that up just to placate his Jamaican suppliers," Shane said. "Only thing I know for sure is, conscience isn't one of his high points. Hugged me like I was his brother before we left, staring at me with those black eyes as I took off. I should have known something wasn't right." He glanced wistfully out the window at the palms being shuffled by the easy onshore wind, then turned back to us, becoming serious. "If I were you, I'd be thinking about a vacation — a month or two the hell away from here. Find someplace where the drinks are frosty and the women are warm. Get in one of those airplanes of yours and slip out of here quietly. Let Jacko's goons wear themselves out trying to find out who you are for a month or two. It's not exactly like he's going to forget what you've done, but he's a busy guy. He can only split his attention so many ways." Our friend narrowed those green eyes, staring at us. "You stay here, someone's going to figure it out. Someone's going to find you. And then, the best you can hope for is to be dead."

After leaving Shane, Will and I dropped the medallion into a safe deposit box we kept at First State Bank. We had decided to have dinner in Key West, and with the setting of the sun, see if we could find someone to fondle us. It had been a while since either one of us had been fondled to our content.

It had only been a few months since I'd lost my lady, Marianna, the remarkable Caribbean temptress and former Cuban intelligence agent. We had shared a passionate love affair, but somehow it had failed to endure. Even now, I didn't quite understand, or maybe I just didn't want to deal with it. Marianna was a Cuban woman to her very heart. She loved the music, the food, and the fellowship of her island culture. But most of all, she was deeply religious, and her faith shaped much of who she was. It was a strong and beautiful faith she carried, one that had preserved the world and given comfort and provided succor to millions of people around the globe for centuries. She gladly gave of herself to Mass, confession, fasting, and the rites and other sacraments of her religion — even small pilgrimages.

We also often went up to Miami to attend some of the Cuban celebrations and street festivals, which she needed and I enjoyed greatly. I had always found a special place in my heart for the Cuban people — their zest for life and their struggle to free their country. The problem came about when Marianna began to want me to attend church with her and accept her faith. I never saw it coming, but at some point she confessed to me that she needed a mate who shared her beliefs. While I found her religion comforting in many aspects, it simply wasn't what completed me. I suppose I could only define myself as something akin to a Buddhist with an attitude. The truth was, I had always seemed to find myself the closest to God while watching a backcountry sunrise blush the rim of the world in pinks and oranges. I felt Him in the gentle breeze as I sat on the bow of my boat as well, my fly rod across my knees, and it was often in those moments that I spoke to Him, and I think He listened.

She began to spend more time in Miami with friends, and I drifted back to my semi-profession as a bonefish guide, because I needed something to do, and I still carried a passion for the occupation. One day she came home, and with tears in her eyes, told me she had found someone else.

My partner, Will, suffered much the same fate. Cass, the remarkable lady he had fallen in love with while we were being chased across the southern hemisphere by a rogue agency of the government barely a year ago, had recently stepped out of his life, as well. Cass was a free spirit, and although I was certain she had come to love Will, her definition of the word may have lacked the solidarity that my friend envisioned. Cass was a martial arts expert, and she had opened a dojo for Krav Maga, the Israeli fighting art, in Key West. (They lived in Key West aboard an old shrimp boat that Will had converted into an attractive live-aboard.) She soon became surrounded by muscular admirers, and as my friend eventually discovered, she wasn't quite cut out for monogamy. It wasn't that she didn't love Will — I truly believe she did. She just couldn't resist an occasional *affaire de coeur*. God knows Will and I had chased women in more countries than I could count. But having met Cass, he put that behind him — only to find himself cuckolded. He packed up her things and set them on the dock, then called me, and we flew to Costa Rica for a couple weeks of forgetful debauchery.

I looked at my old friend sitting across the table from me at Aunt Rose's Italian Restaurant. He was a little older, but still very much the crazy, carefree fellow with whom, just a dozen years ago, I had moved to the Florida Keys to become a commercial diver and a tropical fish collector. We had just finished college that year, but unlike our peers we just couldn't buy into the nine-to-five routine. We saw sails on the horizon and we couldn't resist their beckoning. Adventure called to us like the sirens to Ulysses, so we moved to The Keys to find it, and good Lord, we did. Adventure or misadventure seemed to dog us at every turn, from part-time pirates and Voodoo *bokors*, to wacky Jamaican soothsayers and drug smugglers. Adding even more flavor to that Caribbean brew was our learning to fly a variety of airplanes, and the discovery of a couple of lost treasures, as well. Then there were the girls — the ones we found, the ones we loved, and the ones we lost along the way. It had been a lot of things, but it hadn't been boring.

My buddy really hadn't changed much over the last 10 years. He was tall and thin, like a backwater heron, but tightly muscled from his work as a diver, with a mane of unruly blond hair that fell to his shoulders, and clever blue eyes that easily bordered on mischievous.

We were pretty much the opposite in looks. I was stocky and fairly well muscled from hours at the local gym, with long, sun-bleached brown hair and hazel-green eyes, but I had nowhere near my friend's height.

I pointed a fork of pasta in his direction and grimaced. "I hate to say it, but I think Shane's right. I think we need to get out of here for a while. What the hell, it's not like we can't afford it. We made a fortune off the gold bullion we dragged out of that cave in Cuba. We can take your twin-engine Cessna and scoot south for a while. Costa Rica, Panama. It's nice there this time of year."

Will mulled that over while washing down some lasagna with his wine. He nodded and got that classic mischievous grin, eyebrows bouncing. "I like it. Good excuse to raise a little dust south of the border." He thought for a moment. "How about San Blas? The San Blas Islands off Panama? We haven't been there since we were wet-behind-the-ears fish collectors. That's off the beaten path, there's some fabulous diving there, and we can slip across to Ustupo, or even Colon — find out if the women are still as accommodating as they used to be."

We were feeling good when we left Aunt Rose's, the wine and the thought of a new adventure having lifted our spirits. We were enjoying ourselves so much we failed to notice the big fellow at the bar get up as we were paying our bill and place a quick call on the payphone in the lobby. Afterwards, he waited until we had settled into our car before getting into his big Oldsmobile and following at a discreet distance.

We decided to make a stop at The Crooked Crab Bar on Duvall, which was famous for its cool crab races and its hot women. A few drinks, some entertainment, and the possibility of a liaison with someone warm and accommodating seemed like just the right combination. We parked our car just off Duval Street and entered the smoky, boisterous saloon. We didn't notice the big Oldsmobile that slid into the curve just down the street from us. The driver — slicked-back black hair, a guayabera shirt, and blue jeans — found a payphone on Duval and made another call.

Inside The Crooked Crab there was a centered oval bar where bartenders were sloshing out drinks with frantic, methodical cadence; and a bandstand in one corner, where a quartet consisting of a conga man, lead and bass guitars, and a wild harmonica player were enthusiastically hammering out Pat Benatar's "Hit Me With Your Best Shot." The place was full, but not sardine-packed, and the crab races on the far side of the room were already drawing a boisterous crowd. We found a table in a corner and ordered drinks from a shapely waitress. We had just received our drinks when I noticed the big guy in the guayabera shirt come through the saloon-like doors and pause for a moment. His eyes scanned the bar quickly, but lingered just a moment too long on us. He took a seat in the back, three or four tables from the bar, then ordered a drink.

I leaned casually toward Will, who was already making eyes at a college coed two tables away. "Don't want you to be too obvious, but I don't like the big guy with the dark hair over there — a little too interested in us."

Will shrugged, hardly taking his eyes from the coed. "Remember, Kansas, this is Key West...where everybody loves everybody."

"It's not that kind of attention."

Reluctantly, Will glanced over, then turned toward the band and spoke out of the side of his mouth. "He's a bit out of place, isn't he?"

"Yeah."

About that time two more guys entered the bar — one a light-skinned black man with dreadlocks, maybe five foot 10, wearing khaki shorts and a tie-dyed shirt; and a smaller fellow with dirty blond hair and cold eyes, dressed in a green tank top and white jeans. He was thin, but hard-looking — tight muscle groups in his arms and shoulders. They panned the audience until they found the big guy who was paying too much attention to us. There was an almost imperceptible acknowledgement in their eyes before they took a seat near the crab races, with a good vantage point.

While I was looking at the two who had just entered, I noticed a familiar face well above most of the crowd at the crab races table. "Little Mike" — six foot seven, shaved head, attired in denim, chains, and tattoos — was the unadulterated image of a manicured gorilla. It had been a long time since we'd seen him. We had experienced both the bad and the good side of Little Mike many years ago, regarding the possession of Lucky, a very special hermit crab that did his finest racing while high on cocaine.

Will was a quick study. He hadn't missed any of this. "We might have ourselves a problem here," he said cautiously. "I'm thinking Jacko Slade may be better at finding people than we thought."

I nodded. "Yeah. If we're going to get out of town in one piece we're going to need a diversion." I thought for a moment. "You see Little Mike over there?"

"Yeah."

"Okay, I think I've got a plan. We're going to use the old 151 trick..."

Will smiled.

When the waitress came over to check our drinks, I asked her to bring us a half-dozen shots of 151 Rum in a whisky glass, a rum and coke, and a pack of Crooked Crab Bar matches. I explained we were tourists and that I collected matches from the different places we'd been. When the waitress showed up with the drinks, I asked to borrow one of her order slips and a pen. I wrote out a note, gave her a five-dollar bill, and told her to take the note and the rum and coke over to the girl Little Mike had tucked protectively against him (as they cheered their present crab on to victory). I told the waitress to tell the girl it came from the two dudes who were watching us. Then I explained to Will what he needed to do. He got that mischievous grin.

When the waitress departed to deliver the rum and coke to Mike's girlfriend, Will got up, took the whisky glass of 151, and excused himself, sipping casually and moving toward the restroom on the far side of the bar. None of Jacko's boys moved. The one closest to our table continued to cover me. Will lost himself in the crowd and circled back behind that same guy. The other two had just noticed a commotion at the crab races table — a huge, bald-headed guy with muscles and tattoos everywhere was yelling something unintelligible as he bunched up a note from the waitress and threw it on the ground. He turned, found his target, and began a slow, methodical lumber toward the two fellows who had been watching us, pushing people and chairs out of his way with the single-mindedness of a wounded bull elephant. Even as crowded as the bar was, the event wasn't lost on a number of people. One of those was the guy who had been tailing us. He realized there was a serious problem when Little Mike stopped at his friends' table, reached down, and picked up the smaller of the two men by the throat. While holding that guy high enough that his feet were dangling off the ground, and throttling him like a chicken (the fellow gurgling and turning a vivid purple), he reached over, grabbed the other fellow's beer bottle by the neck, and smashed it against the side of the man's head.

Now this, of course, had everybody's attention, including the guy who was supposed to be watching us. Over the music and the mayhem, Will managed to come up quietly behind him and toss the glass of 151 on his back. Before the guy knew exactly what had happened (he was locked in the spectacle of watching Little Mike, who had become bored with strangling the smaller man and was now tenderizing the other with open-handed slaps while he held him by the front of his shirt), Will lit a match and tossed it...

The fellow's back flamed up like a Boy Scout bonfire, and while it wasn't life threatening, it was sure as hell distracting. He started screaming and stumbled into the chaos that Mike had created — bartenders and waitresses yelling, bouncers moving in cautiously (nobody wanted a piece of Little Mike), people scattering, tables going over, and drinks splashing/shattering on the floor. Mike, a complete berserker at this point, saw a flaming person screaming and charging in his direction, so he broke a chair over the guy's head. Through the pandemonium I managed to catch Will's attention and we inconspicuously made our way to the front doors.

We eased out of the saloon and down Duval toward the car. Behind us, people were pouring out of the exit, lost to an amalgam of fear and excitement. The warm night air, filled with honeysuckle and jasmine, was like a balm to our senses and I took a deep breath, exhaling slowly.

"Well, after all these years, Little Mike hasn't lost any of his charm," Will muttered. "What'd you put in that note? Sure got our boy's attention."

I spoke without looking at my partner. "Dump the tattooed gorilla and join us for a drink. My friend and I will screw you till you think you've died and gone to pecker heaven."

Will shook his head and smiled. "Yep, that would have done it all right. That's pushing all the right buttons." But he quickly sobered. "I caught the accent on the black guy — Jamaican. You know what that means…"

"Yeah, Jacko's found us. He's a quicker study than we thought." I glanced up at the full moon, pale as a dove's egg, with long, soft-white cirrus feathers whisking past it. "I'm thinking it's time for us to grab some diving gear and our toothbrushes, and head for Summerland Key Airstrip — you've still got the 310 there, right?"

My friend nodded somberly. "Yeah, that's the place. Take me by my boat and I'll grab what I need, then we'll head up The Keys."

Two hours later we were loading our gear in the twin-engine Cessna. Will had called Key West International and received a weather report for the Caribbean Basin. It looked good. We'd hop across to Cancun and spend the night. From there we'd cross over Honduras and Nicaragua, refueling in Costa Rica. Then we'd make the final run into Colon, Panama, to clear customs; then hop across to the San Blas Islands chain — hundreds of small islands, only a few of which were inhabited by the indigenous Kula Indians along with a handful of enterprising foreigners who had set up diving resorts. The water and the diving were spectacular, but best of all, it was pretty much off the map for most people. Just what we needed while we figured out how to deal with Jacko Slade.

CHAPTER 3

The flight over to Cancun went without a hitch. I hated flying over water without filing an Instrument Flight Plan, but we didn't want any record of where we were going. We grabbed a taxi after landing and found a quiet little motel. By eight a.m. our 310 was back in the air. The waters off the Yucatan Peninsula and the Gulf of Honduras were a deep, crystal blue, and there was hardly a cloud in the sky as we soared along the first couple hundred miles. After refueling in La Ceiba, we climbed over the mountains of Honduras and Nicaragua, which brought back less-than-pleasant memories of a crash landing on a river deep in the Nicaraguan jungle in Crazy Eddie's Grumman Goose. But this trip went well, and by late afternoon we were landing at San Jose's main airport in Costa Rica. Another night at a comfortable hotel and a delicious breakfast of ham and eggs with exotic fruit and fresh Costa Rican coffee, and we were on our way again. By noontime Will had us landing in Colon, Panama, clearing customs for our hop to the San Blas Islands.

Years ago we had stayed at Jerry's Dive Resort on an island about the size of a football field. (Okay, it was a little larger than that.) It was a near-perfect circular island with a lovely sand beach all the way around and a short landing strip cut through the center. His only neighbors were a small Kuna Indian village (the indigenous natives of that region).

A half-hour flight had us dropping in on the tiny airstrip, and before the props quit turning, Jerry stumbled out and greeted us as if we were long-lost relatives. Like ourselves, he was older now, but little else had changed. He wore a battered pair of surf shorts, a flowered shirt, and flip-flops. His weathered straw hat was still perched on a tangle of blond tresses, covering a darkly tanned face crinkled with squint and laugh lines. Jerry was a bit of a stoner, his droopy "Custer" mustache perpetually stained with pot resin, but he didn't let that affect his ability to conduct business. The story was, he'd made a big hit in the late '70s — a two-week boat trip to Jamaica that paid really well. Unlike so many others who blew what they made on booze, women, and more drugs, Jerry took his money and bought a tiny island in the San Blas Archipelago. It wasn't much, but it was his, and his tourist/diving business managed to pay what few bills he had.

"Well, I'll be damned!" he cried as we climbed from the plane. "Bill and Texas!"

"Will and Kansas," I reminded him, as my partner whispered, "He could be Rufus's white brother."

We had another friend in The Keys, a Jamaican Rastaman named Rufus, who had been the nexus of a number of our more interesting adventures. Rufus could never get our names straight, either.

Ignoring the correction, Jerry plowed on, "Great timing! The deep reef is clear as bath water right now, and as pristine as ever — never seen a crop of rock beauties and royal grammas like this last season, and the yellow-headed jawfish in the sand, in and around it, are just unbelievable! Thousands of heads popping up out of the sand like jack-in-the boxes. You gotta see it, man! And the grouper are everywhere." For a moment the smile faded and the humor melted from our friend's face. "Nobody screws with Jerry's reef. We had some dynamiters try to work my area. I can show you where their boat is now. It's gonna be a nice new reef addition in a couple of years."

There were those who had taken to dynamiting reefs — to kill food fish. One stick of dynamite will rupture the bladders of everything within 50 feet. The fish float up and the culprits snatch them off the surface. Quick and easy — except that it not only kills the fish, but the reef, as well. We had seen reefs in a number of places that were subject to this conscienceless treatment — nothing left but a white, dead coral graveyard. Jerry had obviously given the bad guys a taste of their own medicine.

"So, what do you dudes have in mind?" Jerry continued. "You want a bungalow, right? And I imagine you're gonna want your own boat."

"Right on both counts," Will said. "But we're looking to just lie back and relax for just a little while, maybe rent your cabin cruiser, if you've still got it, or something like that. If the weather holds we might explore a little, check out some of the other islands in the area."

"You got it," our host replied. "I got a nice 35-foot Chris Craft with a small forward cabin and twin inboard Mercs — just what you want. I use it for party fishing and diving in season, but as you can see," he said, motioning around at the mostly empty tiki huts, "things are slow right now."

I looked at Will and he nodded. "That'll work."

Will unlocked the nose storage compartment and we pulled our gear from that and the cabin. Jerry called over a couple of his native helpers and they took our gear to the tiki hut he had chosen for us. We spent the rest of the day organizing our gear and catching up with our buddy.

That evening we shared a seafood feast that would have put a smile on a bona fide Key West Conch — Nassau grouper, split lobster tails, and hogfish grilled over hardwood coals, along with yellow rice, black beans, and fresh finger bananas for dessert. We watched the dying sun ignite mottled cotton cumulus on the horizon, infusing them with pink and orange, then compressing those colors into heavy reds and purples, while the edges softened and morphed to silver and grey. We drank dark rum, smoked a little of Jerry's killer weed, and by the time the brilliant yellow moon had slipped off its zenith, we were lost to a nepenthe haze that cloaked us in euphoria, filled us with confidence, and bound us inextricably to nature, friendship, and spirit. It was a damn fine night.

The next day Jerry showed us his Chris Craft and we all took it out for a test run to make sure we were comfortable with it. By the end of that day we had all our gear stowed and were ready for a week or two of adventure and exploration. That evening we feasted again on a fresh dolphin (mahi-mahi, not bottle-nosed) that Jerry had caught on the reef. We drank Balboa beer and burned another of Jerry's left-handed cigarettes, then watched as the sun buried itself in the distant mountains of the mainland and the stars climbed out of the ensuing darkness, glistening modestly in their timeless symmetry.

I had hardly thought about Jacko Slade all day.

There are nearly 400 small islands in the San Blas Archipelago, some of them uninhabited and many seemingly filled to capacity with palm-thatched huts of the Kuna Indians. They rise out of the crystal-clear waters and are often surrounded by pristine reefs. We spent the better part of the following week drifting aimlessly between islands, diving, drinking Panamanian beer, and living on what we speared or caught, along with some of the supplies we had purchased in Colon. We probably drifted farther south than we had intended, and in the distance we could just see the mountains of Panama and Colombia. It was late in the afternoon — the sun was being dogged by rain-filled cumulus, creating cool shadows across a softly rolling sea, when we saw a boat, perhaps a quarter-mile off. Even at that distance it appeared neither tight at anchor or cutting a wake. We decided to have a look. As we got closer it was apparent the boat wasn't anchored or under power, but simply adrift, and listing slightly to the port side. It was an old commercial fishing craft, about 30 feet long with a small center wheelhouse/cabin. We hailed it, but there was no answer. Will looked at me.

"Yeah," I said. "Let's check it out."

We tied off to the stern and climbed aboard. There was no one on deck, but I immediately noticed what appeared to be splotches of dried blood. We followed them toward the cabin. We found him there, curled up on a filthy mattress, back against the wall, legs drawn up, his clothes bedraggled and bloodstained, hair matted, several obvious wounds showing — slashes and punctures on his torso and arms. He sat there clutching a leather satchel of some sort, eyes distant, even though it was obvious he saw us. We moved in slowly and knelt beside him, and he tightened against the wall.

"We're not going to hurt you," Will said. "Let us help you."

My partner looked at me and motioned for something to drink. I slipped out to our boat and grabbed some water. When I returned, Will lifted the bottle to the man's lips and he responded, drinking a little, but it was obvious that his situation was critical. "What happened to you?" Will asked.

A bitter smile touched his lips, and his eyes lit with distant memory, strangely fearful and yet triumphant. "I found it," he whispered, turning slightly and looking at us. "I found it," he whispered again. *"La cueva de esmeralda."*

Both Will and I spoke Spanish fairly well.

"The emerald cave?" my partner said, cocking his head and looking at me.

"One thing at a time," I replied, motioning Will to give him more water.

The fellow drank again, gaining some strength from it. He was middle aged, maybe in his mid-40s — dark hair, perhaps of Spanish descent, brown eyes, a wiry physique, but the wounds he had sustained and the obvious trauma he'd been through had drained him. We tried to move him, to make him more comfortable, but he fought us.

"No, no, I must talk," he said. "Someone must know. I was right..." He grabbed my partner's arm with a fierce desperation. "I studied the archives — the Spanish — they forced the Darien Indians to mine the emeralds, and the gold..."

Will looked at me, eyes displaying a sudden interest that extended well past humanitarianism.

"It was true, all of it," the man gasped, eyes wide in desperate fervor. "The Scots and their failed attempt to colonize the isthmus...the Spanish and their fort..." He took a deep, shaky breath. "The attack on the Spanish outpost...the gold and the emeralds stolen. It happened just as Aengus McFerson said."

Will tried to calm him. "Relax friend, relax. It's all right..."

But the fellow was having none of it.

"The archives...read the archives! Read the notes! The limestone spire...the limestone spire..." He choked again and gasped, eyes widening with anguish and shock — as if he had held onto life only in hope of passing on this bizarre chronicle. He clutched Will's shoulder with the desperation of a drowning man, and at the same time sought my friend's palm with his other hand. He forced something into Will's hand, and then, as if his course had been run, he coughed, eased back against the wall, and sighed. *"La cueva de esmeralda,"* he whispered again. He stared at us, and one side of his mouth lifted in an ironic smile. In the next moment his eyes lost their focus and he was gone, still clutching his leather satchel to his chest.

After a moment, Will closed the man's eyes and moved back slowly, still on his knees. He sighed heavily and looked at me. "What the hell was that all about?"

"I have a better question. What the hell is *la cueva de esmeralda?*" I said.

It was then that Will opened his hand and glanced down at what it contained. It was a rough, brilliant-green gem, all sharp angles and planes, just about the size of a large marble. "Whoashit!" he whispered.

"If I were to make a wild guess, I'd say that's an emerald," I muttered incredulously.

My friend nodded. "Want to make another wild guess where it came from?"

We both looked at each other and spoke simultaneously, *"La cueva de esmeralda."*

We spent the next two hours looking through the papers in the man's satchel. His name was Lector Mileston. He was apparently an amateur archeologist who, while searching through the archives in

Saint Mary's Cathedral in Edinburgh, Scotland, came across an interesting and little-known story regarding Scotland's short-lived attempt to challenge the English and the Dutch for colonization of the New World. In 1698 the Kingdom of Scotland established a colony called Caledonia on the Isthmus of Panama at the Gulf of Darien (what would now be the upper part of Panama on the gulf side). Unfortunately, almost from the onset the undertaking was hampered by bad leadership, lack of provisions, disease, and attacks by the Spanish, who had already established a fort in the region and didn't take kindly to newcomers. The colony was abandoned in 1700 after a final clash with superior Spanish forces. Only 300 of the original 1200 settlers survived, and only one of the three Scottish ships made it back to their homeland. But this was where the story got interesting.

The Spanish also had a fort on the Darien Peninsula. Fort Saint Andrew was maintained for one primary purpose: it was the staging area for the shipment of emeralds and gold back to Spain. The Spanish had established an outpost, located far up the Fangaso River, in the mountainous jungle interior. They had somehow established relations with the Indians of the area, possibly because the Indians thought they were gods of some sort, which wasn't unusual for explorers of that era. They had the local tribes mine gold and emeralds for them, trading glass beads and other trinkets, along with goods such as axe heads, knives, and tobacco for the gold and emeralds. Once every three months they would collect their bags of emeralds and an estimated 200 pounds of gold they had smelted into 10-pound bars at the outpost, and take them through the jungle and downriver by canoes to the Spanish Fort.

However, just before the Scots decided to give up and retreat back to Edinburgh, one of their leaders came up with a bold plan. They knew the Spanish had connections with the Indians upriver, and they knew gold was coming out of the area, but they didn't know how or when. But timing is everything. Three weeks before the Spanish were to receive their quarterly shipment of gold, the Scots caught and tortured a Spaniard, who provided them with the location of the outpost upriver. The Scot leader figured he could avoid being hanged for the mission's failure if he brought the King of Scotland a few boxes of gold and emeralds, so he sent a raiding party of 20 men upriver to ambush the Spaniards after they left the outpost. According to the archives, the plan went perfectly...at first.

The Scots raided the small Spanish contingency as they slept, during their second night away from the outpost. They killed the dozen Spaniards, but they also made the mistake of killing the Darien natives who were with them. What would have been a successful effort of thievery and murder became a running battle with the Indians — nasty small folks with poison darts and blowguns — not to mention the elements of an unforgiving jungle and dangerous portages from one point to the next. Two days later they were down to three men, who, late one moonlit night, hid the gold and the emeralds, which were weighing them down to begin with, and made a run for it downriver.

In the end, only one man returned alive. Unfortunately, the experience had left him all but a raving lunatic. Apparently no one believed the story of the hidden gold, but oddly enough, on the ship's return to Scotland, the tale was recorded by a priest, who listened to the man's confession — and that was how the information ended up in the ancient archives of Saint Mary's. Even better, the man provided a series of landmarks to the hidden gold.

Lector Mileston, the luckless individual we'd failed to save, claimed to be a distant relative of one of the original settlers in Caledonia on the Isthmus of Panama, and had been fascinated with the ill-fated attempt to settle in the New World. He traveled to Scotland to study the archives at Saint Mary's, and it was there that he found the obscure information regarding the whereabouts of a lost treasure.

Fortunately, Lector also kept a diary, and it was his diary in the satchel that supplied us the information on the Scot's ill-fated expedition of thievery against the Spanish. That same diary also held the landmark clues for the lost treasure that were mentioned in the archives of Saint Mary's. His writings went on to explain that Lector had hired a guide in a border town called Puerto Obaldia, who had a big boat — probably the one we found him in — and they took it up the river as far as it could go, to one of the rough mining towns that had sprung up with the finding of gold in the local rivers. There they hired a couple of natives with a large, outboard-powered canoe that could be portaged. For a week they fought their way upriver and across short but wicked jungle portages, still following the course and the landmarks described in the archives. In the end, the landmarks were still there, the most important one being a limestone spire that rose out of the top of a cliff just above *la cueva de esmeralda.*

Long story short, Lector found the cave, and surely as there's a bell in Saint Mary's Cathedral, there were the gold and the emeralds. But that's when things started deteriorating.

Will took the diary he'd been reading from, set it on his lap, and began to describe... "He leaves his people at the boat and moves up into the jungle, keeping his eyes on the limestone spire, knowing the cave is at the base of it. When he reaches the cave it's like a spiritual experience for him — a substantiation of all his wildest dreams. He explains that the emeralds had been held in leather bags that had deteriorated, the gold had been hastily stacked on the floor next to them. But it's then that he realizes there's no way to bring the gold and emeralds out of the cave without his guide and the native porters knowing about it, and probably wanting to kill him. He realizes then that he never really expected the tale to be true. So he stuffs a few emeralds into his pocket and goes back down to the boat. Night is falling, and he doesn't feel the need to make any major decisions. But there's a heavy buildup of thunderheads on the horizon..."

My partner turned a page or two and continued. "That night a tropical storm sweeps in with torrents of rain, and while they're in their camp near the river, they hear a roaring sound. The natives immediately start to go nuts — they know what it is. Actually, while the others are trying to get out of their hammocks and sleeping nets, Lector is running for the boat to salvage his diary. It's the only reason he survives, and not too well at that. He's in the boat when the tumultuous, 10-foot-high wall of brown, churning floodwater slams them. Somehow he manages to hold on to the canoe, lying in the center, diary stuffed in his field jacket, as the flash flood rockets him downstream, carrying uprooted trees, animals, and his luckless companions as well, who are by this time, very much dead.

"Somehow Lector Mileston survives the night, and by morning he is totally lost and being carried along at a rapid pace toward the sea. Three days later, starving and exhausted, but luckier than he probably deserves, he finds that with the high water he has apparently drifted through a temporary channel over the main portage site and is now well downriver, passing by the very mining town where the guide left his big boat. He yells for help and they pull him in and feed him, and he manages to find the guy with whom the guide had moored his boat. He's desperate at this point, so he offers the fellow one of the small emeralds he has left in his pocket to let him take the boat and disappear with few supplies, telling the man his friend — the owner of the craft — is surely dead. The good news is, the guy accepts. The bad news is, the guy changes his mind at the last minute and decides he wants the rest of Lector's emeralds. There's a knife fight that ends badly for the fellow who got greedy, but Lector is wounded as well, in several places."

Will paused for a moment, scanning some of the pages and wiping the sweat from his forehead. The sun was setting, burying itself in streaks of grey-blue cirrus on the horizon and the cooling breeze had faded. He turned the last couple of pages in the diary and spoke without looking up. "That's pretty much it — just a few last words about running out of gas and drifting downriver and out to sea, too weak from loss of blood to flag anyone down. I'm guessing the prevailing winds and currents just continued to carry him out, and he just got unlucky at the end — no one saw him or bothered to check him out until he was too far from shore..."

I shook my head incredulously. "Lord! What a tale! Like something out of a movie."

There was a pervading silence for a moment, then Will spoke the words that were hanging in the air. "Sure would like to find that cave..."

Our eyes met.

"Yeah, sure would..."

There was no point in trying to tow Lector's boat back nearly 100 miles, and certainly not with his dead body in it. There were numerous drawbacks there, from serious bloating and smell, to days of explanation with the Panamanian authorities, and perhaps an investigation. After we had thoroughly searched the craft and found nothing else of interest, Will slipped into the water with a pole spear and a 20-gauge powerhead. One shot against the bottom of the hull blew a clean, three-inch hole in the bilge. Half an hour later Lector Mileston and his boat were headed toward the bottom of the Caribbean Sea.

"God bless you, Lector," Will said quietly as we watched the last of the bubbles rise to the surface and dissipate. He held the glittering emerald up to the light and the last of the sun's rays danced through it with mystical allure. My friend shook his head, then turned to me. "As our old friend Rufus would say: 'We all be part of the great cosmic pinball machine. Sometimes it is tiny levers that deflect ball bearing of fate just a little…'"

I smiled and finished the sentence. "You and me…and Lector Mileston…tiny levers…"

CHAPTER 4

Jacko Slade sat in one of the oversized couches in the salon of his yacht in Kingston Harbor and stared coldly at the three men in front of him, the sun from the open window lightening his grey dreadlocks, his black eyes kindled with rage. "Tell me why I shouldn't kill you now. Tell me why. You had them and you let them get away. You say they performed some sort of dog-and-pony show and walked away. Walked away?"

The taller of the three winced and shifted slightly, his shirt rubbing against the raw skin of his back where the mild burns were just starting to heal. There was more of a defensive whine to his voice than he intended. "They had this big guy run interference, and the place went crazy. Everyone was trying to get out the damn building and we lost 'em in all the panic. But we'll find 'em, boss. Their plane's gone, like we told you —"

"Yeah, yeah, I know," Slade barked, cutting him off. "I've heard all the excuses already. I got people on that. Their flight path indicated they were headed for Mexico. From there they headed south — stopped in Costa Rica and then Panama, then flew east. We're figuring that out now. I'm probably gonna send the Griffins. Let them work this out for me."

There was a respectful, almost nervous silence from the three men in front of him when he mentioned "the Griffins." There were some things in life you just didn't screw with, like bubonic plague, nuclear weapons, and the Griffins…

Slade riveted the three men in front of him with a brutal stare. "I want you back in The Keys. If they come back unexpectedly, I want to know about it — you understand? You learn anything, I want to know about it before your drink leaves a wet ring on the bar. No excuses this time."

It took us three days to get back to Jerry's island, blessed — or cursed — with a new challenge. My partner and I had spent a lot of time discussing the pros and cons of trying to find a cave in the mountainous jungle of Panama. We didn't need the money, and Lord knows, with Jacko Slade and his goons, we were up to our necks in intrigue as it was. On the other hand, the jungle of Panama was a great place to disappear for a while, and as Will had said, holding up that remarkable gem, "You can never have too many emeralds."

"If we do this, and that's an *if*, I think we're going to need Crazy Eddie and his Goose," I said, sitting by the dying embers of the campfire. The stars were effervescent, dotting a stygian sky, and the moon was a cool blue-yellow. There was just enough of a breeze to make it pleasant and keep the mosquitoes at bay. It was just my friend and me. Jerry had retired early — he had a diving party coming in the following day.

"Yeah, Eddie's a wee bit nucking futs, but I like the dude," Will replied after a moment's thought. "The Goose could take us a good way in and we could use it to try to find some of the major landmarks Lector mentions. The guy was painstakingly methodical, if nothing else. But looking at Tommy's charts of that area, Eddie probably can't get us more than halfway in — no farther than the mining camp where Lector left his boat."

Will saw the pensive look in my eyes and shrugged.

"We could just flip a coin. Lord knows we've flipped a coin on some pretty important things before." He smiled. "A couple of girls come to mind. Remember Vanny and Carina?"

I did, and smiled. Will pulled a coin from his pocket, but I stopped him with a wave. "We need to stay disappeared for a while, no matter what. Maybe the DEA will nail Jacko in a few weeks and our problems will be solved. Anyway, I don't think we can hang out on this postage stamp of an island very long before we end up bleary-eyed, rum-stained, and talking to the conch shells on the beach." I paused and grinned at my friend. "Besides, I think you're right. You can never have too many emeralds."

Earlier that day we had shown the emerald to Tommy, who was an amateur silversmith and enjoyed shiny things. We didn't offer an explanation and Tommy had been around long enough to know better than to ask. He was appropriately impressed, and the following morning he offered Will a silver chain and a cradle he had fashioned overnight for the stone. In less than a half hour he had locked the stone in the cradle and Will slipped the chain over his neck. It was very impressive, but as our friend mentioned, it was best worn with discretion.

The next day we flew to the mainland (Panama), and placed a call to Crazy Eddie.

Edward Jackson Moorehouse, Crazy Eddie, was a dude unto

himself — a character straight out of a Kurt Vonnegut novel. He'd been a pot smuggler in the early '70s, and if half the stories were true, he'd become the Robin Hood of pot smuggling, giving much of what he made to friends in need. But Eddie gave up the business in the late '70s. The story on the street was he'd made a big run and received a serious chunk of money along with a really nice Grumman Goose floatplane, and apparently he knew when to hold up, fold up, and walk away. While that was true, it wasn't the only reason he quit. He never ran cocaine or heavy drugs, but shortly after his big run he was so full of himself, he did, one time. In the process it cost a young life. He never flew drugs again. In fact, he ended up flying regular relief missions to Haiti and Central America. He cut a deal with a friend of his to keep the plane on his buddy's property on the gulf side of Ramrod Key, and rented the back bedroom/bathroom of his friend's house, but he practically lived in his plane.

Edward Jackson Moorehouse was an eccentric personality. Some would say bald-ass crazy. Nonetheless, he was fearless and clever, and probably the best pilot I'd ever met. He and his first Grumman Goose had been part of one of our earlier "experiences." The adventure had cost Eddie his airplane, shot out of the sky by a Blackhawk helicopter, with us in it. Somehow we survived it all, and Will and I bought our friend another Goose.

Eddie wasn't Jamaican and he wasn't black, but he'd spent a lot of time on the big islands back in the old days, leaving him with a vernacular somewhere between black Caribbean and '60s Haight-Ashbury. He was in his late 30s, early 40s, tall and gangly, and hardly ever seen in anything but a pair of khaki shorts and a fruit-juicy shirt. He had a short-trimmed beard, long, sun-bleached blond hair that cascaded down to his shoulders, and a thin, slightly crooked nose that looked as if it might have been rearranged in a disagreement somewhere along the line, but he was still a fairly handsome guy. He had a perpetual tan and an easy smile, and he had taken to wearing, almost perpetually, a Jimmy Buffett "Margaritaville" ball cap that he claimed was given to him by Jimmy himself after they shared an evening of drinking in Key West. Everybody liked Crazy Eddie because he did crazy things, and nobody had better pot than Eddie. Strangely enough, his eye patch actually added to his persona rather than detracting from it.

Eddie was a casual guy, but he was nobody's fool.

There was no question that we would make this worthwhile for our friend, but we both knew the idea would appeal to him so much he'd probably do it for a bag of bottle tops. The boy just liked "the jazz."

The phone rang three times before he picked up. "*Hola,*" he said. "What it is?"

"It's me, Kansas."

"Hey, Kansas, my man! How's it hangin', dude?"

"Good – actually, really good. Got a possible gig you might be interested in — another adventure, like the one a few weeks ago."

"What are we lookin' at? Give me the skinny, bro. Don't be shy."

"Can't say much, you know, now, but we're talking about a trip up a river in Panama. And maybe some shiny green stones — the kind the Aztecs liked." I knew Eddie was somewhat of a Central American history buff.

There was a smile in his voice when he came back. "Shiny green is Eddie's favorite color. Where and when?"

"Meet us in Colon, Panama, in two days. There's a hotel there called El Estereo, about two miles from the airport."

"Groovy. Eddie be there."

"Eddie, we're going to need some other stuff as well — some food supplies, some fresh water containers, camping equipment, and some things you may want to tuck into those special places you have on your bird…"

"Eddie digs, man. It's cool. Give me the skinny."

When I was finished, our friend muttered, "Sounds like a wicked gig, brotha. Maybe even more on the edge than the last one." There was a pause, and I could almost see him smile. "We gonna squeeze the juice from the orange of life again, huh?"

"Drink the juice, eat the pulp, and dance on the rind."

"Right on, dude. Catch you on the flipside."

Forty-eight hours later Will and I were standing on our narrow hotel balcony listening to the sounds of Colon — the hawkers and vendors with their small carts, European cars rolling noisily over the cobblestone streets, the lively music from windows and doors — all of this blending of cultures and races into a frenetic yet melodic orchestra, when a taxicab stopped out front and Crazy Eddie exited. Attired in standard garb — a fruit-juicy shirt and shorts, he looked up and nodded almost imperceptibly, then continued into the building. Three minutes later we were all seated at the little table in the small, living room/kitchen.

"Any problems?" I asked.

Eddie shook his head. "None at all, man. Cool flight down, tailwinds all the way."

"How about the stuff we needed?"

"Got it all." Our friend smiled, his deep tan offsetting a collection of ivory-colored teeth. "I met up with your old buddy, Bobby Branch — the crazy Vietnam vet. Dude's seriously backlashed, man, but he's got more things that go bang than the sheriff's department. The government will never know how much stuff that boy shipped home while assigned to the local armory in DaNang." He chuckled lightly. "Timing was good. He'd just gotten out of jail for using an RPG to blow up the plastic dragon on the top of the Wok and Gong Chinese restaurant on Truman. Still swears they're all commies trying to take over Key West. He offered us AR16s with 30-round mags, and a couple semi-auto shotguns. Hell, he wanted to throw in grenades. But dude, even I can only hide so much stuff, and if they catch you with heavy armor in places like Central and South America, you're never gonna see the light. I settled for a trio of Smith and Wesson nine-millimeter handguns — same caliber so we don't have to screw with different ammo. I also brought my Vietnam vintage handheld radios, so we can stay in touch."

"Excellent," said Will. "Mucking fagnificient!" He held his hands out, palms up. "But I'm hoping we won't need anything that goes bang. This is probably going to be just an in-and-out thing. No Rambo stuff."

"Yeah, tell that to Lector Mileston," I said.

"Who's Lector Mileston?" Eddie asked.

I looked at Will and he nodded. "Well, Lector's the fellow who gave us the story we're about to tell you. Sit back and get comfortable, my friend. You're in for a tale..."

Twenty minutes later Eddie pushed back his chair from the table and blew a low whistle. "Whooo, man, sounds like a John D. McDonald novel." Then he smiled. "But this could be a righteous gig, dudes — a righteous gig."

Puerto Obaldia in the Kuna Yala Province of Eastern Panama was a hole in the wall by anyone's standards — a ramshackle border town with a couple of bars, one or two hostels, and a lousy restaurant. Surrounding all this was a plethora of decrepit, garish-colored shacks and shanties that staggered off the beach and up the side of the mountain, the tin roofs doing their best to keep the torrential rains and the relentless tropical sun from the locals.

Benito Tito, most commonly known as "Benny La Rata," was perched on the gunwale of a derelict net boat half buried in yellow beach sand, having another conversation with himself. This had become a pretty regular thing, but not necessarily a good thing.

Benny the Rat had received his nickname as a youngster. He was small and thin then, and could wiggle his way into or through just about anything — windows, screen doors, loose floorboards — and in the business of thievery, this was a plus. He was still as wiry as a starved terrier, with long, dark, hair and a swarthy complexion, a slightly hooked nose, and quick brown eyes that never settled. In his business it didn't pay to become complacent — there was always someone who wanted a piece of him, from the local *policia* and the people to whom he always owed money, to the landlord of the tin-covered dog house he called a residence.

He plucked an ant off his brightly colored but seriously weathered T-shirt, studied it for a moment with disdain, and flicked it away, wiping his fingers on his ratty canvas shorts. Things just hadn't gone the way Benny had planned. He had seen himself more like the *bandito* Zorro (he had seen the movies once or twice at the theater in Colon), robbing from the *chitbag* rich, living in a fine place, and screwing long-haired, dark-eyed, big-breasted women who loved him because he was Zorro and had a huge *carajo* the size of a zucchini and a tongue like a snake on cocaine.

Yeah, that's how he saw it. But instead he was living in this dung hole of a town, and stealing from stupid hippie tourists who got too high to know their own bloody names (he stole that word from an Englishman tourist just before he stole his wallet).

But lately things had gone from bad to worse. About a week ago he sneaks into a local hostel at night and steals a pocket watch off the dresser of a tourist. The *hombre* wakes up and Benny has to make a hasty exit, but at this point nobody knows what he took. He makes it to the front porch and sees the local constable headed toward him. The guy upstairs is yelling now. Benny panics and does the only thing he can think of; he stuffs the watch in his mouth and swallows it, chain and all. Beats spending three months in the local jail, where even the rats die of malnutrition. For days he can hear the bloody thing ticking in his stomach as it works its way through his system.

Each day he goes to the crapper, but no watch. Finally, with considerable discomfort, he feels the pocket watch reaching the end of its journey, but once again Benny's bad luck strikes. All that comes out is the foot-long chain — the rest of the watch is stuck up his ass — and now he has a gold chain dangling out of his butt. He tries pulling on the chain but it was a pretty good-sized watch and the pain is excruciating, so for the next few days he goes around with a gold chain hanging out of his ass. He makes a mistake of telling a friend, and a day later everyone in town is pointing and laughing at him, asking if they can yank his chain.

Then, last night he tries to rob an old couple on the beach, and the guy kicks him in the *cojones* — kicks him twice. Benny's eyes roll back in his head like a *brujo* in a trance and he passes out. When he comes to, his bloody *cojones* are the size of cantaloupes — two bloody cantaloupes between his legs! And the pain! *Madre de Dios!* He has to crawl all the way home, tears running down his cheeks, moaning like an unrewarded whore, *cojones* the size of cantaloupes and a chain hanging out his ass! Just another week in paradise...

We spent the night going over plans on how to approach this caper, poring over the maps that Eddie had brought. Lector Mileston spoke of the Rio Fangaso several times in his writings, and we found it on the map next to a small Panamanian town called Puerto Obaldia. This was apparently his starting point, so it became ours. We loaded up the airplane with some supplies we had purchased locally — canned goods, some fruit and yams — and with everything else tucked securely in Eddie's secret hiding places, we boarded. Eddie was a human packrat with a '70s stoner mindset. The interior of the plane had big peace symbols spray-painted on the interior, and posters of the big 60's and 70's rock groups duct taped to the walls — Janis Joplin, The Guess Who, and Three Dog Night. (Duct tape was Eddie's favorite tool.) There were boxes of eight-track tapes, fishing and diving gear, an old television, a couple folding chairs, and a huge pile of floating fishing net (the stuff used to gill mullet) stuffed in one corner.

"What's with all the fishing net in the back?" I asked.

Eddie sighed angrily. "I was gonna take that out, but I got busy and forgot. Belongs to the guy who owns the land where I keep my plane. He's a fisherman — nets mullet — but he can't leave his nets out after they've dried because of the freakin' mangrove rats. They chew up everything — the line, the floats — so he keeps a couple in the plane." He huffed bitterly again. "Freakin' rats! I hate 'em! Eat the damned tires off the freakin' plane!"

It was a beautiful, clear, early summer day, and the sunlight filtered through the windshield, warming the cockpit and buoying our confidence. I took the copilot's seat and Will belted into the seat right behind the cockpit. Eddie methodically worked his way through the preflight, checking magnetos and altimeters, carburetor heat and fuel pumps, setting the transponder, and double-checking flight controls. Then he set his mixtures to rich and fired up those big twin, air-cooled Pratt & Whitney engines. While he gave them a second to warm, he pulled a doobie from his vest pocket, lit it, and exhaled. He offered us a hit, and when we refused, he shrugged, picked up his mike, and got taxi clearance from the tower. Three minutes later we were sitting at the end of the runway. Eddie pinched out his joint, exhaled a rich, grey cloud with satisfaction, and stuck the doobie behind his ear. He looked at us and grinned. "Hold on tight, *amigos!* The Emerald Express is leavin' town!"

The flight from Colon went smoothly, and before we knew it Eddie was pointing down at the little ramshackle town of Obaldia, backing off on his throttles and dropping flaps. Seconds later the familiar slap of the hull on water could be heard as the plane slowed and Eddie aimed us for the marina. When we got the hatch open, the familiar third-world Caribbean smells assailed us — ocean and beached seaweed, fish and nets drying in the sun, diesel fuel, and poorly contained refuse. There was a handful of beat-up fishing boats moored at the marina, a couple sports fishermen up from Acandi, Colombia, and a fishing boat or two that were way too clean, with exhaust ports indicating big engines. Smugglers probably. As odd as it might seem, it was all somehow strangely comforting. The Caribbean Basin was our playground — always had been.

Benny La Rata stood on the beach and watched the big floatplane as it arced across the blue-green sky and set down in the mouth of the Rio Fangaso, taxiing over to the small marina perched at the edge of the river. The floatplane tied up at the rickety pier and three *gringos* climbed out. *Thas' a nice plane,* he thought, scratching his butt through his white cotton *pantelones,* inadvertently fingering his ass chain with a frown. *Sure as monkey farts smell like bananas, something in there worth stealing...*

We explained to the owner of the marina that we would need to moor plane for perhaps a week, maybe longer, but for the first day or so we would be making forages up the river. He knew better than to ask why.

The plan was to run the Goose up the Fangaso to see if we could spot any of the landmarks that Lector spoke of. Two of these were distinct — a small waterfall that broke onto large boulders that looked like the backs of turtles, about halfway into the journey; and most importantly, the limestone spire that rose out of a cliff in the jungle. Just below that was *la cueva de esmeralda.* If we could find these ahead of time, from the air, it would make the task at hand a hell of a lot easier. We had mentioned to the owner of the marina that, in a day or two, we would need a skiff that could get us upriver to the large mining camp Lector Mileston had mentioned, where he had rented his canoe with the outboard and his guide. We had been told the river narrowed too much only a few miles from Puerto Obaldia for Eddie to get his Goose in comfortably, but there were a few places upriver that widened out briefly. We could try to find these with the Goose, so Eddie could become an emergency backup if necessary.

Jacko Slade was standing on the porch of his Jamaican mountain home, staring out at the repairs taking place on his storage facility. The explosion and fire set by the assholes who stole his medallion had set him back weeks in deliveries, but the damage to his reputation was far greater. He'd have his revenge. He was a patient, methodical man.

The phone rang and his houseboy brought it to him. He listened for a moment. "Good," he said. "I was certain the Griffins would take the job — something challenging for them."

It wasn't their real name, of course. Rumor had it the moniker was taken from the legendary creature with the body and back legs of a lion and the head and wings of an eagle. Sounded just about right for the Griffins.

"We've been able to get a location on the two we're after. They were in the San Blas Islands for a while, but our contact in Panama said they left Colon yesterday for a hole called Puerto Obaldia, on the eastern coast. Far as we know, that's where they are now. Give the Griffins my best. Tell them I want these people to suffer, understand?"

In truth, Slade knew he had little to worry about on that account.

After we took care of the docking and the locking of the plane, there was little else for us to do but find some lodging for the night, and hopefully a restaurant and a bar. Adventuring is a thirsty business. The two hostels and the main bar looked like something out of an 1800's Western town — tall, square, slant-roofed edifices with second-floor balconies and slat-wood walkways. The restaurant was built closer to the beach, but was still, in the kindest of definitions, garish and motley. The inside was little better than the outside, with small wooden tables and chairs, and a vinyl floor that looked like it might have been installed about the same time the Model-T Ford was becoming popular. But the food proved to be acceptable. We had chicken and yellow rice with black beans, and a beer each. You didn't drink the water in places like this — guaranteed to have you living on the toilet with a week's worth of "the screamers."

After dinner we wandered over to the larger hostel and paid for three rooms. Business was slow. Business was always slow, except in the winter months when the hippies and the vagabond travelers came down, looking to experience the real "south of the border" for a while. A week or two in Puerto Obaldia was generally enough for those folks. They couldn't wait to get back to a bathroom that wasn't at the end of the hall and didn't smell like a badger had died in it — where the water coming out of the taps wasn't a blurry brownish-grey, and a ceiling fan wasn't considered a luxury.

By this time, the sun was sliding into the mountains of the Darien Isthmus, casting shadows across the jungle. The ocean had flattened and turned a dark blue, the palms on the shoreline became melancholy silhouettes, the seabirds hushed their calls, and the softest fragrance of night-blooming jasmine wafted through the stillness. I was reminded why I love the Caribbean.

An hour later found us entering the largest of the local saloons. Over our shoulders we could hear the arrival of another floatplane, but it was only on the water briefly before lifting off. I paused to see the Cessna 182 banking a wing into the dying sun as it headed up the coast.

In the room before us there was a smattering of gold miners taking a hiatus from their grueling work in the jungle rivers; a handful of the local working people, from fishermen to guides; and a few people who looked like they owned the fast-looking fishing boats who were just passing through. They all gathered in knots at the small, round tables, or at the long, hardwood bar. The place had that subtle tang of poorly kept saloons — a medley of old beer, spilled liquor, and sweat, with a slight smack of less pleasing odors wafting from the half-open door of the men's room. Ceiling fans turned in lazy swirls, pulling up and dissecting the smoky blend of cigar, cigarette, and reefer, while a handful of local girls kept the customers in drink.

We found a table in a corner and sat. The waitress, a rather attractive Kuna Indian girl, took our orders with a beguiling smile, and a few minutes later she was back with our beers. She looked at us in an unabashed, sensual fashion. "You wan' anythin' else, you ask for Maria. I take care of you."

As she walked away, Eddie focused on her swaying hips and mumbled, "I might like to be 'taken care of' later on."

We were on our second round of beers and I had just mentioned my curiosity about who might have been on the plane that just landed, when two men came through the swinging doors of the saloon. They were huge by anyone's standard, nearly matching our Key West friend, Little Mike, in size and girth, but there was a brutality in their eyes — a coldness that Mike didn't possess. Dressed in T-shirts and jeans, they weren't muscle-bound necessarily, but there was a sense of power about them and a confidence in their stride that said they knew they were the big dogs — the kind of guys whose favorite drink was Everclear and radiator coolant. There was enough similarity about them that they might have been brothers — heavy jaws; hard, dark eyes; swarthy skin; and long, black hair. It was almost like in the movies, where everyone stops and looks, and even the piano player stumbles. The two men stood at the swinging doors for a moment and panned the room, then stepped in and found a table in the back. One of my first thoughts was of Jacko Slade. But I shook it off. There was no way he could have found us this quickly.

Will put a voice to my concerns. "You don't think…"

"Nah," I said, shaking my head. "Not possible. We're too far under the radar."

My partner shrugged. "Yeah, you're probably right. Guess I'm just feeling a little neurotic."

We had been drinking for about an hour, telling stories, and hitting shots of bourbon in between our beers. We were starting to feel no pain, but were still paying a little attention to the big guys in the corner. It seemed to me they were glancing over at us more than I cared for, but I reminded myself of the odds on that, and how easy it is to be paranoid when there's a price on your head.

Just then, the saloon doors opened again and two women strode in — probably having arrived on the commercial floatplane that came in earlier with the two big guys. They had cameras slung over their shoulders and were overdressed for Obaldia — Banana Republic shorts and the short-sleeved khaki shirts that all the big game hunters wear in the commercials – probably tourists who got one of the overdone brochures on this place. They were a little hesitant when they got a look at the bar, but entered anyway, finding a table near us. They weren't bad looking. One had a mane of soft red hair, a prominent but not overbearing nose, and wide green eyes; the other, longish blond hair tied up in a ponytail, pale blue eyes that displayed little emotion, and a wide mouth that almost extended past sensuous and into peculiar. But in a place like this they were both good catches. It wasn't long before Will, with his propensity for gab, had started up a conversation with them.

Margo, the redhead, explained that they were from Fort Lauderdale and worked freelance for several vacation magazines. This was their latest assignment, "Although God knows why," she added, looking around with a touch of disdain.

Kendra, the blond, had focused on me, and that was okay — she wasn't a bad port for this storm. Being the observer that I am, I noticed how well built the ladies were — the small but impressive muscle groups in their arms and legs. Actually, it was nice. Besides, I figured they didn't get where they were by being wimps. Meanwhile, Eddie had begun to get to know our little waitress, so it was all working out nicely.

We talked for about an hour. The girls explained that they would stay for a week — plenty of time to get acquainted, as Kendra put it with a smile in her eyes. We explained that we were following up on a lead on a lost friend of ours, Lector Mileston. (Better to offer some truth with your lies.) We were enjoying the conversation and I had the beginning visions of sugarplums dancing in my head, but unfortunately, our lady friends decided to make it an early night, explaining that it had been a long flight from Miami to Colon, and then to Obaldia. They suggested we meet for breakfast at about 8:30, and we eagerly accepted.

Watching them go, I realized they were quite a pair. While more striking than attractive, they moved with a stealthy grace, like ballerinas on steroids. Throughout the whole experience the big guys to our right hadn't left their table. They drank mechanically, if not sparingly, and watched everything.

As tomorrow would be a busy day, making our first foray over the river and the jungle in Eddie's Goose, we decided to call it a night, as well. Eddie reluctantly told his little *señorita* to keep her schedule open for the following evening.

Benny had watched the *gringos* eat at the restaurant, then head over to the bar. This looked like a good time to see what they had in their plane. He was halfway to the docks, walking along the old dirt road, his weathered sandals kicking up dust between his brown toes, when he spotted a car coming his way — an older American Ford, still a good distance off. "Son a bitch!" he whispered vehemently, immediately trying to find someplace to hide, but he was too late. The car was already picking up speed.

The driver, Rico Menta, was one of the middle-range fences in the area, selling stuff that disappeared from tourists' rooms and cars. He had his ear to the ground all the time and he often gave people specific jobs. A week ago he had given Benny one of those jobs — a wealthy couple on a sailboat that had docked in Puerto Obaldia. They were said to have a collection of expensive cameras, and Rico wanted them. Benny broke into the boat and found the cameras, but "The Rat" could divorce his integrity like a hermit crab changing shells, and he decided to cut out Rico by selling the loot himself. His partner in crime found out about it, and now planned to do a little cutting of his own.

Benny scurried off the road and into the jungle as the car slid to a halt, and Rico, along with one of his arm-breakers, scrambled out, yelling curses at him. Benny grimaced, his ass chain still dangling between his legs as he ran. (*Three days without a decent chit!*) They weren't likely to catch him in the jungle, but this definitely fouled up his plans for the airplane.

As we left the bar I casually glanced back and saw the big guys still studying us intently. I started to turn to my partner.

"Yeah, I know," he said uncomfortably, not looking at me. "I know..."

The town was built off of one main road, just a few hundred yards from the beach. Houses and businesses were scattered down side streets for about half a mile. There were a number of dark areas, walkways, and side streets we had to traverse before reaching our hotel. About halfway into the 10-minute walk I was certain I heard footsteps from the alleyway behind us. Seconds later, a cat yowled and bolted from the alley coming up on our right. I looked at Will and Eddie, and their eyes reflected the same concern. The moon was just rising out of a band of dark clouds, casting furtive, eerie shadows across the walkways and buildings, and increasing our heightened sense of uneasiness.

Again I heard movement in the alleyway behind us, more distinctive now. Stealth being replaced by expediency — not good. Suddenly, to our right a door opened, casting an amber shower of light into the gloom, and an old man dragging a trashcan stepped out. The fellow was a startled as we were, but the American 20 I quickly produced eased his apprehension.

"Sir," I said in Spanish, "would you cry out for the police as loud as you can for this?"

He smiled and croaked, "I would cry out for the devil himself for that."

I picked up a rock by the side of the road and unceremoniously threw it through the window of the local cathouse just across the street, then gave grandpa the money and whispered harshly, "As if your life depended on it — wake the devil!"

The old fellow earned his money nicely, with a strident falsetto, and it was amazing what one rock could do — people came pouring out of the brothel as if someone had kicked an anthill. In the confusion, we bolted down the street like lizards on crack. Another five minutes found us gratefully stumbling onto the porch of our hotel. It certainly wasn't the nicest hotel I'd ever stayed in, but I couldn't remember feeling more pleased to be inside the doors of an establishment.

Benny was tired and sweaty after an hour of playing jungle tag with Rico and his goon, but both his arms were still intact and there were no knife wounds to be found anywhere. He sat underneath an outcropping of marlstone in a small clearing on the side of the mountain and smoked a cigarette, flicking the ashes away so they didn't get on his brown cotton shirt or his white pants. It was growing dark. There was no returning to town until Rico had run out his anger. He leaned back against a sun-warmed rock and relaxed. Might as well get a few hours of sleep. He would sneak over to the airplane just before dawn and see what he could find.

Some people lack mooring — to ideas, principles, and even to other people. Mooring helps most of us find equilibrium. It doesn't mean we can't move vertically or laterally, but like a boat line at a dock, it keeps us from drifting away. Benny was a quart or two low on mooring...

I awoke just as the morning sky was softening from indigo to pale sapphire. You never rest well the first couple of nights in a strange place. The last of the stars still speckled the western horizon, and the east was just turning pink. I dressed quickly and checked on the others. They were awake, as well. We decided to take a walk down the beach to the Goose before breakfast, just to make sure everything was cool.

It was a beautiful morning. The sea was a blue mirror, just beginning to reflect the fleshy splendor of reds and yellows from the rising sun. The cool dampness of sunrise cast swirls of mist over the calm shoreline waters. It was so remarkable we had ceased conversation and were just enjoying this gift of Mother Nature as we approached the plane from the docks. It was then that Eddie put a hand on my arm, brow furrowed, and pointed with his other hand. The hatch door to the Goose was slightly ajar.

"I know I locked that," he whispered cautiously.

Benny knew he was running late, but there had been a lot of "good chit" in the plane. He had found a gunnysack and was filling it with two-way radios, a camera, and some high-end foodstuffs. But in the process, his long-overdue bowels started rumbling and cramping. The bloody watch seemed to have shifted somehow and he needed to take a crap, now, before he popped like a slapped *piñata*. He found the small head in the aircraft — more like a closet — closed the door, ripped down his pants and squatted on the commode. He was grunting and moaning with delivery-room fervor, but the bloody watch was still blocking the path of nature.

We cautiously opened the door to the plane and peeked in. Things had obviously been moved around. There was no one to be seen but there were some serious noises coming from the toilet. Will eased into the cabin with Eddie and me behind him, and crept forward. He grabbed the door handle and looked at us. We nodded tensely. He flung it open and drew back his fist. There on the toilet was this long-haired, skinny dude, pants down around his ankles, with eyes the size of manhole covers.

Benny, completely freaked out, screamed and involuntarily jerked upright. Unfortunately, the chain in his ass caught under the toilet seat as he stood up, and he shrieked again, eyes rolling back in his head as the sizeable pocket watch was jerked out of his butt. Benny dropped to his knees in agony, and fell face-forward out of the toilet at our feet, writhing and moaning.

Eddie looked over at the commode and saw the watch still attached to the seat by its chain.

"If I didn't know better, I'd say that boy just pooped a watch out his ass!" Eddie knelt and grabbed the guy by the collar, then drew him up, face to face. "Are we gonna have to wait for you to shit the cufflinks to go with that, or are you done?"

"Done," groaned a thoroughly miserable Benny. "Done..." as he tried unsuccessfully to pull up his pants.

Eddie ignored his efforts. "What the hell are you doin' in my plane, you freakin' runamucker?"

"I need a place to take a quick chit, man," our new acquaintance pleaded. "I had a bloody watch cloggin' up my ass. Benny was gonna esplode!"

Eddie let him go with a shove and sat back on his haunches, not done with our boy just yet.

I reached over and grabbed the gunnysack of our things. "And these? What are these all about?"

Our friend was recovering a little now, reaching for his pants at his ankles. "Dis place was a mess, man. I was jus' cleaning up a little."

All three of us looked at him, hard.

"Okay, okay," the guy said. "The truth is dey call me Benny el Zorro."

We looked at each other, then back to the fellow struggling to get his pants up with one hand, while holding out the other. "Yeah, man, I'ne almos' a legend in my own time. I steal fron' da rich and give to da poor."

"You don't look much like a legend, dude," said Eddie dryly.

Benny shrugged, still clutching his act. "My good clothes are at da cleaners."

"I say we take him to the local police and let them sort it out," Will said.

"No! No! Not a good idea!" our guest cried adamantly, holding up his hands. "Dey don' like Benny…Zorro." He gulped in a breath and tried another tactic. "Look, Benny know everyplace aroun' here. You wanna go son'place, Benny know how to find it. I take son' time off fron' my Zorro job and be your guide. What Benny don' know aroun' here don' matter…" He looked up at us, somewhere between pleading and confident, then the façade faded again. "Don' turn me into *la policia*. Dey hate Benny."

I paused for a moment, staring at him. "Do you really know this area? Like, farther upriver?"

The fellow nodded vigorously. "Oh yeah, man. Chu betcha! I work panning gold for a while in de tributaries of de Rio Fangaso. I know de mining towns and many of de people. Benny live here all his life!"

"So why aren't you doing that now, instead of the Zorro thing?" Will asked. "Panning gold sounds like a pretty lucrative profession."

Benny scowled. "Too damn hard work, *compadre*. Dere be snakes, and big cats, and biting lizards, and ants, and bloody mosquitoes! Zillions of 'squitoes! Benny get bumps all over his body like he got son' kinda disease and he itch and he stink all da time!" Our new acquaintance got what could only be defined as a confessional smile. "I rather rob fron' da rich and give to da poor."

"So you're a thief," said Eddie.

Our new acquaintance shrugged. "Only part-time. I'ne taking correspondence courses to be a bullfighter." He smiled. "Bullfighters — now dey make da big bucks, man — get the da hot *chiquitas!"*

Will rolled his eyes.

"Okay," I said. "Let's get back to reality. We may have to go upriver for a few days, maybe a week or so." I glanced over at the others, then back to Benny. "Do you really know the Rio Fangaso well enough to help us?"

Before the little thief could answer, Eddie interrupted, "Don't lie to us, runamucker. You do that, we'll duct tape your hands and feet and throw you outta this airplane somewhere over the jungle."

Benny visibly blanched at that, but recovered quickly. He was beginning to realize that this could be a win-win on a couple of levels. First off, this could get him out of town and away from Rico Menta and his arm-breakers for a while. Secondly, these *gringos* were up to something, and that probably meant money in one fashion or another. Benny applied the most contrite, honest expression he could muster. "Chu betcha! Chu betcha! I know da first names of da tree frogs, know which snakes gwenna bite chu and which not. Benny's *madre* was a Darien — she teach me how to use blowgun, mix poison for darts, to make you *muerto...*" He rolled his eyes, and hung his tongue out of his mouth in a fashion to indicate death. "...or jus' make you sleep for a while. I know what you can eat and what eats you, and I can help you at da mining camps." He paused, serious. "Dey some scary places, man. You gwenna need *un amigo*."

Again I glanced at Will and Eddie, then back to the little thief. "Okay, here's the deal. We're gonna run our airplane up the river today. We'll be back before nightfall. In the meantime, we're gonna give you a chance to prove yourself. You find us a boat we can rent that will get us to the mining camps upriver. From there we're probably going to need a couple of canoes with small outboards. We'll tie up with you tomorrow morning, here at the docks. You think you can do this, for sure?"

Benny nodded vigorously. "Oh yeah, man. Chu betcha!"

As planned, we met the girls for breakfast at the one decent restaurant in town. Margo, the redhead, was dressed in blue jeans and a Bee Gees T-shirt. Kendra, the blond, was wearing khaki shorts and a short-sleeved blue shirt with a couple of buttons casually undone in the front. Breakfast was enjoyable, but marred by our incident from last night.

Margo and Kendra were seriously put off by the idea of Americans being stalked in the streets and were considering booking a flight back to Colon as soon as possible.

"We came here to shoot some photographs, not get mugged, or worse," Kendra whispered seriously. "They don't pay us enough for that. Hell, they don't pay us enough to stay in that chicken coop they call a hotel."

Will was in a panic. The only really acceptable women for 100 miles and they were talking about leaving already. "Maybe the police will find out who did it," he offered.

Margo huffed, unconvinced. "Yeah, right. Have you seen the police chief? He looks like he'd have to struggle to get out of his own way. Way too many tortillas…"

It turned out that leaving today was a moot point anyway. We found out from the waitress that the plane that brought them in would probably not be back for a couple of days, regardless. During breakfast, we explained that we were going upriver. The girls seemed genuinely disappointed.

Margo put her hand on Will's arm. "You're going to leave us here and go gallivanting off? How about taking us with you? We could take pictures…"

We explained that, unfortunately, this wouldn't be possible, and when they asked for more details, we got a little loose-lipped, as men do around women they want to impress (I was reminded that ego has a voracious appetite). We told them we were following up some historical evidence about gold and gems being buried in a cave up the Rio Fangaso in the late 1600s. The ladies were duly impressed.

"That would make a fantastic theme for a shoot!" Margo cried, looking over at her friend.

Kendra nodded. "Our boss would love something like that, if it were true…"

"Whoa, whoa," I said, holding up my hands, palms out. "Publicity is the last thing we want in something like this. We don't need the rest of the world knowing we found a bag or two of emeralds."

The girls were disappointed, but excited by the concept, and it all provided interesting breakfast conversation. We agreed to meet for dinner on our return from the day's flight. Our new friends said they would like us to consider letting them do a short shoot of us in the jungle — maybe just a few pictures of real, intrepid 20th-century adventurers without mention of gold or emeralds. Our egos were duly impressed. We said maybe…

By midmorning we were loaded aboard the Goose and ready to depart. We hadn't seen any sign of the men from the bar last night. Maybe they were late sleepers. Regardless, the odds were growing that they might be associates of our pissed-off Jamaican friend. Not good…

Will and I threw off the moorings as Eddie turned over the big radials. Bursts of grey smoke fired from the exhaust ports and the huge, three-bladed props began to whirr in slow synchronization as we leapt aboard through the cabin hatch. In moments our buddy had us bouncing along the river against the rippling current, the hull providing its familiar slapping sound until the airspeed and the flaps gave us the lift we needed. We soared up off the water in that exhilarating moment that all pilots cherish, when man shakes off the limitations set on him by the gods and lifts into the heavens to share the thrill of flight with the creatures of the sky. Kingfishers and herons along the shoreline fluffed their feathers and shook their wings with indignation. A flock of startled ibis burst into flight below us like black and white confetti, while parrots and toucans cried out insults at the intruders. Once again we had found our element, locked into the thrill of the moment, intrepid 20th-century adventurers that we were.

For the first 15 or 20 minutes there was little more than the winding muddy river below us, snaking its way out of the mountains in the distance and pouring toward the sea. There were, of course, small Indian villages off the banks — thatched huts gathered in ungainly squares, generally with larger communal structures in the center. Soon those began to appear less and less often, as the jungle claimed all the territory along the river. Finally, we came to the first of the mining communities inhabited by those incredibly hardy men and women — amalgams of early Spanish descent, local Indians, and the few European frontiersmen of this area, along with a handful of industrious if not mercenary Chinese. They mined gold and some emeralds from the rivers, or from sparse veins in mountains, incorporating picks, handheld pans, and rickety sluices. Most of the camps had jerry-built docks on the water — little more than raw posts and rough-cut planking angled along the water's edge like precarious wooden centipedes. The houses were dilapidated, tin-roofed wooden creatures built on stilts to accommodate the rise and fall of the river. There was always a thatched-roof bar or two — because mining is a thirsty business. Occasionally, we spotted a few better-built houses a little farther from the river, belonging to those who had hit the small lotteries of the occupation but hadn't left, tied to the profession, entangled in the clinging vines of greed and hope like all the rest. This wasn't a lifestyle for the faint of heart. The busiest enterprise, next to bars, was the undertaker.

After another 20 minutes into the flight, the mining towns were gone and the river had narrowed. At this point we had reached a higher elevation with rising terrain, and the watercourse below had tapered to the point that it was no longer possible to set the Goose down.

It was then we saw the falls...exactly as Lector Mileston had described it. Great boulders rose out of the pools below the plunging waters, looking just like the backs of turtles, but the river widened briefly and went around the falls as well, so we could still negotiate it in a boat.

"I'll be damned," Will whispered reverently as Eddie circled the tumbling 50-foot drop and the pools, which gradually returned to a flowing river. "There they are, just like Lector said!"

"Keep us with the river, Eddie," I muttered, studying the terrain in the distance. "In a few miles we should see a five-mile hairpin turn that comes back on itself. That's where Lector, and the Scots before him, portaged across to save time."

We hadn't been flying another 15 minutes when again, just as Lector had said, we came to the hairpin turn, and realized it would indeed have to be portaged. There was probably a half-mile stretch of low terrain inside the hairpin, and it looked as if there was some sort of small village in the center. Portaging across would save us at least a day of upstream effort.

"Now we're looking for a spire of limestone on our right side, sitting on an outcropping well above the river," I said, having difficulty containing the excitement in my voice.

We didn't have long to wait. Ten minutes later it happened just as Lector said. The river made a wide turn to the right and in the crux of the turn, a limestone cliff rose out of the bowl. There, at the apex of the cliff, was a spike. Battered by storms and winds for centuries, it was no longer as pronounced as it had been at one time, but it was, without a doubt, the spire we were looking for.

There was a spontaneous cheer in the cockpit and Eddie whispered excitedly, "Far out, dudes! Radical to the bone!"

We couldn't set down — the river was much too narrow. But Eddie made several passes while I used our binoculars, looking for a tree-covered ledge 50 feet below the spire that concealed the entrance to a cave which held several hundred thousand in gold, and conservatively, another half-million in emeralds. Things were looking up.

Upon our return that afternoon we met with our new assistant, Benny, who proudly proclaimed he had found a boat worthy of our caliber, and he was more than ready to serve as our humble guide into the backwaters of the Rio Fangaso. After meeting with the owner, we agreed that the slightly weathered, 24-foot, center console

Mako would work just fine. It had been modified with a large forward, covered hatch that would allow some sleeping protection if necessary. The price was high — $200 a day plus gas, but the owner was letting Benny use it, so I figured that drove the price up considerably, just out of pure speculation and concern. Benny had changed into a clean pair of cotton pants and a fresh T-shirt. He had a gunnysack of belongings over his shoulder, and seemed more than eager to depart. He was genuinely disappointed to hear we weren't leaving until the following day.

"So why haven't we heard from the Griffins?" Jacko Slade asked over his shoulder while staring out at the jungle around his Jamaican compound.

The tall man behind him with military-short hair and cold blue eyes replied, "Don't know. I know they made it in — our people talked with the pilot. Evidently there were a couple of tourists with them in the plane." He paused. "Word has gotten out on this contract and I suspect there'll be some independents working it, as well." His face stretched into a feral grin. "I don't suppose it matters to you who kills them."

Slade turned and looked at his companion. "No, it doesn't, just as long as it happens and it's painful. But before it's all over, I want the medallion."

CHAPTER 5

It was already well past noon and we still needed to gather equipment and supplies for the journey upriver, so there was no leaving today. The good side of that was we could probably arrange a date with Margo and Kendra before we left. Eddie had informed us he was taking his chances and meeting with the pretty little *señorita* from the bar that night. The bad side was still the two fellows who were probably on Jacko Slade's payroll.

Eddie came up with a possible solution to our dating problems. He dragged out a chart in the Goose and spread it before us. "How about we do a little picnic this evening?" he said as he pointed to a couple of small islands about five miles offshore. "I talked with 'Benny/Zorro' today and these two islands are mostly uninhabited — just a fishing village or two. There's a nice beach here," he continued, pointing. "We could do a little romantic luau and not have to worry about someone trying to gut us like fish in a private moment — bring some blankets, get some chicken and yams from the local market, maybe even spend the night…"

Will looked at me and got that lascivious grin of his.

"Yeah, not a bad idea," I agreed with a smile. "If we can talk the ladies into it. Besides, if we can stay away from the deadly duo for a few more hours, we'll be headed upriver in a fast boat. That's assuming those guys were actually after us last night. We never really saw them. We could be doing a Chicken Little act here. Maybe the sky's not falling at all."

My partner shrugged. "Actually, you're right. I still can't imagine Slade being able to find us this quickly, way out here in freaking nowhere. I'd put money on those guys being some sort of *banditos,* but that doesn't mean they're our *banditos.*"

The girls thought a beach picnic was a great idea. So, for the rest of the afternoon we transferred gear from the plane to the boat, preparing to leave about midmorning the following day. Benny volunteered to watch the gear, saying he would hide in the forward hatch and guard everything. It seemed like strange dedication from such a mercenary fellow, but we accepted the offer.

Sigmund Freud was fascinated with childhood and its influence on character and personality. Freud would have found Maldo, and

50

his brother Valt, a fascinating study. They were the product of a 20-minute union between an expensive Cartagena whore and a wealthy importer. She had an impressive clientele of judges, politicians, and upper-class criminals. He was an importer — cars, refrigerators, stereos, air conditioners, and cocaine. Sometimes he imported the cocaine in the cars or the refrigerators, doubling his money. Life was fast for her and she didn't realize she was pregnant until the end of the second month. She knew, somehow, who the father was, and breaking all the rules, she decided to have the baby. But it was two babies, and a difficult birthing killed her. The children were handsome boys — not identical twins, but clearly gifted with the same hair, eyes, size, and temperament as their father, who was killed in a gunfight with police only two years after their birth. They were raised in a whorehouse, and later in the streets of Cartagena, which was a hard but valuable education. Valt was fond of quoting Sigmund Freud, who once said, "One day, in retrospect, the years of struggle will strike you as the most beautiful." They hadn't reached that point yet.

Valt and his brother had watched the *gringos* load into their plane in the morning and return in the afternoon — no chance for anything up to that point. They had missed them the night before due to the distraction the trio had created with the old man and the cathouse. It would be easy enough to kill them, but there was apparently a medallion involved that the client insisted on recovering. Now the *gringos* were loading a boat with supplies. It would certainly be better to kill them before they went anywhere else, but no one ran up a river like the Fangaso at night, so they had some time. It was a small town with few places to hide.

They were discussing their next step when someone knocked on the door of the little bungalow they had rented at the edge of town. Maldo opened the door cautiously, hand resting on his hip near the Smith & Wesson at the small of his back. His face took on a puzzled expression — not unpleasant, just puzzled. He tilted his head and asked, "And what can we do for you?"

As we lifted off in the Goose that afternoon, God was smearing swaths of grey putty across the edges of a brilliant western sky. The sun worked its way through the patches and reflected off a gently rolling, green summer sea. In less than five minutes we were circling the pair of small, picturesque islands with circular white sand

51

beaches that Benny had told us about. So far, our boy was earning his keep, once again emphasizing that he would sleep in the forward hatch of the Mako to protect our gear. Had we known, we would have realized it was little more than a gesture of self-preservation. Rico Menta, the fence Benny had ripped off, was practically going door to door in town.

Eddie brought us down lightly and eased the Goose onto one of the picture-perfect beaches. Margo and Kendra, dressed in shorts and loose T-shirts, were ecstatic, already burning up rolls of film as we unloaded our gear. Sandpipers hopped along the shoreline, playing tag with the gentle roll of the surf, scavenging up what each wave revealed. Cormorants bobbed out just beyond the roll of the small shore break, sneaking quick dives for luckless minnows and watching us with interest. A curious osprey observed our intrusion with cool indifference, soaring in perfect circles above. In the jungle, tree toads bleated mournfully, land crabs scurried amongst the brittle mangrove leaves, and we could hear the cries of monkeys and parrots, angered by this invasion of man, but sufficiently well acquainted with the relationship to understand there may be something in it for them.

By the time the sun was entombing itself in Panama's mountains and rose and mauve embers of dusk had closed in around us, we had built a fine coral-rock fire pit, and the coals of a cooking fire were glowing contentedly. I was discovering that Kendra was a treat; quick, smart, and totally without airs, and her features — the strange, pale blue eyes and the extraordinarily wide mouth — seemed to be growing on me, becoming less liabilities and more attractively distinguishing features. Her perky blond ponytail lent her a bouncy coed look without the vapidity that sometimes accompanied that stratum. Hell, the truth was, I liked coeds...

Will seemed to be doing just peachy with Margo, who was an attractive lady in her own right. With that caramel hair, those green eyes, and a nicely proportioned figure, she was a good catch as well. Her nose was just a little large for her face, but her broad smile caught your attention and pulled your eyes from that slight flaw. Again we noticed how firmly muscled both women were, but that certainly wasn't a flaw. Maria, Eddie's "catch of the day" from the bar, was quite attractive as well, with long, dark hair and big brown eyes, and a figure that required a second look. So all in all it was shaping up into an interesting evening.

The girls laid out blankets around the fire and we ate grilled chicken and coal-baked yams, with some sweetbreads that Maria had made, finishing it off with mangoes the girls had brought. In the process, we drank three bottles of wine. No one was feeling any pain by the time the heavens darkened and the first evening stars appeared. We talked for a while, told stories, offered some history, and we discovered that the girls were originally from Homosassa, Florida. Actually, they were half sisters (same father, different mothers).

Eventually, conversation wore down, slowing, then halting tenuously, like an impatient child holding open the door to the next room. Kendra snuggled up against me in one of those moments, as we watched the coals in the fire soften and the stars in the sky harden.

"It's awfully crowded here, don't you think?" she whispered, her voice a sensual purr, her lips against the lobe of my ear, sending tingles down my neck.

"Just thinking the same thing," I said with a smile as we picked up our blanket and grabbed another bottle of wine from the cooler. Glancing at our friends, I added, "We're going to study the mangroves at the other end of the beach."

Eddie took Maria's hand and pulled her up. "Have I ever showed you my cockpit?" he said, nodding toward the plane.

Maria, whose conversational English was less than perfect, replied, "No, not yet. But if I touch it, it's extra."

For the next few hours that silver moon slowly rolled across the sky, casting silky shadows over bough and water, and the jungle gradually grew still and quiet — with the exception of low moans of pleasure, or cries of ecstasy that wafted across the dark sea like enchanted spirits.

By 10 o'clock the following day, the last of the gear was loaded into our Mako. We had bid our ladies goodbye, telling them we would be back in three or four days if all went well. Kendra said they would probably escape to the mainland for a few days of photo shoots around Colon, then return to Obaldia toward the end of the week. As we had agreed, Eddie was to stay in Obaldia with his base VHF radio on the plane. We would use the VHF on the boat to stay in communication, with established daily contact times. He might have to take the Goose up to get a signal as we got deeper into the mountains, but one way or another we would have voice contact. He was our ace in the hole if things got ugly.

So, with the sensual images of the previous night and the possibility of fat green emeralds dancing in our heads, we shoved off into the unknown. The rich sights and smells of the river engulfed us. Exotic greenery and constant rebirth, lazy alligators sunbathing on muddy banks, colonies of cormorants and herons perched in the guano-splattered trees, and chattering monkeys flitting from limb to limb on the far shore. All this was offset by the myriad legacies of man — the refuse at the water's edge, the pearled prisms of gasoline on the surface of the river, and the constant sound of generators producing the energy needed to steal what nature had so kindly offered without a price. As we pulled away from the dock, Will sliding our broad-bowed Mako into the center of the brown river, the most excited of all seemed to be Benny, near the stern. He kept glancing back, then looking forward with a smile.

Will looked at me and called out over the rumble of the twin 125-horsepower Johnson outboards. "The boy's a born adventurer — look how excited he is to be headed into the unknown. Maybe he'll do just fine."

Benny was smiling because in the distance he could just see Rico Menta pulling up at the docks in his old Ford, shouting unintelligible curses and beating on the steering wheel as he recognized Benny in the departing boat.

The first part of the day went well. The spring rains were passing and the green-brown river flowed steadily seaward without the intensity of months before. We had prearranged communication times of 8:00 a.m., 2:00 p.m., and 8:00 p.m. The 2:00 p.m. contact went without a hitch, but Eddie had some startling news for us. The town was in an uproar (as much of an uproar as Puerto Obaldia could manage). Apparently the local police had spent the morning at a crime scene — a little bungalow on the edge of town, where a maid had discovered the renters lying on the floor of the living room — two large, dark-haired men who had been shot to death.

I glanced at Will and Benny, then came back to the mike. "Eddie, you don't think…"

"Yeah dude, that's exactly what I think."

"Whoashit!" Will whispered. "There was a boat that came into the harbor last night, just about the time we were taking off — a small fishing boat. I didn't think much of it…"

I keyed the mike again, speaking to Eddie and Will. "Okay, okay, we're jumping to conclusions here. We don't know who it was that got popped yet. There's probably a thousand people in Obaldia."

"And some of them are whacking each other to get a chance at us!" Will muttered sarcastically. "I don't like being this popular." He looked over at me accusingly and waved his hands. "All I ever wanted to be was a tropical fish collector. Nobody shoots tropical fish collectors. But you — you and Rufus, our crazy Rastaman buddy — every time I turned around you two had some new harebrained scheme."

I waved him off. "Ahh, c'mon, man. You like 'the jazz' as much as the next guy." I held up a hand. "Okay, maybe not at first — at first, the harebrained schemes scared the crap out of us both. But we got a little addicted. We wouldn't be here now, in this freakin' boat headed up a river full of alligators, leeches, and all kinds of biting, stinging bugs, with crazy natives and God knows what else —"

"I'm here for Lector's emeralds and the gold, not necessarily the jazz," Will replied, and as soon as he had said it he realized what he'd done.

Benny had gone from interested in the conversation to suddenly very interested in the conversation, perking up like someone had just plugged him into a 110 line. "Gold? Emeralds?"

Will sighed angrily. "It's a long story, and you're on a need-to-know basis."

I was about to reply when we were interrupted by the blast of a steam whistle. In the distance, coming downriver, was a garishly painted low-draft steamer, probably 40 feet with a center wheelhouse and a canvas-covered forecastle. In the shade of the forecastle, sitting in a gaudy-red velvet lounge chair was an absolutely huge man being cooled by a skinny native with a large heron-plume fan.

At a ponderous 300 pounds, Tu Phat Shong was the product of a Chinese mother and an adventurous father who had been half Hebrew and half Darien Indian. This combination had given Shong connections with the backwater Darien Isthmus tribes, a shrewd respect for money, and the cleverness of the Asian mind. He had small places of residence in two of the three larger mining camps on the Rio Fangaso, and a more permanent bamboo and mahogany home in the jungle, guarded by Darien tribesmen. Much of the area into which we were traveling was controlled by him, and he possessed an extraordinary coconut telegraph. If it happened on the Fangaso, Tu Phat Shong knew about it.

Our immediate conversation was interrupted as we navigated to the side of the river to let the steamer pass. The heavy man sitting in the chair watched us with interest as we passed. He had a shaved head, with the exception of a long lock of black hair that sprouted from the back, right side of his head, and dropped to his shoulder (like ancient Egyptian royalty). He wore a colorful Chinese silk vest that struggled to enclose his enormous girth and a pair of pale blue cotton pants. His skin was closer to the reddish color of the Darien Indians, but lightened by his other heritages. He didn't wave or nod, or acknowledge us in any fashion. He just studied us, as one might study an unusual bug they've come across; those slightly slanted, black eyes devoid of any emotion except curiosity. After we had passed, Tu Phat turned to his secretary, a small, attractive woman with long brown hair and similar black eyes. "Send word up and downriver. I want to know who they are."

Lector Mileston's fight with the mining camp dockmaster a couple of weeks ago had not gone unnoticed. A brilliant, uncut emerald was found in the dead man's pockets and the rumor of a hidden cave with emeralds and gold once again came alive in the camps and villages along the river. Everyone lived for dreams of wealth along the Rio Fangaso. Life was hard and unyielding, but every once in a while someone hit it big. There was a legend about a cave of gold and emeralds, handed down from the Spanish and the natives of the area. It was the El Dorado of the Darien Isthmus — a story no one really believed, but everyone *wanted* to believe. *La cueva de esmeralda.* The mining camp incident and the discovery of the emerald had worked its way back to Tu Phat Shong, and he was not a man to let any opportunity, however remote, slip through his fingers.

While all this was happening, Benny the Rat was weighing his new good fortune. Gold? Emeralds? Now this was the kind of "steal" he was looking for...

I signed off with Eddie, who agreed to find out more and speak with us at 8:00 p.m. We continued on upriver, into the falling sun.

Four hours later, Benny pointed to the rickety docks of the Puerto De La Esperanza Mining Camp (Port of Hope), just as the last of the sun was eclipsed by the treetops of the jungle. "Thas de place for to stay tonight," he said authoritatively. "Tomorrow we get to camp where we take canoes upriver."

The gilded river was greying in the shadows and the night creatures were just beginning their plaintive calls. As we tied up at the dock, we were met by a small, wiry man with short, grey hair and bright, dark eyes, along with a large, brutish fellow who had hands the size of hams, unruly hair, and a jagged scar that ran from eyebrow to cheek, where his left eye used to be.

"Welcome to Puerto Esperanza," said the small man, dressed in the soft *pantelones* of the area and a seasoned T-shirt, his straw hat in his hand. He quickly assayed us, and our boat. "You will be here overnight?"

We nodded.

"Yeah, I guess so," Will replied. Looking around, he asked, "Is there someplace to stay?"

"*Si*, a guest house of sorts, in the camp. If you are not too particular..."

I gazed at the shabby docks and the small shack that served the dockmaster. "How much for overnight docking, and what about our stuff?"

The little man shrugged. "Twenty, American, for overnight. Thirty if you want your stuff to be here in the morning."

"We'd like it all to be here in the morning. All of it."

The little man shrugged again. "Okay, 35."

"You just said 30."

"*Si*, I know, but if I tell you 30, something will probably be missing. But if I tell you 35 and give the five extra to Pablo..." He gestured to the one-eyed gorilla at his side. "...everything is here in morning."

I started to argue, but Will grabbed my arm. "Would you try to steal from a motivated Pablo?"

I paid the man and we took our radios, the canvas bag of weapons, and our Loran. Will patted big Pablo on the shoulder as we started down the docks. "Keep an eye open tonight, okay?"

We found the guesthouse, if it could be called that. It was a barracks-like building that had been added on to a deteriorating hardwood shack about the size of a Chevy van, all on four-foot stilts. The whole thing was set up like boot camp — bunk beds, about a dozen of them, with two naked electric bulbs in the ceiling and a wooden table with three chairs at the end of the room that looked like they might have come from the Civil War. The owner was a wizened, old Chinese woman who spoke pidgin English with a leaning more toward pigeons. Dressed in a simple cotton shift adorned with stains, she looked at us, hands on her hips, weighing us. Finally, she nodded.

"You wanna sleepy sleep, yeah? How many night?" Before we could get a word out she launched off again, hands in the air, wagging her finger at us. "No girly girls. No ficky-ficky here. Sleepy here. I no need sticky sheets to clean. Understand?"

I opened my mouth, and one more time she beat me to the punch, again pointing a finger at me. "Twenty-dollar deposit — you breaky chair, bed, you no get back."

"Lovely," muttered Will, as I paid Mrs. Chiang Kai-shek and she held the 20-dollar bill up to the light, looking for ink smudges. The good news was, each bed came with a heavy wooden chest and a lock, the key supplied by our personable owner, the chest bolted into the wall. We put away our gear, examined the beds for lice, and decided to check out the town and the local watering hole. I would need a drink or two before bedding down with whatever lived in that mattress.

With the exception of the dull drone of generators, one at each end of town, it was as though we had just stepped back in time 150 years. Along the main street half a dozen lamps, enveloped in swarms of bewitched insects, cast an anemic yellow light and brushed obscure shadows onto decks and alleys. There was a walkway of sorts built about four feet off the ground that ran from the guesthouse to the main street in town. Almost everything was built on stilts and accessed by plank walkways. The jungle was only a stone's throw at any point. The compound was a simple affair — one main street with buildings on both sides. The more mundane businesses — blacksmith, butcher, storehouses, stable, undertaker, and minerals assessor — were all on one side. The other side was reserved for entertainment and pleasure — bars, barber, bathhouses, and cathouses.

As we moved up onto the colonnade we could hear bright Latin music blended with the contemporary sounds of American records spilling out from the bars and bordellos around us. We picked the first saloon and entered through the louvered, swinging doors.

Will and I had spent a lot of time in third-world bars, but I thought this one took the cake. The floor was composed of weathered planks, far enough apart to let beer, blood, and other excretions find an exit. There was a long, rough-hewn bar at one end with a pitiful selection of bottles behind it, and a handful of tables and chairs strewn indiscriminately around the room — additional relics from the Civil War. But most remarkably, there was the monstrous trunk of a live Magnolia tree rising up from underneath the planked floor and out the roof of the bar, and there were monkeys slipping in and out of the bar from the hole in the roof. Ghostly rivers of cigar smoke swirled through the room, barely intimidated by the two decrepit ceiling fans. There were probably 20 people spaced about the interior at tables or at the bar, and probably an equal number of monkeys. Several of the customers were openly using cocaine, laying out lines and snorting them with gusto, or smoking reefers the size of Cuban cigars. Three or four scantily clad Darien girls were serving drinks (or themselves, without shame, in the darker corners). The lap dances apparently constituted as entertainment, as well. The monkeys chattered approvingly and applauded with the drunken customers each time an arrangement was brought to a zenith. In one corner a pasty-looking guitarist, a morose African saxophone player, and a skinny Darien woman were performing an almost macabre version of "Nights in White Satin"— music to slit your wrists by — a 911 melody. The only thing that enlivened the place at all was the freaking monkeys.

We had just ordered a second round of beers when Benny leaned in close and said, "So, when are chu gonna to tell me about da gold and da emeralds?"

Will jerked as if he'd been stung by a wasp.

I glanced around, then quickly leaned in and rasped, "Keep your freaking mouth shut, you little mongoloid. You'll get us all killed. As far as you're concerned, there's none of that crap."

"But dere is," Benny replied. "I heard chu say so."

I was just about to reply when the doors to the saloon opened and the porcine Tu Phat Shong entered with a small entourage. Again I was reminded how much he looked like an early Egyptian ruler — the same reddish skin, the single lock of black hair, and the dark, almost almond-shaped eyes.

Tu Phat had just completed a brief transaction downriver regarding a pair of remarkable Long-Winged Harriers — a hawk thought nearly extinct in Central and South America. After a couple of weeks of acclimation, they would be smuggled into the U.S. to a discreet buyer in Dallas. Tu Phat understood something that most of the glazed-eyed, hardcore smugglers had yet to learn — pound for pound, rare birds were worth more than gold, or any kind of illicit drug, and certain reptiles and animals qualified there, as well. In addition, his connections had expanded so greatly that he was now largely able to bring creatures into the States right through customs, by forging the species on declaration forms to represent something non-threatened, and putting a few dollars in the hands of the right people when his shipments arrived.

If, in the event there was a problem, a "mistake in the manifest" could be explained away a lot easier than a couple kilos of cocaine. Life was all about power and money, and Shong had both.

Tu Phat had seen the *gringos'* boat at the docks of Puerto Esperanza, and on a whim, decided to stop there for the night. He and two of his bodyguards, along with his favorite concubine and his secretary, entered the bar and surveyed it for a moment before finding tables, conveniently enough, across from us. The big Darien/Chinese, still dressed in a silk vest and cotton pants, had a small, white-faced capuchin monkey on his shoulder that hissed angrily at the presence of the other monkeys, but relaxed at Tu Phat's coaxing.

The bar grew surprisingly still as the group settled into their seats and Tu Phat Shong offered us the slightest of nods in the process, his rounded face offset by a raptor-like beak of a nose and cold, dark eyes. They ordered drinks, and with some degree of ceremony, a backgammon board was delivered to their table by the bartender. Evidently, this wasn't their first time there. We had no way of knowing, but Shong considered himself somewhat of an authority at the game. Curiously, most of the people who had the audacity to beat him with any sort of regularity often seemed to have accidents — some were bitten by poisonous snakes that found their way into their houses, others were mugged and beaten. Just strange coincidences… But it did have an effect on Phat's game — in a short amount of time he seemed to have become almost invincible. After he had played a round with his attractive concubine, and the band finished a morbid version of "Hurt" by Johnny Cash and took a break (probably to slit their wrists a little so they could get into the next set), Phat's small, dark-haired secretary walked over to our table, accompanied by a bodyguard.

"Good evening, *señors*," she said politely, in acceptable English. "My employer, Mr. Tu Phat Shong, would like to purchase you a drink, and perhaps have you join him at his table."

Will chuckled spontaneously at the name. "Too fat Shong, huh?"

The little lady drew a bead on him, her eyes narrowed, and the charm greatly diminished. "A small word of caution: The last person who publicly found that distinct analogy amusing, disappeared. Most of him was later found on a tiger ant mound in the jungle."

Will's eyebrows went up and his mouth pinched into a grimace. "Whoashit. No offence meant..."

"None taken, by me," she replied, her smile returning. She waved her hand toward her table. "Would you care to join us?"

After introductions, we were subjected to a polite grilling. Beyond common civilities such as where we were from, and what we did for a living, and life in the States compared to Central America, it basically came down to, as Tu Phat put it, "And what is it that brings you to my river, gentlemen?" ("My river," we noticed.)

There was a residue of malice just under the veneer of civility that was almost tangible. I was reminded of a time years ago, at a zoo in Tampa. The animals were in specially designed cages that allowed you to get quite close. There was a young Bengal tiger in a cage, and a little girl, who, fascinated as she was, got as near to the bars as she possibly could, slowly, reluctantly moving past the animal. There was a look in the eyes of that tiger — eyes that never let that child go for a second as the huge creature crept as near as possible, ripples of tension trembling its furred flanks. There was more than just a hunger — it was a sense of power and desire, totally devoid of conscience. It was the same thing I saw in Tu Phat Shong's eyes.

"We're doing some exploring, a historical study on the early Spanish and Scottish influence on the Darien Isthmus, for the University of Miami," I explained. "We're looking for the locations of their early forts. On a personal level we're collectors of antique bottles — 1600s and 1700s in particular. It's been a hobby of ours for years." (The part about the old bottles was true. Again, a little truth in your lies...)

I saw Tu Phat's face light some as I mentioned the Spanish forts, and I wished I hadn't said that. But the interest passed when he saw Will eyeing the backgammon board. "Do you play, Mr. Bell?" he asked invitingly.

Will shrugged. "Yeah, a little."

A competitive gleam suddenly glistened in Shong's eyes. "Would you care for a game?"

Will looked over at me. I was trying desperately to send signals of "No! No!" There was an air about Phat that said losing was something he didn't do well, and Will was quite a talented backgammon player. I stared at my partner, my eyes widening, silently shouting at him.

Will shrugged again. "Sure, why not?" But as he inadvertently leaned forward to touch the carved ivory pieces on the board, the chain around his neck containing our emerald slipped from the throat of his weathered khaki shirt. He quickly recovered, but the moment wasn't lost on his opponent, whose eyes had taken on a more attentive gleam.

"Interesting stone..." our new companion muttered, nodding at it. "How is it that you came about something like that?"

"It was a gift from a friend."

"Was that a friend on this river?"

Will issued an irritated sigh. "I thought we'd already played '20 questions.'"

There was a pause, pregnant with mutual enmity.

"Are you a betting man, Mr. Bell?" the big fellow asked silkily.

Somewhat trapped, my partner replied, "On occasion, I suppose."

Shong smiled. "How about a small wager — perhaps 50 gallons of gasoline... which as you know, is very precious on this river... against the *lavaliere* you wear. It appeals to me."

Will shook his head. "I don't think so."

Phat was still smiling but his eyes had gone hard. "My friend, there are certain...*realities*... on this river. Much like the jungle that surrounds us, there are creatures at the top of the food chain and those who are not..."

"You can't just take my amulet!" Will muttered angrily.

"I am Tu Phat."

"Yeah, I know, but your weight is not my problem," Will spat back.

Tu Phat leaned forward menacingly. "I could take your chain and the gem attached, but I would rather win it, and in this fashion you at least have a chance..."

Will looked at me, but there was nothing I could do at the moment. He returned his gaze to the man in front of him. "Could I have a second or two to speak with my friends? Before I commit to this?"

Our new acquaintance agreed magnanimously with the wave of a hand. The three of us stood and moved to the bar, keeping our conversation hushed.

"I can beat him," Will said. "You know I'm good at the game."

I nodded, looking around. "Yeah, I know, but I'd like to hedge our bet, and even then, I'm not sure it's in our best interests." It was then I noticed the sliced mangos, papayas, and bananas in bowls on the bar. Just down from one bowl a crusty old miner was doing a line of cocaine with every other shot of mescal. He had a small pile of the white powder next to his drink. I came back to Will. "Yeah, you can probably beat him, but I'm going to run interference in the process." I grinned. "I don't have to tell you how distracting a buzzed monkey can be, right?"

I was referring to the incident in the La Concha elevator in Key West, where years ago Will had stolen back a golden Spanish cross that had been taken from us, using a crazed monkey as a diversion.

I turned to Benny and handed him $10 American, pointing to the Darien girl at the far end of the bar. "Go give her this, and tell her to smile and wave when the miner looks at her." Then I ordered another round of drinks for Tu Phat's entourage while Will returned to the table.

My partner looked around at everyone, then sat, focusing on his large opponent. "Okay," he sighed. "I don't guess I have any choice."

Tu Phat nodded, pleased with himself. "A wise decision, my friend," he said as he pushed the board forward between them and began to place his pieces.

About that time I sat down next to the grizzled old miner and nodded. "Buy you a drink?" I said in Spanish.

He nodded. "Of course, my friend," he replied with a smile, as he concentrated on straightening up another line of cocaine with the blade of his pocketknife.

"I was just talking to the lady over there," I said, nodding at the girl at the end of the bar. "She said something about wanting to 'visit' with you for a few minutes." I grinned. "You lucky dog."

He looked up at her and she waved and smiled. He turned back to me, and his eyebrows bounced with anticipation. "Hmmm," he grunted as he picked up his drink and staggered over to the girl.

I grabbed a slice of mango out of the bowl in front of me and mopped up the heavy line of cocaine with it, then set it back in the bowl. I paid for an order of drinks and the bartender set them on a tray for me. When he turned away, I scooped up a half-teaspoon of the cocaine with the blade of the guy's pocketknife, and dropped it into Tu Phat's mimosa, stirring vigorously. Then I picked up the bowl of fruit, sat it on the drink tray, and carried it all back to the table. Benny had already returned, as well, and the two contestants had just completed organizing their backgammon board.

I sauntered over and set down the order of drinks, munching on an untainted piece of mango from the bowl. I stood for a moment near Tu Phat and his simian companion, who still sat on his master's shoulder chattering quietly, picking at the man's hairpiece occasionally, black tail curled casually around the fellow's neck. While working on my piece of fruit, I casually took one out for the monkey (the piece basted with high-grade cocaine). The little creature grabbed it greedily and immediately began stuffing it into his mouth. I offered some to the bodyguards who stood behind Tu Phat, but they stoically refused. I shrugged and returned to my seat at the table, and the drinks were dispersed. The fat line of high-test cocaine would have been enough to give a human a solid jolt. For a monkey...

I bought a little time (allowing the cocaine to kick in) by asking if the rules were different for backgammon here, and inquiring how long Shong had been playing. Our friend implied subtly that this was not a new endeavor for him, and that he was considered "talented" at this game of tactics and luck. In the process, Tu Phat worked his way through three-quarters of his mimosa. I could see the man's eyes garnering a deeper intensity.

Finally, they set about the game, but I could tell the monkey was starting to get a buzz. He went from contentedly sitting on his master's shoulder to chattering incessantly with quick, erratic movements. Tu Phat would occasionally reach up and push the monkey away as the little sucker writhed like a snake down his back and up again, grabbing at his hair lock. At the very least, it was distracting. By the time the game was halfway through, the monkey was nibbling on his master's ears and chattering with the intensity of a nervous hooker. Both of them were acquiring that frantic, electric look.

Fourteen minutes into the game, after an effective "blitz" technique, some lucky rolls, and only 15 moves, Will had killed Tu Phat. Murdered him. Our Panamanian acquaintance had darkened about three shades and his eyes had become incandescent.

"Well," he said with strained civility, "you are quite a backgammon player, and your blitz technique was impressive, but as we both know that approach requires the luck of the roll. Shall we try once more?"

Will looked over at me. My eyes were screaming, "No, you freaking idiot! No!" as I tried to kick him underneath the table.

Will tilted a shoulder in deliberation, then smiled. "Sure. Why not?"

Both the monkey and Tu Phat became more desperate in the second contest, hissing at each other angrily and trading insults. Evidently, the cocaine had hammered them both, but it had attacked the monkey's libido in particular. The little simian began to slowly but enthusiastically hump the back of the man's bald head, wildly grasping the long, single lock of hair like a rodeo rider with reins in hand, grunting out seething epithets of monkey love while drooling on Tu Phat's neck. At that point, the Chinese Darien lost the last of his cool, unceremoniously grabbing his diminutive companion, and with a bitter curse, hurling him across the room. But it was too late. His concentration had been scorched.

Twelve minutes and 14 moves later, Will removed his last piece. Tu Phat, who was miles behind, carefully laid down his dice in a poor attempt at deliberate calm. There was a distinctly purple shade to his complexion that didn't appear healthy, and his hand quavered slightly as he pulled at the wisp of black hair at the base of his lower lip. He blinked, composing himself. "Well, we must do this again sometime, Mr. Will Bell," he said as he rose slowly from his chair.

The others immediately took his cue and followed suit, the bodyguards quickly assuming positions on each side of him. He glanced around at the three of us, but his gaze returned to Will, the menace clearly undisguised. "Your fuel will be arranged for." There was a deathlike pause. "I am sure we will see each other again, along the river…"

"Oh, c'mon, man," I said, trying to mitigate the situation. "It was just a game…"

He stared at me for a moment. "In life, there is no such thing as a game…"

Without another word, he turned and they left — the incessantly chittering monkey following them out, obviously still berating his master for tossing him against a wall, and quickly checking the fruit bowl on the table one last time for another slice of that far-out mango…

The last glance came from the petite, dark-haired secretary — a strange look composed of curiosity, respect, and pity. I didn't like it at all.

When the door of the saloon had closed behind them, I snapped around to Will. "Have you lost your freaking mind? This is a guy who kills people for calling him fat. What do you suppose he does to people who publicly embarrass him — twice!"

"What? I should have let him have our emerald? Just because he wanted it?"

I sighed angrily. "You could have just beaten him gently, instead of massacring him."

Will grinned, despite it all. "The monkey was a big help. You got the little sucker high, didn't you? Just like with the monkey at the La Concha."

I couldn't help but smile in recollection. "Yeah, I guess it was pretty funny, watching him hump fat boy's head like a stoned cowboy. The little dude definitely went guano."

"You're right there," Will chuckled. "I think they're both bat-shit crazy."

Benny couldn't help but snicker as well, but he was clearly shaken by the event. "Chu two de plenty crazy ones," he muttered with a begrudging smile. "But Tu Phat not a good person to have as enemy. Benny no want to end up on tiger ant pile…"

As we lay in our bunks at Mrs. Chiang Kai-shek's boarding house, the pale moonlight drifting through the dirty window screens, all of us trying to come down enough for sleep, Will leaned over on his elbow in the bunk next to mine and said, "Okay, tell me about Kendra."

"Whattaya mean, tell you about Kendra? She's a nice lady. We had a good time."

Will sighed, exasperated. "I don't want the *Reader's Digest* version. I wanna know if she made you go 'oooh-oooh.' I mean, was it just a night on the beach and some sandy sex or did she ring your chimes?"

I thought about it for a moment. The truth was, I liked her, and God, she really was a minx, but with all that had been going on, I hadn't had much time to think about it. "Yeah, I did like her. She's clever and funny, and she has a great sense of timing in conversation, and there was definitely a connection." I paused, thinking back to the night on the beach. "I love the way she smells. She has a fragrance about her, like citrus and cinnamon, and those pale blue eyes...but she doesn't use her femininity as a tool. There's something uniquely capable about her, and I like that."

Will chuckled. "That sounds like 'oooh-oooh' to me."

I turned a little toward my friend's bunk. "Okay, what about you? What about Margo?"

A reminiscent smile found its way to his mouth. "She's very...*hot*, for one thing. Parts of her are hotter than others. I'm tellin' you, when we were finished on the beach, even the monkeys wanted a cigarette. Man, that girl can — "

"I'm okay with the *Reader's Digest* version," I said, interrupting him.

He chuckled in the darkness. "Yeah, okay...I really liked her. It was like, natural with her. No concerns, no demands, and the urgency wasn't frantic, just deliciously paced, and man, I think the woman's mother was a vacuum cleaner, because she could —"

"*Reader's Digest* version..."

"Yeah, okay, okay..." Will exhaled lightly. "And you know what else? She's nice to talk with — a very bright lady. We spent a couple of hours just watching the stars and talking."

"That's gotta be a first for you."

When all had finally gone quiet, Benny lay in his bunk that night, thinking about that oddly shaped stone *Señor* Bell had around his neck. Benny had seen it too, when his new acquaintance had bent over at the backgammon board — beautiful, deep green, all angles and planes. *Dios* knows how much a single *esmeralda* like that would be worth — and they were looking for a bunch of them! These *gringos* were okay guys, as far as *gringos* went, but he knew they were not going to give him any of the treasure they were seeking. No, unfortunately, in this situation Benny would have to look out for himself, as he had always done. Benny had chiseled his character into the hardwood of life for so long that it had become the only pattern he knew, or all he was comfortable with. Take what you could, when you could...

CHAPTER 6

By eight o'clock the following morning we were headed upriver again. The water's course was definitely growing narrower and shallower, and we maintained a constant vigilance for submerged logs or rocks that could damage our lower units and propellers. As I reduced speed on the rolling brown water, the sun was just cresting the jungle on our eastern side, sending prisms of light through the early morning haze and splashing the surface of the river with gold. Troops of howler monkeys were busy in the trees, scavenging for breakfast, and they, along with a plethora of parrots and other wild birds, squawked and screeched indignantly at our passing. River hawks worked the water and the shoreline with a cautious indifference, and every once in a while a crocodile would surface to stare at us with malevolent eyes, or grunt angrily and splash into the river from the bank.

Along the way we passed an occasional village of thatched huts set on stilts in clearings. The inhabitants stared silently at our passing, neither friendly nor aggressive. Outside of the Amazon Basin, the Darien Jungle is the largest tropical rain forest in the western hemisphere. We were entering an area that few 20th century people had challenged — too close to the heart of darkness for most civilized folks. It belonged to the creatures that had owned it for centuries and only one rule applied: survival of the fittest.

The sun rose and stretched across the green sky. The breeze stilled by midday and the humidity soaked us like a sauna as our river wound through the jungle, ever onward, toward the mountains in the distance. At mid-afternoon we pulled underneath a canopy of huge rubber trees to escape the sun, and ate a hasty lunch of greasy meat tortillas purchased in Puerto Esperanza. We pushed on again and by five o'clock we came to the last of the big mining camps, where we would stay for the night. Benny had been right. The water was becoming too shallow to continue on with the Mako. Tomorrow it would be canoes and small outboards.

The sarcastically named, *El Campo de los Tontos* (Camp of Fools), was less sophisticated than the first. We tied up at a weathered strand of pitiful docks and ended up sleeping on the boat, because there was no guesthouse. There was a bar, almost a duplicate of the one at our last stop, but the clientele was rougher (if that was possible). The girls were less comely, and the liquor was made out back in 55-gallon drums. We bought a dinner of rice and beans and some stringy, unidentified meat from the single restaurant, if you could call it that, and returned to the boat. The dockmaster — a tall, taciturn fellow who looked like Lurch from the Addams Family — put us in touch with a guy who had a couple of native canoes for rent, and we made a deal for two of them, each with a 15-horsepower outboard and two 10-gallon gas cans. That would probably be enough fuel — we only had to get upriver. The current would carry us back with minimal power. But we had to portage the half mile of high ground in the hairpin turn coming up the following day.

When I mentioned our plans to the dockmaster, his face furrowed slightly. "Have you been that way before, *amigo,* on that portage?" When we replied to the negative, he continued, "*El Pueblo de las Brujas* — the Village of Witches — lies on that stretch of land. The people of the village there are...strange..." He shrugged. "Perhaps it will be no problem. Most of the time it is not. I myself have traveled through that area without situation, but there are stories..."

"Oh good — freaking jungle witches now," groaned Will from behind me.

"What kind of stories?" I asked, the hounds of superstition knocking down the tent posts of reason in my head.

The man shrugged and held out his hands, palms up. "Oh, one hears tales — in some places reality dances on thin ice. Things are not always as they seem."

"Oh, that clears things up nicely," muttered Will.

The fellow was clearly uncomfortable and apologized again for his lack of solid information. "I suppose there have been stories of people disappearing there." He paused. "Maybe not just disappearing, but *changing...*"

"Changing?" I said, eyebrows up.

He offered one final shrug. "You will be fine. In a couple of hours you will be across the hairpin and on your way. But avoid the village, if you can...especially at night."

The following morning we told Eddie of our plans. He had nothing new to offer us on the apparent murders in Obaldia. We transferred some of our gear and supplies to the dugout canoes (including the two pistols), pulled a battery out of the Mako to run our portable VHF radio, and topped off the jerry cans of fuel. The sun was just cresting the top of the jungle as we slid our canoes into the river, the cool moisture of the morning mist dampening our clothes and skin. Will and Benny were in one dugout, and I, with the extra supplies, was in the other. Mine immediately leaked like an incontinent hooker, but I patched it with some tar the dockmaster had given me.

It was that time of day in an adventure when your confidence level is at its lowest ebb, and no one could deny the challenges that lay ahead.

Benny, who was sitting in front of his canoe, shivered. He wrapped his arms around himself and muttered bitterly. *"Brujas!* Benny no like witches — no like have to drag a canoe for a bloody mile through the bloody jungle, either. Dis becoming a lot like a job... I could be back home studying to be a bullfighter."

Will chuckled. "Ahhh, c'mon Benito, where's your sense of adventure? This is what life is all about — to break from the flock and challenge the hawk. To grab fate by the *cojones* and snatch its wallet for hookers and rum!"

"What Benny gonna get for all dis? All dis adventure chit?"

Will shrugged. "Why don't we wait until we see what we find before we start spending it, huh? Kansas and I have always been generous people to those who help us."

Benny glanced over at Will, then turned to stare at the river. "Yeah, Benny heard dat before."

"Not to worry, Benito," I said, checking the gear in my canoe before we fired up our outboards. "Honor is an important thing with my partner and me — one of the most important things. Genuine honor — integrity — isn't contingent on circumstance. It's not situational. Doesn't matter how much money you have or who you are. In most cases you either have it or you don't." I paused, catching a wave of recollection, then stared at our new friend again. "It's an almost tangible thing, Benito. I've known people who seemed to be born with it, and watched some who didn't start out with it discover it, and occasionally I've seen people sell what little they had. But in the end, when they put you in the ground, your integrity is the one thing no one can take away from you. It's the fabric of real friendship. It's one of the characteristics that defines us as human beings, and on occasion, grants us the ability to be exceptional."

"Wow," said Will. "Where did all that come from?"

I grinned, embarrassed by my loquaciousness. "Don't know. But it's true." I drew in a breath and exhaled, gazing at the mist-blanketed river. "Let's get this adventure on the road, *amigos*."

Benny smiled then, his uneasiness passing with the rising morning breeze. "You betcha, man! Les go grab some *cojones* of fate and get some hookers and rum!"

When we had flown the river in the Goose, we had found a rock promontory to mark our portage across the hairpin. By late afternoon we had found it, and the trail that had been used many times before us. We left the gear aboard and tied ropes forward and aft on the canoes, making the arduous haul through the jungle twice, and having to ford one large creek, as well. With three of us pulling/pushing, the half mile was negotiated quickly.

It did, however, take us by the village.

We were fording the creek for the second time when we noticed the village off to the side, almost hidden from sight. At a distance it was nothing unique, just a gathering of dingy-looking thatched huts with a cleared communal area. It was the singing that brought it to our attention. Well, maybe not singing as much as the chanting of a melody of sorts. It was soft and strangely alluring, and seemed to be coming from the curve of the river by the village. We had stopped for a moment to catch our breath, listening to the voices, when an old woman appeared on the jungle trail, coming from the village and headed toward the river. Dressed in a coarse, dark cotton shift, she nodded to us and smiled, displaying a mouth sorely in need of a few more teeth. Her eyes brightened and she slowed, then stopped, letting us pass on the trail. But as we moved by her she whispered in Spanish, "Aaahh, strangers from a distant island — on a mission." She straightened up, pushing down the folds of her old dress with the almost sensual movements of a much younger person. "Will you not visit with us tonight?" She paused and looked at the sun just above the jungle horizon. "It is near to sunset," she whispered to herself, and gazed at us again. "Will you not stay? The green rocks you seek can wait until tomorrow...and your course is set in stones, regardless."

On the breeze we could hear the melodious chanting from the river, lifting in a flowing, almost entreating chorus, and now I could just make out through the trees a gathering of people standing in the water, holding hands and staring at the sun as it reached for the treetops. I realized then that they were all older women, much like the one in front of us.

We looked at each other in amazement — the green rocks? How could she possibly have known?

"No, Mother," I found myself saying. "We must go on..."

She looked at me. "You will be back, with less than you want, but more than you need." She sighed strangely. "Before your journey is over you will have tasted deception twice, and been challenged by fear thrice. You will lose a friend, and lose what you have found, and find what you thought you had lost."

I didn't know how to reply to that. None of us did. We just stood there, holding the canoe lines.

The old woman smiled slightly. "I must go. I am late for the river. You must go now, as well. It is not your time tonight." In seconds she had shuffled past and was hurrying toward the chorus of voices at the water's edge.

"C'mon," Will said, shouldering his rope. "Let's get the hell out of here. That whole thing gave me the willies."

Benny shuddered, then shouldered his rope at the front. "*Brujas!* I'ne tellin' you, dey all *brujas*. Leave a chicken bone on your pillow and 'poof' chur a frog, or sonthin' worse. I heard about dis place..."

A half hour later we were back in the canoes and had worked our way a couple of miles upriver, but the strangeness of that whole situation had been unnerving. We found a place to camp before darkness took the waterway. Tomorrow morning we would be at the final landmark, the limestone spire, and the crux of this quest.

The next day we swept around a curve in the river, and there, to our right, the jungle suddenly rose up against a steep hillside of limestone. Trees and brush grew out from it in pockets, but none of those was profuse enough to disguise the weathered spire at the top. I looked over at Will, gliding along next to me in his canoe, and pointed. His eyes radiated excitement as he nodded and we headed for the sandy shore below the outcropping, beaching the canoes.

We stood there for a moment, staring up at the spire. Benny was unusually quiet, recognizing that something of significance was happening.

Will finally turned to me. "This is it, Kansas. This is the place..."

Within minutes, Will and I were scaling the gradually inclining rock wall, searching for the small entrance of the cave. Benny was waiting impatiently on the beach as we climbed. Due to the angle of the rock wall, the cave was barely visible from the river, but as we got closer I could see the dark mouth, obscured by bushes and vines clinging to life in the limestone. There was a small, two-foot ledge in front of the roughly four-foot-square mouth of the cave that led to the jungle hillside — easier access. We caught our breath on the ledge, turned on our flashlights and entered, sweeping away the gossamer spider webs in front of us.

It was a small cave, about five feet in height, maybe six feet wide, and less than 10 feet deep. It carried the musty scent of an animal lair and there were bones of small creatures scattered here and there. Cautiously, we cast our lights against the walls, hearts hammering in our chests with a locomotive cadence, eyes trying desperately to adjust to the gloom, and our minds screaming the single question that had haunted us for the last two weeks: could this incredible wild goose chase possibly be real? Could it actually happen for us? Where was the gold? The emeralds? But a sweep of our flashlights revealed nothing — just dirty limestone walls, along with a sandy floor strewn with bone and fur. A rush of fear and failure engulfed me like a tidal wave. My heart thudded against my ribs and I could feel the blood pulsing in my head. Dear God! Had we come all this way and risked everything on a bloody fool's errand? Had someone found it ahead of us? Was Lector Mileston just a madman?

Will fell to his knees in front of me, the picture of desolation and frustration, hands at his sides in the musty dirt of the floor, supporting himself, his shoulders slumped. "Son of a bitch," I heard him whisper hoarsely. "Son of a bitch…"

I painted the beam of my flashlight across the tiny cave one last time, in final desperation, hoping that I had missed something, but I hadn't. I collapsed on the dirt next to my friend, exhausted and defeated, the sheer finality of it all overwhelming me. We sat in silence for a few moments, our flashlights reflecting eerily off the walls.

"We gave it our best shot," Will whispered, as much to himself as to me.

I could hear Benito anxiously calling outside from the canoes.

"C'mon Will," I said. "Someone's got to tell Benito he's going to have to keep his daytime job."

I started to rise, and as I did so I leaned forward and pushed off from the floor — which was composed of several inches of accumulated dirt, animal feces, and sand. My fingers hit something hard and elongated. I stopped, frozen, then gradually closed my hand around the small but very heavy object and worked it loose from the dirt. Will had started to rise but he saw me and paused. I lifted up the six-inch object — maybe two inches wide and one inch deep, and brushed it off as my buddy shined his flashlight on it.

There is something about the weight and the eternal gleam of gold — it is simply incomparable. It is magnetic; totally unequaled in the accompanying hunger and fascination it embodies. It changes the way you see others and the way you perceive yourself in a heartbeat. It can become the mother of all your dreams or the devil incarnate, as it either elevates your sense of magnanimity or banishes your integrity with the slightest caress. I looked up at my old friend and our eyes met, a profound joy and a huge sense of gratification filling our countenances.

Instantly we were burrowing into the soft sand and dirt around us like two lunatic groundhogs. In just a few minutes we had recovered dozens of the gold bars, but at this point I could hear Benito growing frantic, so I stumbled to the mouth of the cave and called to him, letting him know we were okay and would be down soon. For the next half hour we dug and sifted through the floor of the cave. Lector Milestone had buried the gold in the center of the cave floor, and the emeralds, in the six deteriorated leather bags, along the edges of the wall. He failed to mention this in his notes, but in truth I think it was a final measure of protection — in case someone took his diary.

We finally called to Benito and had him come up. There was no hiding this from him, and we had decided he had earned at least a small share of the treasure. *"Madre de Dios..."* he whispered as he stood in the mouth of the cave and we shined our flashlights at the accumulated treasure on the floor. Our friend moved over slowly and bent down, picking up a gold bar in one hand and a fat emerald in the other. He turned and stared at us, the look on his face full of incredulousness, stating the obvious question.

Will answered, "You probably don't have to worry about being a bullfighter anymore, *amigo*."

For the next hour we worked at removing the gold and emeralds from the cave. We transferred up small canvas bags we had brought for the emeralds, then filled them and stacked them — six bags altogether. Then Will and I loaded the gold in slightly heavier bags (about five or six bars to a container) and began to lower them and the emeralds to Benito with a rope. We had instructed him to store them in the center of the canoes in equal amounts.

My partner and I were in the cave while Benito was on the riverbank below. We had finally lowered the last of the gold, and we were packaging the last of the emeralds into the final bag — the rest had already been sent down and loaded aboard the canoes. There was an almost irrepressible aura of elation in the air. We were giddy with excitement, like children on Christmas morning. It wasn't that we needed the money, really. We were still quite well off from a gold bullion adventure in Cuba that had netted us way past comfortable offshore bank accounts, but there's just nothing like the experience of finding buried treasure. It makes pirates of us all. It brings out the core of adventure and yearning in man (and woman) and melts it into a white-hot tangible flux that fills your veins. But the problem is, it's every bit as addictive as heroin. You just have to do it again...

As Will tied off the final bag of emeralds, we leaned against the rough walls of the cave near the entrance and smiled at each other.

"Just like in the movies, dude," Will whispered with an animated reverence.

Once again the gods had smiled on us.

Finally, I picked up the bag of bright green stones and stood. "C'mon, *amigo*, let's go see how Benito is doing."

But as we stepped out onto the ledge and viewed the beach, my stomach dropped three floors. One of the canoes was gone, and there was no sign of our friend.

Ten minutes later, life had gone from impossible elation to unbelievable desolation. Benito hadn't followed our instructions at all. He had loaded all the gold and the emeralds into one canoe, along with a few supplies, and slipped away. He left us a hand-scrawled note from Will's paperwork saying, "I am sorry. Sometimes a man must do what a man must do. This honor thing is not so thick in my blood yet."

We also discovered that Benny had taken the long-range VHF radio, so we couldn't call Eddie, and the fuel line from the gas can to the outboard engine on the remaining canoe, reducing the outboard's operating effectiveness to that of a rock.

We stood there in shock, the sun arching across the sky, reaching for the mountains on the horizon. Will suddenly took the bag of emeralds and tossed them into the canoe, then started grabbing our remaining supplies and tossing them in, as well. "He's got a head start on us and he's got an engine, but he can't portage that canoe by himself, so he'll have to motor around the whole hairpin in the river. We've got paddles. If we get going now and make the portage this evening, we may just catch him on the other side." He huffed angrily. "The little son of a bitch stole from us! I can't believe it!" He looked at me, eyes hot with fury. "I want my stuff back, and I'm gonna get it!"

Inside of five minutes we were loaded and paddling downstream. We had at least an hour to the portage site, and the sun was already touching the tops of the trees.

We reached the *Pueblo de las Brujas* portage just as long evening shadows were claiming the river. In moments we had the canoe pulled ashore, ropes attached fore and aft, and we had begun the arduous task of dragging it along the path. As we reached the village, the last shades of light were being enveloped by a battery of heavy cumulus in the western sky, and a ghostly pale, full moon was ascending in the eastern heavens.

Gradually, we began to hear the voices, rising and falling in a flowing, methodical cadence — eerie, yet strangely beautiful. There was just enough light for us to see the line of women coming back from the river. Behind them, some were just moving out of the knee-high water and following their companions in a slow, rhythmical procession, their voices carrying out over the jungle like the sirens in *The Odyssey*. But I realized something strange had happened.

All the women we had seen in our earlier passing this way had been older and somewhat haggard, but the line of women coming our way, for as far as the encroaching darkness would allow me to see, were quite lovely, young, and slender, with long, glossy hair and perfect golden skin, all dressed in gossamer-like, white cloth shifts. Their voices were beautiful, and as they sang they laughed occasionally, like young girls finding themselves before a mirror. It was all very strange, but none of it was unpleasant. In fact, I found myself gradually relaxing, as I hadn't done for some time. A downy sense of ease came over me, and I felt nearly...blissful.

I looked over at my partner and could see he had been swept up by the same feeling. He was smiling, that goofy grin slashing his face, and his eyes seemed alight with a sense of contentment, perhaps elation. *Maybe it's the singing,* I thought as we set the canoe down and the procession of remarkable women came toward us, parting around us like a breeze. The girls were giggling and reaching out to touch us as they passed on both sides, stroking our arms and faces, whispering to us, and sharing a marvelous-tasting beverage with us from the colorful gourds some carried. I don't remember what they were saying, but I know it was enchanting. All the while, the ethereal hymn they were singing wove itself around us like a feathery web, and at some point I realized we had left the canoe on the path and were strolling along with them, surrounded by their voices, immersed in the vibratory "hum" of the hive.

In moments the village came into sight, but it was different from what I remembered. The handful of dingy, thatched huts my memory held seemed transformed, with tidy thatches, well-swept porches, and inviting yellow lights in the windows. I felt an arm slip about my waist and I looked over at the lovely creature who held me — dark, sensual eyes, a Colgate smile, and honey-brown hair, all wrapped in a pearl-colored cotton shift.

"I'm so glad you returned," she said. "I told you the green rocks you sought could wait until the morrow. Will you not visit us tonight?"

A part of me somewhere in the deep recesses of my foggy brain recognized that something was seriously amiss, because the last time I had seen this woman she was old, and as ugly as sin. But now…

"Will you not visit us tonight?" she whispered again.

The words wafted over me like a warm spring breeze, her breath like that of a candied child.

One of the last things I remembered was Will and me in one of the huts, lying on goose-down blankets with a couple of Ulysses' sirens apiece, drinking wine that tasted as if it was made by the gods and doing things with those remarkable creatures that still make me shiver with incandescent recollection.

CHAPTER 7

You know you've had an interesting night when you wake up in the morning with hair in your mouth, and it's curly, and it's not yours...

The warm morning sunlight brought me around — that, and the less-than-pleasant odor of the room. It was one of those mornings where your eyelids stick together and you have to work to get the blur out of your vision. There was enough hair in my mouth to tie several nice bonefish flies, and an arm that didn't belong to my body was draped across my chest. I wasn't quite up to moving yet, still struggling with my vision. I noticed that the skin of the arm was wrinkled and the fingers of the hand were thin and bony. I blinked a few times, gathering the energy to move. My head felt like someone had poured napalm into my skull and lit my nostrils. Through a concentrated effort, I removed the arm and discovered it was attached to an older native lady, maybe 60 or 65, wrinkled like a Shar Pei, mouth slung open, snoring loudly. The sight was enough to startle me into movement. I snapped upright in the bed, throwing the woman off me, and my head exploded with brilliant, sharp blades of light piercing my eyeballs. I guess my scream woke her.

Opening her dark eyes, she lazily turned her naked body around without shame and leaned her head on a hand — the pose of a much younger woman. "Welcome to the day," she croaked, then her bleary eyes went sly and she murmured, "but I wish it were night again..."

Ignoring the pain, I scampered out of the bed and began searching for my clothes, which I found on the floor. Feeling more in control with pants and a shirt on, I sat in the only chair and combed back my hair with my fingers. "Wha-what happened last night?" I asked.

As she explained in detail things I didn't want to hear, I glanced around. The squalid bamboo room had a dirt floor and a couple of open windows. We had been lying on an old mattress, no sheets. Much of the place was in disarray. There must have been quite a party. There was another old woman apparently passed out by the other mattress. Will was nowhere to be seen, but something odd caught my attention. There was a chicken — a white chicken with a red cockscomb and dark strokes on the wings — sitting on the other mattress, staring at me intently and sitting next to a pile of Will's

78

clothes. When it saw me look in its direction, it clucked — it clucked in an impatient, almost angry fashion, and stood up on its long legs. It was then I noticed that, dangling around the chicken's neck, was the silver chain and emerald amulet my partner wore. The chicken stomped its feet and bobbed its head in an agitated fashion, cackling again, still staring at me.

"Oohh, no, that's not possible," I muttered incredulously to myself. "Not possible. I'm still drunk." But at that moment I was reminded of Benito's last words: "*Brujas!* I'ne tellin' you, dey all *brujas*. De leave a chicken bone on your pillow and 'poof' chur a frog, or sonthin' worse. I heard about dis place..."

"Not possible" I croaked again, as the chicken hopped down off the bed and tottered over to me in a stiff-gaited walk. It looked up at me and clucked again in a frustrated fashion, then pecked at my toes.

"Oh Jesus!" I grunted, moving to the door and looking around outside. No sign of my friend. I came back and the chicken shuffled over. Squatting on my haunches, I stared at the creature. "Will? Will, is that you?"

The bird did a little dance by the mattress, pecked at the floor, then peeped at me again.

"Jesus! They turned you into a chicken!" I moaned, holding my head with my hands. "A freaking chicken!" I looked at the old woman, who had pulled herself up against the wall and now sat with her arms around her knees, indifferent to her nakedness and smiling at me in the strangest of fashions. I glanced at the bird, then back to her. "What happened last night?"

Her smile never faded. "You're timing was right — at the peak of the full moon. You were welcomed into the village, and the night was enjoyed by all." But her expression changed slightly then. "If your soul had not been clean, the experience might have been very different," she said. "We all see what we want to see at the peak of the full moon..."

Still trying to find a path to reality, I looked at the chicken again, then back to her. "Is that...is that..."

The old woman paused, as if struggling with recollection. "As to your friend, I cannot say. I know Kachia was here last night — one of our great *brujas*, and your friend chose someone else over her..." She shrugged. "I have seen stranger things, but I do not know all. I live within the weave. I do not make it."

There was a huge part of me that couldn't even accept the

possibility, but a small portion of my head said, *What if it is Will?* I knew how impossible it all was, but what if it were true? Will and I had been friends for a long time, and through it all, through the thick and thin, we had never abandoned each other, and that was why we were still alive and kicking.

The chicken clucked again and pecked at the floor, moving toward the door, and I remembered Benito, the little thief...

I stood, then reached down and picked up the bird, taking the chain with the amulet and slipping it over my head. The creature seemed quite comfortable in the crook of my arm. I shook my head in disbelief. "No one's ever going to believe any of this..." I muttered. "A freakin' chicken..."

There were two old men — the first I'd seen — sitting in the canoe at the side of the path, right where we had left it, smoking brown, poorly rolled cigarettes.

They looked up and one said in surprisingly good English, "You have slept late, *amigo*." He smiled at the other, then turned back to us. "Full moons are like that here, but we have watched your belongings for you."

And indeed they had. As I glanced around, everything was miraculously still in the canoe — even the emeralds I had stuffed into a biscuit tin.

"We will help you to the water," said the other. He grinned at his friend. "Everyone says you need as much help as you can get."

They were a wizened pair, but tougher than they appeared, and within the hour we had the canoe at the river's edge on the other side of the isthmus. I gave them $10 American, and they seemed very pleased.

"You must visit again," one said as I climbed into the canoe, set the chicken on the floor in front of me, and grabbed a paddle. The fellow grinned again. "These are son' horny *chicas* round here. Es good to have the pressure taken off of us occasionally."

I couldn't make out whether he was joking or telling the truth, but it didn't matter. I had places to be, and a thief to catch.

I realized that by sleeping away half the morning I had missed Benito. He had surely made it around the hairpin isthmus and motored past the village by now. I still had one of Eddie's handheld Vietnam vintage radios, but its range was limited. Without the big VHF that Benito took, there was no way to get in touch with our friend until I got much closer to Puerto Obaldia. I was on my own.

The chicken, in the front of the canoe, fluffed its feathers and bobbed its head, clucking impatiently.

"Yeah, yeah, I know. I'm moving as fast as I can," I muttered as I pushed us off from the bank and began to paddle. "I had a rough night too, you know."

The bird chirped sharply, still looking at me.

I sighed. "Okay, okay, you had a rougher night. This is no time for that one-upmanship you always do."

The chicken chirped contentedly and settled onto the bow. I paddled, trying to get past the pounding in my head and the double vision. *Jeez...what a night...*

Tu Phat Shong sat on a wing-backed rattan chair on the porch of his home, just below the shoddy mining village of *El Campo de los Tontos*. The mahogany and bamboo house was set artfully into the jungle, protected from casual view by a variety of trees and shrubs, yet still providing a fairly good view outward. From his vantage point Tu Phat could see the river as it flowed in slow, perennial fashion toward the distant sea. He sighed and sipped his mimosa, relaxing, as his secretary told him he should. He was just starting to let go of the embarrassing defeat he had received at the hands of the American the other night. He had been unbearable for the last few days — as vicious as a leopard with a paw wound. He beat one of his servants unmercifully for over-sweetening his tea, and forced another to sleep in the jungle overnight for failing to sweep the porch steps of the house. He could still see the triumph in the American's eyes when he was thrashed so easily, and he lost the chain and amulet that he was so certain he would have. Moreover, by the defeat, he lost the dominance he needed to question them about the stone. It was much like the one that had been found in the pocket of the dockmaster who had been killed a couple of weeks ago.

For the past few years he had dedicated himself to the legend of *la cueva de esmeralda,* having read all the information he could on the early Spanish possession of the Darien Peninsula. He had devoured all the old Spanish documents he could lay his hands on, studying maps and trying to determine where the upriver Spanish outpost could have been — the one that had gathered the emeralds and gold from the Darien Indians. He had found proof in the archive reports that a shipment had been lost around 1700, and the rumor written between the lines was that emeralds and gold had been hidden, probably in a cave near the river. He had scoured the upper reaches of the Fangaso and sent search parties along the banks and into the interior without success. And then, inside of a few weeks, rumors were everywhere of a white man who had gone up the river with a couple of guides and come back alone — with emeralds. Following on the heels of that, two Americans show up and head upriver...with a large emerald.

He needed to find those Americans again. He was certain they were somehow tied to the first *gringo* who disappeared after a fight that killed the dockmaster at *Puerto de la Esperanza*. Word on his coconut telegraph said they had rented canoes at *El Campo de los Tontos* and passed through *El Pueblo de las Brujas,* heading west. He had men in every village and bar from Obaldia to where the river churned itself out of the high mountains. Somebody would find them.

As I paddled along the placid river, I began to realize what a pickle I was in — all because of my trust in that fast-talking little thief. I had a couple of days traveling before I would be back at *Puerto Obaldia,* and by that time Benito would probably be halfway to Brazil. After about four hours, the aggravation and the weird alcohol of the previous night had begun a fierce argument with my stomach and bowels. I knew I was going to have to stop. I mumbled angrily to myself about being forced into this detour by the call of nature, and I was reminded of one of Will's favorite rants on the subject: "Defecation is a serious waste of human energy and time — you'd think God would have designed a better system for his 'most perfect work.' The average person spends 10 minutes a day on the toilet. 10 minutes a day times 360 days is 3,600 minutes a year; times, say, an average lifespan of 70 years, is 252,000 minutes or 4,200 hours. This calculates into 175 days — nearly half a year spent on the crapper!"

My friend/the chicken sat contentedly in the bow as we moved along smartly with the current, making much better time. We were coming around a large bend in the river and suddenly, there ahead, was *El Campo de los Tontos*, where we had rented the canoes, and where we had left the Mako. The chicken perked up and cackled lightly. "Yeah, yeah, I know," I said, straining to see across the sun-glared water. "But I don't see the Mako..."

The chicken cackled again, agitated.

"You got that right," I replied. "If he stole the boat, we're screwed."

As I brought the canoe up to the rickety dock and tied off, the tall dockmaster (the one that looked like Lurch of the Addams Family), ambled over.

"*Buenos dias, amigo,*" he said amicably. "Your friend was here earlier. He took your big boat, saying he was sorry for the inconvenience, but he had places to be — son'thing about being a bullfighter in Spain. He seem like a nice person, but I'ne not sure I trust him completely."

The chicken clucked bitterly.

"Yeah, you got that part right," I muttered.

I needed a break from the hard floor of that canoe, a restroom, and something to eat. There was no leaving the chicken with the boat, so, with the bird tucked under my arm, I headed for the bar, which was the only place to get food in *El Campo de los Tontos*. I knew this could be a touchy situation and wished I had a pistol with me, but it too was in the other canoe.

As I moved away from the docks and headed down the walkway toward the bar, a man in the shadows of the dock house, squatting and smoking a cigarette, watched me with keen interest.

I figured I would be in the seriously deep caca, carrying a chicken into a bar — the equivalent of the wimpy kid who brings his pet turtle to school. Neither does well. But as I entered the local tavern, I noticed a number of the men drinking at the bar or sitting at the tables eyeing my bird with regard and curiosity, and nodding at me. A couple even smiled. Two or three others had single chickens in cages. I shrugged, considerably relieved – a pro-chicken village, one where a man can carry his bird under his arm with respect. I guess anything is possible.

I sat down at the bar and put the bird on the chair next to me. "Just keep your wits about you, Will," I whispered out the side of my mouth. "Just sit there and keep quiet."

I also noticed that whoever owned this bar had a distinct interest in chickens — there were photos on the walls everywhere. There were also old photos of Darien Indians, probably going back 100 years, and there were Indian artifacts on the wall — bows and arrows, blowguns, and even a collection of blowgun darts.

As I waited for the bartender to work his way over to me, I grabbed a deck of weathered cards off the bar and cut them, spread them, then rolled the splayed deck back and forth with a single card. I wasn't a card shark, exactly, but I was pretty handy with a deck of 52. Poker and card tricks (or the combination thereof) had paid for a portion of my college experience.

I noticed that the tables and chairs had been cleared away from the center of the room. I thought it was odd at first, but I figured maybe they were having a dance of some sort tonight. After I had ordered a beer and emptied half the bottle with my first swig (paddling a canoe in the hot sun is a thirsty business), I noticed two men leave their table in the back and saunter over. Both were dressed in typical cotton pants and shirts, and wore weathered straw hats.

The big one settled in next to me, and the other next to my bird. The larger one — sun-darkened face, bad acne, and yellow teeth that looked like they were trying to get away from each other — took a swig of his mescal and leaned over, almost conspiratorially. "Thas a nice bird chu have, man," he said.

I nodded noncommittally, sipping my beer. "Yeah, I guess."

The Panamanian edged a little closer. "Chu want to sell him?"

The other guy was checking out my chicken — looking at his beak and touching his wings. (I had come to the conclusion that Will was a rooster — I mean he had spurs and some black in his wing feathers, but that was about as far as my knowledge went. To me a chicken was a chicken.)

"No, I don't want to sell him," I said more abruptly than I meant. "He's not really a chicken — it's my partner. He was turned into a chicken at *El Pueblo de las Brujas*." (I didn't mean to say that — it just came out.)

The guy next to me recoiled a little at the mention of that name. "That is too bad for your friend. But that may make him even a better challenger for *El Condor*. I give you 20 *balboas* for him."

I puffed up a little. "I'm not gonna — "

"My friend could break his neck with just a nod from me — then you have nothing. Or you could have 20 *balboas*."

The guy's eyes were shining with a bold vehemence. I had to think quickly. "How about we cut cards for him? I win, you buy me a bottle of tequila — you win, you get the bird."

The fellow thought about it for a moment, then smiled, displaying those tombstone teeth again. "Okay, *gringo*. We do that."

I took Willbird away from the other guy and put him up on the bar, whispering harshly to him in English, "I'm gonna need a distraction, Will, like the old days, okay? A distraction, at just the right time…" I pushed the cards together, shuffled them a few times, (expertly slipping one into my cuff as my companions received drinks from the bartender), and put the deck in front of my new acquaintance.

He stared at me, taking the top half of the deck, then looked at his card. He smiled confidently and showed me a Jack of Spades. "I thin' I'ne gonna own your chicken, *señor.*"

I reached for the deck, and as I did, the chicken backed up a little, carelessly getting too close to the edge of the bar and stumbling off the bar top with a screech and a flutter of wings. It was just enough of a diversion for me to slip the card out of my cuff and slide my cut of the deck onto it.

"He's clumsy as hell," I muttered, nodding at the bird on the floor. "He's not used to being a chicken." Then I turned over the portion of the deck displaying a King of Hearts. "Well, look at that! I win." I offered a conciliatory smile. "Better luck next time, gentlemen."

I believe they were about to argue the call when the saloon doors opened and a tall, wiry Darien Indian with long black hair and hard grey eyes entered. Unlike the others, he wore blue jeans with his white cotton shirt, and he was leading a chicken on a leather leash.

The guy next to me whispered with sort of a reverence, "El Condor…"

I stared for a moment. This was not your ordinary bird. It was about twice the size of my chicken and looked like a damned Rottweiler with feathers. I think it had teeth, and spurs like little scimitars. I picked up my boy off the floor and held him protectively, the bird clucking nervously. Suddenly, it all became painfully clear — cock fights! My chicken and I had a major problem. I was headed for the door when suddenly two of the larger customers appeared in front of me.

"House rules," said one gruffly. "Once your bird comes through the doors, he fights."

I jerked away. "He doesn't want to fight. He's a pacifist. We just came in for a drink."

The Darien reached for the large knife at his side. "He can fight and win, or die bravely, or I can cut his head off now. Your choice…"

We were definitely in deep caca for the second time in 15

minutes. I glanced around looking for a way out, or an angle. I saw that we were standing next to the collection of Darien Indian artifacts. Among them on the wall was the collection of small blow darts and a brief explanation in Spanish that read: *The wourali poison for Darien Indian darts is extracted from indigenous climbing vines (strychnos toxifera) to which are added fire ants, Indian pepper, and the pounded fangs of the labarri snake — all boiled in a gourd over a small fire until a thick paste is formed. The darts are dipped in this mixture. DO NOT TOUCH THESE — THEY ARE GENUINE POISON-DIPPED DARTS.*

I looked at the two men in front of me, then glanced over at the Frankenchicken my bird was going to have to fight. "Okay, okay. We're in, but I need a few moments, and I want to meet with the owner of the other bird."

When the two headed over to the tall Darien Indian, I casually leaned against the wall, and then, when no one was looking, I snatched one of the darts and broke off the feathers, leaving me with a three-inch splinter of very poisoned wood. I realized the dark-brown poison at the point was very old and maybe not effective anymore, or maybe just a little effective, which would be perfect...

Walking over to the owner of the Frankenbird, I introduced myself. He was taciturn at best. "They fight now," he said abruptly.

"No, no, not right away. I assume you're using Marquis of Queensbury rules for this, where each bird can be examined by the competition before the contest."

"Queensbury?"

"Yeah, yeah," I said. "International rules for cockfighting. Used around the world. I check your bird, you check mine, for metal on the spurs, protective devices under the feathers."

I was making this up as I went along, but apparently I at least had him confused.

He paused. "Then they fight?"

"Yeah, yeah, then they fight." I handed him Will, and knelt next to the other bird, its small, mean eyes staring at me like a hungry fox. I stroked it a couple of times, then felt around the body, palming the dart in my hand, and moving it to my fingertips, then quickly jabbing the big bird in the butt one time. The creature cackled loudly and flapped its wings and I promptly put him down. "Everything looks to be in order to me," I said confidently.

The fellow set my chicken down. "Now they fight."

"Yeah, now they fight." But I needed a few moments for the poison to take effect, if it was going to. "But, as per Marquis of Queensbury rules, we must share a toast." I grabbed a couple of glasses from the table next to us and poured some of my new acquaintance's tequila into them, handing one to him and lifting the other. "To El Condor! To Willbird! To ferocious cocks everywhere!"

Immediately after the toast, Frankenchicken's owner marched his champion out to the center of the cleared room and sat him down.

I picked up Will and whispered to him: "Lots of bobbing and weaving, okay? Stay away from him as long as you can — left jabs and lots of movement. Keep him off balance. Wear him out."

The chicken clucked nervously.

I sat my bird friend down about five feet from his opponent and backed away, and immediately the big rooster charged. Will's technique was good. He shrieked and ran, dashing out of the ring and underneath the tables, squawking loudly. It wasn't exactly the best fight that bar had ever seen. Mostly it was a chase as my boy bounced over and under tables and around the legs of viewers, getting caught periodically for brief sessions of pounding, then escaping with gurgling shrieks again. But I noticed that, early on, monster bird was starting to lose his momentum, and Willbird was starting to fight back — a couple of quick jabs, nice footwork, an occasional roundhouse with a spur, before shrieking into a retreat.

After a minute or two, it was obvious to me that the poison was working. It was too old to kill the bird, which was good, but it was slowing him way down. He'd become like a boxer on Quaaludes — stumbling into chairs, not getting his guard up quickly anymore, a seriously dazed look in his eyes. My boy saw the change, and his animal (or bird) instincts took over. He was moving in faster now, throwing nice left hooks, working the midsection with jabs and pecks, and doing some great roundhouse kicks. He was even doing a little Muhammad Ali after exceptional shots, dancing around, his wings fluttering in the air.

The partiality in the room was changing, as well. The massacre they had expected was morphing — the little guy was winning, and somewhere deep within them, the subtle influence of hope was altering their perspective. They were so used to seeing the big man win, so used to accepting defeat in most aspects of their lives, that this sudden exception put wind under their wings, and in some subtle fashion reminded them that sometimes you beat the odds. That was what their lives, and the bitter drudgery of mining, were all about — being lucky every once in a while, and the little guy winning when no one expects it. Within minutes the crowd was shouting and yelling, splashing drinks on each other as they capered and cheered, standing on tables and crying out encouragement for the small white rooster that was all of a sudden kicking the big guy's ass.

Finally, toward the end, my boy was fully in control, effortlessly tossing left and right hooks, jabbing with an occasional spur and using his body to control his flagging opponent. They had fought their way to the top of the bar — the big rooster, dizzy and baffled, strictly in a defensive mode now, and trying to stay on two feet. As his opponent teetered on the edge of the bar, Willbird backed up and did a flying front kick, both feet landing solidly on the big rooster's chest, sending him soaring backwards as if he'd been shot out of a cannon, slamming him against the wall and dropping him into the open trashcan by the bar. The crowd went wild, and a chant rose out of the ranks, building gradually from a whisper to a roar: "Willbird! Willbird! Willbird!"

I drank for free for the next hour or so, and my boy was given a monster bowl of seed to work on. I was a little higher than I liked by the time we left (Willbird tucked under my arm), and not paying as much attention as I should have been. When we got down the planked walkway to the docks I noticed there was a new boat tied up — a small Donzi-type speedboat with one man by the steering wheel and one standing on the docks. They were big guys in faded blue jeans and T-shirts that strained to contain their muscles. I was about to turn around, my fuddled head realizing we had a situation here, when I felt someone stick a gun in my back.

"Jus' keep moving forward, assahole, and I won' be forced to blow your guts all over dis nice dock."

I stiffened and slowed for a moment, but the jab of the gun again encouraged me forward. The guys by the Donzi looked strangely familiar. Suddenly it came to me, and I groaned. They were the bodyguards for Tu Phat, from the bar the other night, where Will had cleaned Phat's clock in backgammon. "Son of a bitch," I moaned.

When we got to their boat I noticed all my gear from the dugout canoe had been loaded aboard, including the biscuit tin with the emeralds. I moaned again.

One of them shoved me toward the stern, onto a bench seat, then sat in the seat across from me, holding a pistol. The other handled the boat, swinging out into the river and heading downstream.

I looked out at the winding, brown waterway. *At least we're going in the same direction as that little weasel, Benito.*

The guy holding the gun finally couldn't resist. He pushed back his long hair with one hand. "What is with da chicken, man?"

I had placed Willbird on the seat next to me, one hand on him protectively.

"I'm gonna have cards made so I don't have to keep doing this," I muttered.

The guy cocked his head questioningly.

"Look, it's not a chicken. It's my partner. He got turned into a chicken at *El Pueblo de las Brujas* last night."

The fellow stared at me, interested now. "Da tall *gringo* wid' da blonde hair, who beat Tu Phat in backgammon?"

"Yeah."

He smiled, but it wasn't nice. "Then it's good you bring him. Tu Phat will probably want to have him for dinner. After dinner he will probably feed you to da crocs."

I rolled my eyes. "Great..."

The guy chuckled. "Like you *gringos* say, 'some days is a bitch, right from when you get up!'"

I hated to admit it, but so far, he was right.

CHAPTER 8

Tu Phat Shong, dressed in a fresh silk robe and soft nylon pants, was sitting in the shade of his veranda when he saw the Donzi coming up the river. A small smile twisted the corners of his mouth when he recognized one of the Americans in the boat.

We pulled the Donzi up to the river dock at the front of the house and I was hustled off by one of Phat's men, Willbird under my arm, while the other walked behind us holding a gun.

Tu Phat rose slowly from his rattan chair and stood by the porch rail as we climbed the few steps up to the house. "How nice to see you again, Mr. Kansas Stamps," he said in that oily fashion of his. "I have been looking forward to another conversation with you and your friend." He looked around questioningly, glancing at the chicken under my arm. "And your friend? Where is he?"

The guard to my left spoke up. "He claims his *compañero* was turned into a chicken in *El Pueblo de las Brujas*."

Tu Phat's eyes flickered with caution. The name of that village had the same effect on everyone. "A chicken, eh? That is too bad." Then he got that evil smile again. "But you know, I was thinking of having chicken tonight, so maybe all is not lost."

The guard nudged me. "See? I tol' you so."

I recoiled and grasped the bird tighter against me. "C'mon, man. There's no need for this. We haven't done anything to you, we're just passing through."

Phat nodded in an agreeable fashion. "Yes, that is correct, but it is the passing-through part I would like to know more about. Why don't you tell me what you have been doing on my river, eh?"

If his men had discovered the emeralds in the biscuit tin, they would have said something by now, but I was still caught between trying to save a fortune and preserving the life of my friend. I had to gamble — to try a mix of truth and lies. "Okay, okay. Listen, we heard about the legend of a cave upriver that had emeralds, maybe even Spanish gold in it, from the late 1600s. We got into some of the old Spanish archives that told about a shipment that was stolen, or lost, right at about 1700 — thought we'd do some exploring, see what we could find." I sighed bitterly. "But it's tough upriver — too much jungle, everything wants a piece of you, from the mosquitoes to the leopards. It was just too much for us..."

I thought I might be making some headway when Shong stepped over and ripped open my shirt, exposing the chain and the emerald. He snatched it off my neck and held it in his fist in front of my face. "And this? Where did this come from, *señor*?"

When I hesitated, he saw the look in my eyes.

"I am not a patient man, Mr. Stamps," he growled. "But I have another meeting I must attend to now, so I will let you consider your answer for a couple of hours." He got that sardonic smile. "Dinner is at six o'clock. Baked chicken. They will come for your friend at five." He turned to the guards. "Lock them in the boathouse. Both of you keep guard outside, you hear?"

For the next two hours I sat on a bench in the boathouse, talking to Willbird, who clucked in commiseration with me. The boathouse was located on a canal that ran inland from the river. It was being used as a dry dock/storage area for boat parts and engines. It didn't contain any functioning watercraft, but I noticed as they locked us away that Tu Phat did own one other boat, tied up at the canal dock — an Aquasport open fisherman, about 18 feet, with what looked like a 125 Mercury at the stern.

I continually glanced at my watch as the minutes ticked off. The boathouse was tight as a camel's ass in a sandstorm, and both of the men outside had weapons. There was nothing I could do. There were no heavy tools inside, nothing I could use as a weapon against the guards. Willbird sat on the floor beside me, clucking mournfully.

At five o'clock, the guards unlocked the door and entered. One held a gun on me while the other came over. We'd run out of time and luck. As the big guy reached down for the chicken, I stood, with my hands out, palms up. "Okay, Okay. You win. You win. I'll tell you where the emeralds are. Just don't hurt the chicken."

At that moment Tu Phat appeared in the doorway, again with that smile that contained about as much sincerity as a hungry leopard. "Well, Mr. Stamps, I'm pleased with your timely reconsideration. A wise choice." He looked at me. "Go on…"

"In the biscuit tin on the Donzi — that's where the emeralds are. We found them buried in the floor of a cave where the river bends, just above *El Pueblo de las Brujas*."

Shong stared at me for a moment, then nodded to one of the men. "Go."

Five minutes later he was back with the tin. At Phat's prompting he spilled the contents onto a worktable. The afternoon sun shone through the window and brought the green stones to life. The eyes of the big man gleamed as he ran his hand over the hard-angled gems and picked up an exceptionally large one, holding it up to the light.

Still looking at the emerald, he spoke, "This was all? This was all you found?"

I huffed. "What? That's not enough — a couple hundred thousand in emeralds?"

"The legend says more than this," the Panamanian said, turning to me.

I stared him in the eyes. "You'll have to take that up with the guy who wrote the legend."

Phat shrugged. "He's on the list." Then he exhaled with a degree of satisfaction, shoveling the emeralds back into the can with his big hands. "But this will do for now." He turned to the guards. "Tie him up. Bring the chicken."

"No!" I yelled, rising to my feet. "You promised, if I gave you the emeralds!"

Tu Phat shook his finger at me. "You have been reading too many American novels. There is no honor among thieves." He grinned, hands out. "Besides, a man must eat…"

The guard next to me stepped in and in a swift movement swept his hand under the chicken, grabbing it by its feet and turning it upside down by his side. As Willbird shrieked and flapped, I lunged at the guy, and caught a gun butt in the temple for my efforts. As I went down, things growing fuzzy, the big Darien said, "Don't kill the bird. My chef will do that before he dresses it. I like my meat fresh, like the leopard."

In the haze I saw him nod to the other guard and point at me.

"Kill him and throw him in the canal. My crocodiles can dine, as well."

With that, Shong and one of the guards left. The other man turned to me, his face hard. "Get up. We gonna take a walk. I don' feel like dragging you to the water."

"You don't have to do this," I pleaded. "You could just let me go. I'd be on the next plane out of here. Tu Phat would never know—"

"Oh yes he would," the fellow said, dark eyes lighting with apprehension. "He know everything, and then I would be food for the crocodiles tomorrow night." He waved the gun. "Les' go, *amigo*. Now."

It was Woody Allen who said, "You never get used to the

prospect of imminent death." He was right. It's a strange thing. You become desperate at first, prepared to try anything, but as opportunity narrows, you usually end up strangely complacent.

This is it. I should have done more, or I shouldn't have done what I did, or I wish I had told the people I cared about that I cared about them...

The guard pushed me out onto the dock. As we walked along the rickety slats, I prepared to leap into the canal, but his voice stopped me.

"If you jump, I will shoot you at least twice before you hit the water, and the blood will attract the crocs. It will not be so quick then, I promise you."

At the end of the dock, with my back to my executioner, I lowered my head and waited.

"*Lo siento, señor,*" he said as I heard him cock the revolver. "No hard feelings, it's just my job." There was a pause. "It's not a bad job, actually."

I waited for the explosion and the impact, but all I heard was a grunt behind me, and a thump of something heavy hitting the planks on the dock. A second or two later, when there was still no report, I slowly turned around. There was Will — in human form! He held a tire iron in his right hand and the big guard lay crumpled at his feet. I exhaled hard, the fear and the stress draining out of me in one long breath. "Will! You're not a chicken anymore!"

"A chicken?" my friend muttered. "You've been out in the sun again without your hat, haven't you?"

I involuntarily stumbled over to him and touched him. "Oh Jesus, I'm glad to see you! I...I...you were a chicken — turned into a chicken by the witches." I pointed at the house. "They just took you — to eat you..."

"Definitely too much sun," my friend said dryly.

"How? Why?" I stuttered.

"Look, I don't know what happened to you. But I woke up naked early this morning — stars still out — drunk and stoned beyond comprehension. I stumbled out of the hut to pee and took a tumble down the hillside behind the village. When I came to again and could gather my senses, it was close to noon. Everyone said you'd left. So, I found my clothes, took a canoe by the shoreline and came after you. When I got to *El Campo de los Tontos* the dockmaster said you'd had some trouble with a couple of Tu Phat's men in a Donzi and they had taken you downriver, probably to Phat's place. I followed slowly, watching the banks, and finally found the Donzi tied up out front here." He took a breath and smiled. "Timing is everything, dude. I was sneaking up toward the house when I saw this guy..." He nudged the fellow on the dock with his foot. "...walking you down the dock with a gun at your back. The rest, as they say, is history."

"Man, I swear I thought you were a chicken," I muttered incredulously.

"What is with you and this chicken thing?"

I took a couple of minutes to explain what had happened at the village — the chicken in Will's clothes that morning, how it responded to me, the cockfight, and how I ended up in the boathouse.

"You should be writing this stuff down," Will said with a smile. "It would make a great fiction novel." He glanced toward the big house set back in the jungle, then toward the dock and the Aquasport open fisherman. "But right now I'm thinking we need to get out of here. Where are the emeralds?"

"Phat took 'em," I muttered. "I had to give them to him or he was going to kill the chicken." I took a deep breath. "Will, I can't leave without the chicken. They're going to eat him." My partner started to speak, but I raised my hand. "I know you're not going to understand, but that chicken and I went through a lot together. I thought he was you, man, and I just can't let them eat him."

Will scrunched his mouth in thought. "That's okay, 'cause I can't leave without my emeralds. We're going to have to deal with Phat boy on both accounts."

Without another word Will pulled the unconscious guard up and leaned him against a dock piling, then he took the man's belt and wrapped it around his neck and the piling, pulling the belt tight and notching it with the buckle at the back of the post — impossible to reach and just one notch below asphyxiation if he didn't move too much. Then he tied the man's hands and feet with docking line.

I picked up the guard's gun and fired it into the water of the canal, then stuck it in my belt.

Will jumped as if he'd been goosed. "What the hell?"

I pointed toward Phat's place. "They're gonna be expecting a shot."

We both turned and headed for the house, walking along the

dock.

"A chicken, huh?" my partner said without looking at me.

"Yeah," I replied with a smile. "You're gonna like him. He's a really personable little fellow, and gutsy too."

"A chicken..."

We slipped quietly across the grounds, moving silently from hedge to tree. I noticed that Tu Phat had a guard by the Donzi we came in on, at the dock on the river. I caught a glance of Phat standing on his back porch, where a table was being set for dinner by a Darien Indian servant. Off to the side of the porch was one of his guards. To the side of the house I saw a stump, its dark-brown stains telling the final story of many a creature. My stomach did a little lurch when I thought about the chicken.

"We need a distraction, Will," I whispered urgently. "Got to get the guard off the porch, so we can deal with Phat boy — and I gotta get the bird. We're going to need a serious distraction."

Will glanced around for a moment, settling on the lawn equipment shed about 50 yards from the porch. He got that goofy grin and his eyes went mischievous. "How about a little of Flip Wilson's Geraldine? You remember? We used it on Conan, the guy guarding our car in The Keys a few years ago." He raised the crowbar he had carried from the dock. "It's tough to ignore Geraldine."

I did remember, and I smiled. "Yeah! That oughta work great."

With a final nod, my partner headed around the house from the other side so he could sneak into the shed.

I hid behind a hedge, keeping an eye on Tu Phat and his sentry. A few moments later there was a cry from the lawn equipment shed — a high-pitched woman's voice. "He'p me! He'p me! Someone he'p me, please!" Pause... "You stay away from me, you black-eyed demon. Don' you dare touch me! Don' you dare take down yo' pants! Don' you...ooohhh my gawd! Yo daddy musta been a gorilla! Lawd, he'p me! No! No! You keep that giant, tuberous thang away from me, you hear? Holy mackerel! You got a permit for that?"

Phat looked over at his guard and nodded toward the shed. "See what that's about. Now."

As the guard sauntered down the porch steps and headed over, the cacophony continued.

"Don' you dare touch me with that thang!" cried the voice, followed by movement inside — something banging against the wall. "Don' you dare! Don' you dare try to put that...ooohhh my Gaaawd!" Now the thumping against the wall was steady, rhythmic. "Ooohhh, Jesus! I been skewered by an anaconda!" shrieked the voice again. "My eyeballs is bulgin' outta my head! I's twitchin' like a shot possum! Ooohh... Ooohhhhh... Don' you dare... Don' you dare... stop, elephant boy! Whoodang! Ooohh Lawd! Give mama aalll dat snake!"

The reference to the possum reminded me of my own pressing issues. I looked over at the stump. Still nothing going on there, thank God.

The guard reached the shed, swung open the door and cautiously stepped in, out of sight. It was quiet for a moment and I thought I heard a thump, then the voice shrieked, "Ooohhh Jesus! Not two of you! Don' you dare... Ooohh my gawd!"

Tu Phat was so engrossed in the spectacle he never even noticed me as I swung onto the porch and snuck up behind him, the dock guard's pistol in hand. I shoved the barrel against his spine and whispered, "Any fast moves, Phat man, and you'll be breathing out of your belly button."

Before he could even consider turning around I grabbed the long lock of black hair on the backside of his head and jerked it down, bringing his chin up at an unnatural angle. "On your knees, now!"

He eased down and I waited for a few seconds while I held him, staring impatiently at the equipment shed. At that moment, Will stepped out and tipped the crowbar to his head in salute, a big smile on his face.

Phat groaned quietly, realizing he was screwed. My partner padlocked the shed door and trotted over. There was at least one more guard, down by the Donzi, on the river dock in front of the house, but it was one thing at a time.

"Okay, Phat man, where are our emeralds?" Will said as I held our prisoner tightly.

"You cannot get away with this," the big man gritted, still on his knees. "I will find you."

I looked at Will and put the gun to Phat's head. "Well, in that case let's just kill him now." But as I cocked the revolver his attitude changed.

"Okay! Okay! They are in my study, in the brown box on the desk! Down the hall, first room on the right!"

I nodded to Will and he slipped away, returning in moments with a grin and a biscuit tin full of emeralds. "Time to say, 'Goodnight Johnny.'"

"Not quite," I replied, reaching for a carving knife on the serving table next to me. The man's eyes grew wide as I turned to him, still gripping his lock of hair. With a jerk I brought his head back to me, eye to eye. "You ordered me killed with no more concern than you might show when choosing your breakfast fruit." I raised the knife. "Now you're going to pay for that." The big man started blubbering, begging not to be killed as I brought the razor sharp blade downward, sawing through this precious lock of braided hair on the side of his head.

There was both relief and horror in his eyes when he realized what I had done. He was still alive, but it was perhaps the ultimate insult to a Chinese. He opened his mouth to scream and I stuffed his pigtail into it while Will cut off the corded sash on the tablecloth and bound Tu Phat's hands and feet.

I was so preoccupied with Mr. Shong that I had momentarily forgotten about the chicken. I ran to the other side of the deck, looked out at the stump, and froze in horror. The cook was at the tree stump, dragging the chicken from a burlap bag, holding it firmly with one hand and gripping a small hatchet with the other. With an involuntary yell I leaped over the balcony and onto the grass, yelling and running, trying to get the gun out of my belt. But I was too late. With a smooth, practiced move, he thrust the bird onto the stump, pinning it tightly, and swung the axe.

The blade whistled down, cleanly severing the chicken's head as the axe head buried itself in the stump. He instantly released the remains of the bird and it tumbled to the ground, flapping and shaking spasmodically, then collapsing. I screamed, hitting him from behind and bowling him over, bitter rage engulfing me with the fury of a hurricane. I hammered him unconscious with the butt of my gun, and Will had to stop me from beating the fellow to death.

When my friend pulled me off the inert man, I sat there on the grass, staring at the remains of my feathered companion, breathing in gasps. I realized it was crazy — that in a very short time I had transferred the affection and loyalty I carried for my friend to a bird. But I couldn't just instantly release those emotions simply because it wasn't true. For a short time, the poor bird had been my friend, my companion. I think, at that moment, Will finally understood. He placed his hand on my shoulder. "I'm sorry, man. I'm sorry..."

I sat there on the grass for a few moments, catching my breath, still staring at the brutalized creature in front of me.

Will touched my shoulder again. "We gotta go, man, we gotta get out of here…"

But as I slowly rose and we started to walk away, I heard a chirp — a soft cluck from the burlap bag next to the stump. It was then that I realized something didn't jive. The dead bird didn't have any black on its wings…

There was another tentative cluck from the bag next to me. Slowly, I knelt, reached over, and opened it…and Willbird came scrambling out onto my lap, peeping and chirping excitedly. "Mucking fagnificent," I whispered with a huge smile, absolutely amazed, and pleased beyond belief.

"Yeah, that is way far out," Will agreed, with that funky grin splitting his face. "But now, we gotta go, buddy."

I snatched up Willbird and tucked him under my arm, and we raced for the docks where the Aquasport was tethered. My partner possessed the unique propensity of being able to hotwire just about any boat or car in minutes. (His brother had been in the business of selling vehicles that weren't his to sell, and had passed on the talent.)

In minutes Will had the open fisherman's 125 horsepower Mercury purring like a big cat, and I had cast off the dock lines. As we pulled away, down the canal and into the river, we could hear one pissed-off Panamanian screaming his lungs out while trying to get himself untied from a patio chair. I was reminded then of an expression I'd heard a guy use at a bar one night — a guy named Frank: *"Any fool can have bad luck; the art is knowing how to exploit it…"*

The 19-foot Aquasport was a smooth-running craft and Will had it carrying us along nicely, but it wasn't a speedboat. I knew we had to take advantage of our lead-time. We'd covered three miles of river before I noticed the Donzi coming around the last bend behind us. It looked like one of the guards was at the helm with Tu Phat next to him, and the other guard was by the rail. Phat and one guard had rifles aimed in our direction.

In short order, bullets were slapping the water around us, and smacking the transom. We crouched down as Will pushed the throttle hard against the wall, one hand on the controls. The twists and turns of the river had helped preserve us to this point, and I had kept our pursuers at bay with the guard's pistol, but now the Donzi was gaining on us.

We needed a distraction. I quickly got down on my knees, rummaging through the equipment locker, and found what I was looking for — the emergency kit with a flare gun and a handful of flares. About that time we took two rounds through the engine cowling, one of which must have ruptured the fuel line. Gas was spraying onto the hot manifold and smoke was pouring out of the exhausts like a Key West mosquito control truck. Our speed had begun to suffer, as well.

We would have been finished at that point but for a small stroke of luck. The Donzi's propeller hit one of the long lines of floating vines that occasionally break loose from overhanging trees and become navigational hazards. Even over the phlegmatic stammer of our engine I could hear Phat screaming as the boat came to a stop and one of his men jumped over the side to cut the vines loose from the lower unit. This bought us the few minutes we needed. We managed to get around a bend of the river and out of the competition's sight.

I leaned over to Will and shouted over the engine. "I've got a plan. It's dangerous as hell, but we've gotta try something. No question Phat boy's gonna catch us now."

Will nodded grimly. "I'm listening."

After I had explained, Will hissed, "Son of a bitch! That's a plan? That's the best you got?"

"That's it, man..."

He stared at me hard. "Okay, let's do it."

Without another word, Will shut down the outboard. I took my pistol and shot a handful of holes in the above-deck fiberglass auxiliary gas tank at the back of the boat, then pulled the plugs from the deck and transom drains. As a final desperate thought, I snatched the VHF radio mike off its clip while switching the radio to the frequency we used with Eddie. I quickly blurted out a message telling him if he was getting this, we needed help now, giving him our approximate position on the river. Meanwhile, Will stuffed the biscuit tin of emeralds down his shirt.

Gasoline was pouring out over the deck and into the water, creating a pearly gas slick around the drifting boat. We could hear the Donzi firing up from the bend behind us, then the roar of its big engine, and the chase began again. Tucking the pistol into my belt, I grabbed the flare gun and an extra shell, then reached into the bait box and grabbed Willbird, tucking him under my arm. I looked at my partner. "Let's go."

We slipped into the water at the stern of the boat, because the current was keeping the accumulated gas on the surface around the bow and the sides. We were being as quiet as possible, trying not to get the attention of the crocs on the shoreline. It was a huge gamble, but this way we might make the shore and have an opportunity to flag down a passing boat — if the crocs didn't get us first.

We were no more than 50 yards from the boat, clinging to a floating log that was working its way downriver, my chicken sitting nervously atop it, when Phat and his boys came barreling around the bend. When they saw our boat they slowed and cautiously motored toward it. They were taking their time and we were drifting farther away from the Aquasport.

It was going to be a long shot for a flare gun. "C'mon," I muttered fiercely. "You can do it."

Finally, the Donzi edged up into the gas slick, coming alongside our battered open fisherman. We had been treading water, holding on to the log the whole time, but I'd managed to keep the flare pistol and the extra round out of the river.

"Now!" whispered Will urgently. "Now!"

I rested my forearm on the log, pointed the gun at our gas-soaked boat, and triumphantly pulled the trigger. The report of the pistol snapped our three antagonists around like frightened meerkats, but there was nothing they could do.

Unfortunately, as our old Rastaman friend Rufus used to say, "Sometimes even da gods get bored, and dey like to play with you."

The projectile passed a foot over the hull and continued traveling another 100 yards, sailing into the jungle before exploding. Suddenly, the whole thing became painfully clear to Phat and his crew. He was screaming to his wheelman to get the craft away from there, but the guy had turned off the boat and now, terrified, was furiously grinding the starter.

With a curse I snapped open the flare gun, ejected the dead shell, and slammed the new one in, but the Donzi had just fired up and was turning away from the derelict hull. I threw my arm up on the log, aimed, and fired. This time the shot was straight and true, slamming the side of the Aquasport's hull and bursting into a red-orange explosion that ignited the surrounding gas on the water with an oxygen-stealing, fiery "whoosh." The good news was Phat and his crew hadn't moved their boat far enough from the hull before the explosion. The bad news was, they had managed to get far enough away to not be totally engulfed by the inferno.

When the smoke cleared, Tu Phat and his men looked like poster children for faulty BBQ grill accidents. They had no eyebrows, their hair was smoking and frizzled, and their clothes were in tatters — but they were still alive and seriously pissed. They spotted us as we swam with the current toward a bank that didn't appear to be packed with crocodiles.

Still, it took Phat and his boys a few minutes to get moving. The boat had stalled and their second and third-degree burns were making things painfully confusing at best. But once they were headed our way, we could tell we weren't going to make the shoreline before they got to us. Tu Phat, in the bow, was already firing, the bullets slapping the water around us. Once again I had the bird tucked against me and I was forced into using a sidestroke.

By the sheerest of grace, the log we had hidden behind hit the bow of their boat as they came at us, forcing them to swerve radically or bust a prop, and the engine died again. As they worked on firing up the Donzi, the crocs on the shoreline were getting interested in the excitement, and began waddling off the bank and splashing into the water, headed our way. It looked like a "six of one" situation.

As we paddled furiously for the far bank, I huffed out a few words between strokes.

"Damn, Will, didn't mean to get you into such a mess."

My friend coughed out a mouthful of river as he stroked methodically for the shore. "Don't go getting all melancholy on me now," he spat forcefully. "You didn't exactly twist my arm."

It was at that moment, with bullets smacking the water around us, and the merciless crocodile eyes just above the surface closing in from the far bank, that I heard it — the throaty roar of two big outboards heading our way. I spun around, treading water, desperately glancing downriver, searching for the impossible. Just then, from around the bend came the Mako we had originally rented in Obaldia, engines screaming full out. As the boat got closer I could just make out the skinny frame and the long dark hair of the person at the wheel.

"Son of a bitch!" Will muttered incredulously. "Is that who I think it is?

"Yeah, it is," I whispered gratefully. "Benito!"

We threw up our arms and started waving, and our little buddy saw us, waving back and turning the boat in our direction. In seconds he was beside us. Will clambered over the transom. I handed him the chicken, and climbed aboard myself. We all paused for an uncomfortable moment, Will and I staring at our little nemesis/savior.

"Didn't expect to see you again," I said.

Benito shrugged and smiled sheepishly, then he straightened up. "Son'times a man must do what a man must do." He nodded downriver. "I was at the dock in Obaldia, unloading son' last stuff. I heard your call on da boat radio..." His gaze dropped to the deck. "*Lo siento, amigos.* Benny is ashamed..."

I couldn't help but smile. "Maybe there's more of that 'integrity stuff' in your veins than you thought."

Benito looked at the chicken quizzically. "You bring dinner?"

Will shook his head and wagged a finger. "Don't go there, Benny. Don't go there –"

We were interrupted by the roar of the Donzi's engine. Tu Phat and his people were swinging around the bend toward us.

"Let's get outta here!" I cried, and as my partner took the controls I put Willbird in the bait box at the stern, then grabbed the passenger's seat.

Benito settled into the bench seat at the bow. We were alive and we had a new boat, but I had lost my pistol in the escape from the Aquasport. With the twin 125s on the Mako we could make a run of it again, but the Donzi was still faster, and the bad guys had guns.

Within minutes we found ourselves in the same situation again. The curves in the river gave us some advantage, but as it straightened out for the final run into the sea, Tu Phat and his Donzi were closing, and again bullets began slapping the water around us.

"This is really getting old!" Will groaned, crouching down behind the windshield as he steered us. "You got any more ideas?"

A round punched a hole in the windshield in front of me and I screamed like a child. "No, not right off the top of my head," I shouted over the roar of the engines. "We just race them for Obaldia and hope they don't kill us before we get there."

Another four or five rounds raked our transom. A foot higher and someone would have been dead.

"I don't think that's going to work," Will muttered caustically as he continued to swerve the boat, making us harder to hit.

Our old buddy Rufus, the psychic Rastaman with connections to places that most of us have never seen, also used to say, "Da gods, dey bore easily, and sometimes dey keep special people alive strictly for entertainment. We call it amazing luck, but it nothing more than da gods adjusting da rabbit ears on da television of life."

I swear to you, at that moment, when I was certain we were done, I had the strongest impression to look downriver. There on the horizon, just barely in sight, was Crazy Eddie's Grumman Goose.

I grabbed Will's arm hard enough to make him flinch. Pointing out over the bow at the horizon I shouted, "Eddie! It's Eddie!"

With a huge smile, Will pushed the throttle to the wall and we streaked toward the Goose and its wonderful, wacked-out pilot. But we still had to deal with the very angry people behind us. I sincerely hoped the gods had something figured out there, because we were still taking some very serious fire. I snatched the mike off the VHF radio and made sure the frequency was set to 122.4.

"Eddie! Eddie!" I shouted as another round of bullets raked the boat. "We need some help, man. You got anything?"

Our friend's voice crackled through the radio speakers, just audible above the roar of the engines and the gunfire. *"Hola,* dudes! Eddie digs, man. Hold tight. Keep breathing! Eddie gonna have to get inventive. We gonna give 'em some shit, you might say."

Before I could ask who "we" were, Edward Jackson Moorehouse had dropped his mike and the big airplane zoomed over our pursuers and us with a roar — so low I thought his undercarriage was going to hit the windshield on the Donzi's center console. As soon as it was past, Eddie cranked it into one of those crop-duster turns, where all the loose rivets shake and you can hear the wings groan from the G-force. He swung around and dropped the plane to 100 feet off the water well behind, then moved downriver steadily until he was above and just forward of the Donzi, keeping perfect pace with it. I watched the cargo door open, and somebody pushed out the ugly, pink, porcelain commode from the bathroom in the plane.

Eddie was a master with that airplane — a Michelangelo of the air. He timed it perfectly, leading the Donzi below him like a hunter leads a duck. The heavy toilet tumbled out of the sky, rolling slowly as it fell inexorably at its target. The toilet struck just forward of the console and that fancy little boat exploded, shards of porcelain shrapnel spreading out viciously as the craft buckled. The commode drove itself through the hull and most of the way out of the bottom. The driver, who had an ear taken off by a sharp shard of crapper, lost control and the boat swerved sideways, going up on a rail and flipping end over end several times, tossing its luckless occupants into the air like rag dolls.

We had slowed to a stop, watching with considerable wonder. Only a moment ago I was certain we were dead. Yet, in just seconds our pursuers had been vanquished, as if swatted by the hand of God — with the help of a whacked-out hippie who was probably the finest pilot in South Florida, plus whoever it was that pushed out that freaking toilet. There were no signs of any survivors from the Donzi, but I couldn't manage much grief there.

The big Goose swung around in the distance and made another slow pass by us. It was then that I realized who was up there with Eddie. Waving energetically from the cargo hatch were Kendra and Margo. I waved back. Will and Benito were beaming and shouting. Once again we had danced with the gods of fate and walked away with the prize.

My partner turned to me, smiling from ear to ear. "I told you," he said. "You're not dead until you see the devil!"

CHAPTER 9

Will and I met privately with Benito and Eddie. Benito explained that he had hidden the stash of gold and emeralds beneath floorboards of an abandoned shack down by the beach. We took a walk and retrieved them, leaving Benito a bag of emeralds and a couple bars of gold. If he was careful, he would never have to worry about bullfighting lessons again in his lifetime. The rest we carefully hid in Eddie's Goose. The boy had hiding places that would shame a neurotic pack rat.

That night we celebrated wealth, survival, and good friends at the bar in Puerto Obaldia. We ate, drank, and danced, and bought drinks for everyone in the room at least a dozen times. Word had spread up and down the river that Tu Phat Shong had been killed, although no one had found the body yet — unlikely that would happen, with the crocs in *El Rio Fangaso*. It was like the death of the Wicked Witch. The entire community seemed to feel a universal lift of spirit.

It was a hell of an evening. We had to tell the story again and again to Eddie and Benito, and our new ladies. (We left out the part about the drunken debauchery in the Village of the Witches, but we had to tell the part about my believing Will had been magically morphed into a chicken.) Everyone loved it all. The girls begged to take some photos of the treasure (without pictures of us) and we agreed to that — for the following day.

At our insistence, they explained the commode-bomb affair that had saved our lives. When they reached us and saw our frantic race for survival, they had no weapons. It was Eddie who suggested removing the two bolts holding it in place. It was ridiculous and desperate, but a familiar, damned near comfortable zone for our daredevil friend.

Then, there was the news of the death of the two men in the house at the end of town. We assumed they were probably envoys of Jacko Slade's, sent to even up some karmic scales and get his medallion back. The whole thing inferred the possibility of competition. I didn't at all like the idea of being that popular. Not at all.

At the urging of the girls, we had to tell a little of the Jacko Slade story, as well. Will and I were the better part of snockered by this time, and probably told more than we should have, but I felt no angst. We were among friends. Once again our ladies were duly impressed, saying that they were beginning to think they were dating Indiana Joneses, and wanting to know if we still had the fabulous medallion. We did, of course — in our Key West safety deposit box. Again, they wanted photos. Even as drunk as we were, we said not likely.

That night with Kendra was one of the most wonderful evenings I could remember; mind-bending sexual fireworks with the beginning of something deeper — swells of passion and the first hints of genuine emotion. The next morning, we stood on the balcony of my room, hand in hand, watching the sun crest an indigo sea and melt away ribbons of mist while a fresh onshore breeze caressed the lazy beachfront palms with that timeless sense of endearment. I glanced at Kendra, immodestly covered by a pink kimono open in the front, her perfect, arching breasts seeking escape.

She was staring out at the ocean, and while her countenance reflected a sense of poise and contentment, there seemed a flicker of unease within those pale blue orbs. When she saw me looking at her she smiled, warm and inviting, and the flicker faded like the early morning shadows on the beach below. I found myself wondering whether she, too, was thinking that this tryst, this tropical liaison, however passionate, might be coming to an end now that our mission was completed. She stilled my concerns for the moment with a kiss, taking my arm and leading me back to bed.

I awoke to find Kendra gone. She left a note saying she had to meet Margo and gather the equipment they would need for a shoot of the treasure, and that they would want some written information on the history behind the treasure along with a brief narrative of our part in all of this — for their editor. She added that no names or home locations would be used, and that they would like to do the shoot on the island where we had shared the romantic interlude last week. That was a good choice — private and safe. We could have Eddie fly us out, do the shoot, and then put everything away in his hiding places before returning. When I got together with Will at breakfast, he said it was probably a stupid thing to do, but it pleased our egos greatly — a national magazine doing a story on our find.

As we sipped our coffees after breakfast, Will looked at me. "So, after this photo shoot, what happens? We can't exactly return to The Keys. We wouldn't last 48 hours before Slade's goons would have us tied spread-eagle on a beach somewhere and were cutting out the information they wanted."

Before I could reply he held up a finger.

"And...then there's the girls."

I started to speak, and again he interrupted.

"Don't know about you, but I kinda like this one. Aside from her amorous talents, which pale most professional hookers, she's a pretty cool lady, and I'd like the chance, somehow, of continuing to see her."

"Can I speak now?"

My partner shrugged. "Sure. What's stopping you?"

"I feel the same way. I'm just not quite sure where to carry this." I paused. "A lot is up to the girls — they have to feel the same way."

"I don't think that's a problem at my end."

"Don't think it is with me, either," I replied, adding some cream to my coffee. "Okay, here's the deal as I see it; they're from Fort Lauderdale, and that's a big city. Maybe we could hide out there for a while, see if our buddy Shane O'Neal and the DEA nail Jacko. It's an option...but it's still up to the girls..."

We all met at the docks at 11 a.m. — the ladies adorned in camera equipment and Bermuda shorts, and us in our finest khaki shorts, jungle shirts, and Docksiders. Our faces didn't matter, they were never going to be photographed. The treasure was conveniently still aboard the Goose. I threw off the docking lines as Eddie cranked over the big radials, and in less than two minutes we were in the air, Jimmy Buffett's "Son of a Son of a Sailor" swelling the cockpit.

Within minutes the hull of the Goose was slapping the water of the tiny bay where we had picnicked a week ago. While Eddie stood guard with a pistol, the treasure was laid out on a blanket in the sand. There was a strange watershed moment when the ladies finally got to see what we had found — the emeralds laid out in piles or singularly, large stones interspersed with the brilliant sheen of gold bars. It was enough to take the breath from anyone who appreciated adventure and wealth, but there was a strange look that passed between the two girls — somewhere between elated and purely uncomfortable.

After a round of photos of the individual treasures, and some shots of Will and I kneeling by the gold and emeralds — great pictures of our shorts and shoes — Kendra looked at Margo and nodded. Margo called Eddie over, wanting to get him in the pictures, too. Eddie handed her his pistol and turned toward us, but as he did, Margo professionally clipped him behind the ear with the butt of the gun, and he dropped like a stone into the warm sand.

Will and I just sat there on our knees, staring, mouths open like two fat reef groupers looking for a cleaning wrasse.

"Wha...what's going on?" I croaked. "What are you doing?"

Kendra stepped forward, pulling a .380 pistol from under her blouse at the small of her back. She sighed hard. "We have some bad news for you boys, on several levels..." She glanced at Margo, their eyes sharing a look that bordered on disappointment, but was cloaked in determination. "First, we're not exactly who we said we were, and secondly we're not exactly strangers to Jacko Slade."

Will sputtered, "You gotta be kidding me — all of this? It was an act?" He started to stand, and Margo's gun barked out a single round that smacked the sand between his knees.

"Don't make this harder than it has to be," she said.

I stared up at Kendra, bafflement precluding the anger that was building in me. "Why didn't you kill us earlier? Why all this dog-and-pony show?"

"And where would the fun be in that?" Kendra asked, her eyes losing some of their coyness. "We're artists. What real artist would find satisfaction in a five-minute painting? What author could find gratification in writing a book in 24 hours? No, there has to be forethought, orchestration, suspense, and a...climax or two, before the finale." She shrugged. "Admittedly, we would have probably killed you earlier — but somewhere along the line you became... interesting. Not that you're anywhere near as fascinating as you think you are, but while we were enjoying your company, the emeralds and gold thing did catch our attention." She glanced at Margo, as if seeking reinforcement, then came back to us. "Sounded like a nice bonus. Besides, we needed to know where the Jamaican medallion was, anyway."

There was a bravado in her words that didn't match the look in her eyes. Something flickered there. I had seen it this morning on the balcony of my room — an uneasiness, an uncertainty that didn't match her actions, like an actress forced to play a part that no longer suited her.

"I don't believe you. I don't believe for a moment that all that passed between us was 'a job' to you." I shook my head. "I'm not buying it."

She hesitated, as if my words had shattered her armor, but she hardened again. "You don't have a say in the matter."

"We only need one of them to get the medallion," Margo said, the implication quite clear.

"So shoot yours," Kendra replied curtly.

"No, I like mine. You shoot yours."

Will looked up at Margo, and I could see the pain of this deception in his eyes and the concern for our vulnerability. "It doesn't have to be like this," he whispered to the lady in front of him. "We could share all this — this life, together, for as long as it feels right."

Again I could see a nerve was struck, and the will in Margo's eyes faltered. But she shook her head as if breaking a spell and replied caustically, "And what are we supposed to do? Become housewives? Have dinner ready for you when you've returned from your adventures?" She shook her head again. "I don't think so..." But there was still a mote of angst – a hesitation in her eyes.

They both moved forward, bringing up their weapons, only a few feet from us, standing on the blanket we were kneeling on.

I glanced sideways at my friend, face downward, and whispered, "The Three Stooges. You remember?"

There was the slightest of nods. We looked up at the girls again while we placed our hands at our sides on the blanket. "I just have three things to say before you shoot us. One — this has been a remarkable journey. Two — Kendra, I think you might have been the one for me, and...three!"

As the last word exited my mouth, both Will and I grasped the blanket in front of us and jerked. The gold and the emeralds went flying, and our girlfriends/executioners were lifted almost vertically into the air before coming down hard on their backs in the sand. Will and I were on them in a heartbeat. Even with all that I knew, I couldn't bring myself to punch Kendra. With the air knocked out of her, I managed to wrestle the gun away and grab the woman, wrapping my arms around her and squeezing tightly. While I begged her to stop fighting, she managed to elbow me in the chin, brawling frantically, rolling us over in the sand several times, trying for groin kicks in the process. But gradually, as I squeezed the air out of her lungs, her efforts slowed. Through the entire struggle I was begging her to stop. Finally, her struggles ceased and we lay there, face to face. I pulled my head back a little and stared into her eyes. The fire in them slowed, then cooled, and with the realization that it was over, a release took its place — somewhere between relief and grateful acceptance. Those beautiful blue eyes softened and the next thing I knew, she was kissing me passionately.

A voice from the other side of the blanket fractured that most unique moment. It was Margo, kneeling behind Will, with her arm around his neck, holding her gun against his temple. "Let her up," she said. "Move away from her."

But there was something in her voice that had lost its fervor. When she saw Kendra and I look at her, arms around each other in ardor now, not anger, Margo sighed, and deflated. "Oh, what the hell," she muttered as her eyes softened. She lowered the gun and ran her hand around Will's neck down into his shirt in a sensual caress. "Maybe I would enjoy being a housewife," she whispered throatily, as she dusted the sand off my partner's face and kissed his ear. "Where am I gonna find another guy with a donkey schlong like yours, anyway?" She looked over at Kendra. "Crap. You know we're not gonna get paid a dime this way..."

"And if this gets out, it'll screw our reputation," Kendra replied with a smile.

Eddie, who was lying a few feet from the blanket, had just come around. He sat up and twisted his head from one side to side, then tenderly touched the bump behind his ear. "What happened?"

"I think you must have walked into something, Eddie," Will said with a smile.

"But it's all cleared up now," Kendra added. She looked at me and became more serious. "I really like you, Mr. Kansas Stamps. I really do. But this is all new to me..."

"We can figure it out as we go along," I replied. "As long as you promise not to shoot me if I don't get the lawn cut, or the porch swept in a timely fashion."

After finding all the gold and emeralds we'd knocked into the sand during our ruckus, we returned them to Eddie's hiding places on his plane. That evening we let Willbird out for a walk, then went to dinner, and the girls told us more about themselves. They were from Homosassa, Florida, and were really half sisters, but the tale got more complicated from there.

During their third year at the University of Tampa, Margo started dating an older man who became highly possessive and abusive. They tried notifying the police, but they were little help. One night, Margo's boyfriend became violent, and beat her badly enough to require an emergency room visit. That was it for them. They realized they were going to have to resolve this themselves. Two weeks later they lured him to the marl pits just outside of town and Margo shot him three times with a .32 caliber pistol she had purchased at a pawnshop. They weighted the man down with cinder blocks and pushed him into the dark water. The most remarkable discovery was that it hardly bothered them at all.

Around that time Kendra began dating a guy she later found out had mafia connections. One night, two months after the incident, Kendra got really high with her mafia boyfriend and told him about what they had done. He was very impressed. Three weeks later he came to them and asked if they would be interested in doing a contract hit — no one would suspect two innocent college girls...

That's how it all began. They graduated from college the next year but never did anything with their degrees — they were making too much money with their side business. After a couple of years, they took on the *nom de plume* of "the Griffins." Their reputation had grown. They only had to do a couple of hits a year to live quite comfortably.

Kendra leaned across the table at the bar in Obaldia, drawing Will and I in as she finished the story. "You have to understand, most of the time we were provided with rap sheets on the contracts. They were all scum. You pay people to take away your trash. We're in the same business." She paused, exhaling guiltily. "But with you two, the money was so good we couldn't resist. A hundred thousand."

"Money won't be a problem anymore, Kendra," I said. "We'd like you to limit your hunting excursions if at all possible. However, Will and I seem to have a propensity for running into people who want to hurt us, so it's possible you could get some practice now and then."

Margo smiled. "You need somebody whacked, we're your whackers."

"That's weirdly comforting," muttered Will with a grin.

I held up a finger. "One last question, then we'll put this shooting business to bed. The two big guys who came into this bar the other night — the ones that turned up dead in their apartment?"

Kendra glanced at Margo. Their eyes met, and her friend shrugged.

"Competition. What were we to do, ask them to leave?" Margo said.

Kendra sighed. "This is a very competitive business..."

Our ladies were good with the idea of us going home to Fort Lauderdale with them for a while. In the interim, I would contact Shane O'Neal with the DEA and see how they were progressing with Jacko Slade. But before leaving Panama, we spent two days in Colon, getting Benito a visa to visit the U.S. and jump-starting a possible dual-citizenship for him. The boy was in clover — a bag of emeralds and a couple gold bars went a long way to easing the pressures of life, and as he put it, "Obaldia es no place for a rich bullfighter."

While in Colon, Eddie made a couple of calls to connections from "the old days." We were able to cash in one of our big bags of emeralds and a handful of gold bars, and Benito sold a good portion of his stash, as well.

Two days later we said a temporary goodbye to Benito, whose visa was still in preparation, and the rest of us loaded into the Goose (with Willbird, who I just couldn't part with). Eddie cranked up the cockpit speakers and Mr. Jimmy Buffett surrounded us with the reminiscent melody of "One Particular Harbor" (it seemed damned appropriate). Our pilot brought the big bird around with his usual expertise, pushed the throttles forward, and we bounced our way into a huge, orange-red morning sun. Just like in the movies...

CHAPTER 10

I had always liked Fort Lauderdale. It was softer and less intimidating than Miami, with great beaches and terrific nightclubs. It was a good place to hole up for a while and get to know our ladies. We had breezed through customs without a blink. Once again, all of Crazy Eddie's hiding places on the Goose had served him well. Eddie dropped us off in Lauderdale, then headed home to Ramrod Key. We had given him a handful of emeralds and a couple of gold bars for his time.

The only discouraging news came from Shane O'Neal, who explained the authorities weren't any closer to locking up our nemesis, Jacko Slade. As Shane put it, "He's a crafty SOB who has no problem sewing up loose ends with a knife or a gun. Anyone we've apprehended who might have had any information on Slade seals up like a Ziploc bag."

The good news was, our ladies had adjoining apartments in an upscale complex just off the beach in an area surrounded by nice restaurants, nightclubs, art galleries, and bistros. We could hang out at the pool or the beach during the day and take in the nightlife in the evenings. So, after depositing our emeralds and gold in a local bank's safety deposit box, we took the next couple of weeks off and relaxed. We did make a quick run down to The Keys to check on our residences and pick up Will's Cessna 310 so we'd have some air transportation.

In the interim, Benito's visa was approved (partly due to a small emerald that may have found its way into the hands of the official in charge of the paperwork). Benny showed up at the airport dressed like a movie star — a white Panama hat, flashy clothes, and a gold chain that would have made Mr. T envious. We sat him down later and tried to explain that in some cases, less is better.

Benito nodded a couple of times in understanding. "Chur, you betcha. I get a smaller hat."

By the end of the week we had found him a used Firebird, and a nice apartment just off Federal Highway, close enough for us to keep an eye on him, but not so close that he was showing up for breakfast every day.

As for Willbird, I found a fellow with a huge outdoor aviary just outside of town — lots of wonderful birds in beautiful surroundings

— and I paid him $3,000 to take in Willbird and three hens that I had purchased for him. Didn't want my boy to be lonely. As I set him down in his new surroundings, he clucked tentatively, a little nervous, and glanced up at me with a look that begged, "What's going on here, dude?" But when I brought in the trio of hot little hens I had picked out for him, he bubbled over with appreciative chirps and peeps.

The girls immediately strolled over and snuggled with my little buddy. He looked up at me and clucked softly and I stroked his back; then, without another cluck, he gathered up his petite harem and shuffled off toward the garden. I stood slowly and sighed, captured by a wave of melancholy. My boy stopped at the edge of the garden and turned to look at me once more. He issued one final cluck of goodbye, then he and his girls ambled off into their new life.

During this time, another of the characters in our lives — a major player, actually — showed up. I had wandered down to the local surf shop on U.S. 1, just for something to do. There's not much in the way of waves in Lauderdale, but as an old surfer, I knew the breaks at Reef Road, Sebastian Inlet, and Pump House weren't too far away. If you know anything about surfing, you understand that where there's a wave that meets a beach, no matter how tall or infrequent, there's going to be some crazy dude with a board under his arm rushing out to ride it. I bought an ice cream cone and sat on a bench out front, watching the small waves roll in and crest on the yellow sands of the beach. I hardly noticed when someone sat down quietly at the other end of the bench. Moments later I heard a voice, heavily timbered and laced with that Jamaican *patois*, but carrying the lightness of humor and a sense of philosophical enlightenment.

"Hello, hello, my old friend, Texas."

"Kansas," I said with a growing smile as I turned to our buddy, Rufus. "Kansas."

The Rastaman soothsayer grinned. The goofy name thing was a standing introduction with us. It was great to see Rufus again, but inwardly I cringed, because our Jamaican buddy generally showed up in our lives to forewarn us of a coming consequence of some sort — usually a mission that was accompanied by danger, but laced with some sort of reward. He was an incredible character who most definitely marched to a different drum. Rufus claimed to be the progeny of an ancient race, and was gifted with the eerie disposition of oftentimes knowing what was going to happen well before it happened.

Nothing had changed with my friend, who was dressed in his standard Bob Marley T-shirt (very possibly the one I saw him in last), threadbare dock shorts, and weathered leather sandals. He was ageless, timeless — chocolate skin, long curling dreadlocks falling to his shoulders, a wide mouth with broad white teeth that always welcomed an easy smile, and startling grey eyes (that sometimes changed color to suit his moods).

I exhaled nervously. "Oh God, Rufus. It's not that it isn't nice to see you, but every time you show up, our lives become... complicated."

My friend shrugged. "Dere is some truth to dat, mon. But you and Willmon, you be clever monkeys — you steal the banana from life each time without too much of a price."

I humphed bitterly. "After the last gig you sent us on — those Truthmakers out of Cuba — I had a nervous tic under my left eye for three months."

Again my companion shrugged. "Yes, but you have marvelous adventure to tell your grandchildren — you save president's life, and you get all dat gold bullion from gangstermon."

There was no arguing, we did get rich that trip. I sighed in defeat. "Okay Rufus, what's going on this time?"

The big Jamaican waved his hands. "Rufus have no magical journeys for you today. But I see somethin' coming...not so good." His pleasant countenance faded to serious. "You have made enemy recently, true?"

I immediately thought of Jacko...

"Rufus here to tell you dat most times, bad tings don't go away when you close your eyes. You got hard choice to make. You either go to da moray, or da moray come to you." He sighed heavily. "I will help where I can, but da mists of da future have parted enough for me to know dis be very dangerous time for you and Willmon." Rufus placed his hand on my shoulder. "Once again your life egg has broken. May da Great Tortoise grant you a moonlit path to da sea..."

I had never seen Rufus this serious, and it spooked me badly. Suddenly, to the left of us, a car rear-ended another — just a fender bender, but it brought me around quickly given the nervous state Rufus had put me in. The drivers were immediately out of their cars, yelling at each other. When I turned back, Rufus was gone.

That night as Will and I sat around the dinner table with Margo and Kendra, I told them of my encounter with Rufus.

Will exhaled nervously and shook his head. "Man, if Rufus is worried about something, we need to be downright scared. We're going to have to think this one out very carefully."

The girls, of course, offered their services, but we declined, saying perhaps we could do this one as a team, but there would be no solo acts. Slade had a fortress in the mountains of Jamaica, with more armed guards than some small countries. We would need a very unique plan.

But before we could go to the moray, the moray came to us...

Will was an above-average tennis player when I met him, and during the years in The Keys I had taken up the sport, as well. On the court we challenged and pushed each other, and became much better for it. Because we had this weird thing of almost knowing what the other was thinking, we became very good doubles players, enough so to be recognized in Key West circles as a tough team to handle. Not good enough to beat the semi-pros, but certainly good enough to annoy them.

It turned out the girls were tennis players as well, and we began a routine of rising early, having a light breakfast, and heading out to the courts for a couple of sets.

One morning, about a week after my meeting with Rufus, the courts at the complex where we were staying were taken, so we drove to the public facilities at Holiday Park. My friend and I had discovered that Margo and Kendra did nothing halfway. They were tigers on the court, never allowing us to relax.

After a rousing 6-4 set that Will and I barely managed to hold, Kendra excused herself to the restroom. Ten minutes later she hadn't returned, so Margo went looking for her. When Margo came back, her face was etched with concern. "She's gone," she said. "I found her purse in the bathroom, but she's gone — not at the concession, or the pro shop."

My face stiffened with fright. "I saw a big black Mercedes staying with us in traffic on the way over here. I didn't give it too much thought because it went straight as we pulled into the park, but as I turned in here, I watched the brake lights come on..."

It hit Will like a stomach punch, and I saw him recoil. "I saw a black Mercedes pull in behind the concession while we were playing tennis…"

We called Kendra's friends, the local hospitals, then the police, but no one had anything. It was like she'd stepped off the planet. For the next two days we were frantic. I was strung so tight I was humming like a power line. I even called in a private investigator, but with no results. It was a strange thing, but in a very short time we had both developed powerful attachments to our new ladies, and this whole affair was terrifying.

Four days after Kendra's disappearance I was sitting at the kitchen table having my morning coffee and working on more flyers for the city, when the phone rang. I grabbed it. "Hello?"

Will quickly rose from the couch and was standing beside me.

"Is this Kansas Stamps?"

"Yeah," I replied cautiously, motioning Will over so he could hear.

"I have something you want, and you have something I want. I'll trade you the girl for the medallion. Best deal you're gonna get."

I recognized that voice — heavy and harsh, a growl that sounded like asphalt in a blender. Jacko Slade.

"Listen to me, Slade," I snarled, my face a signature of malevolence, spitting out each word as if hurling stones. "If you hurt her, all the money in the world can't stop me — "

"Save the melodrama," barked Slade, interrupting me. "You need to tuck my medallion in your pocket and be on the next plane to Jamaica." There was a pause. "You know where I am. You've got 48 hours. Then I give her to the hired help. You call the police, I cut her up and then give her to my boys."

"If you even — " I hissed. But the line went dead.

We didn't have much time. We had to put together a team and come up with a plan in just a few hours. While I tried to reach Eddie, and Bobby Branch (the wacky ex-Vietnam vet — because this time we were going to need things that went *bang*), Will went to the bank and retrieved the golden medallion from our safe deposit box.

I got Eddie on the phone by mid-afternoon and explained the situation. "I'm not going to mince words here, Eddie," I said finally. "This is going to be dangerous as hell."

There was silence at the other end of the phone.

"If you don't want any part of this, I completely understand, man."

I heard my friend exhale slowly and my stomach did a little flip-flop. Eddie and his seaplane were such a necessary part of my plan, and he was so unflappable when the heat was up.

"You don't have to do this...I know you've got your own things going on," I added, giving him an out.

"Dude, would you just cool your jets for a moment?" my friend groused. "Are you bat-crap, whacked-out crazy? Do you think Eddie's gonna let you do this without him? I'm just tryin' to figure in an oil change on the starboard engine and a new hydraulics seal for the landing gear. I'm gonna need five or six hours."

I sighed with relief. "Cool...you got it. When you're all together, fly up to Fort Lauderdale and I'll pick you up at the airport so we can discuss plans on this. Oh, by the way, Bobby Branch has a package for us. Can you get that before coming up?"

It wasn't 10 minutes later that Benito showed up. He could see that we were in the flurries — that something was seriously wrong. I sat him down and explained what was happening, that we were going to be gone for a while.

"So, when are we leavin'?" he said without any hesitation.

"Benny," I said, "this is really dangerous. I appreciate your willingness to help, but I don't think — "

"Chu don' know everythin' about Benny," he said. "Can chu pick a lock, or slip through a cracked window like a snake? Benny can move so quiet you thin' he's da wind."

"Benito, I can't ask you to take this kind of chance. I mean, have you ever even used a gun?"

Benny nodded. "Oh, yeah. You betcha. I have one for a while."

"Ever shot anyone?"

He shrugged. "Well, once I chot myself, in da foot. Dat's why I got rid of da gun." He paused and took a breath. "But dat no matter. Benny bring his blowgun and darts — much better. When I was a *niño* I feed my family *con* a blowgun. Benny's *madre una Darien* — a native. She teach me how to mix special dart potions — make you sleep, or make you *muerto.*"

He did the thing with his head sideways and his tongue out.

"Benny goin' with you. Dis is his chance to be a real Zorro, to be a bullfighter..." He looked me in the eyes. "Eberyone needs to be Zorro once in dere life."

It was hard to argue with that.

By late that afternoon we had gathered around the kitchen table at Margo's place.

"Here's the way I see this," I said. "I could do just what Slade wants, but as soon as Jacko has that medallion in his hands, I don't think there's a chance in hell he's going to let me or Kendra walk away — not after what Will and I did to him." I took a breath. "I think we're looking at what the military would call an 'extraction,' but we're going to need a huge distraction with this when we're ready."

"What about our buddy Shane O'Neal, and the DEA?" Will offered. "Could they help us on this?"

"No, and no again," I said with finality. "First off, it's out of their jurisdiction, unless some huge deals could be cut with the Jamaican government, and by then I'd bet Slade would have heard about it with all his connections. Secondly, we'd lose all control. We'd be sidelined. They go in hot and half-cocked, and Slade will kill Kendra." I shook my head, looking around at my friends. "No, we're going to have to do this. It's up to us." I paused and everyone knew what was coming next. "And either we gift wrap Slade for the American authorities, and bring him out with us, or we..."

They knew what the alternative was. And at this point, God help me, I didn't care which way it fell.

"But we need to get over there right away — to infiltrate and reconnoiter, figure out what we're up against, what we can do to annoy them and draw attention if we have to. I think that's going to have to be Will and me."

Margo pushed back her chair. "And what, exactly, do I do?"

"I don't know for sure. I hate to risk losing you, too."

She looked at me hard. "She's my sister, and you forget what I do for a living, mister..."

I glanced at Will and he shrugged, knowing he had no control in this situation. "Okay, okay," I replied. "You go, too. We're going to have to come in on the Black River in my 182, well before the cliffs that Will and I jumped off the last time we were there — so they don't hear the sound of the engine. Then the three of us will work our way upriver to Slade's encampment. We might get lucky. We might find Kendra and be able to get back to the river and out of there in my amphibian, but if we can't, we may have to look to another escape route, like we did last time." I turned to Eddie.

"That's where you come in. You're our backup — you'll bring Benny with you, and land down the river, or in the bay, just like last time. I may want to use you and Benny in the major distraction we're going to need. We'll also require a couple of your handheld military radios — to stay in touch with each other. We'll choose a frequency that's not too busy. And a couple of flare guns. Worst-case scenario, you may have to land at Jacko's airstrip and extract us. He's got a 2,500-foot runway. Supposedly he's a hotshot pilot himself." I turned to Will. "If you remember, Shane O'Neal said Slade owns a fully functional 1945 Navy Hellcat fighter, with fully operational machine guns. How in the hell he managed that, I don't know."

Will shrugged. "Money. You got enough bucks, you can have anything you want."

I paused for a moment, thinking, then came back to Eddie again. "Speaking of distractions, how much of that *el tigre,* that 151/peyote/hashish mixture of yours, do you have?"

Eddie thought about it. "Well, man, I just made a new bunch about a month ago — I was gonna let it set for another month or so, and give it away as Christmas gifts in those little airline liquor bottles, like I do each year. I probably got a quart."

Will issued a low whistle. "Holy crap! A quart of that and you could zone out Montego Bay! I put a drop of that stuff on my tongue once, and all I wanted to do was listen to Pink Floyd and study the bumps on a grapefruit skin!"

I smiled. He wasn't far from wrong. "We're gonna need that," I said. "We'll swing through The Keys and pick it up on our run for Jamaica." I returned to my companions. "I know Slade's compound has a well. Water is pumped into a big holding tank and delivered through pipes to the main house and the barracks from there. The *el tigre* would be highly diluted with 500 gallons of water, but if we could get some into that system ahead of time, I'm sure it'll put them off their game a little."

Eddie got that trademark stoner grin and touched a couple of fingers to the brim of his Jimmy Buffett ball cap. "Seriously harsh their mellows, dude."

"Speaking of harshing mellows, did you get the package from Bobby Branch that I wanted?"

Eddie nodded. "Bro, you got some serious shit there. Radical implements. No wonder they put that boy in jail for six months."

"You betcha," I said, imitating Benito. "You got the dynamite and the M-15s?"

My friend nodded again. "Yeah, man, it's all copasetic. Freaking eyeball poppin', kick-your-ass killer." He smiled, his square, ivory-colored teeth showing from under that heavy Tom Selleck mustache. "Heavy metal thunda!'"

An hour later we met at Fort Lauderdale International and loaded gear into our respective aircrafts. We would fly to The Keys tonight, then head out in tandem tomorrow morning for Jamaica.

We left at dawn the following day. I taxied the Cessna 182 Amphibian out of the canal by my home and into Pine Channel, to be greeted by the rising sun. I probably hadn't slept three hours, and I doubted anyone else had done much better. Will took the copilot's seat, and Margo settled into one of the seats behind us. We would tie up with Eddie and Benito in the Goose at Key West International.

It was a beautiful, clear morning, the sun just breaking through a grey horizon, casting long, golden trellises of light across a bold azure sky. A flock of ibis and flamingos broke loose from the adjacent mangroves, soaring out across the little bay in a white and pink collage, and for an instant a wave of nostalgia rolled over me — a wonderful, brief sensation that consumed the anxiety of the moment, painting a blissful glow of glorious times past, and offering an almost spiritual sense of confidence. A small gift from the Big Guy upstairs...

Eddie and Benito were waiting when we arrived in Key West. As always, Crazy Eddie had used his secret hiding places to store the weapons and ammunition. After a few words, we settled into our respective aircraft, contacted the tower for clearance, and were in the air. The first order of business was passing over/through the Cuban Flight Corridor. With prior notification, civilians can pass over Cuba through a narrow aerial corridor. We maintained the required altitude and vectors, and less than an hour later we were past Castro's "Communist island paradise." I had several friends who had failed to follow the flight and sea navigational rules (for one reason or another), and ended up as "guests" of Castro — some for years. I never forgot the words of one friend: "Rice and beans every day, an occasional piece of chicken. Figure on having to fight someone at least once a week — maybe for your chicken. The only good thing was, we got to play baseball nearly every day. The Cubans love their baseball — refusing to deprive even thieves and smugglers of their national pastime."

After clearing Cuba, we doglegged to the southeast between The Caymans and Cabo Cruz at the southeastern corner of the Cuban nation, and headed into a straight, three-hour run to Jamaica.

As we soared along, 5,000 feet above the blue-green, seemingly endless water, I constantly checked our VOR positions while Will entertained Margo with stories of our adventures. Hearing my partner telling those tales with his usual sense of embellishment, I couldn't help but smile. He was truly a remarkable fellow — clever, funny, and loyal as a Rottweiler. Listening to him reminded me of how many times we had been back to back, and how many times one of us had saved the other's bacon — never thinking about the danger, never considering the consequences. Just doing it.

Glancing over at Will I realized there was a class about him that I had always admired. Class is really all about a confidence that comes when you've challenged life and got the better of it a few times, but it still has to be melded with a sense of compassion and a well-checked ego. Most significantly, class is about self-discipline — a consistent display of integrity. We sometimes associate class with knowing three-quarters of the words in a thesaurus or unequivocally understanding which of the three forks to use with each course at a five-star restaurant, but that's not class — that's knowledge. You can train a monkey to pick up the right fork. You can't train a monkey to show character in times of peril, to be selfless, to be kind when there's no percentage in it, or to exercise pride without haughtiness. Those are the elements of class. Those were the qualities my partner possessed.

An hour later the island of Jamaica came into sight. I don't care what anyone says, when you're flying over big water, your instruments may give you some sense of security, but you never breathe easy until you see land again.

Sangster International Airport lies on the northwest corner of the island. The runway's a stone's throw from the Caribbean Sea. The infamous Montego Bay is hooked into the big bay between Hopewell to the west and Rose Hall to the east. We landed without incident, and after tethering our aircraft at the non-commercial end of the airport we cleared customs. We figured it was best to appear legitimate on the trip in, regardless of what our plans were. The truth is, the Jamaicans aren't too particular about their customs checks on the way in, but Eddie was just too much. With all the dangerous, illegal crap he had on that airplane, from a quart of his *el tigre* hashish potion, to semi-automatic rifles, you'd think he would have been as nervous as a lizard in a henhouse. But the guy was joking and teasing with the Jamaican customs agents like they were old friends, asking them where the best hookers were in Montego, and telling them not to look too closely 'cause they might find the drugs we were smuggling *into* Jamaica.

After customs, we took a taxi into town and killed a couple of hours — sipping light rum punches at the local bars and strolling down some of the old cobblestone streets of Montego. But it was tough to work up any gaiety. All I could see was Kendra and Jacko Slade...

CHAPTER 11

Jacko Slade's fortress home was built outside the town of Tombstone — real name, ironically enough, which didn't exactly comfort me. It was four miles inland on the Black River, on the south side of the island. The plan was to fly south from Montego, arriving at Black River Bay in the afternoon so we could get a good handle on the terrain coming in. Eddie and Benny would anchor outside the river mouth in the Goose and monitor their radio. Will, Margo, and I would go in while we still had daylight. We'd find a place to land on the river, then work our way up toward the compound.

The first part of the plan worked well. Eddie landed on the nearly flat, clear blue waters of Black River Bay without a hitch. The golden Caribbean sun was still high, but into its descent as he taxied closer to shore and found a good place to toss out an anchor. Ten minutes later, I brought in the 182 and taxied over to him, dropping an anchor within shouting distance. By that time Eddie and Benny had already pulled everything out of the Goose's hiding places.

Eddie inflated a small rubber raft. He and Benny packed it with two fully-loaded semi-automatic, short-barreled M-15 rifles (an extra magazine duct taped to each stock), and three Smith & Wesson nine-millimeter pistols, with an extra magazine each. In addition, they stowed a half-dozen sticks of dynamite, 50 feet of fuse, a loaded flare gun with an extra round taped to the barrel, two handheld VHF radios, and a quart of Eddie's *el tigre* in a Bacardi bottle, all packed into a couple of military backpacks. I owed Bobby Branch big time. Benito and Eddie climbed into the raft, paddled it over to us, and we loaded the gear into the 182. When we had finished, our new Darien friend straightened up and pulled the hem of his dark T-shirt down over his brown cotton pants in a nervous gesture.

"I'ne ready if chu need me," he said, surprisingly serious. "I wan' to go wit' chu."

I was so proud of him for being so willing to take this chance. I glanced at Will, eyebrows up in question. He did that trademark shrug of his.

"Okay, why not?" I said. "Everyone needs to be Zorro once in their life. Get your gear."

Benito beamed. "Already got it," he said as he reached down and grabbed a small canvas bag and a smooth bamboo tube about four feet long — his blowgun. He hopped from the raft onto the port float, grinning. "Les' go kick thos' runamuckos' asses."

As Margo checked our weapons with the professionalism of a Marine and loaded the gear into the packs, Eddie looked up at us from the raft, his eyes filled with "the jazz," but carrying serious concern for us. "You freakin' runamuckers be cool, you hear me?" he growled. "You get that girl, and get that freakin' jive turkey, one way or another." He took a breath. "You need me, you call, or you shoot one flare, then a second one when you hear my engines. You dig? It's gonna be a clear night and you'll be uphill from me, so I'll see it."

"We got it, buddy," Will said, excitement in his voice as well. "I know we can count on you."

Eddied touched the brim of his Jimmy Buffett cap with two fingers. "Damned right!" Then, without another word, he turned and paddled back to the Goose.

As we lifted off, the sun was well above the horizon behind us. Our timing was good. If we could find a place on the river to drop in with the bird, we would be coming into Jacko's territory with enough light to navigate, but not so much that we could be seen easily.

Will turned to me. "You got the medallion, just in case we need it, huh?"

I opened the throat of my khaki shirt and showed him the chain around my neck. "If we absolutely need a bargaining chip," I said.

We entered at the mouth of the Black River and stayed 50 feet off the water the entire time. In just minutes I recognized landmarks from the last time we ran out in Eddie's Goose (with Jacko Slade's medallion in our hands, and dripping wet from a jump into the river).

Will was studying his watch, using our flight speed and the distance on the map to determine our location. He tapped me on the shoulder. "Okay, okay, find a spot! We don't want to get too close!"

I pulled back the throttle and eased the nose up slightly, reducing airspeed, then dropped 10 degrees of flaps. I could feel Margo's hands clenching the headrest on my seat.

"You sure you two aren't related to Harrison Ford?" she muttered with a bit of begrudging admiration.

"We do all his stunts," Will said over his shoulder.

A moment later, the river straightened and I spotted a beach-like entrance to the jungle 300 yards ahead. Dropping another 10 degrees of flaps I lifted the nose a touch more, and felt her lose the last few feet of air and settle onto the surface of the river. There wasn't much current to fight, so using my float rudders, I moved us over to the shore and onto the small stretch of brown sand, revving just enough at the last minute to push most of my floats up and out of the river.

There was no time to waste. Inside of three minutes we had the plane tied to a tree, the gear unloaded, and Will and I had donned the packs. We had each taken a pistol, including Margo. My partner and I carried the M-15s. Benito wanted nothing more than his blowgun. As we organized, I turned to Benito.

"Little buddy, I'm leaving you an important task. We need you to watch the plane for us. We lose this..." I pointed at the Cessna. "...and we're screwed. Anyone comes along that looks like they belong with Jacko Slade, you blowgun them, okay?" I dug out one of the two handheld radios and handed it to him. "Keep it turned down to where you can just barely hear it, but monitor it constantly. We might need you to have this plane in the water and waiting for us if we have a problem."

I could see he was disappointed, but he understood that he'd pushed his luck to even be there with us. He nodded. "Okay, chu betcha. Benny do it."

The landing spot we had chosen had a trail that led along the edge of the river and through the jungle, taking us to the very cliff we had jumped from the last time we were here. As we came to the throat of the trail that led out to the cliff, I smelled the sweet tang of marijuana in the air. Will, leading the way, caught it as well, and raised his hand, signaling a halt. We moved forward cautiously. In a moment we could see the shadowy outline of a guard — a Rastaman with a large wool cap covering curls of twisted hair, rifle in hand, sitting on the stump of an old mahogany tree maybe 50 feet in front of us. I exhaled hard, nervous to hives. There was a lot riding on our success here.

"We've got to take him out without a ruckus," I said, looking at Will and Margo. "Any suggestions?"

Margo didn't even hesitate. "I'll take care of this," she whispered confidently as she undid most of the buttons on the front of her shirt. Before I could stop her, she crept away from us, straightened, and moved up the trail as if she owned the place.

The guard swung around when he heard her, and she cried,

"Thank goodness I found someone!" She was still moving toward him casually, almost sensually. "They told me there was a Starbucks on this end of the island. I haven't had a good cup of coffee in a week. Can you help me?"

The guard brought up his gun, confused by the banter and the beautiful woman who had just materialized. "You stop dere, woman!" he said, his face still displaying a baffled look, but not taking any chances.

"I can be very grateful," she said, pulling at the front of her blouse and moving closer.

But at this point the sentry placed the barrel of his rifle against Margo's chest. "Stop, I say, woman!"

His eyes drifted down to the push-up bra and what it contained. That was the moment Margo was waiting for. Quicker than a Jamaican fer de lance, she slapped the barrel aside and popped him in the throat with the blade of her hand. The guard's eyes went wide. He coughed once and collapsed.

"Jeez!" Will muttered to himself, half in dismay and half in amazement. "Why do I always end up with women who can kick my ass?"

I grinned, remembering Cass, his last lady, who was a martial arts expert.

Margo came over, buttoning her blouse. "Show's over, boys. Tie him up and let's get going."

As we bound the Rastaman, I grabbed his wool cap and tossed it to Will. "Put this on your head and tuck your hair into it. That blond hair of yours is gonna stand out as we get closer..."

We both had dark tans and I had chosen a jungle hat that hid my sun-lightened brown hair fairly well. My partner grimaced at wearing the fellow's hat, but pulled it on.

As we moved closer to the compound, we came to Slade's "airfield." There was a twin-engine DC3 (the workhorse of large smuggling operations) parked on the airstrip, as well as a Beechcraft Baron with an enlarged cargo door. And there, in an open-ended hangar near the end of the runway stood the fighter that Shane O'Neal had mentioned. The Grumman F6F Hellcat, produced from 1942 to 1945 for use on aircraft carriers in the Pacific Theater, was the Navy's answer to the Japanese Zero.

Working our way around the hangar, we got a good look at the old bird. It appeared to be in excellent shape, and was still armed with its

Browning M2 machine guns in the wings. Once again I was reminded that Shane said the Hellcat had fully functioning weapons.

I saw Will slow down and gradually come to a stop in front of the Hellcat. We were both World War II fighter plane buffs, but my partner had the bug worse than I. He had actually spent a week at the annual national fly-in located in Oshkosh, Wisconsin, dedicated to pilots and planes everywhere. During that time he spent 10 hours in a Hellcat simulator — he did it with a Hellcat and a P51. While it cost him a $100 an hour, he claimed it was the best money he'd ever spent. Couldn't wipe the smile off his face for a month.

"First thing's first," I muttered. I turned to my friends. "Let's start by finding that water tank and giving them a dose of *el tigre*."

Will glanced at the sun just above the mountains. "I think we may have to speed things up on that project. You remember the cook shack and the mess hall the last time we were here?"

I nodded. "Yeah, dinner at six p.m., sharp — and 90 percent of the camp shows up for it. Slade and his people have their own chef, but the rest of his crew eats there."

My partner checked his watch and got that lopsided grin. "Maybe we can spice up dinner, as well."

As I pulled the radio from my pack, I whispered a few words to Benito, making sure he was still okay, then we headed toward the mess shack. As we neared the complex grounds I saw a few sentries posted on the perimeter, but we managed to slip by them. We were sitting at the edge of the jungle looking at the cook/mess shack about 100 yards away. No more than 75 yards to the north was the water tank. The barracks were just west of that.

Will turned to me and his eyebrows bounced like Groucho Marx's. "Two birds with one bottle..."

"Yeah," I said, studying Jacko Slade's large, mahogany wood mansion on the hill behind all this, knowing that was where Kendra would be held. "Okay, we'll need a small distraction. You got any suggestions?"

Will thought for a moment. "How about a little fire?" He pointed toward the bath complex, which consisted of toilets and showers.

I shrugged. "Sounds good. How?"

"Give me a stick of dynamite."

"What? You gonna blow it up?" I moaned. "Not a good idea at this point."

"Nah, man," Will said. "Gonna cut the stick open, take out some

128

of the powder and put it in the electrical box inside, with a couple of rags or paper towels. It'll make a lot of smoke, same as an electrical fire. Just want to get their attention for a few minutes while I season dinner. That should give you enough time to hit the water supply." He looked around for a moment and found a discarded beer bottle. He held it out. "Give me a quarter of the *el tigre*. You take the rest."

After I had doled out Eddie's killer juice, Will pulled his Rastaman wool cap down on his head and gave Margo a quick kiss. "You stay hidden for the moment," he whispered. "If something goes wrong with our plan and we get snatched, we'll need someone on the outside."

With that, we were gone.

Margo had barely settled against an old rubber tree when volumes of black smoke began to pour from the doors and the windows of the bathhouse. The 30 or more soldiers and workers in the complex were just filing in to dinner. They immediately ran for the bathhouse, grabbing buckets and dragging hoses.

As Will slipped into the mess hall kitchen, I sauntered over to the 500-gallon water tank. My job was easy — I just reached up and quickly twisted off the cap, then dumped the *el tigre* into it. Even with all the tension, I couldn't help but grin, imagining what this camp was going to be like for the next few days.

Will, however, ran into a bit of a problem. As soon as the mess hall had emptied, Will nervously pulled his cap down again and slipped on his sunglasses, so no one could see his blue eyes. He casually walked over to the rear entrance, where the food preparation was done. He opened the door and peaked in. Empty... but dinner was bubbling away in big pots and rice was steaming. Will noticed the cook was evidently worth his salt — he had whipped up a couple huge pots of *pilau*, a native dish containing rice, chicken, some shellfish and a variety of vegetables, along with another Jamaican favorite — red peas soup.

My partner had just set the lid aside on a pot and was reaching for the bottle of *el tigre*, when a harsh voice stopped him. "What you doin', mon? What you doin' in my kitchen?"

The cook, a bulbous ebony giant who had apparently foregone visiting the fire to tend supper, had just come out of the walk-in pantry with some celery and a long knife.

Will turned and huffed. "Dis better be damn good tonight, mon! Jacko hear you were makin' *pilau*, and he say he want some."

This confused the fellow. "Boss Slade don' eat my food," he said cautiously, not wanting to insult his boss, but taken somewhat by the big man's request for some of his prized *pilau*. "He got his own cook."

Will humphed. "Mon, let me tell you somethin'. Jacko Slade eat whatever he want ta eat. Now, you don' wanna give him some, it okay with me, mon. I go back and tell Slade. No problem." He turned for the door.

"Wait, wait!" cried the cook. The man exhaled heavily and put his hand out, palm up. "I don' wanna cause no bangarang with Slade. No mon. I be not that damn, bloodclot crazy. Da man want my *pilau*, he get some."

Will paused and straightened up. "Den go, you! Get me a container for some-a dat damn stew!"

While the cook hastily rummaged the pantry, Will pulled out his half-full beer bottle of *el tigre* and dumped it in equal proportions into the three large pots on the stove. He'd just dropped the bottle in a trashcan when the cook returned with a Tupperware container. The fellow stirred one of the pots well, then ladled a healthy portion into the plastic bowl, snapped the lid on it and handed it to Will. "You tell Boss Slade I be honored."

From the kitchen window, my buddy could see the bathhouse fire was already out and the men were returning to supper. "Slade say feed dem boys well tonight. Empty dem pots for dem." And with that he was headed out of the door with his container of *pilau*.

The man nodded somberly and called back. "Dey get all dey want tonight!"

Will started down the walkway with the Tupperware bowl, then stopped. Suddenly, he turned around and headed back up the trail toward the gated fence at Jacko's home, where two sentries stood. Will handed them the bowl. "Dis come from dey cook. Fresh, hot, and good *pilau*. He say bring you some so you don' miss out."

The guards smiled with pleasure. "Dat Delone, he be a good mon," one said, as he eagerly took the bowl.

Ten minutes later, Will and I had returned to a nervous Margo at the edge of the jungle. "I saw the smoke and the confusion. Everything go as planned?"

"Oh yeah," Will said. "There's gonna be some seriously screwed-up people in this compound in less than an hour. I'm talkin' stiff-legged zombie boys who are mesmerized by the shape of coconuts, transfixed by their own image in a puddle of water, and thoroughly fascinated by the sound of words like 'bungalow' and 'goombah.'"

Both Margo and I had to laugh.

"Okay, so we wait for a while, maybe a half hour or so," Margo said. "Then we make our move on Slade's house?"

I nodded, watching all the people who worked for Slade filing into the mess hall. "Yeah, that's about right."

We'd been sitting quietly for about 20 minutes, watching a few people beginning to exit the mess hall. There was no question everyone was moving a little slower than normal, but the *el tigre* was just entering their systems. The best, or worst, was yet to come.

Will glanced back toward the airfield for a moment, then turned to us. "I'm thinking maybe about the time we move on Jacko, one of his airplanes might blow up." Will bounced his eyebrows. "That'll suck just about everyone out of this camp for a while." He got that loopy grin. "At least those who can still walk and can remember where they are, or who they are."

"Very nice idea!" Margo said, putting her arm around him. "Clever. I like bright men. Especially those with huge —"

"Okay, okay..." Will replied, uncharacteristically embarrassed. "Dig me out a stick of dynamite from the pack, with a coil of fuse and some duct tape."

"Let's blow the DC3," I said. "It's the farthest from the camp and it's his major workhorse." I grinned. "Let's hurt him as much as we can."

"You two stay here," Will said. "I'll go back, tape a stick under the wing tank, and rig a 10-minute fuse. If I hurry back that should give us enough time to be outside Slade's place when it happens."

In moments Will was gone, slipping quietly into the jungle. Margo and I remained hidden in the foliage, watching the camp, engulfed in a heavy silence. After a few minutes, she spoke quietly.

"Do you know how rare it is? What you have — you and Will — a friendship that transcends ego, the honesty you share?" She looked at me, the last of the sun filtering through the high trees and reflecting in her eyes. "I know you two compete for just about everything — including women. It's a guy thing. I understand. But he would do anything to protect you, and for all the bantering between you two, he admires you probably more than anyone in the whole world. Do you know how lucky you are to have a friend like that? Not someone below you or above you, but an equal who harbors no need to be more than that, and puts you first, before himself, in nearly everything."

Her heartfelt words washed over me like a wave, cleansing out ego and filtering pride, and in the process I realized how right she was. I realized that I felt exactly the same about my friend. I thought about all the wild competitions we'd gone through over the years — admittedly mostly with women — and the excruciating fear that had overwhelmed me when he almost drowned in a small Texas town two years ago. I knew also that, while it might not be an easy choice, I would protect his life at the cost of my own, because, as Margo had said, there was no question he would do it for me.

In the humid, summer stillness of the jungle I turned away and muttered, "Yeah, I do know…"

For the next five minutes we sat in an uneasy silence. I was just going to ask her a question about Kendra when the moment was shattered by gunshots somewhere toward the airfield. I could see the fear in Margo's eyes. I was sure it reflected in my own, too. For another few minutes we crouched, listening to an occasional burst of gunfire. Then I heard footsteps coming down the trail behind us and Will burst through the foliage. The first thing I noticed was the blood soaking his shirt on the upper part of his left arm. Margo was up in a heartbeat, bringing him over and pulling him down to look at it.

"How bad is it?" I asked tensely.

"Which part of it?" he hissed with his usual sarcasm. "The part about the plane, or the part about being shot?"

Margo was reaching for the first aid kit, but Will stopped her. "Don't bother. It's just a nick, and we don't have time. After I planted the charge and was headed back, I ran into some of Jacko's guards." He dragged in a breath or two. "Persistent bastards. We gotta get out of here."

But before I could reach for my rifle, the jungle parted in two or three places and a handful of big Jamaicans with short-barreled AK47s stepped out. I stood, trying to keep this from becoming a massacre. "My name's Kansas Stamps. Jacko Slade is expecting me."

The biggest of them, a dirty red beret cocked on his head, stepped forward. "You be damned right about dat, mon," he said, as he swung the butt of his rifle up at me, and the lights went out.

132

CHAPTER 12

When I woke up I was being dragged along the trail by two of Jacko's men. I moaned and they jerked me to my feet.

"C'mon, duppy mon," said one. "You walk now. Boss Slade be waitin' for you."

My head was clearing as we trudged through the camp and I looked around. The *el tigre* was definitely having its desired effect. The good news was, much of the place looked like *Island Zombies II* — people shuffling around aimlessly, or staring at the fading sun, or engrossed in the study of common items like bananas or beer cans with an intensity warranted for space rocks. The bad news: not everyone had drunk the "Kool Aid." We would still have to be on guard if we were going to find Kendra and figure a way out of here.

I glanced back at Will and his lady, marching behind me, and got an anxious smile from Margo.

Will whispered, "Hang in there, *amigo*. We're headed in the right direction."

He was right. We were coming up on the gates of Slade's home. "What happened with the 'bang' at the plane?" I whispered.

"Don't know," Will muttered, making sure no one was close enough to hear him. "I set a really long fuse. Maybe they found it…"

When we arrived at the gates, the two guards never even looked up. They were sitting on the ground off to the side, guns discarded, each with a stick, playing tic-tac-toe in the dirt.

"No question they enjoyed their stew," Will muttered.

The leader of our escort told two of his men to replace those at the gate, then took us to the large mahogany doors on the manor and knocked. A moment later, two huge, bald-headed white guys, who appeared to be twins, opened up and allowed us, and the leader of our group to enter. The last man was told to watch the front door — no one was to enter. I was surprised that they hadn't bound us, but I guess they figured it wasn't necessary. Everybody had guns but us.

Our captors led us into a large living room with sliding glass doors that looked out over the complex. The house was high enough to see the sun still working its way toward the horizon, painting the emerald sky with streaks of rose, mauve, and amber. Any other time I would have been in awe of such a wondrous work of nature, but we were busy at the moment.

Given the distractions, I almost missed him, standing in the shadows by the bar, a drink held casually in his left hand — Jacko Slade. "I was beginning to wonder if you were going to show," he said as he stepped out from the dimness and came over, stopping in front of us. Nothing had changed with him. He was still pale white with shoulder-length grey dreadlocks, and dead, obsidian eyes. He was about five foot 10, lean and hard, dressed in an open-necked white shirt and grey slacks with expensive leather sandals. But everything about him was cold, from his eyes to his smile, and even his voice.

"Where's Kendra?" I said. "I want to see Kendra, now."

"You're not in a position to be making demands," Jacko replied sharply, in control. He looked over at Will. "And you, maybe you'd like to see my daughter again, huh?"

"No, no, actually not at all," Will stuttered, glancing over at Margo. "Not that she's not a nice girl," he said, holding up his hands, palms out. "Well, nice is maybe the wrong word, but…"

"Quit while you're ahead," muttered Margo.

Slade turned to me, interrupting Will. "You have my medallion?"

"It's close, but first I see Kendra."

Slade turned to one of the bald-headed guys and nodded.

My lady was dragged from a bedroom, angry and frightened, but anger was winning out. When she saw me she broke loose from the guard and rushed over to me. I met her halfway and we held each other tightly for a moment.

"Okay," said Slade. "Enough of the happy reunion. Now, my medallion…"

Meanwhile, the two new gate guards at Jacko's little palace had spread out, one on each side of the entrance. The original two had given up tic-tac-toe and moved off. They were 50 feet away, using their sticks to stir up an anthill, purely fascinated with the results.

Suddenly, one of the new sentries grunted lightly and reached up to his neck. He plucked a feathered dart from his carotid artery and glanced around quickly, more angry than frightened. Nothing was out of the ordinary. He looked at the dart again and rubbed at the bloody spot where the dart had entered. He turned to his friend on the other side, but before he could speak, his eyes glazed, his knees buckled, and he dropped face-first in the dirt.

The other sentry quickly stepped over, glanced around cautiously, and knelt. An almost identical dart magically appeared in his neck. He brought a hand to his throat, grasped the small projectile, and slowly pulled it out, then stood with his weapon ready, grabbing his radio and searching the perimeter. He had managed to get the radio to his mouth before his eyes glazed and he fell forward silently.

The big Jamaican guarding the front door of Jacko's place had found a lawn chair and had settled into it on the veranda. He had failed to notice that the guards at the gate were no longer visible. The fellow had almost dozed off when he heard a methodical clicking coming from the stone walkway. He quickly rose and moved to the front of the porch. A smallish fellow with a reddish-brown complexion and long, dark hair was coming up the pathway. Apparently, he was blind; his dark eyes were staring sightlessly ahead and he tapped a long piece of bamboo on the ground in front of him.

"Stop now, little mon," barked the sentry. "What you want here?"

The small man turned his head in the guard's direction. "I thin' I be lost, an I got a problem — I got sonethin' stuck in my stick. Can you look in it for me?" he said as he pointed the stick up at the guard and gazed off above him.

Cautiously, the man grabbed the end and looked into the mouth of the hollow piece of bamboo still being held by the little fellow. "Yah mon, it blocked."

"You betcha," said Benny as he placed his mouth over the other end and blew.

The guard was still staring into the hollow bamboo tube as the dart struck him in the forehead. He pulled away quickly. "What you do, mon?"

But as he reached up to pull the dart out, Benny stepped forward and kicked him in the *cojones* — hard. The Jamaican's eyes bulged, his legs gave out, and he fell to his knees. He tried to bring up his weapon, but the little Darien snatched it out of his hands and tossed it on the lawn.

"Wait! Wait! Don' pass out yet!" Benny whispered urgently as he turned his back and pulled something from his pocket, quickly tying it on his face. When he turned back around, he had donned a thin, black cloth mask with two eyeholes cut into it. Benny did that wide-footed stance of superheroes, hands on his hips, and said "I'ne Benny El Zorro! I'ne da protector of da —"

The guard's eyes glazed and he fell face-forward onto the wood deck.

"Sonabitch!" muttered Benito. "Dat was my big entrance."

As Jacko and his three armed guards stared at me, I realized we had few cards left to play. I reached into my shirt and lifted the golden medallion and its heavy chain from my neck, handing it to him. "How about we call it even and we just leave?" I offered.

"I don't think so," Slade growled as he studied the medallion, making sure it was the real thing. "I'll tell you when I think we're even."

There was a knock at the front door. No one moved. Jacko looked at one of the big bald-headed twins.

"Go."

As the man lumbered away, Slade turned back to us, pulling a pistol from his waist. "Paybacks are a bitch," he muttered with a malicious smile.

"Let the girls go," Will said. "They didn't have any part in this. Just let them go."

Jacko shrugged. "You know, there's a part of me that would like to do that, but how, exactly, do I tidy this up with witnesses? You understand, don't you?" He motioned to the other big twin and the man opened the sliding doors to the balcony. "Don't want to mess up the rug," Slade said as he motioned us toward the outside.

We were moving slowly through the doors when the big twin who had checked the door came stumbling back into the room, a bamboo dart with a fluff of feathers protruding from his neck. He raised a hand and opened his mouth to speak, but nothing came out. His eyes suddenly went wide and he simply collapsed.

Looking back on all that happened, I'm reminded of that quote by our Rastaman buddy Rufus. "Da gods, dey bore easily, and sometimes dey keep you alive strictly for entertainment. We call it amazing luck, but it be nothing more than da gods adjusting da rabbit ears on da television of life."

As the fellow collapsed there was a huge explosion toward the airport, and a mushroom cloud of flaming gas, tarmac, and multiple pieces of a DC3 rose out of the jungle in the distance. The sound was deafening and the shockwave a physical thing. It caught everyone off guard. I'd like to say that it was me or Will who took advantage of that situation, but it was Kendra (who had a little pent-up animosity over the whole thing to begin with) who spun around, snatched the medallion out of Slade's hand, and side-kicked him in the chest — hard enough to knock him through the bamboo room divider at the bedroom's entrance. Slade's other bodyguard, who had been kneeling by his partner, swung around with his pistol, but as he did, Benito, Zorro mask and all, came around the corner with a cricket bat and whacked him into center field. Our little buddy turned around and grinned. "Eberybody chud get to be Zorro once in dere life!"

About that time, a couple shots from the bedroom took out the mirror next to Kendra and me.

"Time to say 'goodnight Johnny,'" Will called as he grabbed Margo's hand and we all made a dash for the balcony.

It was an eight-foot drop to the hillside below, but my adrenaline was pumping so hard I barely noticed it. In seconds we were all on the ground and barreling through the "village of the zombies." In the distance, I could hear Slade screaming...

We reached the jungle path that led to the airstrip and paused. It was about a mile to my 182 at the river. I caught my breath, grabbed Kendra, and pulled her into me, kissing her passionately. She finally pulled away, gazing at me, and I loved the look in her eyes.

"Damn!" she muttered. "Indiana freakin' Jones!"

"I don't know about that," I replied modestly. "You're the one who kicked Slade's ass when we needed it."

"So we make a good team," she said, a new gleam in her eye as she tossed me the golden medallion and I slipped its heavy chain over my head.

"Hey, what about me?" cried Benito. "I musta chot 20 people wiff darts today, not to count da one I kick in da *cojones* and one I whacked wiff da weird baseball bat."

"Yeah! You too, dude," I said with a chuckle. "You're the hero of the day, no damned question! How in the hell did you find us, anyway?"

"When you no come back, I was coming to see what happened. I see dem catch you on da trail."

"Okay, okay, you guys," said Will, arm around Margo's waist. "Let's quit complimenting each other and get the hell out of here. I hear a rum punch calling."

It took us 10 minutes of marching along the edge of the jungle to make the airstrip. We had reached the place where the open-ended hangar sat that held the Navy Hellcat F6F fighter plane. I saw Will slow down and study the old war bird. He looked over at me.

"I could fly that, you know. I could do it. I've had the time in a simulator. I even flew second seat in a specially modified version — for 15 minutes."

"What are you talking about?" I said nervously, afraid of where this was going. "We need to get out of here."

"We didn't take out Slade," Will said. "Most of his camp's still intact. He's just gonna come for us again."

"No, Will, I don't think so..." I said. "You flew a simulator for 10 hours. This is a real airplane. You'll kill yourself just trying to get it off the ground."

"No, the landings were what usually killed people," Will replied.

"That's supposed to make me feel better? Let's just get out of here. We'll worry about Slade another day."

Margo suddenly realized what we were talking about. "No way, Will! C'mon, let's get out of here. Let it go!"

But I could see he was starting to drift over toward the hangar.

"It may not even have real ammunition," I argued. "Then none of this matters. Or maybe the canopy is locked."

"Let's find out," my partner said, his blue eyes intense now.

With a sigh I followed him into the hangar and we slid back the canopy, then quickly crawled under a wing, unsnapping the swivel locks on the starboard ammunition locker and pulling the door down. Much to my dismay, there were rows and rows of live 12.7mm ammunition on the feeding belts.

Will closed it quickly with a devious smile. "I'm gonna get the son of a bitch, and even if I don't, he's gonna have a serious mess where his house and his compound used to be."

I tried again to talk him out of it. So did Kendra and Margo. But there was no getting my buddy around this, so in the end, we laid contingency plans.

Will was to fly out over the coast for a few minutes, making sure he had a handle on the plane. The rest of us would make our way to the 182 on the river and get into the air, where we could observe. Will was to do his thing on the house and the camp as quickly as possible, then we'd land the planes at the airstrip and he'd hop into the 182 with us.

We'd lost our radio when we were captured, but Benito had miraculously held on to his, so I contacted Eddie and told him of our plans.

"You dudes are as crazy as craphouse rats!" he moaned. "I mean, you're a sandwich short of a picnic here! Even I wouldn't do this, dude, and they call *me* crazy!"

There was a plastic laminated chart in the cockpit that provided the prep and start-up procedure. I helped Will through that. When we finally had Will belted in, and the big propeller blades were whirring in sync, my buddy shifted himself forward and took the control stick. Offhandedly, he pressed the red button on the top of the stick. There was a roar as the machine guns on both wings opened up, and the fronds on a palm tree on the other side of the field disintegrated. We both lurched in fright and my buddy instantly released the stick. After a brief silence, he muttered, "Well, the guns work…"

"You know you're freakin' nuts to be doing this, right?" I said. "I can't believe I'm letting you do this."

He looked at me, fully aware that I was terrified for him. "It's okay, buddy. I'm scared crapless too, and I won't do anything stupid."

"More stupid."

He grinned nervously. "Yeah…more stupid." He put his hand on my arm. "You take good care of yourself, okay? And the girls —"

"Don't be making this sound like an Alamo thing, dude. You're making me nervous."

He squeezed my arm, then put his hand on the canopy crank. "I gotta go now." He smiled once more. "It's like our little Darien buddy says, 'Sometimes a man must do what a man must do…'"

As we watched Will taxi that huge, lumbering war bird out of the hangar and down the strip to the threshold, I kept telling myself I should have stopped him. I should have done whatever was necessary.

He pushed the throttle forward and the big plane lurched outward, the tail coming up as it sped down the runway. But when the aircraft began slipping to the left and yawing slightly — all the telltale signs of a failing crosswind takeoff — I found myself trapped in a muddle of self-loathing and terror. *How could I have let my friend do this? How could I have been such a coward – not to have stood up and said, "No, damn it, you're not going to sacrifice your life on the altar of ego and revenge."*

He was halfway down the field, running at full power, but he had slipped so badly, the aircraft was nearly off the runway. One of the wings was higher than the other — a sure sign of impending doom.

"Rudder and ailerons," I moaned. "Correct your rudder and ailerons!" I shouted, knowing it was useless, watching that huge airplane, that flying bomb filled with gasoline and ammunition, starting to slide off the runway. "Full power!" I yelled at the wind. "Get some elevator into it. Get off the freaking ground!"

The starboard wing was tilting downward so badly I was certain my friend had lost control, that he had panicked like so many inexperienced pilots do in a bad situation. When you reach that point, either terror or training take over, and only one of those allows you to survive.

He was two-thirds of the way down the runway and the palm trees at the far end were coming up fast. His right wheel was off the tarmac and into the grass. His left wheel was coming off the ground, forcing the right wing down toward the earth. "Oh Jesus…Will…" I whispered, knowing that I was seconds from watching that starboard wing bite into the earth, seeing the plane roll and crumple, and explode. I was witnessing the impending death of my closest friend, and there was nothing I could do about it.

Margo was crying silently, and the terror in Kendra, holding my hand, was tangible. She was crushing my fingers.

The starboard wing wasn't a foot from the ground when the wind that was lifting the other wing suddenly lulled. Finally doing something right, Will added some starboard aileron and compensated with a hard opposite rudder, and the plane righted itself. A second later the wheels left the ground and the big bird started to rise, wings waggling precariously.

But my partner had used up most of the small runway in the process of getting airborne. Now he had to clear the jungle at the end of the strip.

"Get the gear up!" I muttered harshly. "Power! Elevators! Altitude, you asshole! Get the nose up!"

I was certain he was going to fly into the canopy of dense jungle. To this day I'm sure I saw the undercarriage of that Hellcat scrape the palm trees at the end of the runway. But once again, the gods must have been bored, and they bought their entertainment by preserving my friend.

As we watched the Hellcat soar up into the sun, then bank and roll out toward the ocean, Benito shook his head incredulously. "That one *loco* sonabitch," he muttered shakily. "I'ne telling you, *totalmente loco…*"

When Will was safely headed toward the ocean, we began our run for my 182. Inside five minutes of steady trotting down the jungle paths we came to the clearing where we docked the Cessna. Thank God, none of Jacko's men had found it.

I got the girls seated in the rear bench seat, which brought the back of the pontoons down into the water, taking the pressure off the front. This made it easier for Benito and me to slide the plane into the river. Three minutes later we were rising off the placid waters and headed for the airport. I climbed to 1,500 feet and picked up my mike, setting the radio for 122.4 (the frequency we had agreed to use). "Hellcat, this is Cessna, do you read me?" There was no answer. "Hellcat, do you read me? Come back."

Suddenly, the radio crackled. "Cessna, this is Hellcat. I'm on your southwest quadrant, two miles out."

Sure enough, there he was, a dark-blue silhouette at about 2,000 feet, closing fast.

The radio crackled again. "Cessna, Hellcat, this is Goose, still on the pond, dudes. Ready when you need me."

Eddie!

I smiled and glanced at Benito and the girls in the back seat. We were ready. "Hellcat, Hellcat, how are you doing with the bird?"

"Good, I'm doing good." I could hear the nervous exhilaration in Will's voice. "It's a little bit of a trick getting used to it all. It ain't a freaking Cessna 152, you know? It's like going from a Volkswagen to a Ferrari — with machine guns! I've fired a few rounds, trying to get used to the circled gun sight forward of the cockpit on the engine cowling. But I've decided I'm just going to get down so close that I can't miss."

There was a pause.

"Okay, everyone ready?" I said into my mike.

"Let's go," said Will, as I watched him bank the big blue fighter and drop down toward the interior of the island and Jacko's compound.

Jacko Slade was nearly apoplectic. Three-quarters of his crew were walking zombies and he had no idea what had happened to them. Half of his best men were out of commission, drugged into a comatose state from the darts that little Indian asshole had shot them with. His DC3 was gone — a smoking hull at the airport — and no one had their act together enough to figure out what had happened to the team who had done this to him. He was now convinced the two

141

guys, whoever they were, were probably special agents for the U.S. Drug Enforcement Agency. On top of all that, he thought he had heard his beloved Hellcat take off from the airport.

"Nah, it's not possible," he grumbled to himself. *Nobody just crawled into a Hellcat and flew it away. Nobody.*

He was standing in his front yard, gathering a crew out of what was left of his men, planning to go after the DEA agents and their girlfriends, when he heard what sounded like that big 2,000 horsepower Pratt & Whitney on his Hellcat, about a mile away and closing.

He scanned the horizon, and there, coming in off the ocean was a large, blunt-nosed, dark-blue aircraft. "I'll be damned," he whispered. And he was…

In a matter of seconds the Hellcat closed to firing range, the gun ports in the wings lit up, and twin rows of destruction raced at him, shredding everything in their path.

His new Mercedes at the entrance to the driveway was the first sacrifice, jumping and buckling under the impact of the large, heavy rounds. It exploded as the rounds continued their path of destruction toward him. Jacko Slade suddenly lost all sense of that cool demeanor, screaming and running as the trails of mayhem raced by and into his million-dollar home, barely missing him. Aside from cutting open his house like a chainsaw slicing a melon, several rounds hit the propane tank in the back, and that added a whole new dimension to the mayhem.

Circling at 3,000 feet above, we watched as Will passed through the camp, guns blazing like in a John Wayne war movie. His hitting Slade's house so perfectly was more luck than talent, but my partner gladly accepted it. He pulled the plane up, ran out a half mile, rolled into a tight turn and came back again. This time he picked out the fuel storage facility and the fuel truck for the airport. He was starting to get a handle on how to aim the guns using the circular gun sight. A couple more passes and he was hitting what he wanted, avoiding people and concentrating on buildings. He was doing well.

Jacko, on the other hand? Not so well. Most of his compound was in flames, the mansion was burning like a tinderbox, and the majority of Jacko's people had long since run screaming into the jungle. But it was the last pass that bought Will trouble. A handful of Slade's gunmen, knotted together by the cook shack, laid some heavy automatic fire into the Hellcat as it made that final pass.

Will heard the muted staccato pop as bullets slapped into his aircraft. The canopy just behind his head fractured with an explosion and he shrieked in shock, nearly losing control of the aircraft. At that point my partner decided he'd stretched his luck well beyond the gods' desire for entertainment, and he banked out for the airstrip.

"Cessna, Cessna," Will called. "I'm done. Let's go home. Meet me at the airstrip."

"Hellcat, this is Cessna," I came back. "You go in first. Get on the ground and out of the way. As soon as you're out of your aircraft I'll be touching down to get you. We want to make this quick — in case any of Jacko's men are out that way."

"Roger that," Will replied. "I'll be setting up a long final in a minute or two."

I hit my mike button again. "Goose, come in Goose. You ready to go home?"

"Ready, dudes," replied Eddie. "Righteously packed and set to blow this scene! Gonna put this bird in the air as soon as I see you."

I allowed myself a feral grin. By some miracle, or several miracles, we had done it. Jacko Slade's camp looked like Rome after the Huns arrived — everything was in flames, and there was a good chance that Will had finished Slade in the process. Now all we needed was to get my partner through a landing, and we were out of here.

I circled off in the distance as Will approached on his long final. I kept watching for landing gear on the Hellcat, and when the plane was a quarter-mile out and still no gear, I picked up my mike. "Hellcat, this is Cessna. What about your gear, man? Get that down!"

It was a moment or two before my partner came back, but there was a tenseness in his voice that I didn't like. "Yeah, yeah, I know. I'm working on that. I'm doing it by the book. I've thrown the lever for the hydraulics on the landing gear, but nothing's happening."

"Do it again!" I said nervously.

Moments later Will came back, voice strained. "No good. The light's not coming on. The gear's not coming down. I would have felt it or heard it." There was a pregnant silence. "It may have taken a round or two. I'm gonna have to belly it in," my friend finally said. "There's no other way. We've got to get out of here pretty quick. We've made a lot of noise in this part of the country, and the smoke from the fires is going to have the authorities here on the double." He paused again. "And I'm smelling gas. I think a tank may have been punctured."

"Yeah, yeah, you're right," I sighed, angry and suddenly frightened again. "But belly-landing that plane on the tarmac of that strip is really taking a chance. Totally unforgiving terrain. One spark and your toast." I paused, my mind racing. "You're going to have to ditch in the water, out where Eddie is. Hellcats were aircraft carrier fighters, designed with reinforced undercarriages for sea ditchings. Gonna have to keep your landing in really shallow water, so the plane won't sink and drown you if you have trouble getting out."

"Thanks for all the positive input," Will muttered sarcastically. "All I have to do is crash a shot-up, 10,000-pound aircraft into the sea, and try not to drown in the process. Great…"

"Yeah, but who would have put money on you making it this far?" I said with a chuckle. "Use the same little bay we came into, not five minutes from here, okay? We'll come down right behind you in my Cessna. And remember to crank back the canopy before you hit the water, so the impact doesn't jam it closed."

"Yeah, yeah, sure," said Will, the uneasiness in his voice as thick as syrup. "Piece of cake."

It was then that I noticed the stream of white smoke starting to streak from the bottom of his engine cowling, winding outward like willowy streamers. "Hellcat, Hellcat. I've got more bad news. You need to get down as quickly as you can. Looks like one of those rounds must have nicked a fuel line. You've got gas splashing on your manifold. You've got no choice now. You need to get that plane into the ocean, like now!"

My stomach was knotting with panic again as I stayed up and behind the diving Navy fighter. Smoke was billowing out the exhaust ports of the engine as my friend closed the last two miles to the sea and set up a straight-in landing onto the little bay.

"Keep the gear up, and use full flaps to slow you down, and get your nose high just before impact," I gritted into my mike. "But most of all, keep those wings level. You don't want to roll…"

"You got more instructions for me than my ex-girlfriend in bed," Will muttered. "Unless you're going to tell me what to do with Big Willie at this point, take a break. I got it under control."

"When someone says they've 'got it under control,' they usually don't," I replied tersely.

There was a pause. "You sound just like my ex-girlfriend."

I mentally switched tracks and contacted Eddie, explaining our latest situation. "Get in the air." I said. "Just circle us and keep an eye out for anybody coming our way from the camp or from Montego. When we get Will down and out of that plane, I'll taxi over and get him. Given this situation, I want to make sure he's safe before anyone leaves."

"I can dig it," Eddie replied. "We'll split as soon as our boy is in our hands. But that needs to be soon. I've been listening to the traffic out of Montego. The fuzz has had its ears on and they know something funky's goin' on here. They're putting birds in the air as I speak."

Once again, I found my pulse hammering and my breath coming uneasily as I watched Will and his Hellcat make his final approach on the bay. I decided to land the 182 in shallow water a few hundred yards from shore. After quickly settling in, I told Will to put down as close to us as possible so we could taxi over and get him. As we were gathered in the cockpit and on the starboard pontoon of my plane, watching, Will's words kept echoing in my head like a doomsday bell. "It was the landings that killed most people..."

"You're looking good," I said encouragingly into my mike as his aircraft dropped over the bay and down to 300 feet. "Wings level, some more flaps now." The dark-blue fighter's wings were wagging, and the aircraft was yawing a little. I could see my buddy in the cockpit — a smear of yellow hair and fear. He had dropped another 100 feet, but it was then that the plane and pilot seemed to lose their composure. The wings were suddenly wobbling, the nose was up too high, and the altitude and speed were failing.

"Jesus, Will!" I groaned, totally helpless. He was going to stall the son of a bitch! "Get the nose down! Now!" I yelled. "Give it some power!"

Inside the cockpit, rivulets of sweat were streaming down Will's face, into his eyes, and blinding him. His hands were shaking, and his left leg had begun a nervous staccato beat of its own accord. Smoke from the manifold was pouring in through the heating vents, and it was becoming difficult to see. He had gone from frightened but secure, to terrified. Everything was happening way too fast. He backed off the power some more, and suddenly the plane began to fall radically — and he made the critical mistake that has killed more pilots than bad weather. He pulled back the stick instinctively without offering more power.

He could barely see the water through the cockpit smoke, and the monstrous airplane was suddenly unresponsive, dropping flat like a failed elevator, nose down more than it should be for a landing. He pulled back on the unresponsive stick again and screamed as the water rushed up at him.

I sucked in a breath and held it as the plane fell more than flew the last 100 feet. Its nose dug into the water and the port wing caught, cracking like cannon shot, spinning the mortally wounded bird sharply to the left and bringing it up at a hard angle, the good wing pointing up at the gilded horizon.

Will was thrown hard against the instrument panel, but after a moment or two, the well-built bird did what it was designed to do — it floated for a few seconds, and I saw my partner push back from the panel and shake his head, then release his harness and begin to climb out. All this was good, but there was the fire in the engine cowling that was spreading toward the shattered left wing and its fuel tank. Slowly, as the craft took on water, the angle diminished until the Hellcat was almost level. It was resting in about eight feet of water.

"Get out of there," I muttered, raising myself out of my seat, still holding the now useless microphone. "Get the hell out of that plane!"

Will's movements were slow and fuddled as he climbed out onto the right wing, on the opposite side of the major damage, and struggled to get to his feet on wobbly legs. He looked around, dazed, then saw us over the fuselage. He tried to smile and waved.

At that moment, the ruptured fuel tank on the other wing blew with a roar and an orange ball of flame. The last sight I had of my friend was his body being blasted backwards, hurled into the water. Margo, next to me, screamed.

I fired up the engine on the 182 before realizing I'd done it. Everyone in the plane or on the pontoons held on tight while I taxied over at a speed just under takeoff. Shutting down next to the smoking remains of the Hellcat, Benny and I threw out the anchor. Before the line was taut I had kicked off my shoes and was in the water, swimming over to the far side of the craft where Will had been standing. I was sure Margo and Kendra were right behind me.

There was no sign of my friend. The surface was slick with oil, and smoke still lay like morning fog around the wreckage. I dove down and searched the shallow water, but there was no Will. When I surfaced, the girls were nowhere to be found. I drew another breath and dove again, working around the coral heads and sea fans that were now littered with aircraft debris. Most of the hull lay to my right, the starboard wing still attached. It was the port side that had blown. Grabbing another breath I dove down again, this time working myself under the submerged wing still attached to the fuselage, thinking perhaps he was there.

But as I wiggled my way under the appendage, I failed to notice the Pitot tube beneath the tip. This is an L-shaped, pencil-like pressure device mounted under airfoils or on noses of aircraft used to determine their speed. As I swam beneath the wing, I got too close to the Pitot tube and the point slipped between the collar of my khaki shirt and my shoulder. Realizing I was caught, I struggled, and the pointed end of the tube punctured my shirt, effectively hooking me under the wing. I was already low on air, having been down for the better part of a minute, and my struggles were soon taking the last of my strength.

Trapped under the wing, I had no leverage. I was beginning to experience that heavy, pressurized sensation in my lungs — the first stage of asphyxiation. As I struggled desperately, glancing about wildly for a savior, adrenaline surged into my veins, enhancing the panic. My heart was hammering with a reckless cadence, and a grey mist was growing at the edge of my vision. There was no way for me to get a purchase. Caught by the scruff of my neck like a choleric cat, I flailed madly with the last of my energy, trying to get my shirt unbuttoned with numbing fingers, finally ripping at the heavy fabric, clamping my mouth shut, refusing to succumb to the seductive craving for air and inhale. But that only works for so long — and it's just exactly as they tell you – eventually your body says, "Breathe!" And you do…

The next thing I knew, I was bent over the fuselage at the tail section of the destroyed Hellcat, half in the water and half out, and someone was hammering me on my back. In between throwing up breakfast, coughing up seawater, and gasping in sweet, incredibly wonderful air, I glanced behind me to find my partner slapping me again, while Kendra and Margo held me out of the water.

When Will saw that I'd regained consciousness, he quickly turned me around and leaned me against the fuselage. The panic in his fire-scorched face dissolved, and relief blossomed in its place.

Kendra pushed the hair out of my eyes, then kissed my forehead, her hand caressing my face. "God, Kansas, you scared us…"

Will leaned in and patted my cheek. "Glad you're back, *amigo.*

Did you see the devil?"

"Yeah," I croaked. "And he wanted to know where you were."

CHAPTER 13

Within minutes we were back at the 182, crawling up onto the floats and organizing things. I felt like hell. My head was still spinning and I was nauseated, but we needed to get out of Dodge. Will was pulling the anchor and I was settling into the pilot's seat when Eddie's urgent voice crackled over the radio.

"Cessna, Cessna, you have a bogie coming in from Jacko's compound! Looks like the twin-engine Beech Baron from his airstrip."

I groaned and Will barked an expletive from the copilot's seat. "I knew I should have shot that up, too," he said. "But Lord, it was such a pretty little aircraft…"

I was racing through the start-up procedure when, in the distance, I saw light from the sun glinting off the wings of the approaching plane. "Pretty or not, it's coming our way, and that can't be good." It was falling out of the sky, clearing the island, and leveling out about 50 feet above the water. The pilot had reduced speed on the aircraft to just above stall. At that moment, I saw the big cargo door open on the side facing us.

"What the hell?" I stammered. Then I saw him — Jacko Slade — at the controls. Crouched in the interior of the aircraft were three of his men with AK47s.

Slade brought the plane right down onto the flat, calm water, lining up and coming in not 100 yards from us, and as the Baron roared by, the men with the AKs opened up. I watched in horror as pluming tufts of spray from the automatic rounds marched across the surface toward us. Suddenly, it was pandemonium. The windshield in front of me and the window next to Will exploded, splashing shards of glass across everyone, and I could hear bullets slapping into the aluminum floats and the side of the aircraft. As the 182 trembled from the impact, I heard Margo cry out in pain.

In less than five seconds it was over and the Baron was rising up, running toward open water so it could turn around for another pass. To my right Will was shaken and pale, cut by glass on his neck and shoulder, but apparently unharmed otherwise. I threw myself around in the seat to see what had happened to Margo, and gasped. She was slouched in her seat against the wall of the plane. She had taken a round in the shoulder and blood was spilling from the wound.

Kendra was already trying to staunch the bleeding with a T-shirt. Miraculously, Benito, who had been on the port pontoon when the attack came, had fallen into the water between the pontoons and was unharmed.

There was no way for Will or me to reach Margo in the small cabin. The plane was shot to hell, and Slade was making another wing-over in the distance. Suddenly the radio crackled — miraculously, it still worked.

"Cessna, Cessna!" shouted Eddie. "Come back to me!"

I grabbed the mike. "Eddie, get out of here, now! If you throw the throttles to the wall you might be able to outrun Slade as far as Savanna-la-Mar or Negril. I know he's seen you. Run for it, man! Someone's got to tell what happened here. How...how we —"

"You're out of your rabid-assed mind if you think Eddie's leavin' you. You just get your bags packed. I'm comin' down!"

"Man, you can't!" I cried. "Slade will shoot you to pieces on the water."

"This is a tough old bird. She's been shot at before. Now shut up and get ready." He paused. "You got any guns left in there?"

"I grabbed an AK from one of the downed guards in the camp as we came through."

"Okay, when Jacko passes, you annoy him with that as much as possible. All of you, get in the water, behind the floats on your plane. I'll come in on that side. All you have to do is swim over to the hatch and I'll pull you in. Dig?"

"Eddie..." I whispered gratefully.

"Shut up and do it! I'm gonna be slapping the water in one minute."

The mike went dead. I couldn't help but shake my head in wonder. I was reminded that the amalgam of friendship and courage is an amazing thing, and only those who have witnessed it under fire can truly understand it.

I guess Slade took his time on his downwind run. I'm sure he was savoring the whole thing. There was nowhere for us to go. But in the couple of minutes it took him to run out over the ocean and turn around for another pass, Eddie had manhandled that big bird of his onto the water and was taxiing over. I suppose Slade was surprised, but a 30-year-old Grumman Goose certainly didn't represent a threat, and he probably viewed it as a "two-for-one" package.

Before Slade could hit us again, we had all slipped into the water behind the port float. Will and Kendra had found the first aid kit and had secured a bandage over Margo's wound, but the lady was still bleeding badly and nearing shock. Kendra gave me a nearly painful hug and kissed me passionately, then pushed me back and stared at me, eyes full of ardor and fear.

"Don't you dare get yourself killed, you son of a bitch!"

I took a position in the water at the front end of the port pontoon, resting the AK on it for stability. Eddie had pulled up behind us, allowing my shattered Cessna to provide some cover. As Will and Kendra swam Margo over to the Goose, Slade came in for his second pass. Benito was in the water next to me, holding onto the float.

"Get out of here!" I yelled tersely. "Get over to the Goose!"

Benito shook his head harshly. "No. Benny stay. Maybe you need help."

There was no time to argue. The big Beech Baron was leveling out, not 10 feet above the flat surface of the bay. It came screaming toward us, its occupants already opening fire, AKs on full-auto. Again I watched their bursts stitch the water with angry spouts, and my beautiful aircraft began to pop and shake from the impact of the big bullets. But this time I could fight back. Long before Slade brought his plane even with mine, I was firing, marking range by the slapping of my bullets in the water. I led my fire right into the aircraft, watching the plane's flight path flutter and the wings roll slightly. As they passed in front of me, I got off another solid burst. One of the men at the cargo door collapsed and dropped his weapon.

My 182 was being torn apart, and Eddie's Goose was catching it, as well. I risked a quick glance back and saw Kendra and Will pulling Margo into the aircraft. I had flames coming from my engine compartment and the whole thing was already listing badly to the starboard, nose down. It was time to go.

Benito and I made some sort of Olympic record for a freestyle swim and were at the hatch on the Goose in seconds. In the distance, I could see Slade racing downwind again so he could come around and bring his gunmen to bear on us once more. Will dragged us aboard as Eddie rushed to the cockpit and fired up the big engines. The wind was coming from offshore and it allowed him to take off straight into Slade, as he came in at us. This would cut the time that Jacko's shooters would have to hammer us, but I knew that hardly mattered. Eddie's aircraft could no more escape that sleek Beechcraft than a fat goose could an eagle. All we could do was run, and hope that maybe the cavalry would show up in time.

As Slade closed, we got Margo into one of the four seats behind the cockpit. Will took the seat next to his lady and held her, compressing the wound with the bloody T-shirt, kissing her forehead, and whispering assurances he didn't feel.

I settled into the copilot's seat and Kendra and Benito buckled into the last two seats opposite Margo and Will. Eddie was already pushing the throttles to the wall and setting 20 degrees of flaps. We surged forward, and in moments the hull was into its rhythmic slap against the sea. Eddie pulled back on the controls and I felt that moment of release as the hull left the water. He didn't climb, but held his throttles to the wall, giving him all the power he could get, taking advantage of the ground effect and forcing Jacko to come down to him.

I could see the Baron in the distance, coming at us almost head-on. Just as the planes passed each other, and machine gun fire erupted from the cargo door on the Baron, Eddie drew the yoke back hard and to the left, jammed a solid left rudder, and dragged the big bird into a wing-over that would have scared a stunt pilot. He threw the aircraft up and over the gunfire and the other aircraft, minimizing the assault. In the middle of the fray, with bullets smacking the hull like popping corn, and the wings shuddering from G-force, he threw back his head and howled like a wolf. As he rolled the big plane around and leveled out, Eddie looked at me, eyes ablaze with the passion of chance, and grinned.

"Them runamuckin' jive turkeys ain't got us yet!" he cried.

There are those who live for sunsets, still waters, and frosted drinks — content to garner their excitement from the pages of books, and cinema screens. They're satisfied with viewing storms on the horizon, and never weathering them.

Then there are those who live for the hurricane — to dance in the howling wind, and feel the driving rain sting their faces, to roll the dice and take the chance — because it gives them perspective and adds spirit and dimension to their lives. They live that way because they have to – to satisfy themselves. Well, that, and the barroom stories...

And that was Edward Jackson Moorehouse.

Eddie swung the big plane around and headed north along the

coast toward Savanna-la-Mar, the closest sizeable town. He had customized his engines and had his wing spars reinforced to afford him better performance in bad situations. It had paid off to this point, but a very pissed Jacko Slade was coming up fast behind us. I had burned up the only magazine in the AK47 trying to defend us as we made it to the Goose.

Eddie shouted from the cockpit, letting us know Slade and his Baron were moving up. Crazy Eddie, the old smuggler that he was, had installed mirrors on the sides of the fuselage near the cockpit, as the fighter pilots of World War II had done. It gave the pilots an idea of who was trying to sneak up on them. "He's staying beneath and behind us, sliding up in our slipstream, so he can hit us by surprise!" Eddie yelled. "Hold on tight. I'm gonna roll away from him as he comes up even with us."

A moment later the Baron roared up alongside and a fusillade from the two remaining gunman raked us. Eddie rolled away and down from the fire as he had planned, but some of the rounds still ripped through the cockpit and cut stitches in the soft metal down one side of the old Goose. As the glass on Eddie's side of the cockpit shattered, I heard him grunt in pain, and I felt a stab in the calf of my left leg. We were falling wing-over at the ocean, and there was white smoke streaming from the engine on the pilot's side.

We lost 1,000 feet of altitude before Eddie manhandled the plane back into straight and level flight, reducing power on the wounded engine and compensating with ailerons and rudder. I reached down and touched my leg, and my hand came away wet.

There was something about the way Eddie was hunched over the controls that wasn't right, but the others in the back were crying out. I was out of my seat and into the cabin in a heartbeat. Will, still bleeding from the glass shrapnel in the 182, was clutching Margo tightly, covering her with his body. He looked at me, and for one of the first times in my life I saw terror in his eyes. "We're losing her," he whispered harshly.

The plane was leveling out. Kendra was unharmed, pulling herself out of her seat and giving me a brief hug before kneeling next to Will and his lady. Margo was conscious, but there was the distant glaze of the badly wounded in her eyes. She managed a weak smile.

"Shoulda just shot you two in Panama and gone home." She looked at my partner and chuckled dryly. "If I get out of this alive, you're gonna owe me big time."

Eddie's voice from the cockpit broke the moment. "Hold on! Here he comes again!"

As the Baron pulled up level with us and another barrage hammered the craft, our incredible pilot cut the power, dropped 10 degrees of flaps and almost stopped us in midair, simultaneously rolling us down toward the ocean – minimizing the attack. As we fell out of the sky, Eddie brought his gallant bird under control once more. I moved back up to the cockpit as the Baron arched across the horizon and began moving in behind us again. The wind was whistling through the holes in the Plexiglas cockpit and I noticed that Eddie was hunched over so much he was practically lying against the side of the cabin and the controls. It was then that I saw the blood pooling on the metal flooring at his feet — heavy and red, jiggling with the vibration of the trembling aircraft.

I quickly knelt next to my friend and eased him back in his seat. There was a blood-soaked hole in his shirt, below his ribs on the left side. He looked down at the damage, then out to the smoking port engine.

"Bummer," he grunted. "Sons of bitches are shooting me and my girl to pieces." He checked his mirror. "They're coming again just below and behind us, in our slipstream. Don't think we can stand another round..."

I glanced around in sheer desperation, realizing that the final moments of life were upon us. There was no getting out of this. But as I frantically scoured the cabin, I saw the pile of netting in the back of the plane—the mullet gill net that belonged to Eddie's friend.

I was suddenly reminded of a story Eddie had told us about a smuggler friend who always carried a 50-foot-long net in his Mako when making midnight pot pickups from Gulfstream freighters. If he was being pursued by the Marine Patrol on the return, he would drag out that old mullet gill net with Styrofoam buoys on it and cast it out behind the boat, into his slipstream. There was no way for a boat behind him to miss it. That netting ate a couple of Marine Patrol propellers, saving his bacon on more than one occasion.

I put my hand on my friend's shoulder and told him what I was thinking. Through the trauma and pain, he offered a grin. "I'll watch the mirror. When they're just right I'll raise my arm. Get them freakin' runamuckers!"

"Kendra! Benny!" I yelled as I moved toward the rear of the aircraft. "Help me, quick!"

As Benito and I dragged the netting from the back of the plane toward the cargo door, I shouted to Kendra, "Get the cargo door open! Now!"

My lady never missed a beat. She staggered over in the bouncing airplane and unlatched the door. I knew it was a one-in-100 chance. The net had to open enough and fall just enough to hook a wing or touch the props on the Beechcraft below us. But if it just touched them…

We reached the hatch just as the Baron was making its move, coming up behind the Goose, and swinging up and out of our slipstream. The wind whipped and clawed at us. Eddie, hunched over in the cockpit, raised his hand, waving as best he could. Both Benito and I were struggling to keep a grip on the sides of the door while shoving the netting through the hatch without being dragged out of the aircraft. When the wind finally caught the netting, it ripped outward as though it were attached to a freight train.

I leaned out the door as far as I dared, trying desperately to get a look, the wind pummeling my face and hair. There was the Baron, just making its break from the slipstream to finish us off. The net ripped out of the opening and unfolded like a giant, elongated spider web, twisting and turning in the air, dropping down toward the Beechcraft. But Slade saw it before the net engulfed the plane and threw his aircraft upward, right below and just behind our right wing. The netting soared underneath the Baron, drifting downward like a fallen palm frond.

I cursed. Benito collapsed against the inner wall by the hatch as Eddie looked back. His shoulders sagged, knowing this was the end. Slade was coming up again, right underneath us. There was no hurry now. There was no place to hide in this shot-up old bird. I took Kendra's hand and drew her into me, holding her tight. From the cockpit Eddie looked back at all of us, his face a mask of pain and sorrow, but his eyes held us. He brought two fingers to the tip of his prized Jimmy Buffett cap, touching it in a final salute.

Slade moved his killing machine up at us, coming in close enough for us to spit on him. He was enjoying this. God, I hated him.

In our panic to get to the nets, we had overturned several boxes of supplies from our Darien/Panama adventure. An assortment of items were scattered across the floor, from camping equipment to canned goods. At that moment, a large can of Campbell's Pork and Beans rolled across the floor and bumped Benito's foot. In an amalgam of desperation and fury, he picked it up and hurled it out of the hatch at the Baron just below us — the final act of a desperate man.

"Sonamabitche!" he screamed.

The can soared out and was sucked into the slipstream, and for as long as I live I will never forget that moment. The large can of beans tumbled through the sky almost in slow motion, unerringly plunging in a descending arch, an innocuous missile of destruction, right into Slade's starboard propeller.

It doesn't much matter what kind of plane you fly, propellers are just not designed to be struck by a three-pound metal can traveling a 100 miles an hour.

I'll never forget Jacko Slade's face as the heavy metal container struck the whirring blades and exploded. It was the look of incredulousness, then terror. It could have been that there was a hairline flaw in one of the three propeller blades on that engine. It happens occasionally. But the second that the can struck, all hell broke loose. The damaged, now imbalanced prop practically tore itself off the shaft and a foot-long tip of one of the blades snapped off and hurled like a dagger through the cabin window on Jacko's side.

To this day I don't know if it struck him, or just provided the finishing touches to a bad day, causing him to lose control of his aircraft. It doesn't matter. As we pulled away, I watched the Baron struggle for straight and level flight, then gradually roll over and fall into a spiraling dive. Moments later, it struck the calm sea, nose first, in a foamy explosion. Within seconds it was gone.

As I stood there, bleeding and exhausted, yet exhilarated to still be alive, I felt a hand slide around my waist. Kendra's arm encircled me tightly, and I reached over to Benito, clasping his shoulder. Somewhere in the back of my mind, I could hear my old friend Rufus' words regarding the gods' entertainment, and their adjustment of the rabbit ears on "da television of life." A small smile touched my lips.

"Damned amazing throw," I muttered.

My Darien friend shook his head and offered an incredulous smile. "A 100 years from now, my children's children will still tell dis story! How dere papa killed an airplane wit' a can a beans."

Up in the cockpit, Eddie brought us from our reverie as he sagged in his seat, groaned, and simply fell sideways onto the floor. The plane lost its flight path and began to glide downward at an angle.

156

Kendra and Benito rushed to the cockpit with me. They pulled Eddie out of the way and dealt with his wound as I took his seat and fought to bring the plane back to straight and level. We were losing the left engine. Smoke was pouring from the exhaust ports and it was sputtering and hissing like a maddened tomcat. Will started to rise, torn between helping me and holding his lady, but I yelled at him. "Stay where you are. I got it! You just take care of Margo."

I reduced the power to the damaged engine, manually adjusting the trim, and applying the correct rudder to keep the plane level. Benny and Kendra pulled Eddie into the cabin and stretched him out on the floor. He had taken a round in the side and was bleeding out. My old friend looked up at me and tried to smile, but it morphed to a grimace.

"Talk about harshin' my mellow..." he muttered painfully.

His eyes blinked, then lost their focus and slowly closed. My chest constricted in fear.

Only a few feet behind me Will held his lady, stroking her forehead and keeping pressure on the wound in her shoulder. I figured we had about 10 minutes before people started dying on this plane.

It had been a couple of years since I'd been to this area of Jamaica. Will and I generally stayed in Negril when traveling down this way. But I remembered spending a few days—and nights—in Savanna-la-Mar with a particularly attractive Air Jamaica stewardess. I remembered that the hospital was about a block from the end of Great George Street—the main street in town. By the Goose's DME, we were about 10 minutes out of Savanna-la-Mar.

August was the month that Savanna-la-Mar celebrated its Sugar Cane Festival, which included a week-long revelry of feasts, speeches, rum, parties, more rum, and a huge parade down Great George Street. Timing is everything, they say, from commando raids to orgasms...

Henri Baracoste, the mayor of Savanna-la-Mar, and his wife, Loretta, sat in positions of honor on the single float at the head of the Sugar Cane Festival parade. It had just begun to undulate its way down Great George Street to the cheers of spectators on both sides of the avenue. The mayor's white summer suit contrasted with his cocoa-colored skin in a striking yet elegant fashion.

His wife had chosen a light blue, low-cut cocktail dress that displayed some of her finer attributes. *And why not?* she thought. She was proud of herself and her husband.

Baracoste had done well in life. He had come from old money to begin with, and he had made new money on land, sugar, and a few discreet investments in midnight deliveries of burlap-wrapped bundles. Life was good.

There was a high school marching band behind them, followed by a handful of long-legged, baton-twirling majorettes, a motley crew of slightly drunken pirates throwing candy to the crowd (because every costal town in Jamaica had a history of pirates), and an entourage of colorfully dressed "cane cutters" swinging their machetes and gyrating wildly. The parade was just beginning at Independence Park and was headed to the docks at the other end of town. The mayor and his wife gazed out at the crowd and waved benevolently, enjoying the spectacle and the position of prominence. But something in the distance caught Baracoste's eye—a speck coming in off the sea, with a trail of smoke following it.

As the speck drew closer, he realized it was an airplane tumbling out of the sky, one engine bellowing smoke. He pushed back in his seat, puzzled. *Could this be part of the festivities? Surely not.* But the plane came on, wings wagging precariously as it left the sparkling ocean and crossed the beach, a half mile away.

As we sailed over the outdoor market near the shore at Nesbitt and Great George streets, the left engine coughed phlegmatically and died. I drew back the last of the power on it, pushed the throttle on the good engine to the wall, and stood on the right rudder, trying to keep us in the air, but at this point it was just a matter of where we crashed. In the distance I could see the big white hospital building across from the park. But right next to it, dead ahead, was the parade. As we soared past the courthouse on the left, then the Westmoreland Parrish Library on the right, I dropped 20 degrees of flaps, yelling at everyone to hold on.

The driver of the float, hidden beneath the sugarcane and tropical flowers, had slowed, then halted as he watched the giant aircraft drop to less than 50 feet, coming off the ocean and straight down Great George Street, right at the parade. Baracoste's eyes went from curiosity to concern and he slowly stood, still not quite able to grasp this bizarre situation. Loretta's mint julep had stopped en route to her lips as she, too, stared in disbelief. The participants in the parade behind them had gradually lost their exuberance, all gaping at the impossible sight. Batons bounced on the ground as perky majorettes missed their catches; pirates slowed then stopped like statues, candy falling from their hands; and cane cutters stumbled from their gyrations to pause and gape at the oncoming leviathan.

The spectators on the sides of the road had gone from boisterous to curiously uneasy. As we closed to within 1,000 yards of the hospital, I dropped another 10 degrees of flaps and lowered the gear. Now the spectators slid from curious to panicky and began a wholesale retreat into alleys, side streets, and fields. We dropped another 15 feet and the wings on the plane began taking out lampposts on both sides of the street like a cane-cutter's scythe, the staccato pop of electrical explosions accompanying each strike. At that point, the party broke up completely, and everyone behind the Baracostes' float—the pirates, the majorettes, and the cane cutters—disappeared in a screaming melee.

With eyes the size of mangoes, Loretta stumbled into her husband's arms. Henri's mouth hung open, his eyelids blinking to the rhythm of the collapsing light posts.

I cut the engine and pulled the nose up, and we slapped Great George Street viciously, bouncing once and sailing for about 50 yards, then coming down slightly askew and hard once more. The port landing gear snapped and folded, sending the plane into a sideways slide, right at the lead float where Henri and Loretta were holding each other, wailing in terror and disbelief.

Kendra and Benito, still holding and protecting Eddie on the floor, were slammed forward into the cockpit in a jumble. We continued to slide, metal screeching on pavement in a shrill, ripping cacophony, blending with the cries inside the aircraft, not the least of which were mine.

The plane ground its way down the street for another 100 yards, closing on the float with the determination of a charging rhino while I clutched the useless yoke in a death grip. Gradually, I felt the velocity of the aircraft begin to diminish, and as we narrowed the last 50 yards, the old Grumman Goose turned slightly, slid up to the front of the float, and begrudgingly ground to a halt. When I looked up there was a man holding a woman in his arms, both frozen statues, not 10 feet from the nose of the airplane. We were a block from the hospital.

Before the Goose had quit trembling, Will had thrown open the

159

hatch and bounded onto the float. "Sorry about your parade," he said, as he snatched the mint julep out of Loretta's hand and downed it in a gulp. "But we've got injured people and we're commandeering your ride. Now get the hell off!"

Minutes later we had Margo and Eddie in the small emergency/trauma room, with the only two doctors in the facility working frantically to save them. I paced up and down the hall, terrified that the gods of fate were making choices I couldn't live with. Outside, a crowd of hundreds had gathered around the remainder of our aircraft and the hospital. This would be a Sugar Cane Festival parade that would go down in the history books of Savanna-la-Mar.

After a frantic half-hour, one of the doctors came out, a somber look on his face. My stomach lurched. The local constable was with him — a big, burly, very unhappy-looking fellow. I suddenly found I couldn't get a breath. They paused in front of us and the doctor exhaled hard, his countenance offering no assurance. He shook his head grimly and I thought I was going to throw up.

"I don't know how," he said, "but your friends have survived. They are on the cusp of life, but they are stabilized."

A flood of relief washed over me and my knees suddenly felt weak. Kendra's hand found its way into mine and she squeezed hard enough to make me wince. I put my arm around Will's shoulder and could feel some of his tenseness dissolve. All this was good news. The bad news was, the constable took us away in handcuffs until the situation could be explained.

Even though we offered a quickly concocted story of being shot out of the sky because we were caught in the middle of a drug war situation between Jacko Slade and another organization, the authorities still searched our plane for contraband, finding nothing. In the end, there was little they could charge us with, except destruction of public property while in the process of crashing an airplane. When we agreed to help with restitution regarding new streetlamps and the removal of Eddie's totally destroyed Goose, they decided to let us go.

That evening we gathered around Margo and Eddie's beds in the hospital. Both of them were ghostly pale from loss of blood, but they were going to survive. Will was sitting on Margo's bed, holding her hand. Kendra was sitting on the other side. Margo looked at Will, eyes diffused with passion and heavy pain medication.

"Damn. This being shot thing really sucks," she croaked. "I'm usually on the other side of this." She grinned lasciviously. "Hey, lizard tongue, you gonna sneak in later and make me feel better?"

Will smiled, but shook his head. "Not tonight, babe. You need a few days to recover."

I stood between the beds, next to Eddie. "You scared the crap out of us, you know that?" I said to my old friend, glancing at Margo, as well.

Eddie offered a tired grin, comfortably high on Demerol. "Eddie gonna have to quit hanging out with you dudes," he whispered. "There's such a thing as havin' too much fun. I was starting to feel like one of those wooden ducks in a freakin' shooting gallery." He became serious. "You owe me another Goose. This'll be the second one, dude, and I want a killer stereo system in the cockpit. I wanna feel Janis Joplin standing next to me when she yells, 'Take another little piece of my heart, now baby!'"

Everyone chuckled.

I nodded emphatically and put my hand on his shoulder. "Damned right, *amigo*. You're gonna think she's sitting on your freaking lap!"

We spent the next 10 days in Savanna-la-Mar while Margo and Eddie healed sufficiently for travel. In the interim, the authorities met with us two more times. There were not a lot of credible witnesses, due to the *el tigre* in the water system and the food at Jacko's camp. Many of those interviewed immediately afterwards were still so high they thought it was an attack from outer space. In the end, it looked much like what we had said — that someone had gone after Jacko Slade and his organization in a big way. The authorities figured it was either a hit from one of the Colombian cartels that thought Slade was becoming too significant, or maybe the DEA had decided to get creative. In any event, we were off the hook — considered tourists who had been caught in the middle of it.

During that week, Will and I had surreptitiously met with the officials at the National Museum of Jamaica in Kingston, returning the treasured medallion that was a talisman of the enslaved and a symbol of freedom for the country.

When Margo and Eddie were released from the hospital, we boarded a chartered Beechcraft Queen Air in Montego Bay. Once again, my partner and I were headed home after another wild adventure.

As I paused at the threshold of the cabin, I stopped and turned, taking one last look at the island that had held such intrigue for us. The palm trees were being caressed by a soft, afternoon breeze, and the ocean in the distance sparkled blue-green and inviting. I stood there, reminded of the power of gold and greed. But glancing into the cabin at my friends I was also reminded of a quote from my old Rastaman friend, Rufus: "Friendship, love, and luck; dey constantly moved by da current of life, but like da little wrasses dat clean da moray's teeth, dey grow stronger each time dey swim away from da eel's mouth. Never forget, we all be part of da great cosmic pinball machine. Some of us levers, some of us tiny balls…"

Once again we had cleaned the moray's teeth. It was time to go home to rest and recuperate. To "find a groove and cool our jets" as Crazy Eddie would say, and to find our buddy a new Goose.

After taking Margo to a physician in Fort Lauderdale for a final checkup (she was healing remarkably well), we spent a week finding Eddie a replacement for his Goose. As luck would have it, Eddie found a well-maintained 1959 Grumman Goose in Tampa. I wrote the check for it (and an additional check for a "killer killer" stereo system). There was no one chasing us anymore, and the Darien emerald adventure had secured our financial future, so we took some time off and brought our ladies home to The Keys.

We spent a couple of weeks introducing the girls to the glory of the ocean, teaching them to scuba dive, and roaming the crystalline waters off Big Pine Key. We were enraptured by the infinite grace of manta rays as they glided through the water beside us, marveling at the effortless spontaneity of porpoises and flying fish soaring in tandem with our boat, and captured by the stunning elegance of the summer reef, with its tumultuous riot of colors and shapes.

Elegant staghorn and elkhorn corals, monstrous brain corals, and billowing sea fans provided a stunning backdrop to it all, only to be enveloped by a sinuous, weaving body of multicolored small and large fish, all inexplicably, almost neurologically, connected by a sense of simultaneous instinct. The entire reef was a flowing ballet of tranquility and serenity periodically interrupted by sudden waves of blurring movement, all orchestrated with milliseconds in between. I'll say it again. Whether it took a few days, or millions of years, the ocean is God's finest work — sheer creative artistry combined with the imagination of Michelangelo on acid.

We wandered from the soft, current-scrolled sands and inner patch reefs of Hawk Channel out to the reef line, and trolled for mahi-mahi dolphin along the weed lines that curled lazily out to sea, the brilliant sun tanning us like natives. We were immersed in the wonder of it all, like children of Eden.

We caught our dinner each day, feasting on grouper, dolphin, and lobster in the evenings, then watched the sun melt into the purple and rose gauze of the horizon from the deck of my home. We partied on Duval Street until the early morning hours, danced at Sloppy Joe's, played pool at The Green Parrot, and, pleasantly smashed, ate divine desserts and drank champagne at Louie's Backyard. We became regulars for breakfast at Island Jim's on Big Pine Key, and chased the elusive bonefish in the backcountry off our key in the mornings. Margo loved Will's converted shrimper in Key West (which had been made quite luxurious), and Kendra was equally taken with my home on Big Pine. It wasn't long before The Keys had worked their magic on our ladies and they decided to come live with us.

The girls agreed to reduce their work schedule to maybe a couple of whacks a year — to keep them in spending money. What were we supposed to do, tell them to give up their profession and become canasta-playing housewives?

Kendra put it best: "We can't just become something we're not overnight — nice little housewives attending the book club at the library on Friday afternoons and having dinner ready a five p.m. That's just not our style. What if we said you had to give up being adventurers? No more searching for gold or lost relics, just stay home and play backgammon and mow the lawn." She took a breath and exhaled slowly. "You have to understand. There's more to this than just whacking strangers. The people we take out need to be taken out. They're bad people. And we're good at what we do. There's a sense of pride. Besides, everyone needs a hobby."

Benito was enjoying himself in Fort Lauderdale, becoming quite the man about town, and had decided to stay up there temporarily. Eddie had recovered nicely from his wound and was back to his wild and cantankerous self, immensely enjoying the new custom stereo system in his latest Goose. All the harshed mellows seemed to be past.

Life was good, very good, but looking back on it all, I should have been reminded of one of Will's favorite expressions: "Just about the time you're strolling down the street of life, not a care in the world, somebody pushes a piano out of a fifth-story window..."

CHAPTER 14

Rodney Whitcomb (known as Sundance), originally of Vancouver, Canada, lately of Eglin Federal Prison in Central Florida, sat on one of the tables during yard time with a dog-eared notepad and a small piece of pencil. Let the muscled morons lift their weights, toss leather balls back and forth, or thump their chests at each other like gorillas on steroids. He had better things to do. Besides, God knew what kind of bacterium would be teeming on all that sweat-laden equipment — the spores, viruses, parasites — swarming legions of disease just waiting to assault a person. It was a bloody miracle he'd survived over two years in this human catastrophe as it was, with its filthy cells, the horrid food, and God, the restrooms — he had seen more serviceable latrines in Guatemalan whorehouses. The whole place was a bloody zoo. But aside from the constant fear of disease (he was fairly certain he had contracted tuberculosis while here — he had noticed a slight fever recently, night sweats, and fatigue... yes, probably tuberculosis), he had managed to maintain his focus. Yes, his focus. He had stayed true to his mission, had kept track of the people who put him here. He had not lost his purpose. It wasn't long and they would have to let him out — good behavior, overcrowding, and all that — and then he would seek his reward...and his revenge.

Sundance eased his large, stout frame away from the wooden table and went over his notes. He pushed his thick, straw-colored hair back from his forehead, his pale blue eyes scanning the pages that contained all the information he had gathered on his quarry; a scrapbook you might say. With the help of a companion on the outside, he had followed their accomplishments over the last few years. They had done quite well since he had first met them in Costa Rica. Penniless they were, destitute after the sinking of their boat, and he had taken them in, given them an opportunity to earn some money. True, he'd been in the process of robbing a bank at the time and that seemed to put them off. They were such whiners. No *esprit de corps*. After the bank job they had the audacity to desert him. Well...he did try to shoot them. Maybe that had something to do with it. Later, their paths crossed again, in a contest over who should possess a small, very ancient, golden pyramid. In the end, they threw him off the back of a boat in the dark of night — food for the sharks.

Then the authorities found him and when they ran a check, well, a number of indiscretions did surface, and he ended up at Eglin.

He owed them, and payment was coming. Yes, an eye for an eye and a tooth for a tooth. Sundance had taken to reading some of the Bible, given to him by one of the door-to-door religious salesmen they allowed in occasionally. He realized he liked the book— lots of cliffhanger situations that led to miracles, and lots of smiting or smoting going on. David smote the Philistines, the Lord smote the Egyptians, Moses smote the Amorites, Chedorlaomer smote the Rephaims, and Balaam smote somebody's ass (although it was unclear who's ass that was). Sundance liked smoting. There was a sense of retribution and finality about smoting that really pushed his buttons. He was going to do some serious smoting when he got out of this hellhole.

Some time back Sundance realized he could probably use a crew of sorts to help with the heavy lifting— and maybe some of the smoting, depending on how smoothly things went. So, he began to watch his fellow inmates, looking for a couple of likely companions in the business of piracy and plunder, for he realized from the newspaper clippings and inside information he had received that there might well be some serious plunder to be had.

Apparently, his "old friends" had found a treasure or two. Gradually, he began sorting out and dismissing possibilities. Many of his fellow incarcerates were simply one coffee bean short of a cappuccino — liabilities to themselves as well as others — and that would never do. Others were smart enough, but too competitive. There could be only one captain on this voyage. Some were capable, but just plain lunatics — bobble-eyed psychos. Finally, after cautiously wading through several dozen people, he found Coco Odan, and his partner, Weasley Johnson.

While Coco and Weasley thought of themselves as professionals in the world of crime, they had really been more like inept scoundrels, always looking for an easy mark, not wanting to work too hard or risk too much, skipping along on B&Es, robbing drunk tourists, and getting in on an occasional small drug deal.

Weasley was a rotund five foot eight, with coarse, red hair that hooked behind his ears and fell to his shoulders, and listless blue eyes that constantly looked like they didn't get the joke. He was doing two years at Eglin for getting careless on a pot deal—it turned out the buyers were narcs. His name was actually Johnson Weasley, but while in prison (where there's no such thing as privacy, especially in the showers), it was discovered that Johnson had an extraordinarily ugly penis due to an accident with a chemistry set and a fire as a child. Johnson's Johnson looked like a Mexican Gila monster with no legs — all motley colored, and lumpy as a Baby Ruth Bar, and what pubic hair he had was reminiscent of Everglades saw grass after a summer swamp fire. So at Eglin, everyone just reversed his name. He became Weasley Johnson, and it stuck.

After a while, even Johnson accepted it, and as strange as that might seem, it gave him some credence in a place where any credence was better than none at all. While at Eglin, he had taken to gluing a pair of those jiggling dime-store eyeballs on each side of the head of his slightly disfigured member. *Here's looking at you, kid...* He came to realize that you had to be weirder than the weirdoes to survive there. In prison, you're either fish, or bait...

Coco Odan had come to Miami in the Mariel Boatlift in 1980, along with 125,000 other Cubans. He was tall and thin with slicked-back, black hair; Bela Lugosi-on-Quaaludes eyes, one of which had a lazy slant to it; a long, pointed nose; and a wide, heavy-lipped smile that was a couple of teeth short of pretty. His features made him appear like a caricature of himself. His grandmother had been a Haitian and she had given him the soft cocoa in his complexion for which he was nicknamed. He hadn't been in Miami for much over a year before he got nailed for stealing a car. Grand theft auto bought him 24 months. He was Weasley's cellmate. Both were getting an early out in September — conveniently enough, just like Sundance.

Sundance had encouraged Weasley and Coco to join him in his little foray into newfound wealth and much-needed revenge, when they were released two weeks hence. He stared out over the yard, his field of dreams coalescing nicely — except for the tuberculosis he might have — that, and the yellow jaundice. He'd noticed a bit of a yellow tinge to his skin lately. Perhaps his bilirubin was high. He should see the hospital doctor. What a supercilious, unsympathetic hack the man was; refused to see him more than once a week, called him a hypochondriac. Doctor? Hah! The idiot couldn't pour water out of a boot without instructions on the heel. For God's sake, the unmitigated debasement he had to bear in this foul dungeon.

CHAPTER 15

"So, tell me about yourself," she said as we lay in bed, the moon hanging just under the eve of my house, its cool luminescence splashing the window and bathing the room in soft chartreuse. The air conditioner was offering asylum from the humidity and heat, but I had our window open slightly, allowing the subtle fragrances of evening jasmine and key lime to waft in. A tight mesh in the window screen denied the legions of tenacious no-see-ums and mosquitoes, the bane of The Keys. Somewhere a gull called mournfully and another answered.

"You first," I replied. "I hardly know anything about you. We've barely had time to talk in the last few weeks. We were either fighting for our lives or making mad, passionate love — not much in between. Fill in the gaps for me."

Kendra chuckled, sensual, throaty — she had a voice that could conjure melody from syllables. She snuggled closer, her blond hair flowing over the pillow, those pale blue eyes turning from me to watch the ceiling fan in its lazy swirl, that nectarous scent of citrus and cinnamon emanating from her. "Not much to tell, really. I grew up in Homosassa. When I was two, my mother left my father. Dad always said it was a traveling salesman. A year later he married my mom, the one I remember, and about a year later Margo was born. We lived near the river — beautiful, clear water. Margo and I could swim before we could walk. We grew up, went to high school — not part of the in-crowd, but not unpopular either. It didn't seem to matter to us. We knew, somehow, that we were different from the other girls. They could see weddings, babies, the husband home at five — the whole white-picket-fence scenario. Somehow, that just didn't work for us. There was a big world out there — things to see and taste and experience..." She turned to me, a smile caressing her lips. "You understand perfectly, don't you?"

"Yeah, I understand. I never had any desire to belong to the 'in-crowd' in high school or college. All I wanted to do was strike out into the wilderness of life — feel the surf breaking across me and my board at sunrise, explore, and as you said, experience." A sigh escaped me. "I broke the heart of a girl who loved me once, back then — my first love. She risked falling in love because she was certain I would change. She wanted the church wedding, lots of kids.

Nine-to-five didn't bother her at all. But it terrified me." I drew in a breath of recollection and exhaled melancholy. "She couldn't change me. I couldn't change me. I couldn't stay, live like that, without stunting something deep and vital within me — something that had to expand — a pure, unadulterated need to see what was over the horizon."

Kendra nodded somberly. "I have to admit, your life and Will's seem straight out of a Travis McGee novel. To have done what you have...it's a miracle you survived it all."

"There's that word, 'miracle,'" I muttered. "It encompasses everything from divination and inexplicable preservation, to the face of Jesus on tortillas. I've always had a faith in a greater power — somebody or something paying close attention to us — that's for sure." I eased back on my elbow and gazed at my lady, running a finger down her cheek. "Let me tell you what I think about miracles: I have watched a small, brittle, speckled eggshell crack open and seen a tiny, mottled sparrow crawl haltingly into this life. That's a miracle. I have seen courage rise in the eyes of a common man and watched him sacrifice himself to save those around him, and that's a miracle. I have fought monster, hull-crushing storms at sea that, for no logical reason, didn't kill me. I've been face-to-snout with sharks, blood from a recent kill still flowing through their gills and staining the water. I have crashed airplanes, and challenged men with weapons intent on killing me, but somehow I'm still here to relate these stories, and you can't tell me there isn't a miracle or two in that bag. So forgive me if I'm not so impressed with the supposed face of Jesus on a tortilla."

Kendra chuckled again. "Amen," she said quietly.

The phone rang on the nightstand. I really didn't want to answer it, but there was an insistence. "Sorry," I whispered as I shifted my arm free from my lady and rolled over to pick up the receiver. "Hello?"

There was silence on the other end for a moment, then a ponderous sigh. "Life is such a fascinating affair, as we cascade down the rapids of experience in fragile crafts of dreams and desires. They say it's the journey, not the destination that matters. But I'm not quite sure of that."

The accent was clipped, almost British, but carrying the occasional inflection and cadence of someone who had spent time south of the border. I felt like I knew that voice. "Who is this?"

"Why, I'm hurt — positively shattered you don't recognize me," the voice continued. "We shared so many...unique experiences..."

Damn, the voice was familiar, but I just couldn't place it. "Sorry buddy, but I don't have time for 20 questions with late-night lunatics."

"We are all lunatics in one fashion or another, but he who can divine his illusions is considered a philosopher, no?"

I started to speak but the voice interrupted me.

"Not to worry. Won't keep you now. Just wanted to say hello. I'm certain we'll be seeing more of each other in the near future."

Click.

"Who was that?" Kendra asked as I sat the phone in its cradle.

I shook my head, mystified and a little uncomfortable. There was a subtle undertone of intimidation to that whole thing. I knew that voice from somewhere...

We were moving into late summer/early fall in The Keys, when the skies become a rich azure, and heavy cumulous batteries build at the edge of the horizon, lightning exploding in their bellies in brilliant flashes. The weed lines on the reef begin to fade and move out, the water becomes eerily clear, the wind falls to an occasional whisper, and you can see forever across the blue expanse. It's my favorite time of the year, normally...

We were all doing well. My relationship with Kendra was growing stronger every day. She had gone from lover to friend, and while she was a willful woman, she accepted what was becoming a partnership in the decisions of life. Margo was back to her old, precocious self, apparently wearing out Will, who had a reputation for sexual fortitude.

"She's like a mink in heat — all the time," he muttered with a mouthful of eggs. He had come up from Key West and we were having a late breakfast at The Big Pine Coffee Shop while the girls were off for some shopping in Miami. "She's freakin' insatiable. Tucking fenacious." He took a sip of his coffee and pointed the cup at me. "I'll wake up in the middle of the night and she's down there..." He nodded at his lap. "...crotch dancing with Willie, or doing the lollipop. I mean, I like sex as much as the next guy, but this is above and beyond the call. I need to sleep a little."

"Have you spoken with her about this...appetite?"

Will shook his head. "When was the last time you told a girl you didn't want to do the dirty so much? How well did that go?" He took a sip of coffee. "I mean, I really like her — she's a very cool lady, but..."

"So, what are you going to do?"

"I'm gonna ride up to Marathon today, to the Chi Cho's Health Foods, and buy some vitamins. Maybe this is sort of like breaking a bronco; if you hang on long enough, the horse begins to ease up to where you can just ride it occasionally, instead of doing the crazy all the time."

I took the day to clean my boat. With all the fishing and diving we'd been doing, it needed a little maintenance. Will left for town about 11 o'clock, cruising across Henry Flagler's magnificent legacies — the Bahia Honda and Seven Mile bridges.

A morning sun reflected off the water with a sparkling brilliance. Pelicans and cormorants perched on the bridge rails, holding their wings out to dry like sun-gilded statues, or glided effortlessly alongside the pilings in search of the luckless fish too close to the surface. Frigate birds and ospreys swirled above, locked into endless thermals, and seagulls — the perennial tricksters of air and sea, constantly on the lookout for an easy meal — swirled and dove in perpetual movement. Will, caught up in the medley of nature, hardly noticed the dark-blue Ford Fairlane that managed to stay just a car or two behind him.

He found the health food store at the little strip mall in the center of town, just down from the theater, and after a few minutes of picking up bottles and reading labels, a diminutive, older Asian lady came over to him. "Can help you, yes?"

Will shrugged, then sighed. "Yeah, yeah, maybe. I'm looking for something to give me a little more energy. Vitamins maybe..."

The lady was very astute, noticing he was holding a bottle of "Herbal Male Fortitude."

"You want more energy to play tennis, swim in ocean? Or you want have more energy for dangling noodle?"

Will winced like he'd been pinched. "No, no dangling noodles, exactly —"

"I got fresh shark fin powder. Make you like gorilla!" she interrupted, raising her forearm with her fist clenched. "Knock down doors with your *jiba*. Make you so hard you crack conch shell —"

Will took a step backwards, hands out, palms up. "Don't want to crack conch shells or knock down doors. I just want more energy..."

She smiled "Ahhh, you got zing-zing tiger mama. Huh? Huh?"
Will shrugged again, embarrassed. "Yeah, tiger mama."

"Okeydokey," the little lady said as she turned on her heel and
moved to the end of the isle, pulling down two bottles, then turning
to him again. "Take two these each in morning and two in evening.
Give you energy for two tiger mamas! Huh? Huh? Plenty powerful
vitamin. Got little *jiba* medicine in it, too."

Will paid for his vitamins and, with new optimism, left the store.
As he reached the car and was digging into his pocket for his keys, a
van pulled up into the parking place adjacent to him. Suddenly, there
was a tall Cuban standing next to him. The fellow had slicked-back,
black hair, a long pointed nose, and weird eyes, one of which had a
lazy slant to it, as if it were fascinated by something on his shoulder.
It would slide slowly downward in that direction for a moment, then
snap back into place. Very disconcerting.

"Hegh man, chu got a light?" the fellow said with a distinctive
Cuban accent, presenting a dark cigarillo. (The left eye started to slip
down as if attracted to the side-view mirror on Will's car.) "Two
years in de slammer, I no have a decent cigarillo."

"Aahh, no, I don't," said Will, not relishing how close the Cuban
was standing to him. About that time he heard one of the doors on
the van open behind him, effectively blocking the view from the
road.

He started to look back, but the Cuban reached out and poked a
finger in his chest, keeping his attention. "Chu ever been in prison,
man? Everywhere you look, man, dere is bars, an' *estupido* assaholes
everywhere. It sucks, beegtime, man."

"Yeah, I bet," Will replied, taking a step back. "But I gotta go
now…"

"Why, my old friend, in such a hurry," said a voice from behind
him. "Always so anxious to dispose of those who merely want to
share life's bounty with you."

Will swung around. That voice was painfully familiar. There was
Sundance stepping from the van — the lunatic sociopath he and
Kansas had inadvertently become entangled with in a wild trip
through Costa Rica almost three years ago. The last they'd seen of
him was when he'd stolen an ancient golden pyramid from them.
When they managed to get it back, he tried to shoot them on the deck
of a shrimper in the Marquesas Keys, but they got the better of the
situation and had the pleasure of forcing him overboard.

The man had changed little, other than being somewhat less ponderous. He still looked like an overweight Humphrey Bogart with pale blue eyes. He was only about five-nine, but weighed close to 200 pounds — not so much fat as heavy, in a formidable fashion. He had found a new version of his favorite outfit—a white sports jacket, white pants, a collarless shirt, and tennis shoes. The jacket was already showing signs of careless eating. Sundance never went anywhere without a couple of Almond Joys stuffed in his pockets. His long hair was still straw yellow, jutting out underneath a white Panama hat.

"Sundance..." Will sputtered. "What are you...the last I heard you were..."

"Yes, I was, but I got out," Sundance said. "Good behavior and all that. While you've been gallivanting gaily about, discovering ancient gold crosses and Spanish coins in the Bahamas, or gold bullion and emeralds in Central America, your old partner has been collecting new diseases in a hellhole in Central Florida." Sundance did that inadvertent twist of his neck — jaw one way, then the other. "Not the least of which is yellow jaundice, possibly even hepatitis."

"You were never our partner," Will replied stiffly, but surprised by how well-informed Sundance was. "We spent most of our time trying to get away from you — or trying to get back the stuff you stole from us."

Sundance shook his head slowly. "There — that's just the ungrateful attitude I expected. Not a single kind word for an old comrade in arms."

"You tried to kill us."

"Simply a misunderstanding at the time."

"More than once!"

"We mustn't dwell on the past."

Will felt a sting in his right arm and turned to see the tall Cuban removing a needle, the syringe he held, now empty.

"What the hell?" Will muttered, realizing he was hemmed in, the Cuban behind him and his rather large acquaintance in front of him. Everything was getting a little fuzzy around the edges. He could just make out a third guy climbing out of the van.

"Not to worry," Sundance replied. "I'm trusting Kansas will want to share your newfound wealth with his old partner, too."

"You're not our...you never..." But at that point, a grey fog blossomed in Will's head and his body went all warm and buttery.

Ten minutes later Sundance turned to Weasley Johnson, who was driving the van, and Coco Odan, in the back with Will. "Tie him up tight. You have the wire cutters, right?

Coco nodded.

"Johnson is dropping me off at the motel. You two know what to do. Get back to me when you're done with your little task. An index finger will be just fine. That should get everyone's attention."

After dropping off Sundance at the Holiday Inn in Key West and trussing/gagging Will, Coco and his partner headed downtown, their captive, awake now, lying behind them on the floor of the van.

Johnson looked over at Coca. "We flip a coin, okay? To see who has to do it. You know, cut off the finger."

Coco shrugged. "Yeah, okay."

Will's eyes flashed open as if he'd been plugged into a 220-volt line, and he began a furious debate about this plan, but the gag prevented him from presenting a viable argument.

"Relax," said Coco, looking back at Will from the passenger's seat. "This all be over in a little while."

Will began an argument again, probably relating that having a finger cut off is not one of those things you can comfortably relax about. But after a short drive, the van halted.

Johnson exhaled. "Okay, this is the place. Let's get this done. Flip the coin."

A moment later Will heard Coco's relaxed chuckle. "Okay, dude, you da lucky winner. Let's get this over with."

Will was once again presenting adamant, muffled arguments as to why he should get to keep all his appendages, when the two men got out of the van and walked away.

Bilmort Funeral home was quiet. It was a Wednesday, and Wednesdays were generally slow. There was a secretary out front in the reception room. Marcus Bilmort, the mortician — a small, taciturn man with large brown eyes — was busy preparing his latest customer in the back. Johnson and Coco strolled in. Coco ambled over to the desk where a diminutive but not unattractive secretary sat.

"Hey baby," said the tall Cuban, that right eye sliding off to the side. "We need to see the dude what runs da place. We gotta friend who's gonna die. We need some arrangements."

At the sight of the two, the secretary involuntarily slid her seat back a little and glanced at the door to the preparations room.

"I...I'm sorry. Mr. Bilmort is busy...preparing a loved one. Could I take your name and —"

"*Es* cool, little mama. In fact, dat's perfect," Coco said, nodding, catching the direction of her eyes. "We only gonna need a minute or two."

Johnson was already heading for the door. Coco followed.

"You can't...you shouldn't..." bleated the girl, starting to rise.

"*Es no problemo, chiquita*," Coco said as he waved a finger over his shoulder, walking away.

As the doors to the preparation room opened, Marcus Bilmort turned from the man on the table, his eyes wide, gloved hands speckled rose with the remains of his client. "I'm sorry, sirs, no one is permitted —"

"*Es* okay, we're permitted," repeated Coco, pulling out a pistol. "Jus' go stand over dere, by da wall."

The mortician hesitated. "You...can't... You —"

"Now!" barked Coco, bringing up his gun.

Johnson, pulling out his cutters, stomach doing little flip-flops, stepped hesitantly over to the fellow on the table. He reached out and picked up the man's cold, stiff hand while grasping the wire cutters, his scrambled eggs and Rum Runner breakfast gurgling uncomfortably in his stomach. He looked at his partner, eyes seriously unhappy about his luck of the draw.

"C'mon dude, get with the snippin'," hissed Coco nervously.

"You...you can't do this!" wailed the terrified mortician. "You're defiling —"

"I gonna defile your face, you no shut up!" growled the Cuban.

Johnson placed the blades of the cutter around the pale, hard index finger. He closed his eyes.

"Do it, chickenshit!" chided Coco, eyes gleaming maliciously, the right orb losing its grip again.

Snap went the blades. *Whoosh* went Johnson's breakfast, up and out, Rum Runner and scrambled eggs everywhere.

The door to the van slid open and Johnson stepped in, pale as a specter and still holding the wire cutters. Will squirmed like an epileptic centipede, mumbling for clemency under his gag.

"Shut up, you freaking idiot," barked Johnson, wiping his mouth again with the back of his hand. "Today's your lucky day."

They drove up to Big Pine Key. On the way, Johnson put the

finger in a small cardboard box, then scribbled an address on it. There was a note in the box, written by Sundance. They found the mailbox they wanted, stuffed the container into it, and immediately headed south, stopping at Murray's on Summerland Key for a six-pack of Busch and some Snackmaster Beef Jerky.

I checked the mail about three o'clock and found the box. There was no return address. I took it back to the house and pulled up a patio chair on the deck. A handful of seagulls were chasing each other over a ballyhoo they had pilfered from my neighbor's bait box as he cleaned his boat, their vociferous squawking and aerial circus intruding on the stillness of the day. The wind was a pleasant six to eight knots, the yellow-orange sun had passed its zenith and was falling toward the horizon.

I opened the package. There was something wrapped in tissue paper. I turned the box over and dumped it on the deck table.

Five minutes later my hands were still shaking. I had just finished reading the note from our old nemesis, Sundance.

Greetings and Salutations, Kansas,

I can only hope this finds you in slightly better spirits than your good friend, Will, who's feeling a little disjointed at the moment. Ahhh, but better times are coming for all of us, if you simply do what is required of you. We could be the tres amigos again, and share our wealth — after all, you garnered this fortune of yours while I languished in prison. Had we still been partners, I would have received my share. Simple, rudimentary reasoning, no? On the other hand, if you choose, you can lift no finger to help your friend, or you can point the finger of guilt, in which case you'll receive another finger tomorrow morning. However, I would recommend you don't let this opportunity slip through your partner's fingers, so to speak.

What I want is simple. A large bag of uncut emeralds and 50 pounds of gold — some of what you stole from the pauperized people of Panama — what I figure would have been my share if we had still been the tres amigos.

"We were never the *tres amigos,* you asshole!" I whispered savagely.

The letter continued: *Now I imagine you're arguing vehemently the parameters of our partnership, but I should remind you that it was I who rescued you in Costa Rica, when we first met, and it was my guiding hand that provided you with the resources to return to the land of your registry.*

"Yeah, by robbing a freaking bank! Then, when we tried to get away, you tried to kill us!"

Yes, yes, I'm sure you're muttering something about misunder-standings, but nonetheless, this is the situation, and now I require the above stipend — soon — or I give you the finger... again.

Now, I'm sure you know where the old bat tower is on Sugarloaf Key. You will arrive there between eight and nine p.m., with the above-mentioned items in a briefcase. Set it underneath the tower, then drive away. If you try to ferret out my intention — if you linger there — you will get two fingers tomorrow, maybe an ear, depending on my mood.

If you do as required, I will return your friend tomorrow.

Sundance

P.S. If you're curious as to how I became so well informed, let's just say I have had a pen pal over the last year or so, who has paid attention to all your activities. And your friend, Crazy Eddie, is as loquacious as a parrot on crack when he drinks — which is often...

I knew where the bat tower was — an old, wooden assembly of shattered dreams, a flight of fancy built in 1929 by a Keys fishing-lodge owner named Richter Clyde Perky. Mr. Perky figured if he constructed a huge tower and filled it with imported bats, those bats would fly out each sunset and devour the mosquitoes (which were eating the fishermen at his lodge). He built the tower, captured thousands of bats, then introduced them to their new home. At sunset one evening he opened the hatch, and all those little leather-winged, bug-eating denizens happily flew out — never to be seen again. Not a single one returned, leaving a final score of mosquitoes, a zillion — bats, zero. Nothing sucks more than that pivotal moment when you realize you've been duped by your own ego.

CHAPTER 16

"You know this guy is dead — dead as yesterday's grouper," Margo gritted as she sat her drink on the table at the front window of Captain Tony's in Key West. "It doesn't matter where he goes, I'm gonna find him. I'm gonna feed him his nuts, and —"

"First, let's worry about getting Will back," I said to her and Kendra.

"You're gonna pay him what he wants? A bag of emeralds and 50 pounds of gold?" Kendra asked.

I nodded. "If that's what it takes. My first stop is our bank here in town to get the ransom. We only have a few hours. But I'm going to look for a weakness in his game, as well. The optimal situation is to get Will back and keep the loot. The trick, I think, will be to follow this guy discreetly when he leaves Sugarloaf after getting our loot. I think I'll call Crazy Eddie, put him in the air with his Goose. Maybe he can track Sundance for us, so we can find the goods after we get Will back."

"And then we kill the son of a bitch," growled Margo, her green eyes alight with fire.

Johnson and Coco were holed up at the Holiday Inn in Key West, waiting on word from Sundance, who was two rooms down from them. Will was still bound hand and foot in the van.

"Maybe we should go down and feed the dude, or give him some water," Johnson said, sitting on his bed cross-legged, shirtless, wearing blue jeans and drinking a beer. "He's been in there all day."

Coco, who was standing in front of the mirror combing his long, dark hair with his fingers, and checking out his new ZZ Top T-shirt, thought about it, then shrugged it off. He picked up the bottle of José Cuervo on the counter and took another shot. "Cheez!" he hissed, slapping the bottle down, still looking at himself in the mirror as he replied. "You don' wanna get to know him too good, *amigo,* in case we gotta toss him off Bahia Honda Bridge, like Sundance was sayin'. Trust me, the less pictures your brain has of him, the less you gonna see him when you try to go to sleep later. You need to be more worried dat Sundance finds out we didn't cut the dude's finger off."

Johnson nodded thoughtfully. "Yeah, man, you're right there. But

177

man, that would have been some messy shit. I had a tough enough time snippin' off that stiff's finger."

"Yeah," replied Coca, smiling. "You nearly pussied out on that." He straightened up and turned to his accomplice. "But with jes' a little luck, we be done with this gig in a couple hours, and have son' serious cash in our pockets."

While Johnson and Coco were in conversation, Sundance stood on his balcony, watching the sun slip into the cumulus clouds in the distance. He did that typical neck twist thing — from one side to the other — and sighed wretchedly. *Bloody humidity is obviously exasperating my hypothyroidism.* "Cursed with disease after bloody disease," he muttered. "No wonder my temperament edges toward the intellectually morose."

Coming to a decision, Sundance turned and closed the glass door, then went to the phone and called his "compatriots," packing his bag as he spoke. "As per our plan, I'm going to rendezvous with our money now. Soon you and your confederate will be rich men, and I will be slightly richer, which is only fair, as I have done all the heavy mental lifting."

Coco nodded, eyes sparkling with the thought of impending wealth. "Yeah, man, sounds good to us." But he paused, his brain struggling with a couple of variables. "But how come you go pick up the money? Maybe we should come with you, man."

"No, not necessary," said Sundance with finality. "I told you, we'll meet at the Casa Mexicana in Marathon and split the loot there. First rule of successful pilfering — get away from the scene immediately."

Coco wasn't quite comfortable with this, but he didn't have a better plan. Now he was wishing he had given this more thought. His head flipped over to the second variable. "What about the dude in the van?"

"I've given this some consideration," said Sundance carefully. "Unfortunately, the man can identify you — quite possibly put you back in the asylum from which you've been so recently released."

That gave Coco pause. An ugly shiver cascaded down his back. "Uh-huh..."

"I think it's best that you simply toss him off the Bahia Honda Bridge on the way to Marathon. Let the currents, and Old Moe, the hammerhead that haunts those waters, determine his fate. Wouldn't want my dear companions to end up back in prison."

There was a lull at the other end as Coco took that in. "Yeah, I thin' maybe you're right, man. Jus' a quick toss and we done."

Sundance smiled. All was working out quite well as he captained his "confederacy of dunces." "Wait until the sun is down. I will meet you at the Casa Mexicana in Marathon at 9:00 p.m."

"Okay, man." Coco hung up the phone and looked at Johnson. "Looks like our buddy gonna be food for the sharks after all."

Johnson's stomach did a little flip-flop at the news. It wasn't what he signed on for. But he didn't let it show on his face.

Will, still tightly trussed and gagged, thought he'd died and gone to hell. He figured it was close to 100 degrees inside the van and he was nearing dehydration. He had rolled around in the vehicle and offered muffled shouts through the gag, hoping someone would hear him as they walked through the parking lot, but no one noticed.

I had retrieved a bag of emeralds and 50 pounds of gold bars from the bank. It required only four bars, each six inches long, two inches wide, and one inch deep. Gold is heavy, and throughout history has carried a heavy consequence, as any buccaneer (past or present) will tell you.

Following Sundance's instructions, I prepared to leave for Sugarloaf Key and the bat tower. Meanwhile, I had contacted Crazy Eddie and put him in the air, circling that island innocuously in his latest Grumman Goose. I had also picked up three of his Vietnam vintage handheld radios. Margo was parked outside The Sugarloaf Lodge, watching the road going south with one of them. Kendra was a mile or so north, just across the bridge on Cudjoe Key with another. I had the third.

I arrived at Sugarloaf Key just after sunset, taking the small, unmarked road back to the bat tower. Perched on its four weathered, wooden legs, and silhouetted against the last light in a western sky, the tower rose up ominously like a scene from a Hitchcock movie. Its sun-bleached, grey shingles were fading to black, and the dark, open hatch reminded me of a huge mouth from which thousands of bats had streamed outward and upward into the humid summer darkness over 50 years ago — one time.

I stopped by the tower and waited for a moment, letting the shadows grow, then got out, carefully searching the area for any sign of movement. When satisfied I was alone, I pulled the gold and emeralds from the trunk and placed them underneath the tower. With a final look around and a brief entreaty to the gods of flimflam, I returned to my car and drove away.

When I reached U.S. 1 again, I paused and picked up the radio on my seat, keying the mike twice as a signal to my companions. "I'm moving away, headed north, toward my place on Big Pine. It's up to you now."

As I set the radio down, I heard the distant roar of a small plane taking off. My stomach suddenly dropped three stories. The freaking Sugarloaf Airport! Not a half-mile from the bat tower! How could I have been so stupid! It was nothing more than a few hundred yards of runway bulldozed out of the coral with a little cinderblock building for an office, but there were several planes there, and one was just taking off. I threw open the car door and stumbled out. There, lifting off and heading into the sun was a small, twin-engine Cessna. I watched it turn, as if taking a final look at me, wagging its wings with mockery, then it rolled around and headed west. I suddenly knew, unequivocally, who was in that plane. Quickly I grabbed the radio. "Eddie! Eddie! Do you read me? Come back. Come back."

"Yeah dude, I got ya. What's the skinny, man?"

I exhaled gratefully. "How close to the Sugarloaf airstrip are you?"

"About a mile north right now."

"Can you see the small twin rising up out of there?"

There was a pause as my friend scanned the horizon. "Yeah, dude. I got it." There was another pause. "Let me guess. That's your buddy, Sundance, huh? Sonabitch out-foxed you."

The plane was growing smaller in the darkening distance. "Yeah, looks like it. Can you follow him? See where he goes?"

"Negative on a long chase. I only have about a third of fuel on my mains and I haven't had time to install auxiliary tanks in this puppy. Besides, that twin is a whole lot faster than this fat old bird."

With a dejected sigh I watched Eddie and his Goose follow, but at best he would only be able to provide a direction. Sundance could be headed anywhere, from the Texas coast, to Mexico or Central America. There was no doubt he had hired a pilot who knew his way around the Gulf.

Will was startled out of a reverie of thirst and heat when the van doors opened and a waft of fresh, early evening air blew through. His captors were back, getting into their seats.

Coco looked back at Will with a grim finality. "It jus' not your lucky day, *amigo*." He offered an ugly smile. "Son'times you eat da shark, son'times da shark eat you."

It took the better part of 45 minutes to reach Bahia Honda Bridge — the tall, magnificent archway built by Henry Flagler that was decommissioned in the early '70s. A new, lower bridge had been constructed to take its place, but the new one was still high enough to allow some commercial fishing traffic to pass under it. It was a weekday night and the automobile traffic was fairly light. The sun had been swallowed by heavy, cumulus banks half an hour ago, and darkness had settled in across the black water, which rippled with current as it surged between the two islands that the supported the almost-mile-long bridge.

Coco backed off on the accelerator and let a car pass him. There were no headlights in either direction now. "Okay," he grunted as he pulled over against the railing and stopped. "Time to do dis thing."

They dragged a protesting Will out of the back doors of the van and over to the railing. A heavy orange moon was just coming up on the far side of the ocean. Slivers of grey clouds slipped across its face, blinding it from the act that was about to take place. The wind was rising and the smell of the sea — Sargasso weed, salt, and mangrove — wafted in the air. But all this mattered little to the three men: two about to sacrifice a third to the gods of the sea and the creatures within it.

Will's muffled cries were lost to a rising wind and the cries of night birds. Realizing the obvious, he struggled furiously. His feet were still securely tied, but all afternoon he had been working on the bonds at his wrists, and while raw and bleeding, he had made some progress. The fury of terror added to his impetus, and as he writhed and tossed around, trying to break the grip of the two men as they carried him to the railing, he managed to free his hands. As they dragged him up onto the railing and unceremoniously pushed him outward, he reached out and grabbed Coco by the front of his shirt, just as Coco's momentum was moving forward in the toss. The Cuban lost his balance and tumbled over the rail behind Will, a shriek of terror burbling up and out as he realized he had just become part of the sacrifice.

What happened next is best prefaced by the words of Rufus, the mystical Rastaman, who was often heard to say, "We are all part of the great cosmic pinball machine. Sometimes it is tiny levers that deflect ball bearing of fate just a little — da gods adjusting da rabbit ears on da television of life."

Will was tumbling in an almost slow-motion freefall, arms flailing, his back toward the ocean, looking up at the star-filled sky and still listening to the drawn-out wail of Coco somewhere to his left. It was only about 20 feet, but it seemed like forever, and in the periphery of his vision, for the briefest second, he thought he saw/felt a huge shadow on the water, coming at him. He waited for the impact of the water, terrified by a night swim to shore in a channel known for its sharks, but instead of a wet impact, he suddenly slapped down hard on a mattress of what appeared to be tightly packed bundles.

The impact knocked the breath from his lungs and he lay there, helpless, for a moment or two. Almost immediately, he could feel the vibration of a big diesel engine and he sensed forward movement. *God in heaven! I've fallen onto the deck of a boat running without lights!* In the next moment two men had his arms and jerked him to a sitting position.

"Who the hell are you, and how in the name of Neptune's hairy balls did you get on my boat?" hissed the larger of the two, his big frame stretching a Key West Turtle Kraals T-shirt.

"Sonabitch musta jumped off the bridge as we passed under," said the other. The fellow grabbed a shock of Will's long hair and pulled him up. "You DEA? Marine Patrol?" he asked harshly over the low rumble of the engine.

Will was just starting to get his breath back, and beginning to realize a couple of salient facts. First off, he could smell the sweet, overpowering aroma of pot, and quickly came to the conclusion that the bales he was sitting on most likely originated in Colombia or Jamaica. The boat was running without lights, and most importantly, Coco had apparently "missed the boat."

"No man, no!" Will sputtered. "Some people just tried to kill me — tossed me off the bridge! In some sort of bloody miracle I fell onto the stern of your boat." He looked at them, realizing that he was going to have to quell some fears posthaste if he didn't want to end up in the water again in about 30 seconds. "Guys, I don't give a rat's ass what you're doing. I wish you the best of luck. Just don't throw me back in the water. Hell, man, I'll even help you unload…"

The moon pulled away from the clouds for a moment and illuminated the craft — a small long-liner, somebody's working boat, usually after swordfish and mahi-mahi...but not tonight. The bigger fellow looked at his friend.

"We only have a couple choices here... and we could use the help offloading, that's for sure..."

"Good choice! Good choice!" Will spat out.

The other guy huffed angrily, but the fear and anger in his eyes had abated. "Okay, okay. What the hell, can't very well feed him to the sharks." But he grabbed my friend by his shirt again. "When this is done, I'm going to give you 500 bucks, cash, and you're going to forget this ever happened. You understand?"

Will exhaled in huge relief. "Oh, man, do I freaking understand! I never saw you and I never want to see you again!"

The fellow turned to his partner. "Tell Ted to pick up his north north-westerly course now, and start watching for the flashing light on the back side of No Name Key. I'm sure our friends are getting impatient." Then he untied Wills legs and pulled him to a standing position. "Dust yourself off. You're about to have an interesting night that never happened."

Old Moe, the giant hammerhead that had terrified divers and swimmers around Bahia Honda Bridge for years, felt the vibrations in the water dancing along the lateral line on his huge trunk and setting off primordial signals of a possible evening snack. Something was thrashing around on the surface not too far from him — something weak, and in distress, and probably tasty. He followed the signals as unerringly as a bloodhound, and sure enough, above him on the moonlit surface was one of those tender creatures that generally had enough intelligence not to thrash around at night, when his sense of prey-taking was at its height. He swam slowly but purposely over to the target, just barely below the surface, his dorsal fin almost breaking free of the water, long tailfin leisurely waving behind it. The creature was crying out in Cuban (not that it mattered to Moe), treading water frantically in an enticingly slow spin, pushing all the right buttons for the monster below.

Coco never knew what hit him.

The moon had buried itself in a huge bank of cumulus clouds and Weasley Johnson lost sight of Coco as the Cuban drifted with the outgoing tide between the new bridge and the old, heading out to sea. Weasley could still hear his partner yelling, but there was nothing he could do. He had heard the rumble of a boat below as well, but it had passed quickly. A moment or two later he heard Coco shriek, then nothing. The hair on the back of his neck stood up and he shivered. There were cars coming in both directions now. He eased out a shaky breath, returned to the van, and drove away. There were things you just couldn't do anything about. "Sometimes you eat the shark, and sometimes the shark eats you," he muttered with a cheerless finality.

Johnson made his way to Casa Mexicana and sat at the bar drinking tequila sunrises for the next four hours, until closing, realizing that this had been the mother of bad days. He had lost his partner, and Sundance had obviously duped him.

While Jimmy Buffett crooned from the jukebox about sons of sailors, the bartender, a moderately attractive lady in the later years of her bloom, slid over and told him it was last call, hitting him with a little more tequila in his sunrise without being asked. She had been watching him most of the night. "Bad day, huh?"

"You got no idea," Johnson muttered cradling his drink.

"Why don't I take you home with me, and at least we can end it well" she said straightforward, matter of fact, the only betrayal a slight sparkle in her eyes.

Johnson sighed. "Lady, that sounds like a great offer, but I may not be the catch of the day." The tequila muddling any pretense, he muttered, "I got a wanger that looks like a Gila monster. Not pretty. Just being up front."

She smiled. "It's okay. I like lizards..."

In the interim, things had become "interesting" for Will and his new enterprise as a part-time marijuana off-loader. As soon as the shrimper was clear of Bahia Honda Bridge they took a northwest course, staying with the shallow channel as much as possible, and headed into shallower water just east of No Name.

As the boss had predicted, there was a flashing light near the middle of No Name where the single paved road on the island ended at the water's edge. From the mangroves, three small, low-draft skiffs with sizeable engines shot out and slid up against the shrimper. There were some tense greetings, then everyone got down to the business of loading the skiffs, which sped toward the dead-end road on No Name to commune with two dark-colored vans that awaited them.

Will helped load each boat from the shrimper, which filled the first van. It pulled away without lights, down the long, straight road (Watson Boulevard) and across No Name Bridge to the small development called Doctor's Arm at the end of Big Pine. From there it was a straight shot down Key Deer Boulevard to U.S. 1. Then the boss man sent Will to the shore to help offload into the last van. Everything was going smoothly. The last skiff was being emptied on the shoreline and the small longline boat was already headed into the backcountry to clean up any residue or seeds onboard before returning to Key West.

Suddenly, Will heard a yell from one of his smuggler companions. The fellow was pointing down Watson Boulevard, where they could see a silent string of flashing red lights entering No Name Key. Across the water, coming from Spanish Harbor, Will could hear the roar of large engines and just make out in the moonlight two Marine Patrol craft headed their way.

"Party's over," said the pilot of the bonefish skiff as he tossed one of the last bales to his buddies. "Time to boogie."

Will was left with a quandary — stay with the boat or take his chances on shore. He took one more look at the string of lights headed toward them on the road and quickly moved back to the bench seat behind the console. "Get us out of here!" he yelled to the pilot.

The organized affair quickly became an every-man-for-himself situation as people scattered into the surrounding mangroves, and boats sped away with a handful of occupants.

A fall front was moving in from the north. The wind was rising and clouds were beginning to obscure the orange harvest moon, which was good — less visibility. Will's pilot, a tall, skinny fellow in Hang Ten Shorts and a khaki "fishing guide" shirt, slammed the throttles to the wall and the little skiff fairly leapt out of the sea, only a few feet of the transom and the lower unit of the engine touching the water. But one of the Marine Patrol craft had singled out Will's skiff and broken away. The chase was on.

Will's helmsman stood at the console, grasping the steering wheel comfortably, knees flexed, eyes alight with anything but fear, a slight smile turning up the edges of his mouth.

The son of a bitch is enjoying himself! Will thought as the fellow turned to him.

"Having fun yet?" he yelled over the roar of the engine.

"No, not exactly," Will replied, maintaining his death grip on the stainless steel rail at the side of the console, flexing his legs at the slap, slap, slap of the water on the hull.

"Relax," said the smuggler. "As long as they don't put up a bird, we'll kick their ass."

Will understood. If they could stay ahead of the larger boat, they could squeeze through the westerly side of Mayo Key and Big Pine, then up through the tight, shallow channel at the tip of the island, between Annette and Howe Keys and Big Pine, and disappear into the hundreds of islands in the backcountry. The Marine Patrol boat would be forced to reduce speed to negotiate the tiny, winding channel, if they could make it at all. But the variable was the new, twin 225 horsepower engines on the patrol boat. It was gaining, and if it caught them before the narrow channel, they were screwed.

Sure enough, Will's worst fears were realized well before the northern tip of Big Pine. The Marine Patrol had closed the gap to 50 yards and an officer was yelling at them with a bullhorn to stand down. Both boats were entering the shallow, narrowing conduit that preceded the tiny channel at the top of the key. Outside of that small pathway, the water was very shallow, with endless coral heads — bad news for lower units on engines.

Will decided to take things into his own hands. There were two bales left in the back of the boat. He stumbled his way to the stern, grabbed one, and tossed it over, forcing the craft close behind them to swerve out of the narrowing, 10-foot-wide waterway. There was a change in pitch as the big propellers on his pursuer's boat dug into the sand and muck. As the moon was sucked beneath a dark battery of clouds, Will quickly threw out the other, and the gods (bored and looking for some entertainment) directed it perfectly, right at the bow of the larger boat, just as the pilot was fighting to get back into the slender channel. The bale slammed into the bow and the pilot reacted before thinking, snapping to the right and out of the channel, where a lone coral head awaited, just a foot and a half below the surface. The noise of the lower unit striking the head was a physical thing. The lower unit exploded and the big craft swerved violently, rolling onto its gunwales on the port side, nearly ejecting the occupants. As the Marine Patrol officer threw back the power on the ruined engine, the momentum took the boat over a second head, and the crunching of metal propeller on coral was audible. (There's nothing more mischievous than bored gods.)

Will's new friend at the helm risked a quick look back when he heard the explosion, and saw the patrol boat gouge the second head. He slowed the boat to a stop and looked back again, to make sure the Marine Patrol officers were okay. Will realized that, for him, this was nothing more than a game. He wanted to win, but he didn't want anyone hurt in the process. The fellow grinned broadly and shook his hair back, waving goodbye to the stranded officers. He turned to my friend. "Not bad, dude, not bad," he said. "I owe you a cold one."

By midnight Will and his new buddy, Ted, had negotiated the tiny channel at the top of the island and run down the backside of Big Pine, then across to Little Torch, where Ted lived. After a couple of cold beers and a boisterous recounting of their adventure (getting better each time they recalled it), he drove Will home to his renovated shrimp boat in Key West.

I was still outside on my deck, watching the moon, just past its zenith, struggle with a tenacious front of cooler air and heavy clouds, still worried to death. I knew that for all his feigned aplomb and decorous prose, Sundance was just a few degrees short of being an unbridled sociopath. He had obviously done something with Will — probably had incorporated a witless partner somewhere along the way and had them take care of the nasty work. My brain fizzed with ugly scenarios. There was no way I was going to sleep. I just didn't know what to do next. I couldn't exactly call the police without opening myself to questions regarding emeralds and gold that we wouldn't want to answer, and chances were, they would do very little about a possible missing person for the first 24 hours.

For all our bantering about decisions and our constant competition for the fairer sex, that moppy-headed, lanky dude with that Lee Marvin grin and those crazy blue eyes was by far, my best friend in this life. I stood there staring up at the moon, asking the Big Guy in charge of tough decisions for a little help, when the telephone rang. I dashed off the porch and through the front door to the phone in the kitchen.

"I have another interesting story for that book you're always talking about writing," said Will.

My pulse slowed with relief and I exhaled with the pleasure of having my world back in balance. "Yeah, I bet. Good to hear your voice. I was beginning to wonder..."

"I was beginning to wonder, several times," replied Will. "Why don't you meet me at The Bull and Whistle in a half hour. It's been a long day and I don't feel like driving back up to Big Pine — and I need a drink or two, or three..."

I had to ask. "Will...your hand...your finger. Are you all right?"

"Whataya mean? What about my finger?"

"Well...I mean, he cut it off and sent it to me. We paid the ransom..."

There was a confused pause on the other end of the line. "What the bloody hell are you talking about? No one cut off my finger. What ransom?"

"Sundance," I blurted. "He kidnapped you and demanded emeralds and gold. I got a finger in the mail. Your finger, I thought."

"Well now, that's really freaking amazing," grunted Will. "Yeah, he snatched me, that's for sure. But I still have all my appendages." He paused. "And he's got our gold and emeralds?"

"Yeah, some of them..."

"Son of a bitch!"

Eddie followed the light twin Cessna for a half hour, then turned back and landed his Goose in the channel by his home on Ramrod Key. I got his call just as I was closing the front door, headed for Key West.

"They left out on a westerly course, but it wasn't long and they left me in the dust," Eddie explained. "A very fast little Cessna. I'm guessing they're headed across the pond, but that straight line out could have been for my benefit, and they could be cutting over to the Gulf Coast — New Orleans, or Galveston, who knows?" He paused. "But if I had to put money on it, I'd say Mexico or Central America."

"Yeah, those are Sundance's old haunts," I said. "That makes more sense to me, too."

I sighed hard in disappointment. We'd been had by our old nemesis, and we'd lost well over a $100,000 in emeralds and gold. But at least Will was safe. I grabbed my hand radio and notified the girls, whom I realized were still staking out U.S. 1, telling them that Will had escaped and we were meeting at The Bull and Whistle. They were ecstatic that our boy was safe, but a vengeful Margo was providing graphic detail on her plans for Sundance. Even after I explained the finger thing, she was still offering seething scenarios. Nobody cut a finger off her man and got away with it.

Floody bucking amazing…

CHAPTER 17

That night we rendezvoused at The Bull and Whistle, and Will told us his tale.

"So now you've added drug smuggling to your repertoire, huh?"

"Inadvertent drug smuggling," Will corrected with a smile. "But it was a unique experience. Does make the ol' heart hammer a little. You have no idea how light a 50-pound bale of pot is while your system is being mainlined with adrenaline and fear."

I chuckled. "Something else to tell your grandchildren, who will consider it all a combination of age, imagination, and bald-faced lies."

Will extricated himself from Margo's protective grasp and leaned forward, elbows on the table, looking around at us all. "So, what do we do about this rat turd who burned us to the tune of a $100,000?"

Margo, dressed as hot as her temperament in a red tube top and a black miniskirt, immediately started to offer some additional graphic suggestions when Kendra held up her hand.

"We go after him. That's what we do." She turned to me. "Don't you have a DEA friend? The guy you helped out a while back after he was hurt in an airplane crash? I remember you telling the story."

I nodded. "Yeah, Shane O'Neal. Why?"

"I'm betting he can take advantage of Fat Albert, the drug interdiction radar balloon on Cudjoe Key. He should be able to tell us where Sundance went — at least close to where he ended up."

"Yeah, good idea. Probably won't be able to follow him all the way to his destination, but Shane should be able to give us a real close approximation. Here's how I figure we can..."

I stopped in mid-sentence, my jaw dropping, flabbergasted and terrified all at once. There, struggling his way out of a limo on the far side of Duval Street, was a huge Chinese with the beginnings of a new, black lock of hair sprouting off the side of his head — Tu Phat Shong, formally of the Darien Jungle. Obviously, he was nowhere near as dead as I had hoped.

The others saw the big man and the look on mine and Will's faces.

"Who is that?" Kendra asked. "You look like you've seen a ghost."

"I would have preferred a ghost," I muttered, still watching Tu Phat as he headed into a small eatery, his entourage around him as usual — two heavies, his secretary, and his favorite concubine. "That's our old adversary, Tu Phat, from Panama. This really ramps up the game."

"Yeah, you're right there," Kendra agreed. "Apparently the dunking in the river after the speedboat chase didn't finish him. Not good."

"We're going to have to readjust our plan a little," I said, still watching the Panamanian. I turned to my lady. "Tu Phat doesn't know you. We need you to follow him, find out where he's staying, what he's up to, if you can. We have to be ahead of the curve here."

Kendra nodded, a strand of blond hair falling over her face, and for some reason, making her look very sexy to me. "You got it," she said. "I'll see you later tonight. Don't wait up for me."

"Maybe I will…"

I turned to my partner. "You've had a rough day or two. Go home. Catch up on some rest. We'll all meet tomorrow at The Big Pine Coffee Shop about 11 a.m. By then, maybe I'll know something from Shane." I glanced over at the limousine across the street, from which Tu Phat had just disembarked. "Maybe getting out of here for a few days is a really good idea. I'm thinking as soon as possible."

Margo put her arm around Will protectively, eyes glistening with a carnal sheen. "I'll take my baby home, nurse him a little, work out his kinks…"

Will glanced at me, his eyes possessing a look similar to a sheep being led to slaughter. He knew, and I knew, he wasn't going to get much sleep tonight.

I stopped at Dion's on Summerland Key on the way home, grabbing a bag of their famous fried chicken and a six-pack of beer. I sat out on my deck for a couple of hours, sipping cold beer, munching on drumsticks, and watching the stars glisten in the dark heavens. The night was hot and still, with a slight fragrance of honeysuckle and bougainvillea, the only sounds an occasional splash of mullet jumping in the canal out front, or a lone night bird calling from the adjacent mangroves. I realized without question that we were headed into another adventure, whether we liked it or not. This one left us with *two* antagonists — we had to move ahead blindly after Sundance, while watching our backs for Tu Phat…

I saw the lights from Kendra's little MGB coming up the road at about midnight. She had spent the evening fending off wannabe

Caribbean cowboys looking for a real "Key West experience" to take home with them, while discreetly following Tu Phat and his people. She actually spoke with them for a while at Captain Tony's, playing the innocent tourist. They were staying at the Pier House, and were on "a quest" as Tu Phat put it — "looking for a rematch in a backgammon game..." It wouldn't be long before Tu Phat's people found out where we lived. It was time to get out of Dodge.

We sat on the bed as she recalled the evening. The lights were dimmed, nothing but the rustle of the wind in the palms outside and moonlight from the window, painting the tiled floor. As she finished, that errant strand of blond hair tumbled down across her face again — the epitome of sexy. Kendra raised a hand to pull it back and I stopped her.

"Don't," I said softly, as I took my lady's hand and pulled her into me...

The following morning an exhausted-looking Will, along with his lady, entered The Big Pine Coffee Shop. We waved from a table in the foyer at the front. After they were seated, the waitress, a cute little thing my friend and I had known for years, delivered menus and coffee.

"Hi Kansas. Hi Will," she said. Then turning to Will with a bright smile, she added, "Haven't seen you for a while. You doin' okay?"

Margo locked her arm in his possessively and gazed at the woman with just a touch of menace. "He's good. Real good. Now bring us some cream, would you?"

"How you doin', buddy?" I asked, softening the moment as the waitress moved away. "Recovering from your latest ordeal?"

"Which one?" he asked wearily.

"Well, I got a little insight on Tu Phat last night," Kendra said, leaning forward conspiratorially. "But none of it's particularly good. I think the best thing we can do is get out of town as soon as possible."

"Which fits into the plan," I added. "I got in touch with Shane, my DEA buddy, early this morning. The bogie that went out of Sugarloaf Airport about nine p.m. yesterday maintained a fairly straight course across the pond. He couldn't say where it landed, but his guess was central Mexico, probably in the area of Cancun."

"That makes sense, now that I think about it," Will added. "I remember Sundance talking about spending time in Cancun —

actually, an island just offshore there, called *Isla Mujeres* — Island of Women. Not much there, just a couple of hotels, a restaurant or two, and a handful of bars. A good place to hole up for a while, maybe cut a deal on the sale of some emeralds."

I nodded emphatically. "I think you're both right. Let's find the son of a bitch and get our loot back. Meanwhile, we can get away from the Phatman, and lay some plans for dealing with him, as well." I looked at Will. "How about we take your 310? I feel better in a twin engine when crossing the big water."

"No problem," my friend said, sipping his coffee. "We'll pack some clothes, fuel in Key West, and be on our way." He glanced at the ladies. "Sound okay to you?"

Margo pulled him in a little closer, nearly spilling his coffee. "You know me, baby. As long as I can 'reach out and touch you,' I'm fine."

"Yeah, I know," Will said, the corners of his mouth grappling with a smile.

After breakfast Kendra grabbed some stuff from my house and the girls drove back to Will's shrimp boat to pick up a few things.

My partner and I took my pickup and headed over to the Summerland Key Airstrip, where Will kept the Cessna 310, to make sure all was in order mechanically before the flight. As we drove, I glanced over at Will, who was unusually quiet. I suddenly realized that his chin had fallen onto his chest and he was sleeping.

He awoke with a start and looked over at me blearily. "Sorry man, I got about two hours of sleep, maybe."

"Rough night, huh?" I said with a knowing smile.

Will sighed hard. "You got no idea. Most of the night I felt like a blow-up doll at a porn convention." He turned to me. "You know, I like being a little kinky, like most guys, but that woman's got things in her purse you only find in stores with wire mesh windows — spiked leather chokers, dildos the size of baseball bats, handcuffs... and that's just the stuff I can talk about." He exhaled again and looked at me. "I got teeth marks on my balls, man! They're still stuck to the sides of my legs from the honey she poured on me. I got peanut butter in my ass cheeks!" He took a breath and sighed shakily. "I need a little break, you know? To sleep for a few hours, at least." He paused and looked out at the road ahead. "I'm beginning to think I've gotten myself into more than I can deal with here. She was fun at first, but things have gotten a little out of hand." Will turned to me again. "I'm thinking...she may not be the one...you know? But let's face it, Margo's not the easiest person to consider breaking off a relationship with. She's a bit...frightening. Like, spooky, dude. I mean, she kills people for a living, and from what I can gather, she may have whacked a couple of folks who just pissed her off."

"Oh, c'mon, man. Surely she can't be that bad. She'll understand. She wouldn't hurt you, I don't think — "

"Yeah, well it's not your ass we're gambling with here, is it?"

I ran a hand though my hair nervously. "Maybe when we get back from this little affair in Cancun, you can let her down easy — tell her you'd still like to see her, but more as friends."

Will looked at me and blinked incredulously. "Yeah, right. When was the last time that actually worked for you? When was the last time you tried that with a woman who cleans her gun each night before she goes to bed? She's an affectionate creature, no doubt, but it's all too damned weird for me."

"We'll get you through this, but for right now, given the situation we're about to go into, we could use their help here. You need to just do your best to ride it out."

"Easy for you to say," he muttered. "You don't have peanut butter between the cheeks of your ass and bite marks on your balls."

By three that afternoon we were in the air. Will was bushed, so I took the left seat and let him nap in the back with Margo. Even Kendra, after chatting quietly with me for a while, opted for a brief nap. She lay against the window, her long blond hair flowing down across her breasts, breathing easily. I held her hand as I flew — nothing much for me to do but watch the VOR and keep us on course. The engines hummed with mesmerizing synchronicity, the sun warmed me through the Plexiglas, and the instruments assured me all was well. Immersed in the cocoon of modern flight, I relaxed for the first time in a while. It was a beautiful day, with the sea a silky turquoise and the edges of the horizon rimmed with wind-strewn, satiny altostratus clouds, stretching up into the stratosphere like white feathers.

Time passed quickly and quietly, with the exception of Will's snoring. Before long I could see the bulbous shape of Mexico's Yucatan Peninsula emerging from the mists ahead. I got on the radio and set up an approach with Cancun International, and 20 minutes later our wheels were touching down on the weathered runway, a cooling sun nestling into the green mountains to the west.

After clearing customs, we headed down the long, single concourse corridor, assailed by hotel and timeshare promoters, excursion couriers, and taxi drivers on each side. One fellow, small and thin with large dark eyes and curly hair, made a more pronounced effort than the others did to get our attention, walking beside us and promising to "take us wherever we wanted to go for practically nothing — a very, very few pesos." When we told him we were interested in going to *Isla Mujeres*, his animation bounced up a notch, assuring us that he could get us to the ferry in time for the last run of the day.

As we worked our way toward the airport entrance, Renaldo introduced himself and asked where we were from, and we told him Key West. He immediately recalled picking up a man from Key West just yesterday evening.

That got our attention.

"What did he look like?" I asked.

"A big, heavy man with yellow straw hair," he said. "With a white coat and pants, and a Panama hat."

That really got our attention.

"Where did you take him?" I asked.

"Oh, he no stay," Renaldo replied. "I take him for a dinner in town and then he come back and get on plane again. He fly away," he said, motioning with his hand like a bird. "He fly away. To Canada, I think."

The mutual sigh was audible.

"Son of a bitch," muttered Will, echoing all our sentiments.

But, there was something in the man's eyes that just didn't work, more like a satisfaction than a disappointment.

"Too, too bad, huh? Flicking shame, *señor*. He fly away. He gone," Renaldo said. But it seemed almost rehearsed.

Margo stepped over to him. "What restaurant did you take him to?" When the guy hesitated, she moved in closer. "What airline did he leave on?"

Again, the fellow floundered, not expecting this. "Aahh, maybe it was Trans American…"

In a heartbeat, she closed the distance on him, almost face to face. "He didn't go anywhere, did he? He paid you to bullshit us."

As Renaldo stumbled back a step or two and started to stutter another excuse, she straightened her hand into a blade and popped him on the neck at the carotid artery, quick as a snake. His eyes went wide, then fluttered, and his knees collapsed. Will and I caught him and put the fellow's arms over our shoulders, carrying him toward the closest restroom. No one paid any attention — just another tourist getting a head start on his vacation.

"He fly away. He fly away," Will muttered sarcastically with a flittering hand movement. "The son of a bitch was given our descriptions and paid to divert us."

I nodded as we dragged our boy into *el baño de caballeros.* "But the good news is, Sundance is here, sure as Mexican frogs eat Mexican flies."

When Renaldo came to, we had him sitting on the toilet in one of the stalls. It was a little crowded, but he was the most uncomfortable.

Will grabbed him by his hair, pointing his head up at us. "We can do this the easy way, or we can do it the hard way." He took out an American 20. "Tell us where he is and you get money and we don't beat the piss out of you, then drag you over to the authorities for jacking tourists."

"I...I don' know — "

"Yes, you do." I said fiercely. "Last chance before you end up in jail tonight."

With that, his willpower evaporated. He shrugged. "All I know is I take him to the ferry for *Isla Mujeres* and tell him to stay at *Posada Del Mar*, de best place on the island. He pay me 40 American to watch for you, and den call de hotel and tell him quick-quick, if I foun' you."

I gave him the 20. "Understand, Renaldo, you try to warn him about us and we're going to know. Then I turn the *mala mujer* loose on you." I nodded toward the concourse outside. "She is not a nice person. I doubt they'll even find your body. Do I make myself *claro, amigo?*"

He gulped and nodded. *"Si, señor. Muy claro."*

We checked with one of the excursion promoters and found we needed a taxi to Puerto Juarez, which was 15 minutes north of Cancun. From there we had to take a ferry across to the island. We were on our way before the fellow had completed his last sentence. The last ferry left at 8:00 p.m. and it was 7:30.

Hailing a taxi and paying the driver double to drive like a bat out of hell (which they did normally), we made the dock just as they were casting off lines.

Fifteen minutes later, we were docking in *Isla Mujeres* — as picturesque a place as you'd care to find in Latin America, with fishing boats lazily canted on yellow sand beaches, nets drying in the sun, and ragged old hardwood piers leading into the crystal waters. Thatched-roofed huts mingled with colorful cinderblock houses, and a few bars speckled the shoreline, adorned with palms and flowering plants such as bougainvillea, hibiscus, and honeysuckle.

The island was an amalgam of old Spanish architecture and fishing village motif, interspaced with a few modest hotels and restaurants, but by and large it still held a quiet charm. *El Central* (downtown) was nothing more than a four-by-six-block area of older buildings to the north of the docks. There were only a couple of taxis — most people got around on motorbikes or bicycles. We managed to share a taxi with a couple from England, and had the driver take us to *El Posada Del Mar*. The fellow told us we were lucky on two counts. The ferryboat had thrown a piston just as it was docking. No one was leaving or coming until morning. And tonight was the annual celebration honoring the original Mayan inhabitants of the island. It was the biggest affair of the year for this couple of acres of sand and coral. "*Mucho tequila, el grande* parade, *baile* in de streets." Any other time, this might have been fun.

I spoke with the front desk clerk of the hotel, telling him that we were friends of Sundance's, and we wanted to surprise him. An American 10-spot greased the way. Kendra and Margo stayed in the lobby, making certain no one left in a hurry, and no one interrupted our visit. When we reached the room, I quietly checked the doorknob and found it unlocked. With a quick, slightly nervous glance at Will, I opened the door slowly.

Actually, I'm not sure what we expected, but it wasn't what we found. The room looked like it had been struck by a hurricane. Furniture was overturned, the mattress was off the bed and slit open, and Sundance's personal things were strewn everywhere. However, it was our old nemesis who won the "holy crap!" prize. He was tied spread-eagle on the bedsprings, arms and legs bound to each post. He looked like he'd lost a fight with a salad shredder. His face was an amalgam of blood and bruises and his chest had been used as an ashtray, repeatedly.

I released the gag and pulled the sock out of his mouth. He looked up at us and tried to smile, but settled on a grimace. "You're late.

The party's over," he mumbled through bruised lips. "I'm sure you're disappointed."

"That all depends," I said. "Did they get what they came for?"

He sighed bitterly. "Not at first. But they were persistent bastards."

Will glanced around the room, then back to Sundance. "You got ripped off, huh?"

Sundance spit out a little blood, most of it dribbling down his chin. "No, I'm a masochist. I do this two or three times a year, just for fun. Next month I'm planning on having someone break my legs in Switzerland."

I felt my stomach fall three stories. "They got our emeralds? The gold?"

Our battered rival nodded, and spit out part of a tooth. "So much for trusted compatriots. However, I've got an inkling of where they're going. After this score they'll probably retreat to their little den of iniquity in Mexico City. I could find them."

"They're not going anywhere tonight," I said. "The ferry's down, engine problems, and they've only just started to build an airstrip here. We've got the night to find them."

"I'll require a finder's fee...to help you find them," Sundance said nonchalantly. "I can identify them."

Will fuzzed up like a fence-rail cat. "A finder's fee! Are you freaking nuts? You're the frazy cucker who put us in this situation! Screw you! You tried to kill me! And you stole our emeralds!"

Sundance shook his head slowly. "Actually, to be perfectly correct, your partner gave me the emeralds and gold as somewhat of a promissory note regarding your health. It was all a misunderstanding. In addition, the companions I hired may have misinterpreted my intentions for you. I'm convinced now that they were both depriving some village of an idiot."

"I'm not paying you squat," Will spat. "You can take your finder's fee and — "

"Do you want to sit here and banter about semantics, or do you want to get our gold and emeralds back?" Sundance said.

"It's not 'our,'" I said. "It never was 'our.'"

"I'll take 20 percent," said the bandit on the bed.

"Twenty percent?" Will shrieked.

"God, this whole thing is depressing me," I moaned.

"Depression is simply anger lacking in enthusiasm," Sundance muttered, spitting out another piece of tooth. "I have enough enthusiasm for all of us. After all, I may have suffered irreparable damage to my outstanding good looks. It's personal now."

"Five percent" I said.

"Whoashit!" Will yelled. "You're giving him our money? That he stole?"

"He can identify them," I countered.

"Ten," said Sundance.

"Christ on crutches!" cried Will. "He — "

"Done!" I said.

The sun was nearing the distant mountains, gilding the still waters of the little bay near town — a small slice of paradise that had a great history of ancient Mayans and their artifacts, Spanish conquistadores, pirates, and lost treasure. Francisco Hernandez de Cordova sailed from Cuba and "discovered" the island in 1517. He gave the place its name because of the idols he found there — Mayan goddesses carved around a small temple at the southern end of the island. The statues are long gone, victims of Spain's religious indignation, but much of the temple had managed to survive the ravages of time, and man.

After allowing Sundance a chance to clean up and patch his wounds, we all headed to the bar at the *del Mar*, gathering around a small table on the patio by the main street. Will, whose personality hadn't quite recovered from the deal we struck, was bitterly complaining about the mosquitoes being big enough to stand flat-footed and screw a mud duck. Sundance, dressed in a fresh pair of white pants, a tropical shirt, and his ever-present white Panama hat, was on his third rum and coke, without any particular effect. Margo was silently eyeing our new partner with malevolence, but maintaining her best behavior. She hadn't cut him or shot him yet.

Around us, the ambience was heating up as villagers and tourists mingled in a slightly drunken collage through the streets, restaurants, and bars. As the annual parade began to move along the main street, images of favorite saints led the way, followed by *piñatas*, and fiery pinwheels held high and twirling, showering out multicolored sprays of sparks and smoke. Adults cheered and children dashed alongside, lighting individual firecrackers with playful enthusiasm — typical Latin American holiday entertainment. Several of the kids worked up enough courage to ask for a dollar or two and we shared a little money with them. One was so pleased he gave us some of his fireworks.

Will stuffed them in his vest. "Maybe we'll have our own celebration on the beach later tonight," he said.

The old yellow moon, obscured for a moment by drifting wafts of smoke from the fireworks, looked down with indifference. It had seen it all before. People come, people go, but the moon is the moon.

"So, I'm betting they had to get a room, if they could find one," I said to my companions.

Kendra shrugged. "This isn't exactly a tourist Mecca, and this," she said, nodding at the small parade, "isn't exactly Mardi Gras. There can't be more than half a dozen hotels here. We check them."

I was about to answer when I heard an airplane coming in from the mainland. "I thought there was no airstrip here," I mumbled to no one in particular.

"There isn't," said Will, pointing at the last of the light in the eastern sky. There in the distance was an amphibian Cessna 182, just like my own back in The Keys, already nosing downward about a mile from us, where *Isla Mujeres'* protected lagoon lay.

"Son of a bitch," said Sundance, slowly enunciating each word angrily. "I should have thought of that."

The parade was past us, working its way north. The street was clearing somewhat. Across the street, leaning against his vehicle and smoking a cigarette, was one of the few taxi drivers on the island. All five of us were up and running in unison. I waved two 20-dollar bills at the startled, older man.

"All yours, if you can get us to the lagoon in three minutes!"

At the sight of the money he quickly regained his composure. "*Si! Si!* For that I get you to Miami in 20 *minutos!*"

A moment later we were barreling down the poorly paved road at breakneck speed, racing by startled tourists on bicycles, and locals heading out of the town toward their small, tin-roofed houses along the beach. I could see the aircraft dropping its flaps and leaning in toward the flat waters of the lagoon in the center of the island, which was surrounded by mangroves, and a few homes here and there on higher ground. Because of the wind direction, the Cessna was landing at the closest end of the lagoon, where hundreds, perhaps thousands, of disturbed, angry waterfowl were scattering across the surface (heron, ibis, cormorant, flamingo) in a frenzied effort to get airborne. In moments they had lifted off in unison creating a huge, elongated cloud that flew the few hundred yards to the other end of the water and settled in again. It wasn't the first time a seaplane had disturbed them. They had a routine.

Ahead of us, off in the distance, I could see another taxi parked at the edge of the inland waters, about midway down on the lagoon. There were two men — big guys with short dark hair, in short-sleeved shirts and blue jeans — waving at the aircraft as it touched down a couple hundred yards from them.

"Go! Go!" I yelled at the driver, pointing frantically at the plane.

The girls were shouting at the fellow, and even the generally taciturn Sundance was thumping the dash with his fist and yelling for more speed. The old Chevy Impala was bouncing dangerously over the ruts of a road that had turned mostly into marl rock. Pedestrians were throwing themselves clear of the thundering vehicle while shaking fists at us and screaming obscenities.

The Cessna had completed its landing and had turned immediately, taxiing toward the men on shore.

Suddenly, I had a thought. "Do they have guns?" I yelled at Sundance.

He shrugged. "I don't think so. Knives. They had knives!"

The plane had reached Sundance's associates and the two men were wading out, scrambling into the craft.

"Crap!" I hissed vehemently. "We're not going to catch 'em!"

But the aircraft didn't have enough distance left to lift off, and was forced to taxi back to the far end of the lagoon and turn around for a takeoff run.

By the time we reached where the Cessna had met the men, the two thieves were already aboard the plane and it was taxiing back to the far end of the tidal pond for takeoff. With a nasty smile, one of the men shot us a one-fingered salute.

"That cuts it!" muttered Will angrily as we all scrambled out of the car. "They're gonna fly away with our loot while we stand here like tourists and wave to them!"

I glanced around frantically, trying to think of something — some way to stop them. But there was nothing we could do short of throwing rocks. It was then that I noticed all the waterfowl had settled at the opposite end of the lagoon — thousands of them. As I said, they knew the drill. I glanced over at Will, who was staring at the very same thing. "You remember Pete Timbers, who lost his airplane to flamingos off Johnson Key?" I said.

He grinned that old lopsided, mischievous smile he was famous for. "What are we waiting for?"

While the seaplane swung around in the distance and the pilot did a hasty preflight check, we quickly explained our plan to the others. It was a hell of a long shot, one-in-100 odds, but we had nothing to lose by trying. In seconds Will and I had dashed to the other end of the seaway and started wading in quietly toward the zillions of waterfowl in the marsh and on the water. Will had pulled the gifted fireworks from his vest, passing me a couple strings of firecrackers. He broke a punk (a smoldering fire stick used to light things with fuses) into pieces and gave me half.

"Work your way into the center of the marsh — quietly," he whispered while lighting our punks from some hotel matches I had taken off the patio table. "As far as you can get, without spooking the birds."

The pilot in the distance was good to go, and was pushing his throttles to the wall. The 182 surged forward and in seconds broke onto a plane. We were already wading well into the marsh, birds around us everywhere beginning to get skittish, near to taking flight. I could see my partner sloshing almost noiselessly deeper into the marsh, up to his knees, the whole body of perhaps two or three thousand birds beginning to squawk and chirp nervously.

We waited until the plane had reached the halfway point — the point of no return. To stay into the wind the pilot had to come right over the top of us. I looked over at Will and lit two strings of Black Cats I'd tied to mangrove branches. He lit a Roman candle and aimed it upwards. The pilot was pulling back on the controls; the plane was 200 yards downwind from us, rising upward.

The Roman candle "popped" in Will's hand, and a plume of smoke and fire emitted a green fireball, then another. The Black Cats began to explode like machine guns in a firefight. Almost in unison, the entire marsh squawked in terror. Thousands of wings beat furiously as terrified creatures slapped themselves loose from the water and the mangroves, and rose into the sky in a monstrous, colorful cloud of pink, black, and white. The entire collage was silhouetted against the last of the setting sun, gilded by its final rays. It was beautiful, extraordinary, and any other time I would have been overwhelmed by its splendor. But there was an airplane coming at us, with a pilot who was fighting to get above the undulating mass of birds that could wreck his craft like the hand of God.

The pilot was good, I had to give him that. While climbing out right at stall speed, trying to get as much altitude as possible, he began to bank, trying to dodge the huge collage of birds, which was beginning to break up in strings and patches. As it lost its cohesion, individual pelicans, flamingos, and ibises spread away from the center and rose out over the land on both sides of the lagoon.

Will and I and our friends could do nothing more. We stood there, frozen in the moment like desperate statues, watching the plane weave through the birds, waiting, hoping to hear the sound of a damaged prop, listening for a broken engine rhythm. But it never happened.

I was certain I noticed one small bird, perhaps a cormorant, smack the center of the nose cone on the prop, and I thought for sure... But gradually the Cessna rose above the dissipating mass of frightened creatures and banked toward the mainland. I saw my friend's shoulders slump. He dropped the Roman candle and it fell, hissing into the darkening water, drowning, like the last of our hopes. I sloshed over to him and we stood together in silence, watching the plane lifting up into the last of the sun.

"Well, we gave it a good try," Will said.

"Yeah," I muttered. "I guess we did, but that doesn't stop me from being wrist-slitting depressed."

"Did you know that depression is simply anger without enthusiasm?" he said, still staring at the airplane.

"So I hear."

Our friends were equally disappointed as they watched the plane gain altitude. Somehow Margo had ended up next to Sundance. She sighed angrily. He glanced over.

"Don't be too distraught, my lady. The trick to life, as I'm sure you well know, is being a survivor." Nodding at Will and me, he continued. "Those are resourceful fellows out there, and I am not without means and determination. We'll find our money."

"It wasn't your money."

He shrugged. "Semantics. Possession is nine-tenths of pleasure." He looked at her again. "If you could get past your immediate desire to cut off my soft parts, you might find that you and I are a lot alike. In the rat race of life, sometimes you have to take what you want and worry about the details later."

"Yeah, but even if you win the race, you're still a rat."

"Semantics," he said, watching the corners of her mouth struggle with a smile.

Will and I turned in unison and began to slosh back toward shore. Just then, we both heard it — a slight change in the sound of the engine on the departing Cessna. The smooth purr was interrupted with a cough, then another. I looked at my partner and he shrugged, still too fearful to accept what he had heard and afraid of being depressed again. But it came once more — two or three coughs and a change in the pitch.

"You know, I was certain I saw a mud duck fly into that nose cone," I whispered. "The air intake is just below the nose cone."

There was a pause and Will, still watching the plane, muttered, "Yeah, you clog that intake — say, with mud duck feathers and guts — and an engine can starve, quit working pretty quickly."

The engine coughed again, three times in a row, and suddenly the aircraft rolled into a bank, doing a 180 and returning toward the island, losing altitude. My friend turned to me with that broad grin of his. "Yep, that looks like a luckless mud duck problem. From the sound of that engine, he'll be lucky if he makes it back to land."

I could see Sundance and the girls waving and shouting excitedly on shore. I grabbed my partner's arm. "C'mon, I want to welcome them back."

But our friends in the Cessna had no intention of cooperating. The pilot was pushing his limping aircraft south, away from the town and any curious authorities. Second-guessing, I figured he was going to land at the lonely end of the island, where the old Mayan ruins were — maybe clean out his air intake, check the engine, then get the hell out of there.

"C'mon, buddy," I said, picking up the pace. "We gotta get back to the taxi."

Our friends had convinced the taxi driver to wait. We all piled into the car, telling our driver to "follow that airplane!" It wasn't much of a task as there was only one major road on the island that led down to the southern end, which, if the guidebooks were correct, was the first place the sun touched Mexican soil each morning. But none of that was important at the moment. We were in a race to get back our goods.

Central American taxi drivers are notorious for their abandonment of roadway etiquette and their affection for speed beyond common sense, but our guy must have been the fellow who taught the course. In fairness, I'm sure he was encouraged by the extra 20 I stuffed in his shirt pocket. We chased the plane at breakneck speed, bouncing and jolting over the terrible road and taking curves at speeds that would have made Richard Petty throw up. But it was a small island, and the pilot needed to set down quickly.

As I thought he would, he chose the very end of the key, running the plane up on the beach not a few hundred yards from the ancient Mayan temple. The sun was burying itself in the distant mountains and a pale, eggshell moon was rising on the other side of the world, casting a blanket of luminescence across a still sea, painting long shadows behind the shoreline palms and the old ruins on the hill. It was beautiful and eerie at the same time. Given my fondness of ancient civilizations, I would have loved to have spent a few hours exploring, but we had business to take care of.

There was no point in subterfuge. We were sure the guys in the plane had seen us chasing them. We got out of the car and walked over in unison. My logic was, there were three of them — two really, because the pilot had no vested interest in this, he was just hired help. There were five of us (not counting the taxi driver). The odds were good and we had Margo and Kendra, which greatly increased those odds.

Our driver parked the car and stayed with it. The rest of us strode over like something out of a bad street gang movie. I felt like I should be chewing gum and carrying a switchblade. Will and I had picked up a couple sturdy pieces of driftwood. The pilot, who had the cowling up on the engine, stopped working and turned. His two clients walked around to the front of the plane next to him.

"You have something that belongs to us," said Will, working up more bravado than he felt. "We want it back. Play nicely and nobody gets hurt. Otherwise, it's likely to get messy."

At that point both men pulled out large, nasty-looking revolvers.

I whispered testily to Sundance, "I thought you said they didn't have guns, man."

He huffed, frustrated. "I said I didn't think so. I'm not a freaking psychic, and I was a little busy at the time."

The larger one took a step forward. "Chu gotta be the most *estupido* people I see in a long time." He put his hands out, palm up in one, the gun in the other, like an old gangster. "What chu gonna do, now? Huh?"

The anger and frustration just got the better of me. "Listen, you bastards. There's no place you're gonna be able to — "

205

The report of the pistol interrupted my useless threat and I felt a stinging jab in my thigh. I looked down and saw blood welling out of the hole in my jeans. Kendra gasped and quickly moved to my side, kneeling and putting pressure above the wound, taking the scarf from her ponytail and tying it around my leg. I realized it was only a graze, but the point was made.

"That wasn't terribly bright of me, was it?" I grimaced as she knotted the scarf.

"Well, you're never too old to learn something stupid," she huffed angrily.

The big guy ran his gaze across us. "Anybody else got sonthin' to say?" He sighed. "Well, it look like our plans get changed a little now, 'cause of chu *idiotas*. Now I thin' we gonna take *las mujeres* with us, just as a little insurance that you no call anyone while we fly back to de mainlan'. Chu be good *muchachos,* we release them in Cancun."

While that would have terrified most women, I saw a brief look pass between Margo and Kendra, their eyes going hard for a fraction of a second — a telepathy of violence.

Margo turned to the men, her countenance changing to dread and fear. "Oh please, please, don't take us. Don't hurt us. We'll do anything you say."

The larger of the two men smiled. It wasn't exactly pleasant. "*Si,* maybe you will, but for now, chu going on a *aeroplano* ride."

Will got a knowing gleam in his eye. "Be careful what you wish for," he whispered out the side of his mouth.

The Mexican *banditos* held us at gunpoint for another 10 minutes while the pilot cleaned mud duck puree out of the air intake, then started the plane and checked all the instruments. When everything was in order, one of our captors held a gun on us while the other ushered our ladies aboard. Margo and Kendra had given us meaningful embraces, but there was absolutely no concern in their eyes.

"Piece of cake," Margo whispered in my ear as she held me.

As the plane lifted off, Will shook his head. "I wouldn't be in their place for all the gold that's been dug out of Mexico."

Lord, was he right. Not three minutes later, while the plane was still in sight, the sliding cargo door opened and two limp bodies tumbled out, twirling listlessly in slow motion for 1,000 feet before slapping the unforgiving dark waters below. The seaplane turned around and a few moments later it touched down in front of us, pulling up on the beach.

The pilot, white as a sheet, was escorted out by our ladies, who seemed no worse for the experience. Kendra handed Will the heavy travel bag containing our emeralds and gold, then took my hand. "Well hon, you ready to get back to town? We need to get that leg looked at." She glanced over at the terrified pilot. "Get out of here."

The guy didn't need any coaxing, but as he was hastily turning to leave, Margo caught his arm. "I want you to take a moment and imagine an empty space where your *cojones* are now." She gave him a second. "That's what it's going to feel like if you tell a soul about this."

As the man fairly ran for his plane, Margo sidled up to Will and put her arm around his waist. "C'mon sweetheart, time to get back to the *hacienda*. All this excitement has made your baby horny…"

We found the local doctor, who cleaned and stitched my wound. It was superficial, but he gave me a handful of pain pills and told me to take one every few hours. We all gathered for a nightcap at the hotel bar before retiring, to take the edge off all the excitement. During that time I noticed the oddest thing — Margo's level of vehemence for Sundance seemed to have receded slightly. I wasn't sure if that was a good thing, or a bad thing.

CHAPTER 18

The following morning we all met for breakfast in the hotel. My leg was sore as hell, but other than that, I was fine. I had been gently coddled by my lady and had slept like a baby — probably something to do with tequila and pain pills.

I couldn't say the same for my buddy Will. He looked like something the cat dragged in. Margo was somewhere between capricious and lethal — her usual self — but she was bright-eyed and upbeat, addressing conversation to everyone, even Sundance. At Sundance's prompting, we agreed to split the loot after breakfast, then return to Cancun and take the 310 back to The Keys.

Will was still resisting that arrangement, muttering that it was like paying someone to beat you with a rubber hose. Sundance countered that there were those who enjoyed being beaten with a rubber hose. Margo added that sometimes a little pain could enhance pleasure; heighten the senses. Will, hunched bleary-eyed over his oatmeal, grunted apprehensively.

After breakfast, the girls and Sundance went upstairs to pack. Will and I decided on a walk down to the beach, to take in a little fresh air and some sunshine. It had been a long couple of days.

The morning sunlight glistened on the water like shards of glass, the sand was soft and warm between my toes, and a perfect five-knot breeze caressed us as we walked. The fishing boats were just making their way out for the day and tourists were gathering at the docks for the first ferry back to the mainland. I took a deep breath and exhaled, pleased as punch to find we were returning home in one piece, with most of our plunder.

As we walked, making small talk or just drifting quietly and enjoying the ambience, Will, still looking at the water, suddenly said, "Kansas, I don't think Margo is the one for me. I don't think this is gonna work."

"Hmmm..." I said, stopping in the sand and looking at my friend. "Still having problems, huh?"

My buddy shook his head and looked at me. "Man, I never thought I'd say this, but I can't keep up with this woman sexually. I mean, I like sex as much as the next guy, maybe more, and a little bit of kinky is okay, but this woman is like a rabbit on crack — rucking felentless. And it's not, you know, gentle sex. It's like lovemaking sanctioned by the *Marquis de Sade*. I woke up in the middle of the night and found myself tied to the bedposts with a racquetball in my mouth." Will sighed again and looked at me. "Man, I'm even smoking after sex, like Margo."

"If you're smoking after sex, you're doing it too fast," I said with a smile, trying to lighten things, but the levity rolled right past my friend.

"I'm gonna have to tell her that I need a break, that maybe we're just not cut out to be a couple."

"Whooo," I muttered. "None of this is good. I'm beginning to think you might be right about her not taking rejection well."

My buddy winced. "Yeah, I know. She mentioned something in passing about a boyfriend who had to be 'taught' to love her, saying something about him disappearing. I don't know if that meant he disappeared on his own, or he 'got disappeared...'"

"You don't think she would really do that, do you?"

Will shrugged. "Who knows? She obviously has a penchant for whacking people."

"So, when do you plan to tell her?"

Will ran his fingers through his hair nervously, then straightened up, coming to a decision. "I'm gonna go back and tell her now. She's in the room packing. Now is as good a time as any. Besides, we're all going back in my plane; it's not likely she'll kill me right away."

Margo stood at the window, stiff, straight-backed, her eyes on the distant harbor. "I know this isn't really what you want. You're just stressed out. It's been a difficult time, being kidnapped and having people try to kill you. That can throw off your psychic and erotic equilibrium. I read that in a magazine just recently." She turned to Will. "I'll give you a little space; let you catch your sexual and emotional balance." She sighed. "I know I can be a little... demanding, okay? You're not the first person who's brought this to my attention." She chuckled uncomfortably, "But let's face it, you can't kill everyone who doesn't like you, can you? I mean there's the police and all the questions..."

The implication made Will's left leg dance nervously.

She sighed. "When we get back to Key West, you take a little time. I want you to like me. I don't want to...lose you. I mean rejection makes me so bitter, and I hate it when I get bitter. I'm not myself. I do terrible things." She chuckled once more, uneasily. "But none of that's going to happen...this time. We'll be all right..."

We took the ferry back to Cancun, and by noontime we were in the air in the 310, somewhere on the road to Key West again. It was obvious to Kendra and I that there was a rift between Will and his lady, but no one broached the subject on the way home. Margo chose to sit in the back with Kendra. Sundance, complaining about the possibility of having received irreparable damage to his nasal passages during his recent beating, curled up in the rear seat. I rode right seat, up front with Will. By five p.m., my friend had us touching down.

After customs, Will took a taxi to his shrimp boat home, and Kendra and I flew the plane back to Summerland Key, where he kept it and where my pickup was parked. Margo and Sundance caught a taxi to the Holiday Inn. Will and Margo had agreed to "a brief hiatus," as Margo called it. "So everyone can catch their breath."

That night, Will knocked down several beers to calm his nerves. By 10:30 he was reaching that place of comfortable, if not nirvanic inebriety. Things were going to be okay. With a little luck, he'd slide out of this relationship like a greasy eel. Let the crazy chick flog someone else's privates. He needed a week off, just for the scabs to heal. *Better love next time, baby...*

He was sitting on his couch, The Zombies on his stereo melodically telling him "She's Not There," when he heard a thump above. Not loud or heavy, more like someone leaping quietly from the gunwale to the deck. He waited, turning down the stereo slightly, but didn't hear anything else. *Nerves. His freakin' nerves were getting him.* He had just settled back into his couch when he heard it again — footsteps, very quiet, moving slowly, but it sure sounded like footsteps, working their way across the deck toward the cabin. He stood, wondering if he should get his pistol out of the drawer in the galley. Key West had its share of bandits. Marinas were popular haunts for them, and there was Tu Phat to be concerned with. Then again, it might be...

The footsteps halted.

"C'mon in," he said loudly. "Nobody home but me and my nine millimeter."

There was total silence on deck for a minute or two. He could hear the wind whistling softly and water slapping against the sides of the old lapstrake hull. The outriggers creaked and there was a soft chafing sound as the fenders rubbed against the dock. Then there was the sound of footsteps…receding…and the night went quiet again.

"I don't think there's any talking to, or buying off, a guy like Tu Phat," Will said the following morning, as Kendra and I had breakfast with him at Two Friends Restaurant on Front Street. "He's not gonna be content until he gets his pound of flesh."

Kendra wasn't happy about Margo not being there with us. Margo brought a lot to the table when it came to ugly business, but my lady understood that a "cooling period" was in order for her sister and Will.

"I think we need to be proactive here," Kendra said. "We either con him or snuff him, soon."

Will grimaced. "I don't like the idea of planning to kill someone. Makes me real uncomfortable."

"How about being dead?" she replied. "How uncomfortable does that make you? Whatever we're going to do, we need to bring it to him, not the other way around."

I sat there, watching the tourists on Front Street go gaily about their vacations in paradise while we plotted how to stay alive, and debated rubbing out someone. I couldn't suppress a bitter smile. Key West always seemed to teeter between the yin and the yang of peaceful serenity and tropical iniquity — anesthetized by ganja and rum while being wired to a quivering pitch by robust Cuban coffee and Caribbean intrigue.

A few blocks away at the Pier House, the phone rang in Tu Phat Shong's suite. One of his heavies answered it, listened, then hung up. He turned to Tu Phat. "They back, boss."

We spent part of the morning foraging for fresh information on Tu Phat. He was still at the hotel and it appeared he'd spent a good deal of time talking with bartenders, fishing guides, and friends of ours. Fortunately, no one knew exactly where we were, but it was just a matter of time. We were considering offering the Chinese/Darien a deal — the emeralds and gold for our lives. But there was no guarantee he would keep his end of the bargain.

Kendra and I decided to go back to Big Pine. We had recently ordered a custom wetsuit and a spear gun for her, and Mary Ann at Underseas Dive Shop had called, saying the gear had arrived. We thought maybe we'd run out to Hawk Channel and check the coral heads for grouper — someplace where we'd be less conspicuous.

Will returned to his boat, pulling up in the marl parking area and glancing around before getting out of his Mustang. He walked to the dock, then down to the shrimper, stepping onto the deck and checking the entranceway for the seagull feather he had carefully wedged between the door and the jam. It was still there. He breathed a little easier as he unlocked the door and entered. Grabbing a beer from the fridge, Will pulled off his fruit-juicy shirt and moved to the closet to hang it up. He opened the door and screamed, staggering back, hand on his heart, the beer bouncing onto the floor and rolling against the floorboards. There was Margo, standing in the closet, wearing nothing but a red-feathered Fantasy Fest mask and holding a kitchen knife, her caramel red hair flowing down over her shoulders, just reaching the tops of her sloping breasts.

"I know I told you I was going to give you some space," she said, holding her hand out, palm up. "But then I got to missing you, and I thought, *What if he's missing me, too? Maybe what he really needs is just an exceptional blow —* "

"Jesus!" Will moaned, leaning against the adjacent bureau, still holding his chest. "Margo, you can't..." He took a breath and collected himself. "You can't just be..." He glanced down at her hand. "What's with the knife?" he asked cautiously.

"I was going to make some fruit salad for you."

"Margo," Will began again, gently. "We agreed to take some time off. Don't you remember?"

She stepped out of the closet. "Is that really what you want?"

Will paused, weighing the situation, then sighed. "Yeah. Yeah, that's what I want. It's what I think we need."

She looked at him. "If you're not careful you could lose me."

Will wanted to say, "Promise?" But he bit his tongue.

"I've been seeing Sundance," she said. "Just as friends. Actually, we have a lot in common."

Yeah, you're both freakin' sociopaths, Will thought.

"He understands the pain I'm feeling. He's been rejected by you, as well."

"Because he tried to kill me, and stole from me."

"He says I need to get on with my life, but I should still probably punish you for causing me such pain." She paused again. "I don't want to hurt you." She flipped the knife in her hand to where she was holding the blade, then flipped it again, back to the handle. "But it's still on the list..."

"Margo," Will said softly. "It's not that I don't still care about you..." *Jeez, you're a lousy liar.* "... but you need to go. I need some time to myself."

Suddenly, she straightened up. "You're just like all the others!" she spat angrily, hand tightening on the knife handle. "Oohh, Margo, you're the one, you're the one, and then suddenly you're not the one anymore!"

Will inadvertently backed up, and her eyes narrowed. "If you're not careful I may have to put you out of my misery." Then she flicked the knife. It whirled through the air and thudded into the cabinet next to Will's head. Before he could do anything else, she swept out of the room and was gone, the cabin door slamming behind her naked, shapely ass.

My friend slid down the wall, sitting on the floor, elbows on his knees. "I could have taken her," he muttered. "I could have." After a moment, he exhaled and shook his head. "Who am I kidding? She would have eaten my lunch and I'd be wearing my balls around my neck now. What the hell am I gonna do?"

Will finally got up, found his beer and opened it, then took a shower. He liked drinking beer in the shower. There was just something about it — a man thing. About an hour later, while making a sandwich, Will felt the boat shift almost imperceptibly and there was a knock on the door. Cautiously, Will got up, tucked his pistol in the small of his back, and walked to the entranceway by the forecastle. There was a small, slightly balding Hispanic man standing at the door. He had almost sad brown eyes, with small wire-rimmed spectacles, and was dressed in tourist shorts and a Jethro Tull T-shirt.

"Are you Will Bell?" he asked.

"Yeah," Will answered cautiously.

"Good," said the small man, as he pulled out one of the new police tasers, stepped in, and stuck it against Will's chest.

When Kendra and I got back from the patch reefs of Hawk Channel, there was a recorded message on the phone from Will. It was important I was to come as quickly as possible, alone, and meet him at his boat. Kendra wasn't happy about my going alone, so she followed me onto Stock Island in her MGB and agreed to wait at The Hogfish Bar and Grill until we knew what was happening. I got to

Will's shrimp boat and knocked on the cabin door. A small, slightly balding Hispanic man answered.

"Are you Kansas Stamps?" he asked.

I nodded cautiously. "Yeah."

That was pretty much all I remembered...

When I came to, the sun was working its way into the sea, turning the cumulus clouds on the horizon into soft, pink cotton candy. The edges of the sky were already going grey, the wind had died, and the air had that warm, humid feel of early evening. I could hear mosquitoes buzzing around me, and smell the ocean and the sweet/sour odor of mangroves. But as I recovered from the painful stupor of being zapped by a taser, there were other major surprises.

First off, I was bound to a piling of some sort, what looked/felt like the remnants of an old pier extending out into a deserted channel, probably on the gulf side of The Keys. The water nearly rose to my chin, and my hands were wrapped around the piling, behind me, secured painfully tight. My feet could just touch the mucky sand bottom.

I immediately realized I wasn't alone. Someone was tied behind me, to the same piling, in the same fashion. I noticed a couple other disconcerting things. Around my neck hung what appeared to be a huge, raw haunch of bloody meat — probably the hock of a pig. Blood from the luckless creature was washing around me and beginning to work its way down the channel with the outgoing tide. Not good...

As I squirmed, I felt the person behind me come to attention. "Kansas? You awake?"

Good Lord! It was Will!

"Yeah, yeah. But I'm gonna try to go back to sleep now, because this is a miserable freaking dream."

"Man, I wish it was a dream," he said anxiously.

I spit out a mouthful of water. "How did we get here?"

"I don't know about you, but some weasely little guy with a taser zapped me at my boat, and the next thing I knew I was in the back of a van all trussed up and blindfolded," Will spat angrily. "I gotta tell you, I'm really over being tied up and left in vans. Anyway, an hour or so later someone opens the van and dumps you in. Then we take a ride for about a half hour. Finally, we go off the paved road onto marl for about five minutes. Then they drag us out and dump us in a little rowboat. I could hear the oars splashing." He took a shaky breath. "Next thing I know, I'm dumped over the side, into the water, and a couple of guys jump in and are tying me to a piling. Then they tie you. Of course, you're still out for the count. Then they put the pig haunches around our necks. I can hear them — Central American accents, joking about us being dinner *para los tiburones.* Most of all, I can hear the guy who stays in the boat giving them orders. Wanna guess as to who that was?"

"Tu Phat," I muttered angrily. "Tu Phat."

"They ripped off our blindfolds just as they shoved off for shore." Will humphed, somewhere between angry and scared. "They didn't want us to miss the show. The way I figure it, we're in one of the backcountry channels. From the timeframe I'd say somewhere near Kemp Channel, by Cudjoe or Knockemdown Keys."

The sun had just slipped under the rim of the horizon and shadows were growing on the water and in the distant mangroves, but I could see the spot on shore where they had come in — an old mud and marl track not unlike the hundreds that exist throughout The Keys, connecting eventually to U.S. 1.

"Mmmm, Kemp..." I grunted. "Known for lots of sharks..."

"Yeah... *mucho tiburones*... and it's starting to get dark. Feeding time..."

As if the devil himself had heard us talking, I saw the first fin break water about 50 feet from us, coming in from the main channel, moving leisurely, cutting a slow "S" pattern as it picked up the blood scent in the water. I don't mind telling you, I peed my pants a little.

My partner's head came around sharply a few degrees to the left. "Ooohh, God! Two fins coming my way..."

I don't care who you are, sharks are the things of which nightmares are born. There is nothing more terrifying than being out of your element and at the mercy of a creature whose singular, most elemental driving force is to kill unmercifully with slashing, ripping tenacity, while simultaneously eating you. But sharks are rarely in a hurry. They're cautious creatures. When their prey isn't splashing or swimming in a frantic fashion, they like to check things out, and will often bump their target with their nose to get a sense of how vulnerable or yummy it is. Blood in the water helps move this process along, and at this point, we were feeling very vulnerable and terrifyingly yummy.

As we struggled with our bonds, I could count half a dozen fins in the water around us. Nothing huge; this was the backcountry and the bigger boys tended to work the reefs. But an eight-foot shark (two or three of those in the water around us) can really make a mess of you.

"Oh, Lord," wheezed Will, his body tensing as a seven-footer passed within inches of him, the fear in his voice a palatable thing. "Of all the ways to go...eaten by sharks! I should have listened to my mother. 'Don't go movin' to The Keys with that rascally friend of yours. You'll just end up in trouble!'"

"Rascally friend? Rascally friend? I thought your mother liked me!"

Suddenly, my attention was drawn to the dark water on my left, as a big one glided to and fro in front of me. From the lazy motion of the large tail, I was guessing a hammerhead. I was so mesmerized with terror, I didn't notice a smaller shark, maybe six feet, come in just under the surface and nudge me with its nose, checking out my edibility, its sandpaper skin scraping me raw. I screamed like a child, now struggling madly at my bonds, experiencing a level of terror I hardly knew existed. But it was no use. Tu Phat's people had done their job well.

In the distance, the top of a huge, orange moon was crawling out of the mangroves on the opposite side of the strait, casting a luminescent swath across the narrow channel in which we were imprisoned. The wind had died completely, and the water, with the exception of the slight movement of an incoming tide, was silky calm. The moon cast a fair amount of light, allowing us to see the hungry denizens moving in, sweeping back and forth in nervous, erratic, ever emboldened patterns around us. But there was one, the big hammerhead, that was growing more and more audacious, making sweeps in and out, getting closer each time, the bloody scent of the meat around our necks growing increasingly irresistible.

"Will," I whispered, frightened senseless, and suddenly faced with my own immortality. "If this is it, I just want you to know — "

"Yeah, back at you, my friend. You've been the best — "

"Actually, I was going to tell you that I slept with Cass after you guys broke up. I ran into her in Key West one day and we had a couple of drinks, and it just happened. I always felt bad about that."

"Hmmmm," my partner said, obviously weighing that insight. "Well, then, seeing as we're probably at the end of the immediate food chain here, I should probably mention that Celeste — you remember Celeste, your first wife who left with Angie, my first wife, to go live in St. Kitts? — Celeste got around a little after she moved in with Angie. Actually, she visited me a couple of times. I always felt bad about that..."

"Son of a bitch..." There was a pause. "Oh well, water under the bridge..."

I watched as the big hammerhead cruised out about 30 feet, then suddenly swirled around. It turned hard and straightened, its dorsal rising out, cleanly cutting the water as it aimed unerringly at us.

"You've been a really good friend...and I always..." Will gritted, terror edging each syllable as the shark came at us.

"You too, buddy..."

It was nothing more now than the toss of a coin, the luck of the draw, and we both knew it, tied to a barnacled post as a primordial killing machine picked up speed for the hit, the blood in the water having finally driven it to the point of carnage. It was the single most terrifying thing I have ever experienced. I watched as the huge creature rolled its hammer-like head out of the water and extended its jaws, peeling back the "lips" around its teeth for the strike. I saw all this in terror-filled, moon-painted, slow motion — the head rising up out of the water, actually striking my shoulder; the huge, black, totally indifferent eye so close to me that I could clearly see the thin nictitating membrane rolling over the eyeball in protection at the last minute. It was truly horror incarnate as it struck me in the chest, slamming me against the piling hard enough to crack a rib, and I remember shrieking mindlessly again and again. Will was screaming as well, because, hell, he was tied right next to me. It could have just as easily been him, and maybe the shark would come back for seconds. Who knew?

But there was one small piece of good news in this whole event: hammerheads have notoriously small mouths for their size, and this one was no exception. He managed to get his jaws around and into the huge haunch of pig against my chest, but not into me. Of course, the shark didn't know this, and he immediately began the savage ripping/tearing that follows a strike, his big tail thrashing back and forth for impetus. He would have probably wrenched me to death with the rope around my neck that held the ham, but his razor teeth sliced through the cord that bound it. After the initial strike and a flurry of twisting, he turned and swam away, carrying the haunch.

I'll admit, there was definitely some poop in my pants, and neither of us could get enough air in our lungs, but there was one other development — the old, weathered piling to which we were tied had been struck with such force that it had cracked at the base and was leaning over. Will was bent downwards, face just inches from the water, and I was leaning upwards slightly, looking at the rising moon.

"Will! Will!" I yelled. "The post, the post! It's broken at the bottom. Maybe we can — "

But my buddy was already responding, straightening up, feet gathering purchase on the sandy bottom, pushing and pulling with his body in almost superhuman fashion. (Being attacked by a shark will do that to you.) I began to help, using our back-and-forth motion to break it loose completely.

"You're not dead until you see the devil!" grunted my partner vehemently. "You're not freakin' dead until you see the devil!"

In just seconds, the weathered, waterlogged wood gave and snapped, and we were standing on our feet, still tied to a piling, but mobile. There was still the issue of about a half-dozen sharks around us, but many were preoccupied with the piece of meat the hammerhead was working on.

"The shore!" I yelled, gasping, trying to keep my head above water (Will had a good five inches of height on me). "The shore!"

Carefully, like some neurotic tubeworm, we began to shuffle toward the beach and the mangroves about 50 yards from us. I could still see fins in the water, moving to and fro, swinging in toward us and circling around, (and Will still had a haunch of meant around his neck.) But my buddy and I weren't moving radically enough to incite attack, and we were quickly stumbling into shallower water — to our waists, then to our knees, and finally we hobbled out onto the sand, collapsing in an hysteria of gratefulness.

We lay there for a few minutes, faces in the sand, being assailed by mosquitoes and working on getting our breathing back to normal — not saying anything, trying to mentally digest what we'd just been through.

"I've got poop in my pants," said Will quietly.

I grinned despite it all. "Oohh, I'm way ahead of you, man. I've had poop in my pants for some time now. Every frightening thing that happens to me for the rest of my life I will measure by this experience."

"We need to get untied from this freaking post," my friend added, his confidence returning.

"Maybe I can help with dat," said a familiar voice from the shadows. We craned our necks like neurotic seagulls and gasped. Rufus! Rufus! It seemed impossible, but there, squatting in the sand at the edge of the mangroves was our old, mystical Rastaman friend.

For the better part of a decade, since Will and I first moved to The Keys, we had the distinct pleasure of knowing, and occasionally interacting with this strange Jamaican. He had the unerring disposition of inadvertently showing up and presenting us with the possibility of bizarre, profitable adventures, or appearing when we were in a jam and providing us with a solution, a suggestion, a potion, or any combination thereof, which generally saved our asses. He was like a gangly, intuitive, guardian angel, part mystic fisherman, part Rastaman, and part free spirit, who for some reason had singled out two crazy youngsters and guided them into adulthood while taking advantage of their talents in certain enterprises in which he was involved. I suspected we weren't the only ones he provided with his remarkable services. But here he was again, not an iota of change in all the years we'd known him — shoulder-length dreadlocks, an aging Reggae T-shirt, haggard shorts – same old Rufus.

As he cut the ropes that bound us, and pulled the meat off of Will's neck, I asked, "How? How did you know we were here?"

He shrugged. "It be a long story. I was coming to see you, to tell you I sensed many unpleasant happenings circling around you, but when I get to your boat, I see Kansas being shoved into back of van. Da van drives off, so I follow. But I lose it in traffic on Cudjoe Key, so I have to backtrack to see where it turn. It take me a while, but finally I find you," he pointed at the water, "out dere."

"Why didn't you come out and get us?" I said with exasperation.

"Dere be sharks out dere, mon."

"But you could have helped us," Will persisted.

"How you know I didn't?" he said with that mystical, bright-toothed smile, his weird, grey eyes lighting up. "How you expect dat old post break so easy in da water? How come dem sharks don' eat you, mon?"

"They sure as hell tried," I muttered, standing and brushing myself off, then offering a hand to Will.

Rufus scratched his nose for a moment. "You tiny wrasses been swimmin' too close to da moray's mouth lately. Da Grand Messenger of da Wisdom of Ganja say sometimes the only real difference between *cojones* and idiocy is living to tell the tale. You little fishes just about lucked out, and this journey you on not over yet." He gazed at us. "You know what I'm sayin'? You got yourselves in some deep caca with da China man."

I glanced at Will. *He knew about Tu Phat! How?*

Our Jamaican friend took a breath. "Da Grand Messenger also say, 'Patience and faith are da hungry monkey's companions while he seeks the virtue of timing.' Patience, little monkeys. Choose your time." At that moment he stood and reached into his shorts pocket, pulling out a tiny plastic bag containing a white powder. "Once again, I have little gift for you. Do you remember what I give you many years ago, for da bad lawyer man in Key West?"

Again, Will and I glanced at each other. He was talking about the attorney, Justin Mames, from over five years ago.

"Yeah, I said. "The magic dust."

Rufus nodded. "Yes, but in truth, it is not magic." He paused for a moment, as if embracing an ancient memory. "It is potion brought to da New World by my ancient people, used for generations, made from da rarest tropical plants in Africa and da Caribbean, used to calm da mind for acceptance of... *suggestion...*"

Will and I traded glances again, simultaneously thinking about our experience a couple of years ago with a strange "truth device" that had similar properties.

Rufus continued. "We have used it for healing maladies of da mind for centuries. But it can be used for other purposes, as well." He looked at me, then my friend, making sure he had our attention. "Pour powder in palm of hand and blow it into face of da person you wish to change. Do not breathe in! Dere is no will but yours with magic dust, mon. What you say, dey will be. You have maybe five minutes after dey inhale dust to bury thought in dere head." He paused. "Dis is good choice for you. No need for people to become dead, mon — bad for your spirit. You know what I mean?"

He put out his hand and I took the small packet of white powder.

I nodded gratefully. I knew what he meant. Getting around this without somebody pushing up daisies would be okay with me...*if* the magic dust really worked.

Our old friend continued. "It maybe wear off at some time in future, but it be many, many moons. By den, who knows?" He gazed at us affectionately. "Cool driftings, mons. May your life eggs break cleanly an' da Great Tortoise grant you a moonlit path to da sea..."

CHAPTER 19

Rufus took us to his ride, a barely reputable VW Bug, but it got us back to Will's boat. He wished us luck, saying that he would be around for a few days, then he would return to his dilapidated fishing boat and head up The Keys. Once again our friend had come to us in our time of need and offered a solution. But we still had to figure out a way to get to Phat, before he got to us.

I called Kendra from Will's, to let her know we were okay. Her tone vacillated from grateful relief to anger.

"Good Lord! I've been terrified. What the hell's going on? I was certain something had happened to you!"

"It had. Tu Phat got to us. Fortunately, an old friend saved our asses. Listen, things are heating up. I want you to get out of the house. Rent a room at The Big Pine Motel. I'll call you there in an hour or so, when we've got a plan worked out."

We were wet and filthy, so Will said he'd get us some clothes. "They'll be a little big for you," he called from his bedroom, but they'll — HOLY CARAAP!" he suddenly yelled.

I came rushing in. "What the hell's going on?"

Will was standing there, naked, his undergarments drawer open. On the floor was a pair of his underpants. They were moving. He took a pen from his desk and carefully flipped the skivvies, allowing us to see inside. Someone had carefully sewn a small tarantula into the garment, and the creature was squirming angrily.

"Freakin' Margo!" he fumed. "Margo! I'm tellin' you the woman is off-the-cliff bonkers. If I hadn't been payin' attention, Donkey Boy and the Twins would have been spider meat." He turned to me. "I don't know what I'm gonna do, but I gotta get out of this situation. There's no persuading her..."

"There are two theories on arguing with women. Neither of them work," I said dryly.

After showers and fresh clothes, we were ready to tackle the next stage of our dilemma — how to get Tu Phat close enough to blow powder into his face without him killing us.

It was actually Will who came up with a novel suggestion. We were sitting on the deck of the shrimper, Jimmy Buffett's "Havana Daydreamin'" wafting up from the cabin, watching the stars glitter on the surface of the water and listening to mullet splash in the

221

harbor. My friend suddenly set down his beer and turned to me.

"A backgammon game. How about I challenge him to a backgammon game? We'll make it enticing. If he wins, we give him the lion's share of the Darien emeralds and gold. If we win, we walk away free men. No more chasing us."

"What's going to make him keep his word?" I asked.

"Doesn't matter. He probably wouldn't keep it anyway. But I'm betting he can't resist another round of backgammon with me — to see if he can beat me and get some of his pride back. Then, of course, there are the emeralds and the gold..."

I grinned. "Pretty fair incentive for a greedy egomaniac. Let's make the call — see if we can set something up. He's at the Pier House."

Will held up his hand. "Not so quick, little hungry monkey. We need a plan to pull this off. It needs to happen where there are lots of witnesses, and somewhere we can get away quickly if things go good or bad."

"Maybe someplace like the Pier House, or a restaurant?" I suggested. "Louie's Backyard, Two Friends? Or maybe that new place, Schooner Wharf?"

"Yeah, maybe," my buddy said. "But you know what I think would work best? Sunset Celebration at Mallory Square. Lots of people, and plenty of room to move if we need to."

"Ya, mon. Perfect."

Sunset Celebration in Key West came about in the 1960s, when "flower children" descended on Key West in search of the proverbial "paradise," often gathering at Mallory Pier to get high and groove on the cloud formations at sunset. Eventually, naturalists, tourists, and a handful of enterprising street vendors joined them. The event reached a pivotal period in the '70s and '80s when it morphed from a pure sunset celebration to somewhat of a flea market (and later to a cruise ship dock). But before it got totally out of hand, an organization called The Key West Cultural Preservation Society drafted some guidelines and negotiated a lease with the City of Key West to manage the "sunset experience" and ensure its "artistic integrity." Sunset at Mallory Square went on to become one of the most popular, well-known aspects of Key West, combining the area's cultural and natural flavor in one event, every evening.

"We need to set it up for about seven p.m.," Will added. "By the time we finish our backgammon game the sun will be setting, the crowd will be at its peak, and we can wrangle an escape. Now, here's what I have in mind for that…"

When he finished, I couldn't help but smile. "So make the call, man."

Tu Phat was lounging on his couch, watching television, enjoying the World Wide Wrestling Federation's latest event. The phone rang and one of his heavies answered, listened for a moment, then brought it over to his boss. Three minutes later, Phat placed the instrument in its cradle. "It's so much nicer when the pigeon comes to you," he muttered with a smile.

After firming up a little of the plan for our backgammon-game cum-magic-dust-assault, I headed up The Keys to The Big Pine Motel, where Kendra was waiting in room number four. When she opened the door, she threw her arms around me, then dragged me in.

"Lord, I'm so glad you're okay," she gasped as we sat on the bed, facing each other. "So, tell me, what happened?"

I told her about Tu Phat's people and the sharks, and Rufus, then explained the plan we had for the magic dust. We'd bring about half of the emeralds and gold to Sunset at Mallory Square, and Will would play one more game of backgammon with Tu Phat. But when the moment was right, we'd distract his heavies (this was probably where Kendra would come in), and give him a faceful of magic dust. A simple but precise command that he "completely forget about us or any desire to harm us, and return to Panama to live happily ever after" would hopefully get everyone out of the weeds — if it worked. If it didn't, we'd turn Kendra and Margo loose…

Kendra chuckled, pleased, but not exactly convinced that this magic dust thing would work. I explained that we had used it before with a Key West Attorney, Justin Mames, and it had been remarkably effective — to the point that we had Mames bouncing around on all fours and barking like a dog every time he told a lie. It ruined his political career, but that was only a sideline to his drug-running business, anyway.

"Well," Kendra said. "I'll be glad to help…" She looked at me. "You sure you don't want Margo and me to just whack him? Wham, bam, thank you, ma'am, and it's done?"

I blew out a breath of uncertainty. "I know you could do that, but it's kind of a karma thing with Will and me. If we can get out of this without offing him, I'd feel better about it."

My lady shrugged. "Your call. I'll do whatever you need me to do."

I smiled lasciviously, reaching for her. "I have something I'd like you to do for me, right now…"

An hour later, we were hungry. I had given Will the phone number for The Big Pine Motel and asked him to call if there were any new developments. Kendra stayed by the phone while I went to The Baltimore Oyster House on Big Pine for a couple of dozen oysters on the half shell, two orders of French fries, and a six-pack of beer. If we had to stick around, we might as well enjoy ourselves.

Around midnight Margo and Sundance were lying in bed at the Holiday Inn in Key West, smoking cigarettes. Bertie Higgins was whispering about "Casablanca" through the portable radio on the bureau, as a ceiling fan twisted up the lazy whorls of smoke.

Out of nowhere, Margo, still staring at the ceiling, said, "Guess what? I know where the rest of Kansas' and Will's gold and emeralds are — or rather, where they're going to be in the immediate future." There was a loud silence. "It seems they're setting up an exchange of sorts, tomorrow, to buy themselves out of a pickle with a Panamanian bad guy. All that gold, and those emeralds…"

She gave it a moment to sink in.

"What if we relieved them of that burden before they gave it away?" She turned to Sundance and ran a finger down his naked shoulder. "That might be an excellent way to punish Will for being so…*inattentive* to me."

That brought an exhausted, if not somewhat ulcerated Sundance around. He had never encountered a woman this relentless — so remarkably bent on squeezing the last ounce of gratification out of every carnal congress. He wasn't sure it was a bad thing, but it was somewhat challenging. Anxious to divert her attention for a while, and certainly intrigued by another shot at the emeralds and gold, he said, "And you know this how?"

Margo stubbed out her cigarette and turned to her new lover. "Kendra called me tonight, while you were out buying wine. She was quite free with the details. But then, I'm her sister. We've always talked…"

"Actually, that might be an excellent way for some restitution," Sundance muttered. "Will is obviously a cad, without conscience, or taste. How otherwise could he neglect a woman of your obvious charms? You could hurt him in the one place that matters the most — his pocketbook. Imagine, my dear, what we could do with that kind of immediate wealth..."

"We?" she said, eyebrows rising.

"Well, my lady, this could be a challenging affair. I would think a partnership would be almost essential to ensure success. After all, the important thing is that we punish him, right?"

Margo thought about it for a moment, then offered a reminiscent smile. There was a part of her that still wanted that lanky, long-haired island boy — *needed* him. Hell, if he came through that door right now she'd be all over him like sugar ants on ice cream. But the part of her where her pride resided had grown ugly. She had been shunned like a two-bit hooker — refused. Again. But if Will was to be brought to his knees in some fashion, he might need her more...

"Yes, let's hurt him, and make ourselves rich in the process," she whispered mischievously as she twirled a lock of Sundance's long, sandy locks with her finger. She grabbed him by the hair and kissed him passionately, then pulled his face slowly downward, toward the part of her that never felt anything but want.

While Sundance was headed down to the place he affectionately called "Twatamala," we were laying plans. It should have been an easy thing. We figured we'd rent a space and set up a backgammon board on an old lobster trap at Mallory Square, near the water, but in between vendors and street performers, so there were lots of witnesses. We'd get Tu Phat to join us there and with just a little luck, Will would eat Tu Phat's lunch at backgammon one last time. We'd blow some magic dust in our adversary's face and tell him he didn't know us, never did, and didn't care, and we'd be drinking toasts to our cleverness at Schooner Wharf by dusk. But just as a backup, that night I called our old Panamanian buddy, Benny, in Fort Lauderdale. You could never tell when a little backup with a blowgun might come in handy.

"Hello, Benito," I said.

"Kansas! *Es bueno* to hear fron' you. Was' goin' on, *amigo?*"

I smiled at the sound of his voice. It's always that way with good friends, and Benny, for all his initial shortcomings, had become a good friend. But he was living the high life in Lauderdale, and I didn't know how receptive he'd be to helping us right now.

"I know you've probably got lots going on — chasing women and becoming the Latin version of John Travolta — but I've got a little situation here in Key West, and I might could use your — "

"Where chu wan' me, *amigo*?" said my diminutive friend without hesitation. "You know Benny be dere."

I grinned again. Friends were the most priceless possession a person could have. "Catch the next flight down to Key West, and call Will when you arrive." I paused. "And bring your blowgun, with a dart mixture that's not fatal. You might get a chance to be Zorro again. Who knows?"

Benito got in at six that evening and stayed at Will's boat overnight. The following morning Kendra rented us a couple of rooms at the Pier House, which was just a stone's throw from Mallory Square — one for Will and Benito, and one for Kendra and me.

By nine o'clock the four of us had rendezvoused and were gathering up a good portion of our gold and emeralds again at our bank, as surety for the plan. Tu Phat would undoubtedly want to see the real thing. After the bank we parked in front of the Pier House. It was time for mimosas at the bar, to celebrate the first stage of the plan.

We made our way to the lobby with the small but heavy suitcase. Kendra stopped at the front desk to help Will and Benito register for the room she had reserved. I strolled along one of the outside corridors toward the room Kendra had rented for us. It was early and still quiet. Most of the guests were at breakfast or still sleeping off a memorable night in Key West. I turned a corner near the rear of the building and a fellow stepped out of a laundry room — a large, slightly rotund man with long locks of blond hair, poorly disguised in a trench coat and a Groucho Marx mask (big nose, bushy eyebrows, and glasses).

"Give me the suitcase and I won't use this," he said, nodding at the small caliber gun in his right hand.

"That's a really crummy disguise, Sundance."

"I'm sorry, you have me mistaken for someone else. Perhaps some other handsome, extremely debonair individual. Now give me the suitcase."

I shook my head, taking a step backwards. "I don't think so. How in the hell did you find us?" I heard a shuffle behind me. I was about to turn when something with a heavy indifference smacked me on the backside of my head, and the lights went out.

Margo, holding a sock filled with pea rock, stood over the prostrate body and looked at Sundance. "I told you it was a stupid disguise." She knelt and took the suitcase. "Welcome to the Karma Café," she whispered. "There are no menus. You get served what you deserve..." Then she looked up at Sundance. "C'mon. Time to find our new future."

I awoke with Will patting me on the cheek. "Hey, Kansas. C'mon, buddy..."
I felt like The Grateful Dead had crawled inside my head and turned up their amplifiers.
When I could see straight, Will asked, "What happened, man?"
"Sundance happened," I moaned. "And probably Margo. I suspect she's the one who whacked me on the head."
My buddy spit out an expletive. "Well, that tears it. Now we're really screwed. What am I supposed to show Tu Phat now?"
I thought about it as I slowly sat up and twisted my head from side to side, wincing. "Maybe he'll just have to have faith." I looked up at my buddy. "You'll have to sell him on you not being stupid enough to bring an attaché case full of rocks to a backgammon game with a man who would probably kill you outright if he knew the truth."
Will shook his head incredulously. "A case full of rocks, huh?"
"Bricks, if we can find them. They're heavier. Besides, we've got Benny here, with his blowgun for backup. He'll fit right into all the crazies at Sunset Celebration." I smiled at my friend. "No offence, Zorro."
Benito shrugged.
"You sound real confident for a guy who hasn't got his ass on the line," muttered Will.
"I've got a plan. I'll be close by, providing a distraction if things get sticky."
"A distraction, huh? For a 300-pound Panamanian sociopath with no sense of humor, and a couple hit-men heavies?" Will ran his fingers through his hair in that nervous fashion of his. "Then there's crazy Margo and Sundance. We have to catch them before they disappear forever with our loot." He exhaled, exasperated. "Where are we going? And why are we in this freaking hand basket?"

I had to smile at my partner's offbeat sense of humor. "We may be in the hand basket, but hell's a ways off yet. We can pull it off. But you're right about one thing — we've got to find Sundance and Margo — like, right away."

Will nodded emphatically but raised his hand. "Let's not be too impulsive here. We gotta think this out. Remember what Rufus says; "The legacy of the hasty monkey is the furry taste left in the lion's mouth."

"The lion here is Margo. Sundance is just a freakin' jackal."

We quickly caught up with Kendra in our room, and explained what had happened. My lady sat on the bed, shoulders slumped. She looked up at me. "I'm so sorry. I...I guess I should have known..." She sighed and gazed up at Will. "You're not the first, of course. There's been a fairly long list of suitors. Sometimes she gets bored, but most of the time she just frightens them, or exhausts them, until they disappear." She glanced out the large glass doors toward the ocean. "I like to think that they just left her, and some, I know, did. But some..." She shrugged woefully.

"Well, whatever happens to Sundance is his own misfortune," I said. "He's a big boy, and no less conniving than her, but I want our loot back."

"Floody bucking right," said Will and Benito, almost in harmony.

The sun felt wonderful on Margo's bare shoulders, and the fresh morning breeze coming in from the window of their rental car was exhilarating — but it probably had something to do with the suitcase filled with gold and emeralds on the floorboard of the car. Just desserts. Life was on the upswing. Now all they had to do was drop off the car at the airport and catch a flight to Miami. From there they were off to Sundance's favorite haunt, Costa Rica — a good place to start a new life with her new lover. She glanced over at him. He wasn't exactly what she had dreamed of, but there was a certain roguish charm about him, and he had a quick wit, not to mention a remarkable tongue. He was still resistant to some of her more flagrant overtures (whips, handcuffs, foreign objects), and he needed to rest more than some of the others, but she was starting to like him quite a bit.

Sundance, on the other hand, wasn't quite as sure about this relationship. The woman was a bit like "The Human Catapult Carnival Ride" on Miami Beach — at a distance, it looked exciting, but once you got into it, you were just hanging on for dear life.

Nonetheless, everything continued on plan. They dropped off the rental car and were fortunate enough to catch a flight going into Miami only 15 minutes later. The gods were smiling on them.

We missed them at the airport by three minutes. We stood at the concourse gate and watched the plane lift off into a blue sky freckled with puffy white cumulus, while Will muttered a number of appropriate expletives.

"Okay, here's how I see it," I said, looking at my watch then up to Kendra and my partner. "We've got to get to Miami International and intercept Margo and Sundance before they disappear. We've got less than eight hours before Will has to be at Mallory Square, so we can't risk taking him with us." I paused. "I just wish I knew where they were going."

"My guess is Central America," said Will. "That's Sundance's favorite stomping ground, and it makes sense for them to get out of the country."

Kendra nodded. "Margo said something about Costa Rica."

I turned to Will. "Okay, we're going to have to split up. Benny and I are going to have to borrow your Cessna and head for Miami. If I push the throttles to the wall, I can nearly catch up with that aging DC3. We'll try to intercept Sundance and Margo at the airport. Partner, you're gonna have to hold tight for a few hours — find some bricks for your attaché case, relax, think backgammon. I want you to beat the son of a bitch, even if he doesn't keep his word. With any luck at all, Benny and I will be back in time to help you."

"What about me?" asked Kendra.

"Hon, I need you to stay here and be ready to help Will if, for some reason, we don't get back in time."

"You don't think I should be there to help you with Margo?"

I shook my head. "No, I don't think so. I don't know where this is going, and she's your sister. I don't want you faced with a conflict of interests."

Kendra wasn't happy, but she knew I was right. "Don't hurt her..." she murmured. "And don't let her hurt you."

"Not part of the plan. I intend to trick them, not injure them." I gave my lady a big hug and a kiss, then turned to go, but I stopped, pulling out the tiny manila envelope our Pier House room key came in. "Hey, Will, drop a little pinch of that magic dust in this envelope for me. Just in case I need a backup, okay?"

Twenty minutes later, we were at Summerland Key Airstrip and I was preflighting the 310. The DC3 with Margo and Sundance was well ahead of us, probably three-quarters of the way to Miami, but Sundance and his lady would have to book flights to wherever they were going and wait for it all to happen. We weren't out of the game yet.

The Pier House was repairing one of their walkways, so it was easy for Will and Kendra to "borrow" a handful of bricks. There wasn't much else for them to do but wait nervously until they heard from their friends, or until the sun began to set.

Margo and Sundance were landing at Miami International while I was just beginning my approach communications. Blissfully unaware of any pursuit, they had spent some quality time in the lavatory of the aircraft, which left Sundance pale and spent. He suffered from claustrophobia to begin with, and had a tough time in "the bloody freaking cupboard they called a bathroom" on the plane. He was beginning to presume he was suffering from emphysema, as well. He constantly appeared short of breath around this crazed, sociopathic nymph. But maybe it could have something to do with being bound like Houdini with a freaking racquetball stuffed in his mouth during sex. What the hell had he gotten himself into?

Margo and Sundance had to hike to a distant concourse for their flight to Costa Rica. Their plane departed in about an hour, and Margo noticed a bar near the gate. "C'mon, lover, let's have a drink or two — help rejuvenate you for the long flight to Central America," she murmured, grabbing Sundance by the arm and aiming him at the bar. "I don't know what it is about airplanes. I get so horny…"

It took me 15 minutes and a 50-dollar bill, but we finally found an accommodating ticket agent who would help us locate Kendra's sister, who "was running away from home with an older man." As we neared gate 15 on Concourse D, I saw the bar. I cocked my head. "I'm betting…"

Sure enough, as we eased toward the bar, staying cloaked in the foot traffic, there was the deadly duo, knocking down a few before takeoff.

"So, was' de plan, *jefe*?" asked Benito, a little nervous, but ready and willing. He had brought his short blowgun, barely over three feet in length, and had a handful of darts in his shirt pocket. He had compounded a concoction for the darts that would knock out a gorilla, but not kill it.

Benito had somehow found himself in the last few months. He was cool, and far more at ease — dressed in Levis and a flowered shirt, his long black hair tied in a ponytail with a rubber band, and his dark eyes bright with excitement.

I glanced around, looking for an angle. I remembered Benito telling us about pretending to be a blind guy when he had darted a couple of Jacko Slade's boys in Jamaica. "You still as good as ever with that blowgun?" I asked, nodding at the weapon he was holding like a walking stick.

My Latin buddy smiled. "Oh, man, chu know it! Benny snip de *cojones* off a cockaroacha at 30 steps."

"Okay," I said with a grin. "Hang on." I approached a fellow sitting at the next gate lounge and offered him 30 bucks for his heavy black shades — the Stevie Wonder kind. A moment later I was back. "Put these on and do your blind act, but be inconspicuous. Get yourself into a position where you can get them both, one right after the other, without drawing too much attention. When you see me raise my arm, nail 'em, *amigo*."

Benny grinned again. He was enjoying himself. Hell, he was in his element. He slipped on the shades, straightened up, and began a halting gait in the direction of the bar, his blowgun stick clicking the floor in front of him. He didn't know it, but Zorro had nothing on my amazing little buddy.

I strolled over to the bar and sat down next to Sundance, who was paying far more attention to his rum and coke, gearing himself up for the four-hour air ordeal with Margo. "So, how's your love life?" I asked quietly as Benito found an unobtrusive spot in the corner of the room.

Sundance jerked when he recognized my voice, but gathered himself together. "I'll give you back the emeralds if you'll shoot her," he whispered out the side of his mouth.

"Naahh, I don't think so," I said as I raised my arm.

Suddenly, a small, feathered dart appeared in Margo's neck, close enough to her ear to be mistaken for an earring. She started, straightening up from her drink at the bar, cautiously bringing a hand to her throat. She glanced at Sundance and me with a puzzled look and opened her mouth to say something, but she couldn't quite get it out.

Benito had said that you go through an immediate stage where everything seems fuzzy and out of sorts, "then, pretty quick, you fall on your face." As she slumped onto her elbows, a second dart struck my Canadian nemesis in the same spot, just below his ear, in the jugular. Sundance flinched as well, and immediately began to rise from his seat, but that wasn't going well with a dart in the jugular, instantly feeding a powerful drug to the brain. I eased him back into his seat.

Margo dropped face-first onto the bar, as if in drunken repose, and by this time Sundance was fading out, but his eyes had the desperate look of a ferret in a leg trap. "Don't leave me..." he mumbled helplessly. "The money, it was going to be my escape..."

I patted him on the cheek. "What do you need money for? You've got love!" I couldn't help a sliver of a smile. "Life's a bitch and then you die. Or maybe you become inextricably attached to a bitch and wish you were dead..."

Either the reality of that remark or the drug finally took its toll. My devious friend's eyes glazed to indifference, then closed, and his head slumped onto his chest. I plucked the tiny darts from their necks while the bartender busied himself with the only other customers at the far end, then I reached under Sundance's seat, grabbed the attaché case, and motioned the bartender over to me. "Before they passed out, I heard these two talking about hijacking an airplane. I think you need to call security."

As I turned to leave, I nodded innocuously at Benito and we headed out of the bar, down the concourse.

"Nice shooting," I said, without looking at him, as we walked away.

"Piece of cake, *amigo,*" he said, smiling, not looking at me.

While Mother Luck had been kind to us, we hit a snag as Benito and I prepared to return to Key West. We had developed a leak in the fuel line on the 310. You could smell fuel in the cockpit as I started the engine. They had to bring over a mechanic from the local Flight Based Operation. I was nervous to hives as we sat in the FBO lounge and watched the sun start to fall toward the horizon.

Will and Kendra were having an early dinner at Louie's Backyard. "The condemned man should get a special meal," Will had muttered with gallows humor. It was late afternoon and the sun was edging into tall cumulus batteries at the far side of the Gulf. Fortunately,

232

they had checked with the front desk at the Pier House and received the message explaining our delay. But it didn't make things any easier.

"Timing," muttered Will nervously. "Timing…" He took a hit of his margarita and sighed angrily. "Jeez — a fuel line! Now, of all times! Did I break a mirror somewhere?"

Kendra patted him on the shoulder. "There could be worse things. My mother used to tell me, 'If you think a few years of bad luck for breaking a mirror is a dirty deal, try breaking a condom.' I was never quite sure whether that was aimed at me."

While I paid for the fuel line repairs and, with the blessing of the tower, hastily taxied down to the runway threshold, Kendra and Will finished dinner and returned to the Pier House. It was time.

"Oh well," Will said with a bleak smile. "The show must go on. Even if you only got rocks in your box." His eyes took on a touch of grim. "I gotta have rocks in my head to be doing this."

"You can do it," Kendra encouraged. "If even half of what Kansas has told me about you is true, you'll be fine. Hell, you know you can beat him at backgammon. You know you can. Just do it one more time and you'll never have to open the case." She moved over and hugged my friend, then, pushing back, she smiled and said, "Besides, you've got a pocketful of magic dust…"

Will, long hair pulled back into a ponytail, dressed in his lucky Santana T-shirt and a pair of blue jeans, bolstered up as much courage as possible and began his stroll through Mallory Square. He was watching for the place Kendra had "reserved" with a 20-dollar bill — a couple of folding chairs and a lobster trap with a large beach umbrella attached to it, close to the sea wall. The vendors were in full swing, offering jewelry, conch shells, T-shirts, and a variety of Key West this and Key Lime that. The tourists ogled and haggled over commemorations of their few moments in the land of sea and sun while cruising the promenade, enjoying Jimmy Buffett wannabes, contortionists, poets, jugglers, the surely strange, and the slightly mad, all paying homage to the setting sun. Everyone was hoping to experience that exotic, almost imperceptible "blue-green flash" as that precious golden orb is drawn into the horizon and disappears in a final blink.

The rich scent of the ocean, along with jasmine, bougainvillea, and conch fritters, filled the air, and the wind fell to a silky breeze as

Will found the lobster trap and the chairs, and settled into a seat. He innocuously scanned the area, gazing at the sailboats and pleasure boats at anchor in the channel between Christmas Tree Island and Mallory Square, the setting sun casting long shadows, painting everything with the soft glint of gold. Kendra wasn't far away, playing "tourist," checking out the potpourri of offerings, but keeping a close eye on her friend.

Moments later, Will spotted Tu Phat and his bodyguards. The huge Chinese/Darien waded ponderously through the crowd, dressed more conservatively than usual in loose-fitting silk pants and a large Cuban guayabera, his favorite white-faced capuchin monkey on his shoulder, its tail wrapped around his neck. When Phat saw Will, there was a glint of triumph mixed with malevolence in his hooded eyes, but he quickly buried it.

Will gulped. "Holy moly, dude," he muttered under his breath.

"So good to see you again, Mr. Bell," said Phat, standing over him.

"You too, as always," replied Will, mimicking the man's formality and pushing a chair over for him, under the umbrella, with his foot. "Please, have a seat."

Phat settled awkwardly into the small chair, his men standing behind him and Will in their white, short-sleeved shirts and dark sunglasses. The monkey settled comfortably on his shoulder. "You have the gold and emeralds?" he said, nodding toward the case.

"No, I got a handful of bricks and a bag of marbles."

When his adversary started, his face hardening, Will looked him in the eyes. "Tell me, would I be stupid enough to come to this situation without the gold and emeralds? Do I really look that crazy?"

"Let me see," said the big man.

"No, dude. I'm not opening this case around all these people. Key West is known for its collection of rapscallions. I'm not losing this before we have our game."

There was an ominous pause while Tu Phat debated.

"C'mon, man, are we gonna play backgammon or are we gonna sit here in the freakin' sun and sweat like tourists?"

It was a good line, because his large opponent was already perspiring considerably. Tu Phat wiped his face with his handkerchief and exhaled angrily. "We play."

In moments the board was set up on the lobster trap, the pieces

Michael Reisig

lined up in place and the first roll going to Will. Because he had easily beaten his opponent twice, Will began with a blitz technique. But blitzes are very committal, and once you begin to attack, you must continue to take risks. Unfortunately, as Rufus would say, "Sometimes the magic works. Sometimes it don't..."

Less than 10 minutes into the game, Will was in trouble. Tu Phat, playing more methodically, but still taking a few risks, had established what is called "a prime game," which involves the creation of a "wall," or a long line of your pieces in a row that your opponent can't get past. It had worked, and Will was, as they say, "screwed to the wall."

My friend couldn't believe what was happening. Tu Phat had begun the methodical process of bringing around all of his pieces while Will remained stuck, not getting the rolls he needed, even as Phat started his final run and successfully began to remove his pieces. Sweat was streaming down Will's face and his hands had become unsteady. Tu Phat was also sweating like a hog, but his countenance was beaming and confident. Eight minutes later the big Panamanian removed his last piece and looked across at Will, triumph emanating from his piggish eyes. "Too bad, Mr. Bell. But to the winner go the spoils." There was a heavy pause. "I will take that case now."

While Kendra was pretending to admire the women's tie-dyed shifts, watching Will and his nemesis play a life-and-death game, Benny and I had touched down in Key West and were dashing madly toward Mallory Square in my pickup.

Will realized he was screwed. He'd lost the game, had no gold or emeralds, and the cavalry hadn't arrived. He was pretty much on his own. He slid the case over to Tu Phat, and as the fellow laid it on the lobster trap and began to struggle with the latches, Will reached into his pocket for his last resort — the magic dust. While Tu Phat and his men were absorbed in getting a look inside the case, Will casually withdrew the tiny baggie from his breast pocket and poured the contents into his palm under the table.

It was a lot of magic dust but he was only going to get one shot. He raised up triumphantly and drew a breath to blow. But at that moment, Tu Phat's monkey leaped from his master's shoulder over onto Will's arm. There was no aggression involved, just the contrary

235

— the animal was simply interested in what Will was doing, perhaps attracted by the sweet smell of the dust.

But Will, already on the edge of high anxiety, recoiled as the creature landed on his arm and the dust went everywhere but where it was supposed to — mostly on Will and the ground.

Tu Phat looked at my partner with a degree of disdain. "I would lay off the cocaine, *señor*, if I were you. It has obviously put you off your game."

As Will brushed the remnants of the magic dust from his face and chest, Phat continued haughtily, "You need to eat more bananas — to increase your resistance to the effects of drugs."

Suddenly, Will felt as if his brain had gone quiet for a moment, followed by sort of a cerebral nudge — and suddenly a banana sounded like a great idea, a terrific idea... But at that moment the case snapped open and his nemesis gasped. It wasn't a happy gasp.

Will was already rising from his seat, but he barely made it to his feet before the heavy behind him grasped his neck, shoving him down and gripping his hair. Tu Phat was a lovely shade of purple.

"Where...are...the...gold...and...the...emeralds?" he said, enunciating each word slowly, with vehemence.

"Man, I wish I knew," said Will.

"You will tell me. But in the meantime, the pain you are going to receive will stagger your imagination." He looked up at his men. "Signal the boat, now! Bring him!"

While all this was happening, Kendra had been watching from behind a nearby clothes rack. When it was apparent that Will had actually lost and they were taking him with them (she could see a Donzi-like boat swinging up to the pier), she started to move.

Suddenly, there was a hand holding her shoulder and she felt the barrel of a gun in her back. "One move — one more move — and I kill you."

But Tu Phat's man, behind her, had no idea what she did for a living, and was a touch more relaxed than he should have been. Kendra just slowly collapsed to the ground in an unaggressive lump, not moving, as if she'd fainted. The guy had no idea what to do, so he instinctively bent down. He shouldn't have...

As he knelt and reached for the inert woman, whose eyes appeared closed, an arm shot out, hand in the shape of a blade, catching him solidly in the throat.

Moments later, a terribly distressed Kendra was enlisting a couple of college boys to "help her husband, who appeared to be suffering from sunstroke." They carried him to the public restroom, and at her request, set him in a stall so he could cool off.

The fellow came around in a few minutes, lying on his back on the floor of the stall, his arms stretched back behind him, handcuffed to the plumbing at the rear of the commode, his feet bound together with his belt. The "Out of Order" sign was on the front door of the restroom. Kendra was sitting on his chest with a four-inch pin she had used to bind up her long blond hair. "I want to know where they went in the Donzi," she said.

"I no tell you squat," the man replied with a heavy Panamanian accent.

"Don't be brave," she whispered, leaning close. "It'll just prolong your suffering, and in the end you're going to tell me exactly what I want to know."

Kendra had learned a long time ago just how much pain you can cause with the common, little things in life. She was right on both counts. Five minutes later she knew everything. It wasn't good. But she knew it.

CHAPTER 20

With the attaché case in hand, Benito and I arrived at the Pier House and dashed across to Mallory Square. There was no sign of anyone — just an abandoned backgammon game on a lobster trap. The sun was setting, the last of it slipping behind a smear of white cirrus, casting brilliant, ethereal rays across a darkening blue sky.

We frantically traversed the bazaar once more, but there was nothing — no clues. I was headed back to the Pier House to see if Kendra had left any messages when I saw her step out of the men's restroom in the distance. She was brushing down her white blouse and tucking the loose ends back into her shorts. When she saw me, my lady straightened up and headed my way at a determined pace. She was in my arms briefly, then pushed herself back.

"You got the goods?"

I nodded, holding up the attaché case.

"We need a boat," she announced. "Now!"

Five minutes later we were at the marina in Key West Bight, renting the fastest skiff they had. In the interim, Kendra explained to Benny and me that Tu Phat had rented a 52-foot Hatteras several days ago, which had been anchored in deeper water behind Christmas Tree Island. His plan had been to kill us after getting the emeralds and gold, then take the Hatteras up to Miami, where he had a connection with the Cuban mafia. The sale of the treasure would be made offshore — less chance of being pinched by the American authorities. He would get his money, drop the Hatteras off in Miami, and be gone, back to Panama.

At the docks I placed a quick call to our DEA buddy, Shane O'Neal and begged a final favor — we needed him to tap into his radar and give us a fix on a large target that had just left the west side of Christmas Tree Island, probably headed around the south side of Key West and moving toward the mainland.

"There's a lot of traffic out there tonight," he said, a little peeved that I was imposing on him again.

"It's a big boat, over 50 feet. Will has been kidnapped and we need to get him back quietly if possible. A lot of authorities in boats with sirens, and our buddy could be floating off Smathers Beach by morning."

"Give me five minutes, then call me back."

It was the longest five minutes I could remember.

"Okay, this is what I got," Shane said. "There was one big target that took the course you mentioned. It moved around the western tip of the island, then took an easterly course, halting in the deeper water on a 90-degree arc out from White Street Pier. It appears to be at anchor now." There was a pause. "I apologize for being sharp, I didn't know it was Will. If there's anything I can do —"

"If there is, I'll let you know," I said. "You've already been a huge help."

It made perfect sense. Phat couldn't stay where he was earlier, or we would have found him. He mingled with the sunset traffic as it departed and innocuously shuffled around to the southern end of the island, still close to Key West, while he figured out how to extort his money from us. He wasn't above killing Will, but he was a businessman, and he wanted the jewels and gold from *La cueva de esmeralda.* They represented a personal treasure — something he had sought for years.

While I had been waiting for a return call from Shane, Will found himself bound hand and foot in one of the forward cabins on the Hatteras. He could hear Tu Phat and his people talking about the most effective ways to loosen his tongue regarding the loot. Damn, he wished he had a way of getting a message to his friends, and he wished he had a banana. A banana sounded really good.

On top of it all, the weather was changing. The dockmaster at the marina said there was a tropical storm moving into Florida. Isidore was gaining strength in the Bahamas and moving rapidly westward. While it was predicted to strike Central Florida, the bands of rain and wind were just beginning to move into our area now. The marina manager told us he wanted the boat back before midnight — no ifs, ands, or buts. (If I hadn't offered to double the fee he wouldn't have rented to us at all.)

As the three of us moved out in the 22-foot Aquasport, the wind was picking up. A waning, pale moon was just rising off the ocean, struggling its way through the oncoming banks of darkening clouds. The sky was coming alive as the upper level winds began to drive high streaks of cirrus, scattering them like mackerel after baitfish.

The cabin door opened and Tu Phat entered with one of his heavies. The Panamanian sat on the bed next to Will. "My friend, we can do this the easy way, or we can do it the messy way, but you're going to tell us —"

"Let's do it the easy way," said Will, and he proceeded to tell Phat the truth about taking the treasure from the bank and having it stolen by Margo and Sundance, then stealing it back. He explained that, by all rights, his partner should be looking for him now with the goods in hand.

Phat had one of his men call the Pier House to see if I had returned. He also left a message at the desk for me to call him on his marine radio. But none of that made much difference, because we were already on our way to the Hatteras in a sea that was growing angry. There was a serious chop and the wind was beginning to whip up whitecaps. I held the wheel while Kendra and Benito gripped the console bars as we beat our way through the waves, the 125 Johnson outboard whining smoothly behind us.

If Tu Phat would have been smart, he would have kept his lights off, but he loved his comfort too much, and the compass reading that Shane had given us from the pier led us right to the anchored Hatteras. I cut our running lights and shifted into neutral as the moon broke free and gave us a good look at the craft, rolling lightly in the distance.

"All right, we need a plan," I said, wiping the salt spray from my face. "Most likely there's going to be a captain and possibly a mate on board, probably people who were just hired with the boat, along with Tu Phat and his two bodyguards."

"I can even it up pretty quickly once we get on board," Kendra said, pulling a small, 22-caliber pistol from the small of her back.

Benny held up his blowgun and smiled puckishly.

"I'd be happier if we can avoid killing people, but I'm not averse to it if it means getting Will back alive."

Kendra shrugged. "Whatever."

I glanced around at the choppy ocean lit by the moon. "I doubt they're expecting company out here. How about we just cut the engine and drift into them? Tie off on the stern and use their dive platform to get aboard. We'll leave the attaché case here," I said, lifting the cover on the bench seat at the front of the console and storing our booty.

I brought us around, upwind to their stern a couple hundred yards, then cut the power. As we drifted closer, we used paddles to keep us aimed in the right direction, and in moments our gunwales nudged the Hatteras' stern. Kendra leapt onto the dive platform with our bowline and tied us off. We were between band lines of the storm. It looked like the front was moving northward and away from us. Good timing. Benito and I followed Kendra's lead and we crouched against the stern.

"Now what?" she said.

"We make a walk, or a creep, around — see if there's a guard, or if everyone is tucked in below."

"And if there's a guard?"

I looked at her. "We make him ... peaceful..."

There was a hard glint in her eyes as she glanced at Benny and he nodded. "One way or another..."

We quietly moved onto the covered aft deck, located to the stern of the bridge. We were inching forward, toward the cockpit, the moon obscured by low clouds, when suddenly I heard something behind us. There was a man holding a large, semi-automatic pistol. He must have been topside on the roof the entire time.

"Hello," I said. "Nice boat." I glanced around and found a second man, with another pistol, coming down from the cockpit. I saw the look in Kendra's eyes. "Don't," I said. "Bad odds."

The fellow next to Benny reached down and snatched his blowgun, which appeared to be no more than a colorful piece of hollowed bamboo. He turned it around, looked at it, and tossed it off the stern.

"Me *madre* made dat for me," Benito hissed angrily.

"Yeah? Well, she can make you another one," the guy said.

The other man stopped at the stairway to the bridge. "Hands in the air."

When Kendra hesitated (I knew she was thinking of going for her gun), the guy barked, "*Ahora!* Now!"

The two men quickly searched us, finding my lady's weapon.

"Well, so much for an edge," she muttered bitterly as the larger one nonchalantly pocketed the pistol.

They took us below to Tu Phat's cabin. When he saw us, I'm not sure whether pleasure or surprise won out. "I truly must be living right," he muttered with a smile. "I beat your friend soundly today at backgammon, and then, the very people I'm looking for drop by to visit." He paused. "Now all I need is one more thing..."

"We can make a deal," I said. "Where's Will?"

"I'll make a deal with you," Phat replied, grabbing a paring knife off the small bar and stepping (quickly for a big man) over to

Kendra. He grabbed my lady by her hair and forced her head back, while she was still being held by one of the guards, and put the blade to her throat, puncturing the skin just enough for a trickle of blood to run down her neck. "You can tell me what I want to know now, or I will cut her throat and you can remember for the rest of your life how her eyes looked when she bled to death in front of you."

It was a ghastly and compelling argument. "No! No...don't hurt her. I'll give you what you want. I can get it for you."

"Where? Phat growled. "Where is it?"

My shoulders sagged. "It's in our boat, tied up behind yours. In the bench seat in front of the console."

Phat lanced one of his people with a stare. "Go!"

I was terrified for my lady, but I couldn't help but notice that the captain of the Hatteras was equally shocked by the whole affair. The look of horror on his face said none of this was in his contract.

In moments the guard returned, carrying the case. At Tu Phat's prompting he placed it on the bed and opened it. Our adversary glanced at the gold and the clear plastic bags of emeralds, and the closest thing to a genuine smile slit his face.

"Good! Good!" he muttered, still holding Kendra tightly, not giving anyone room for a play. He turned to his guards. "They want to see their friend, so take them to him." Then he came back to us. "I have an appointment offshore from Miami tomorrow morning,"

The deal with the Cubans...

His eyes went hard. "Then we'll all go our separate ways..." He smiled, all teeth, no humor. "Yours, unfortunately, will probably be straight down, about 150 feet. 'Concrete block diving,' I think they call it."

At that moment, a scene passed through my mind. Years ago, when Will and I were diving for flame scallops in the old submarine pits on Boca Chica Key, I remembered turning a corner on one of the pits, down about 15 feet, and coming face to face with a large bulldog. Someone had tied a concrete block to the creature and tossed it into the canal. The bulging, milky eyes, still laced with the shock of a miserable death, never quite left me. *Not pretty,* I remembered. *Not pretty...*

They tied our hands with nylon rope, marched us to a small centerline berth that had been turned into a storage room, and pushed us in — four walls, no window, a very solid door and an impeccable lock. There was Will, sitting against the wall, hands tied behind his back, like us. We quickly gathered around him, catching up on our latest experiences. When we were finished, Kendra muttered, "Sounds like lambs to the slaughter, huh? Phat's keeping us alive until he gets his money from the Cubans. No bodies to be found ahead of time and screw up his plans. No loose ends..."

Will shook his head. "There's gotta be a horse somewhere in this bucket of manure." He looked at me. "You make it sound like the captain may have just realized what he's gotten himself into. He could become an ally..."

I shrugged. "Maybe, but we can't count on it. What we need now is an angle."

Benito leaned forward. "Dey take Benny's blowgun, but dey no take darts." He got that Zorro look. "When Benny go hunting, he always put a dart behind each ear. Easy to get quick. Dem damn monkeys be fast..." He turned his head slightly and underneath his long dark hair I could just see the feathers on the three-inch dart.

The message was clear — we had a couple of weapons, if we could figure out how to use them. We were interrupted by the sound of the big twin diesels firing up and the anchor being pulled. The craft was underway.

"In this weather it will be a five or six-hour run to Miami," I said to my friends. "So that's what we've got to figure this out."

We lounged uncomfortably against the wall for two hours before hearing movement outside. Suddenly, the door opened and Phat, with one of his well-armed guards, stepped in. Without preamble he said, "The captain tells me our Loran C is malfunctioning. Could be something to do with the storm, but he thinks it's mechanical or electronic. Do any of you have experience with repairing or maintaining this system?"

"And exactly why should we help you get someplace more quickly?" I said.

Phat took out his paring knife and stepped over to Kendra, grabbing her by the hair. "Do you need me to demonstrate again?"

"Okay, okay! Will and I are good at electronics. We can take a look. But I can't promise anything."

"You had better promise," growled Phat, shoving my lady against the wall.

When we got up to the bridge cockpit I could see the storm had abated, definitely moving north. The moon was rising clear of the low stratus clouds and throwing luminescent fingers across the water. Our captain — an older fellow, maybe 60, with short greying hair, a thin mustache, and worried dark eyes — was sitting in his chair at the wheel. One of the heavies was there with him.

"See if these two can help," Phat said to the captain. "I can't afford to be late for this affair, you understand?" He turned to the guard with him. "Stay. Watch them carefully." Then he was gone.

I looked around. The Hatteras was built with a small bridge/cockpit amidships at the top of the boat, with a few stairs leading down to a long, covered, aft deck. Below that, inside the hull, were the salon, galley, and bedrooms.

"If we're gonna be any help, you're going to have to untie us," I said.

The heavy glanced at the other bodyguard on the bridge and the guy nodded.

Once we were untied, I rubbed my wrists. "I'm going to need a flashlight — small, bright beam — a pencil, and a piece of paper."

The guards hesitated.

"Do you want us to help or not?"

Our sentry shrugged and went looking for a flashlight. The other guard, at the direction of the captain, found us the pencil and paper.

I whispered to Will, "How about one of your famous distractions? I need a word with our captain."

He smiled. My partner enjoyed his distractions almost as much as I did.

We moved up to the bridge where the instruments and the radios were, and where the Loran was bracketed. While Will backed off the plastic-handled screw mounts, lifted the device out and set it down, I looked at the back of the Loran and wrote on the paper. My partner noticed the device had a long cable on it, probably 15 feet, tucked off to the side (in case it had to be remounted somewhere else). He looked at me and his eyes said it was about to be show time.

Will began to whistle quietly as he undid the cable from the box, apparently enjoying himself, but all of a sudden he jerked straight up, eyes doing that Daffy Duck bulge, and let out a burbled shriek, holding out the end of the wire and shaking like an epileptic on speed. He lurched stiff-legged across the small cockpit, "Aahhhh! Holy freakin'...ahhhh! I'm being fried! 'Lectrocuted!"

Careening out of the bridge, still holding the wire away from him with both hands as if it were a poisonous snake, he screamed again. "Aaahh! Bein' cooked like the Colonel's freakin' chicken!" He threw his arms in the air as if trying to dislodge the wire, and went tumbling down the entrance stairs onto the covered aft deck, screaming, "Sweet Jesus! Help me! Help Me! I'm baking like a meat pie!"

Well, this was all fairly unexpected and the guard instinctively stumbled after him (even though anyone with a rudimentary knowledge of electronics would know the unlikelihood of what was happening).

I grabbed the petrified captain. "Listen! We need to get a message to a friend of ours with the DEA. Otherwise this isn't going to end well for any of us!"

"I…I…don't know," stammered the captain. "My boat's just hired by the day. None of this is my business…"

"You know dammed well what they're planning for us after they make their connection offshore in Miami," I hissed quickly. "Do you think for a moment they're just going to let you ride off into the sunset? Do you?"

I could see the fear and confusion, mixed with incredulity. He didn't want to believe…

"I…I don't… I'm not involved in this…"

Will was still screaming like a banshee, tangled in the Loran cable like Ahab lashed to the whale, yelling something about not being able to feel his lips or his fingers, but the guard was dragging him back across the aft deck.

I shoved the piece of paper into the captain's hand. "First chance you get, send this — channel 73 on your marine radio. Ask for Captain Shane O'Neal with Drug Enforcement."

Now the other sentry was coming up from the salon in a rush. I saw the fear in the captain's eyes.

"I'm sorry," he whispered pleadingly. "I don't think I can…"

I exhaled and let him go, disgusted and unnerved, suddenly realizing that we were on our own. There was no cavalry coming to the rescue.

It only took Will and me 15 minutes to find the problem with the Loran — a poorly soldered connection running to a cable coupling, which we were able to fix quickly. In the process, I snatched up a razor knife lying by the instrument panel and stuffed it in the small of my back.

Tu Phat was pleased that he had his navigational system working again. We were pleased because we were still alive, for the moment. They bound our hands again, marched us back to the storage room, and unceremoniously tossed us in.

As soon as the guards had moved away, we gathered together. Will and I explained the good news about the razor knife (in seconds I had cut everyone's bonds), and the bad news — chances of help coming from Shane and the authorities were slim to none. We quickly perused the small storage room — paints, caulking, extra bow and anchor lines, emergency flares, minor medical supplies, some backup electronic equipment, and galley supplies, but nothing to aid our cause.

I looked at my friends. "From what I've seen, there's Phat, two guards, and the captain. We're going to have to draw one or two of the guards to us and try to take them. Phat may be a problem, but the captain won't be. He's terrified and useless."

We rummaged the storeroom for anything we might be able to use, and Benny made an excellent discovery — a handful of PVC piping remnants, which included a three-foot piece of half-inch tubing. He pulled it out and looked at it, put it to his mouth, then turned to us. "Benny got a new blowgun," he said with that Zorro smile.

We sat against the walls for another three hours, laying out a plan and napping. We knew we had to be close to Miami, and it was obvious by the pitch and rhythm of the Hatteras that the storm had abated. If somehow we could get away before this rendezvous took place, we could make a run to the mainland with the Aquasport — if it was still tied to the stern.

"We're only going to get one shot at this," I said. "Here's what I recommend..."

It wasn't long before the craft slowed, then stopped, and the anchor chain rolled out. We heard the footsteps coming. I could hear the captain's voice. He was pleading with them, saying that they didn't need to lock him up. It wasn't necessary. He wouldn't say anything to anyone.

"You're right about that," the guard growled menacingly.

"Show time," Will said quietly.

As the door opened, the captain was resisting, begging a little, clinging to the guard's arm as the man entered the room just far enough to give his prisoner a shove. The guard saw four people squatting on the floor, hands supposedly tied behind their backs.

Kendra was on one side of the door and I was on the other. But as the man extended his arm, pushing the captain, Kendra lurched up, quick as a mongoose, grabbed his wrist, and jerked him forward. I side-kicked his knee and he went down with a grunt. Will added the *coup de grâce* with an auxiliary frying pan to the side of the head.

The captain was both relieved and panicked. "God! What have you done? What do we do now?"

"We tie him up," I said, as Kendra and Will began to rope the guard's wrists. "Then we're going topside, and find a way out of this mess."

"Oohh, God, you're going to get us killed!" the captain moaned, clenching his hands.

"You don't have to worry, you're not going," Will said, standing up, and we all filed out, closing the door in the captain's face and locking it.

I rather expected the man to wail, but he didn't. He was one of those people who felt safest with their hands over their eyes.

We were in the center of the ship, working our way along to the stairs leading up to the aft deck and the bridge again. As far as we knew, only Tu Phat and two heavies were onboard, and we'd taken out one. Will had everyone hold at the edge of the stairs to the aft deck while I peaked over the top.

The last heavy was lounging in the captain's chair, watching a rather spectacular sunrise — brilliant reds and yellows cutting streaming pathways through somber dark-blue and grey cloud banks to the east. North of us, heavy cumulus still worked their way up the coast. There was no sign of our Panamanian nemesis.

I eased back down the stairs and turned to Benito, whose dark eyes were bright with excitement. "I think it's time for you to test your new blowgun."

Benny nodded. "You betcha, *compadre.*"

"One target, in the captain's chair. That's all I can see..." I paused. "You're okay, right? He's got a gun. You miss, we're screwed."

"There be a thousand monkeys that wish Benny had missed," my Darien buddy whispered confidently.

I couldn't help but smile. "Go get 'em, killer."

Benny crept up the stairs, silent as a shadow.

There was a pause, then we all heard the *pffft* of the dart from the tube. There was an exclamation from the guard and I heard him

247

come to his feet off the captain's chair. "What the hell? I gonna shoot somebody's ass...I gonna..." But a moment later there was a confused exhale and we heard the man drop to his knees.

I quickly moved up to the stairs next to Benito, who knelt there confidently. It had been a perfect shot, right in the jugular below the ear. The poison was already coursing into the man's system. The fellow was trying to raise his gun, but the focus in his eyes dissipated and he simply sighed, falling on his face.

I patted my buddy on the shoulder. "Way to go, Zorro.

Benito scrambled over and pulled the dart from the man's neck, tucking it in his breast pocket. "Sontimes, if chu get the dart out quickly, chu can use it again, but de strength is not so good. Take longer to work."

Will and Kendra, unable to stand the suspense, had moved up next to me. Will quickly crept out and grabbed the man's gun, patting him on the face as he took it. "Hope you don't mind. You won't need this anymore, for a while..." He glanced around. There was no one to be seen. He motioned us forward. When we all gathered at the console on the bridge he said, "Now we need to find the Phat man, snatch our loot, and, as our buddy Crazy Eddie would say, split this funky scene."

"Get a dart in the blowgun, Benny," I said. "We're going elephant hunting."

It wasn't much of a hunt. We found Tu Phat in the master cabin, fresh out of the small shower, holding a huge towel around him. The attaché case with the emeralds and the gold lay open on his bed.

"How in the hell..." he muttered incredulously when he saw us.

Without conversation, Benny shot him in the neck with the slightly used dart. "You'll never get away with this...I'll...I'll... find you." Phat was garnering that lovely shade of purple again. "The Cubans will..."

But I noticed his eyes were beginning to get that familiar look of confusion. He sputtered a few more threats, then his countenance gradually began to slip into indifference, the towel fell from his waist (a sight I'm still trying to get out of my head), and he dropped to his knees. "You're really becoming annoying," he muttered breathlessly, just before he collapsed onto the floor.

"I'd have him mounted, but the taxidermist would charge a fortune," said Will dryly as he picked a banana out of a nearby fruit bowl. He started peeling it. "Really like bananas now. Can't figure out why."

"We need to get the hell out of here," Kendra said. "We either crank up this puppy and head for shore, or we take the Aquasport, if it's still at the stern. But we need to go."

I grabbed the case off the bed. "No arguments. Let's get topside."

But as we got back to the bridge, there was another surprise. The Cubans had arrived. A huge Chris Craft motor yacht was just dropping anchor not 100 yards from us.

"I thought I heard another boat," mumbled Will.

"Not good," I said. "We need to do some fancy thinking here. Will, Benny, take the guard we just knocked out and put him in the storage room."

But at that point our marine radio came alive, crackling with static for a moment, then a voice broke through — a deep, heavily accented Cuban voice with a sense of command about it. *"Holidaze, this is Marco Malon on the Osprey. Come back, Holidaze."*

There was an immediate sense of panic, for a number of reasons. Marco Malon was a name you read in the newspapers every once in a while, generally after there was a contract killing somewhere, or an ongoing investigation into drug trafficking.

"Not good," I repeated.

Will stared at the other boat for a moment, then glanced around the inside of ours and got one of his "distraction smiles." "Maybe we could make this a double whammy — get away from the Cubans, keep our loot, and give Tu Phat enough problems that he won't have time for us. But you're going to have to trust me."

Will picked up the mike on the radio, and, adding a heaviness to his voice, spoke. "This is Tu Phat of the *Holidaze*, come back."

Without so much as a hello, Malon said, "Do you have the fish I ordered?"

Will looked at us and put his hand out in a "trust me" fashion. "Yes, *señor* Malon, We have the fish, and I assume you have payment."

"Of course," was the sharp reply. "You can come over to my boat and we will conduct business."

"I am sorry, *señor* Malon, but no, I would like you to come to me. Forgive me, but your reputation precedes you, and I would like the security of my own surroundings for this transaction. I assure you that all will be well."

The Cuban humphed coldly. "I can tell you, *amigo*, I am safe wherever I go. You would not live to see… Your children will not live to see…"

Will let him finish his threats, then came back on the mike. "Let us not argue about events that are not going to take place. If you would give us a few minutes to accommodate you, then board your skiff and come over, we will provide your fish and you will be on your way — all of us alive and well, huh?"

It was a great imitation of Tu Phat and Malon bought it.

Will placed the mike in its cradle and turned to us. "Okay, we have to work fast. I've been thinking about this. Here's what I have in mind…"

CHAPTER 21

We dragged Phat from his cabin and secured him in the captain's chair, but his head kept falling onto his chest.

"I got it! I got it!" said Will as he rummaged in the drawer next to the chair. Triumphantly he came up with a tube of Instant Set two-part epoxy glue. "I saw it earlier when we were working on the Loran," he explained.

Will mixed up a batch — one-half for the back of the chair and one-half for the back of Phat's shaved head.

"They're out of the cabin and headed for the skiff!" Kendra yelled from the door to the deck.

Will pushed the bald nape of Phat's neck against the top of the seat and held it for 60 seconds. When he let go, the Panamanian's head stayed upright. I found the captain's dark sunglasses on the console, slipped them on our boy, put his elbows on the chair arms, then stepped back and smiled at our handiwork.

A moment later we heard the skiff tie up at the stern. I went to escort them in. Kendra, with one of the incapacitated guard's pistols, hid under the stairs that led down to the salon, as backup if we needed it.

Marco Malon was carrying a briefcase containing $200,000. A big Latin sporting an Uzi — the weapon of choice for drug traffickers everywhere — followed him. One of Malon's claims to fame was that he never carried a gun, he just pointed his finger and you were dead.

I escorted them to the aft upper deck, which was a few steps below the bridge. Will stood in the bridge/cockpit, next to Phat, his arm draped around the captain's chair. The Cuban crime boss stopped, looked up at Phat, and nodded. Will surreptitiously bounced the Chinese man's head in a slight nod, hoping the glue would hold.

I interrupted at that point. "Mr. Phat will only oversee this transaction. He will not participate and he will not comment, so that, at any time in the future, it cannot be said that he engaged in anything legally improper. I will serve as his aide and conduct the business today."

The Cuban thought about that for a moment. He was about to complain, but something about the idea appealed to him — the elimination of complicity while still participating. He shrugged and

251

pointed his finger at the Panamanian. "Thas' *muy* clever, *amigo*. I don' mind, as long as I get what I want."

Will grasped Phat's elbow and lifted the arm slightly in an indifferent salute to the comment. I had to hide a smile. There's something intrinsically amusing about manipulating an incapacitated person. *They ought to make a movie about that – two guys dragging a knocked out or dead guy from pillar to post. That would be funny as hell.* As I seated Marco Malon, his bodyguard took a position behind him, the essence of calm, but the Uzi in his hands looked anxious.

Malon and I had just settled into the rattan couch on the aft deck. I asked him if he liked the ocean and he was responding, when I ran a hand through my hair — the prearranged signal. To their left and behind them, Benito pushed open the door to the louvered locker in which he was hiding. He raised his PVC blowgun and buried the last dart in the neck of the bodyguard, then quickly closed the door.

The man reacted identically to the others — he flinched and grunted, and brought a hand to his throat. No one had noticed anything at this point. The man glanced around, unable to find anything out of order. He reached up and felt the feathered dart. "*Cono*," he muttered weakly. The Cuban started to raise his weapon, but there was nothing to shoot, and the potion was already entering his system, shutting down nerves and synapses. *"Jefe,"* he whispered, trying to warn his boss, but as he did, his legs gave out and he dropped to his knees.

When Malon turned to see what was happening, I pulled Tu Phat's pistol from under the pillow next to me, and trained it on the Cuban drug lord as he started to rise. "Relax. Sit back down. Now!"

"You will never get away with this," he growled. "You will be dead before the next sunrise."

"*Lo siento, señor*, but this is necessary," I replied, and at that point I glanced at Will on the bridge, which was Will's signal to pretend to distract Phat with conversation.

While my partner turned and began to speak quietly, gesturing with his hands, and offering loud responses — "Are you sure? Okay, okay. If that's what you want..." I slipped Malon a note.

"Read!" I whispered urgently.

The Cuban did as I asked, keeping it low and away from Tu Phat's view... *Mr. Shong is holding my parents prisoner. My brother and I are being forced to help him steal from you in order to save them. I am sorry. We do not want your money; we only want to save our family. In truth, we met him through a recent business deal, which didn't end well for him, and now, we are as expendable as you...*

Malon cocked his head. "This is true?"

I nodded. "This is true."

Pointing the gun at the VHF radio built into the rattan coffee table in front of him, I said, "You will tell your people on your boat that you are going to ride into Miami with us. Tell them not to follow."

"Why should I?"

I looked up at Phat in the cockpit, then back to him. "Because you are still breathing right now, that's why."

Malon glared at me, but did as I requested, then angrily tossed the radio mike on the couch next to him. "Now what?"

"Now we go to Miami."

Benny helped me bind the hands of Malon and the bodyguard.

"We got more people tied up on this boat than a bondage convention in San Francisco," I muttered.

Malon glanced at my little Darien friend. "Who's he?"

I put my hand on Benito's shoulder. "He's family. He's adopted."

Benny beamed. "Chu betcha."

While we dragged the inert bodyguard to the corner of the aft deck, Will swung the captain's chair around so that it was facing the cockpit console and "he and Phat" fired up the engines, then pulled the anchor. I held my gun on Malon while Benito went out to the dive platform at the stern. He shortened the lines on the two skiffs — our Aquasport and Malon's runabout from his yacht — quickly rafting the boats together so they wouldn't bang into each other's gunwales while we were underway.

We ran until we had about a mile between our boat and the Cuban Chris Craft, then Will (who was "assisting" Tu Phat at the controls), slowed us to a stop. He gradually brought Phat and the captain's chair around, facing Malon and me in the lounge. Will, always the marvelous performer, stood in front of Tu Phat, his back to us (so neither Malon or I could get a good look at the Chinese), and cocked his head. Then he leaned forward, listening, as if Tu Phat were whispering to him. He straightened up, turned to me, and with a dire countenance drew a finger across his throat.

I winced, glancing at the Cuban, who was now a little more than concerned, then I turned back to Will and Tu Phat. "Are you sure? Are you sure we need to do this?"

Will shifted his position slightly, and with a hand behind the chair, cleverly nodded Phat's head once more, providing a nice little flip of the Panamanian's hand in cold indifference. God, he was a master ad-libber!

Malon began festering with anger and indignation, yelling threats of miserable deaths for all of us, starting to stand. I had to shoot a hole in the couch next to him to get his attention.

"It is what it is, so accept it," I said loudly, but as I turned him around and headed him across the aft deck, toward the stern, gun at his back, I whispered, "Relax. Roll with it. I have a plan…"

The Cuban was stiff with trepidation, still not certain that I wasn't going to kill him, but not showing any fear. When we reached the transom and stepped down onto the dive platform, beyond view of the cockpit, he turned, ready to face his fate, looking for an opening.

"Relax," I said, bringing the gun up and firing it into the air twice.

Malon started a little more than he was comfortable with, blinking a couple of times with uncertainty.

"Now you're dead," I said with a grin, sort of enjoying myself. Not many people got to screw with a sociopath and live to tell about it. "Get in your skiff, cast off, and lie on the deck for about five minutes, so if Phat looks back at his wake he'll see your boat adrift." I paused. "Then go get your friends…"

Malon's face went feral. "Oohh, you can count on it, *señor*…" He stared at me for a moment, his hard countenance softening just a touch. "You will be rewarded for this…"

I smiled humbly. "I'm already being rewarded."

When I returned to the bridge, Kendra, Benny, and Will were standing there with huge smiles.

"So far so good," I said. "We've got a very angry Cuban headed back to his boat. In 10 minutes he's going to be geared up and after Tu Phat." I couldn't help but grin. "*Señor* Malon is convinced that Tu Phat used us as unwilling pawns to steal his money. Our Panamanian boy is hip deep in the brown and smelly."

"But we need to get out of here," said Will. "I don't want to be any part of what's about to come down."

South Miami was in sight off our port bow, maybe a three-mile run. My buddy glanced out the windows of the cockpit. "Time to set this baby's autopilot north for Fort Lauderdale, away from us, then grab our loot, pile into that Aquasport, and head for shore. We'll leave Marco Malon's money on the salon table. I'm not touchin' a dime of that."

"Right you are!" chuckled Kendra. "Let's get the hell out of here."

As we gathered our gear, I noticed Tu Phat was starting to come around some. He was groaning and moving his head. I brought my hand to my chest in concern, and felt something in the pocket of my shirt. As I pulled it out, I realized it was the little manila key envelope from the Pier House — the one that contained the touch of magic dust Will had given me.

"Holy crap!" I exclaimed. "Will! You're not going to believe what I have! All this time! We could have worked our way out of this so much easier!"

"Maybe," my partner said as he walked over and took it from me, popping it open and looking into the envelope. "Yep. Magic dust." He shook his head, staring at me. "I can't believe you. I thought you used it on Sundance and Margo." He glanced at Tu Phat, then turned to me. "Go get the boat started. I'll be right there."

Five minutes later, we were bouncing across a light chop in the Aquasport. The sun, yellow and warm, was just clearing bands of gossamer morning clouds on the horizon. It was beginning to look as though we might survive this situation. But as Rufus says, "Sometimes, da gods, dey get bored, and dey fool with you..."

I was at the wheel. Benny and Kendra were on the bench seat in front of the console. Will, next to me, tapped my shoulder and pointed behind us. "I think we may have a situation."

I couldn't believe my eyes. There was Sundance's Hatteras coming up fast.

"How is that possible?" Will moaned. "We shot him with a dart! He should be out for hours!"

Benito turned back to me and shouted over the engines. "We chot him wit' an 'already-been-used-once' dart. It knock him out, but I betcha it wore off way too quick."

"This is not good," I muttered, realizing that four of us in a 22-foot boat being pushed by a 125 h.p. engine in a choppy sea were not likely to outrun that Hatteras.

Tu Phat had found his men in the storage room. He rearmed them with semi-automatic M-15 rifles hidden in his bedroom, and placed them on the bow. The previously reluctant, now terrified captain was at the helm, and the big boat was closing fast. Phat's men were firing a few rounds to check their range, which was already close enough to be seriously annoying.

It was then I noticed the sleek Chris Craft coming up behind the Hatteras — Marco Malon! The Cuban boat was moving up steadily. Phat was so occupied with catching us he hadn't even considered looking to his stern. Malon had told his men to hold their fire until they could "rip the *pendejo* a new asshole."

Rounds from the Phatman's M-15s were smacking the water around us. I had begun to swerve in shallow S patterns to throw off our opponent's accuracy, but that cost us speed. It was six of one...

Suddenly, two rounds struck the Plexiglas windshield, exploding in a huge fracture and throwing out shards like miniature daggers. One of them struck Benito in the ball of his shoulder and he cried out. I slammed the throttle to the wall as if physically forcing it against the metal casing would make the boat move faster.

"Go!" Will yelled at me over the whine of the engine and the sound of rounds striking the transom. "Go!"

In the next moment Will's shirtsleeve ripped open as a bullet clipped through the cloth, nicked his arm, and drove into the windshield again, punching a hole just inches from Kendra's head.

"Get down!" I yelled. "Everyone down on the deck!" I suddenly realized we had gone from a heady victory to a messy end, all in less than an hour.

I crouched at the console, keeping the boat aimed at the beach, watching lines of bullets stitch the water around us. But as we waited for the next round to strike, another staccato sound was added to the cacophony. We all snapped around, peeking out like anxious meerkats. The Cuban Chris Craft was sliding up behind the Hatteras and three men on the bow were hammering Phat's boat with those nasty little Uzi submachine guns. This, of course, caught the attention of the folks in the Hatteras, big time, and while it backed off some of the pressure from Phat's men, the crazy Cubans behind the Hatteras were blasting with such an unabashed frenzy, some of their rounds were finding us, as well.

To top it off (da gods, dey love a stimulating adventure), we suddenly took a round to the engine cowling (Cuban or Panamanian, it hardly mattered at this point), and the outboard started hissing, missing, and belching smoke. We began to slow, and the firefight with the two boats closed in. Bullets were slapping the water around us like thunderstorm hail, and our fiberglass hull was snapping and shattering as rounds found their way to us. I kept the throttle jammed forward, crouched into a ball at the base of the console while keeping the boat fixed toward the shore.

We managed another 100 yards before the engine coughed phlegmatically, and with a final gasp, died. Phat's Hatteras was thundering down on us. A line of automatic fire stitched our boat from transom to bow, a foot to the right of the console. It was a miracle no one was hit. I could clearly see Phat's men kneeling on the bow of his boat. The sons of bitches were smiling, raising their rifles in tandem for the *coup de grâce*. I looked at my friends, hunkered down behind the center console with me, cloaked in desperation. This was it. There was no cavalry coming to the rescue. It was the end.

My eyes showed my anguish. "I'm so sorry I got you into this... I just want you to know, you're all —"

"Not dead until you see the devil," muttered Will triumphantly, pointing off our bow.

There, coming in off the water not 400 yards ahead, were two U.S. Drug Enforcement Blackhawk helicopters. Side by side, noses down and into the wind, big blades slapping a steady rhythm and flattening the water under them, they came forward like two avenging angels, soaring over us, then ripping heavy, terrifying lines of machine gun fire at the two approaching boats, close enough to chip the paint off the gunwales. It was as if God Himself had waved His hand over the whole affair, and every gun onboard the two boats fell silent.

I noticed a Coast Guard cutter, probably out of the Miami Station, moving up from the south at a fast clip. The cavalry had arrived, but the question was, how?

Twenty minutes later Tu Phat and his team, along with Marco Malon and his people, were in custody. We were aboard the Coast Guard cutter, giving a somewhat edited version of what happened, when Shane O'Neal came walking through the door, fresh off one of the helicopters, dressed in DEA fatigues, tall and lanky, his dark hair ruffled from the wind. "I see you two have been entertaining yourselves again," he said, those green eyes of his somewhere between amused and angry. "How is it that two people manage to get themselves in such a constant barrage of bull —"

"It wasn't our fault!" Will protested adamantly.

"It never is."

"How in the hell did you find us?" I asked. "That was spectacular timing."

Shane aimed his thumb in the direction of the other boats, now under DEA and Coast Guard lockdown. "Your captain friend got a message to us this morning. Sounded scared shitless, saying you two were in the deep muckety-muck, so I rallied a team and went looking for you."

I glanced at Will and he shook his head in disbelief. "I'm absolutely amazed the little weasel came through."

"I think at the time he was more interested in saving his own skin," Shane said. "At any rate, this is quite a catch – nothing less than Marco Malon, if we can make any of this stick. He's claiming the fellow on the other boat stole money from him in a scam." He shrugged. "We'll wait and see, but I wouldn't want to be the fat guy he's pointing fingers at." He took a breath and looked over at our attaché case against the wall. "The captain of this bucket owes me a favor, so I'll let you keep that, if you can tell me it wasn't stolen."

"Absolutely not!" Will said. "We...*found it*... legally."

Shane sighed. "Yeah, right. I've never known two people who spent so much time in the grey area of life."

EPILOGUE

Two days later, Will and I were at the Miami Airport, taking a commercial flight to our favorite getaway place, Fernandez Bay on Cat Island, in the Bahamas — no flying ourselves, no undue excitement, no stress of any sort. We were adventured out. Kendra had decided to take a couple of days off and visit her mother in Central Florida. She, too, needed some peace and quiet.

We were sitting in the lounge of our gate, waiting to board, when none other than Tu Phat and his entourage entered the concourse, moving past us toward the gates for Central American departures. We learned that both he and Marco Malon had made bail. They undoubtedly had a judge or two in their pockets. Tu Phat was sporting a large hat and dark sunglasses. There was a constant, nervous shift to his head, and a cautious movement to his gait. It was obvious that the loss of the Cuban's money (confiscated by the authorities) had left him somewhat of a wanted man, regardless of what the law decided. He was getting out of Dodge before Malon found him. But that wasn't all he was dealing with.

Will, with his eternal sense of mischievousness, had planted a couple of suggestions via "the magic dust" at the last minute on the bridge of the Hatteras. The most significant being, "Every time you hear the words "hello" or "thank you," you will scratch your crotch furiously, fall on all fours, and howl like a monkey."

Mr. Shong was having a tough time getting through the baggage check...

The customs agent took his passport and smiled. *"Hello*, Mr. Shong —"

The eyes on the big man went strangely distant, and suddenly he threw back his head. "Hooowoolll!" he howled. "Ark! Ark! Ark!" Phat's hand immediately and enthusiastically grasped his groin. In a flash he was down on all fours, bouncing around like Fido begging for a bone. "Hooowoolll! Eck! Eck! Eck!"

"That's really an excellent imitation of a howler monkey," I remarked as the agent and the people in the adjacent lines around Tu Phat immediately leapt back, as if they'd just discovered a rabid leper. I glanced over at my partner. "You did that, didn't you? With the magic dust."

Will shrugged. "I bore easily."

"Damn stuff really works."

"I think a lot of it is about timing, and the power of suggestion — as with hypnosis. Like Rufus said, it's not really magic; it just opens the channels…"

I smiled. "That dude's channels are wide freakin' open."

When our old nemesis got himself back together and managed to stand, the agent cautiously handed the passport back to what she was certain was a lunatic. "*Thank you*, sir."

Phat's eyes immediately got that remote expression again as he dropped to his knees, flogging his genitals with the fervor of a gibbon with herpes, head thrown back. "Hooowoooolll! Ark! Ark! Ark!"

The customs lady was energetically pushing the security button under her counter. The adjacent agents were reaching for their tasers.

"I think it's going to be a difficult day for our Panamanian friend," Will said.

Suddenly, my jaw dropped. Two lines to the left of Phat, boarding for Costa Rica, stood Sundance and Margo. After the airport bar incident, they had been detained for two days regarding the possibility of being hijackers. Sundance, in shorts and a tropical shirt, was struggling with three bags.

"C'mon, hon, you're lagging behind, we'll miss our flight," chided Margo next to him, dressed to kill in a red miniskirt and a tight-fitting white blouse — no bra. She smiled lasciviously and grabbed his arm. "I can't wait to sneak you into the lavatory…"

Sundance's shoulders sagged and he acquired that same overwhelmed countenance Will remembered so well. His bloodshot eyes blinked like a deer in a car's headlights.

"Our boy is lookin' a little weary, isn't he?" I said.

"Couldn't happen to a nicer fellow," chuckled Will. "But man, is it not incredibly amazing that we should run into both Tu Phat and Sundance at the same airport?" Will held out his hands. "I mean, what are the chances?"

"Rufus says, 'Coincidence is the Grand Messenger's way of reminding us how small the ship of life is, and that destiny sometimes has a sense of humor.'" I paused. "And, 'the gods, they love a clever reckoning.'"

"Right you are!" exclaimed Will as he turned to me and held up his plastic bar glass, while sporting that funky, lopsided grin. "Here's to coincidence, and to another amazing tale that our grandchildren will undoubtedly credit to illicit pharmaceuticals and Alzheimer's."

I clinked my cup against his. "And here's to being somewhere on the road again…"

IF YOU ENJOYED THIS BOOK, BE SURE TO READ THE OTHERS IN THE SERIES!

The Road to Key West
Book I

The Road to Key West is an adventurous/humorous sojourn that cavorts its way through the 1970s Caribbean, from Key West and the Bahamas, to Cuba and Central America.

In August of 1971, Kansas Stamps and Will Bell set out to become nothing more than commercial divers in the Florida Keys, but adventure, or misadventure, seems to dog them at every turn. They encounter a parade of bizarre characters, from part-time pirates and heartless larcenists, to Voodoo *bokors,* a wacky Jamaican soothsayer, and a handful of drug smugglers. Adding even more flavor to this Caribbean brew is a complicated romance, a lost Spanish treasure, and a pre-antediluvian artifact created by a distant congregation who truly understood the term "pyramid power."

Back On the Road to Key West
Book II
The Golden Scepter

Back On The Road To Key West reintroduces the somewhat reluctant adventurers Kansas Stamps and Will Bell, casting them into one bizarre situation after another while capturing the true flavor and feel of Key West and the Caribbean in the early 1980s.

An ancient map and a lost pirate treasure, a larcenous Bahamian scoundrel and his gang of cutthroats, a wild and crazy journey into South America in search of a magical antediluvian device, and perilous/hilarious encounters with outlandish villains and friends along the way (not to mention headhunters, smugglers, and beautiful women with poisonous pet spiders) will keep you locked to your seat and giggling maniacally. You'll also welcome back Rufus, the wacky, mystical Jamaican Rastaman, and be captivated by another "complicated romance" as Kansas and Will struggle with finding and keeping "the girls of their dreams."

Along the Road to Key West
Book III
The Truthmaker

Fast-paced, humorous adventure with wacky pilots, quirky con-men, mad villains, bold women, and a gadget to die for...

Florida Keys adventurers Kansas Stamps and Will Bell find their lives turned upside down when they discover a truth device hidden in the temple of an ancient civilization. Enthralled by the virtue (and entertainment value) of personally dispensing truth and justice with this unique tool, they take it all a step too far and discover that everyone wants what they have — from the government to the Vatican.

Along the way, from Key West, into the Caribbean, across to Washington, D.C., and back to America's heartland, Kansas and Will gather a wild collage of friends and enemies — from a whacked-out, one-eyed pilot and an alluring computer specialist, to a zany sociopath with a zest for flimflam, a sadistic problem-solver for a prominent religious sect, and the director of presidential security.

OTHER NOVELS BY MICHAEL REISIG:

THE NEW MADRID RUN

THE HAWKS OF KAMALON

BROTHERS OF THE SWORD/CHILDREN OF TIME

THE OLD MAN'S LETTERS

Acknowledgements

I would be remiss not to mention my wonderful editing team. My very talented editor and formatter, Cris Wanzer, did a remarkable job of making this a professional work, as always. But I owe a special debt of gratitude to Kathy Russ and Robert Simpson, who took my far-from-perfect writings, shook the wheat from the chaff, and shaped this into an acceptable read prior to final editing. I am fortunate to have such gifted professional friends.

About the Author

Michael Reisig has been writing professionally for almost two decades. He is a former newspaper editor and publisher, an award-winning columnist, and a best-selling novelist.

Reisig was born in Enid, Oklahoma. The first son of a military family, he was raised in Europe and California before moving to Florida. He attended high school and college in the Tampa Bay area. After college, he relocated to the Florida Keys, establishing a commercial diving business in which he served as the company pilot, traveling extensively throughout the southern hemisphere, diving, treasure hunting, and adventuring.

From there he turned to journalism, putting many of his experiences into the pages of his novels and columns, then going on to manage, then own, newspapers.

He presently resides in the Ouachita Mountains of Arkansas where he fishes and hunts and writes his novels, and occasionally escapes to the Caribbean for further adventures.

Made in the USA
San Bernardino, CA
03 July 2017